About the

Peter is a retired lecturer living in Bedfordshire with his wife and family. As well as becoming an accomplished artist since retirement he decided to write a novel. His first novel, The Main Event, is a mix of murder, mystery and suspense.

Peter Arnold

THE MAIN EVENT

EVENTISPRESS

© Copyright 2023

Peter Arnold

The right of Peter Arnold to be identified as author of this work has been asserted by him in accordance with the Copyright, Designs and Patents Act 1988.

All Rights Reserved

No reproduction, copy or transmission of this publication may be made without written permission.
No paragraph of this publication may be reproduced, copied or transmitted save with the written permission of the author, or in accordance with the provisions of the Copyright Act 1956 (as amended).

Any person who commits any unauthorised act in relation to this publication may be liable to criminal prosecution and civil claims for damages.

All characters are fictitious and any resemblance to actual persons, living or dead,
is purely coincidental.

A CIP record for this title is
available from the British Library
ISBN: 978-1-7393286-2-7 paperback

Published by Eventispress in 2023

Printed & Bound by KDP

Dedication

To my family and friends for all the help and encouragement you have given me along the way.

Chapter 1

Steven and Sarah Cooper, a devoted married couple, occupied number 34, Chatsworth Close in Luton. Neither of them had any living immediate family, but Sarah regularly phoned her Uncle Angus, who lived in a Scottish care home. Locally, they enjoyed a friendship with their next-door neighbours, Karyn and Mark Stewart.

Sarah tended the house and garden, and for two days in the week she volunteered at her local Age UK shop in the town centre. She often joked to people that this charitable gesture would serve her well when she got old herself.

At the current age of 40, her looks belied her age. She was a raven-haired beauty looking much younger. Being a shy person, she would feel her face turning red at unwanted attention. Particularly from men passing in the street staring at her.

Steven was very proud of his wife. He didn't mind the fact that other men found her attractive. He was two years older than her, and as handsome as she was pretty. With hardly a cross word between them, they appeared to be a perfect couple.

Steven worked at a local technology company called Kilburn since 1990. Starting as an engineering apprentice, he worked his way up to the current, well-paid, position of Product Specialist.

Kilburn manufactured a range of analytical scanners used in hospitals. Their scanners cost a quarter of a million pounds each. They are commonplace in most hospitals in the UK and across Europe.

As a major contributor to the technology within these machines, they required Steven to travel to sites around the UK and Europe to troubleshoot installations experiencing problems. The trips were usually short. Sarah didn't enjoy being home alone. She would often take time out from her volunteer job at the charity shop to join Steven on a trip. Whilst Steven worked on his assignments, Sarah would spend the day browsing local shops and markets, looking for bargains. Often, they would extend their stay to include a weekend at the beginning or end of a trip.

Steven's life was currently in turmoil though. The discovery of a competitor's product with identical components in its sampler module threw suspicion upon him. The component was Steven's invention, and they suspected he had shared company secrets with a competitor.

Tim Keating, Head of Product Development, helped to point an accusing finger at Steven. Despite pleading his innocence three weeks ago, HR called Steven in for a disciplinary meeting. They placed him on '*garden leave*' whilst the matter was '*looked into*'. The period of leave was with full pay. He worried, not knowing what the outcome of the investigation might be. He was innocent of the charge laid at his door, but how could he prove it? That he still had ten years of a substantial mortgage on his half a million-pound abode would be a particular worry if they sacked him.

Depressed at this sorry situation, Steven was doing little more with his time than mulling over his predicament. Not sleeping at night, he appeared tired and sometimes irritable during the day.

It worried Sarah that Steven was on the verge of becoming depressed.

'I think you should go to the doctor, perhaps he can prescribe a pick-me-up.'

'Oh, stop fussing love. I'm fine!'

Sarah took the hint. She would have to think of other ways to lighten his mood.

Steven was popular with friends and associates. His relationship with Tim Keating, his head of department, was an exception. He was a bully and not good at his job. He had no respect from those he managed. It was common knowledge by many in his team that he disliked Steven. Some believed he got his job through nepotism; his wife was George Kilburn's niece.

Keating was an overweight, middle-aged, balding individual. His heavy dependence on alcohol was clear by his rosy red complexion and bulbous nose with the texture of orange-peel. A regular pill taker to control his cholesterol, hypertension, and type two diabetes, he always looked as if he was a heart attack, just waiting to happen. He came close to it one day during a verbal dispute with Steven. This was the start of the poor relationship between them.

Angered by Keating's incompetence, Steven protested with him in his office one day. A blazing row ensued. Though, in fairness, it was only Keating's voice that bellowed from within the confines of the pokey office. Steven put his case calmly. Some interesting glances, grins and smirks passed between colleagues working in the outer office area. They listened to what was being said in the explosive manager's office. A loud outburst showed that the exchange might be about to end. The office door opened. Steven stood in the doorway.

'That's my decision, and I'll email the customer to tell him so.' He stepped out of the manager's office.

'COOPER! Get back in here now!!!!'

Steven responded, 'It's Mr Cooper to you.'

Heads in the outer office area ducked as if some shrapnel might land from the explosive outburst. Steven shut the door.

'I'll get you Cooper!'

Other expletives, which weren't altogether clear, echoed through the outer office. Threats about Cooper being able to keep his job were clear though. The rantings continued for about a minute. Steven couldn't listen to anymore. He put his coat on before departing. His work colleagues sat waiting for Keating to emerge. It had all gone quiet in his office.

Colleagues talked, 'You don't suppose he's had that inevitable heart attack, do you?'

Keating finally emerged, looking like a pressure cooker about to blow. He walked straight out. The colleagues speculated about what he would do next. 'He'll go across the road to lick his wounds with a beer or two in the Rat and Carrot,' one accurately predicted.

The next day, Keating looked bleary-eyed. He had spent six hours in the Rat (as it was commonly known as) and left the pub a darn sight happier than when he arrived. From thereon in the two men tolerated each other. Keating was the one that bore a grudge though.

Conversations between them were minimal as the feud simmered on. Keating had mulled the incident over, deciding not to turn this into a disciplinary because Steven's case was strong, and it would backfire on him. He would bide his time and wait for an opportunity to discredit him in other ways.

Steven was skilled at his job and respected by peers and those that worked for him, so Keating found it hard to make him culpable. Impatience got the better of him, so he engineered a scheme that he thought would lead to Steven's demise.

Two years of plotting on Keating's part had now paid off. The plan had come to fruition. Cooper would lose his job over this, as Keating's subterfuge prompted disciplinary proceedings.

Steven's angst would soon be over as next Monday, HR would reveal the results of the investigation at a 10am meeting. Sarah sensed the tension rising in her man, so she tried to keep him busy and entertained. Just before leaving for work on Friday morning, she leant over her husband's favourite recliner armchair to give him a kiss goodbye.

'The weather forecast for Saturday is sunny, so I've invited Karyn and Mark round in the evening for a barbecue and a few drinks.'

'Oh, you haven't, have you? I'm not good company at the moment.'

'Rubbish! We'll have a laugh, you'll see. Sunday's a cooler day so you can go for your run in the morning' (a favourite activity of his). 'Then we'll have a pub lunch at The Old English Gentleman' (their local, a short stroll from the house).

Steven resigned himself to the fact she had planned his weekend for him and agreed to the activities.

That evening, Sarah popped into the supermarket to stock up for the planned barbecue. Deciding against those low-fat quarter-pounder beef burgers this time, she chose four pieces of steak instead. She added a bag of ready prepared mixed salad to the basket along with some coleslaw with cheddar cheese that Steven liked. Wine was a simple choice since Prosecco was on special offer, 25% off if you chose six bottles! Both she and Karyn liked this. Steven enjoyed the supermarket's own brand Belgian beer, so a pack containing 24 cans was a perfect choice. She hurried home after checkout to rearrange the fridge to fit in the perishable food and wine that needed to be chilled. Steven was cleaning up the barbecue, which pleased her. Steven turned serious for a moment.

'You know I might lose my job on Monday, don't you?'

'I don't see how you will. You've done nothing wrong, so there won't be any evidence, will there?'

'I suppose not, but I've a niggling feeling that Keating will have stitched me up, fabricating evidence just to get rid of me!'

'We'll cross that bridge when, and if, we come to it, shall we? I don't want you to worry about it this weekend. We've got each other no matter what happens.'

'But the house? How will we pay the mortgage? Where will we...?'

'Shush, shush, shush, you old pessimist you!' She tapped a playful smack on his hand as she spoke.

'Everything will be all right. We'll work things out whatever happens, you'll see.'

She dropped the subject, but she could see that Steven was still sceptical. She loved her husband. He'd never let her down, and she knew he wouldn't now. He was already preparing for the worst. She found an open document on his MacBook two days ago; his CV. She had skimmed over it, and thought it impressive. They shared the final dregs of a chilled rosé before going back inside to relax. Sarah searched Spotify and found a Seasick Steve playlist. Steven loved listening to Seasick. She sent it to the media server and set it to play in the lounge whilst Steven kicked back on the recliner. He shut his eyes whilst listening to *'I started out with nothing and I still got most of it left'*. A minute later, a chilled beer appeared on the table next to him.

'You trying to get me drunk, Mrs C?' he quipped with one eye open and a smile. *That's better,* she thought. *More like himself.*

Karyn and Mark had lived next door for over five years now. Karyn was from Ukraine. Mark never discussed his origins, he just said he had lived and worked all over, no details. He never spoke of family, neither did he seem to have many friends nor many visitors. They seemed very much to keep themselves to themselves. In contrast to Steven and Sarah, their relationship was tempestuous. Sarah and Steven sometimes heard heated discussions coming through open windows on their neighbour's property. Little spats often started between them two as one would relate a story or experience, whilst the other would contradict the stated facts. This behaviour often amused their hosts. There was an embarrassing occasion when Mark went too far. The contradicting turned into a mocking. Karyn got upset and stormed out. The next morning was one of those occasions when they heard raised voices coming from the neighbouring property. Karyn was a fiery lady when upset and angry.

Mark was a freelance film and sound editor. He worked from home. Their property had a large garden backing on to some woodland. Halfway up the garden bordering the fence was Mark's editing suite, a fortified log cabin. (Karyn called it his Man Cave.) Security was essential, as it contained a lot of expensive equipment to do with his job. Nobody was allowed in the cabin. Not even Karyn. Mark was funny like that, stating that a lot of what he did was confidential pre-release material.

'My work's top secret. I've signed confidentiality agreements.' He would say.

Sometimes Mark would have to go away for what he called business meetings. He could be away for several days, and meetings would sometimes straddle a weekend. Karyn never accompanied him, and he would never talk about who he met or what they discussed. Apart from the secretive side to his life and trade, he was friendly enough.

Karyn worked on the checkout at the local supermarket. She had a strong Ukrainian accent and whilst her English was OK, it was nevertheless a second language for her. Because of this, she sometimes had an interesting turn of phrase.

When the Coopers were new to the neighbourhood a *'While you were out'* card was posted through their door. The card notified of a failed parcel delivery left for collection next-door at number 35.

That evening, Steven pulled on his hoody. Sarah was preparing dinner.

'Time to meet the neighbour, won't be long love.' He walked round to the neighbour's front door.

'Karyn answered the door, and they introduced themselves to each other. Steven thanked her very much for taking the parcel in.

Steven relayed their conversation to Sarah. 'She told me I was anytime welcome. Welcome to what? I wonder?'

Sarah gave him a playful punch on the arm, 'Behave you!'

Sarah and Karyn soon became good friends. Karyn received a key to number 34 and would do the neighbourly thing of watering houseplants whilst the couple were away.

Saturday arrived as a sunny day and a promise of 25° C. Steven erected a gazebo on the decking for shade. Late afternoon, the barbecue was lit to prepare for Karyn and Mark to arrive.

The latch on the gate rattled. 'Hello. We have come,' Karyn called out.

Steven slid the bolt across and let his neighbours into the garden. Sarah stood holding a bottle of chilled Prosecco.

'Hi you two. I hope you're both hungry!'

Steven passed a glass of wine to Karyn first.

'Hungry like a horse… Ooooh Prosecco, thank you!'

Mark accepted a cold beer.

The couples chinked glasses. They greeted each other with handshakes and pretend kisses on each cheek. They all made themselves comfortable sitting on the decking to enjoy the food.

Alcohol worked its magic as the evening wore on and the conversation flowed well, punctuated with laughter here and there. Sarah was pleased to see Steven relaxing. It was gone 11.30pm when the conversation died down. The evening had ended. The Stewarts said their goodnights and thanked their hosts for a lovely evening before leaving. Steven started clearing up plates and glasses.

'Leave that love. I'll do it in the morning whilst you are out on your run.'

Sarah grabbed her man by the arm and led him indoors to the bedroom. It wasn't long before they were both entwined in a passionate embrace.

Soon afterwards, the Watcher had tuned in to enjoy watching the very private activities of this loving couple.

Chapter 2

Keating, for the past three months, had lived a lonely existence, his best friend now being the bottle. His domestic association by marriage to the Kilburn family had now ended. It was over the last time he raised his hand to Jessica, his wife, whilst in a drunken stupor. Police attended. He had spent a night in a police cell, lucky to leave the next morning with just a caution. Following his release he collected his belongings from the doorstep of the house he used to call home. The sight of his dishevelled, unshaven self, ferrying several dustbin bags of clothes and personal effects, from the doorstep to the boot and back seat of his Series 5 BMW looked strange.

The neighbour opposite was giving a running commentary to his wife. 'Ha, it looks like Keating's missus has finally given her old man his marching orders. Look at him, loading up his Beemer. I expect he deserved to get kicked out.'

Keating had no friends. Estranged from his family, he was also too embarrassed to visit his ageing parents' house after years of no contact. Animosity existed between him and his sister. She called him two years ago but only to let him know of their dad's onset of Alzheimer's. She was struggling to cope. A plea for help fell on deaf ears; neither sibling had spoken to each other since that day.

In contrast to the Coopers, Keating spent his weekend alone in his rented flat, consuming large amounts of alcohol. This helped him accept the fact that Jessica now wanted a divorce. His mood was happier this weekend though. His master plan to get rid of Steven Cooper was soon to reach maturity.

By lunchtime on Monday, Cooper would become unemployed and would no longer be a threat to his own continued employment at Kilburn's. He was looking forward to taking the credit for identifying Cooper as the guilty party. He would regain credibility with his wife's uncle following his separation from Jessica.

Whilst still sober, sitting alone early on the Saturday evening, he mulled over his covert actions during the past couple of months. *Had he forgotten anything?* He didn't think so. He'd removed all traces of incriminating emails from his account. They'd check phone records in the investigation. Fortuitously, he made the phone call to the competitor from

Cooper's telephone extension. Yes his confidence level that the evidence trail pointed to Cooper was high.

An unexpected email had arrived from the HR lady yesterday. She required his attendance at the disciplinary meeting on Monday. *Excellent*, he mused, he would get to witness Cooper's demise.

As the light faded, the TV flickered, reflecting off the walls. Keating wasn't watching it. He refilled his empty glass to savour yet another celebratory glass of his favourite tipple, Chivas Regal. He finally fell asleep in his armchair, only coming to in the early hours of the morning. He made his way to bed, still unmade from the night before.

Late Sunday morning, he woke to the frantic clicking noise of a pair of magpies in the garden. There was a cat somewhere that needed seeing off, he surmised. Last night's overindulgence signalled it was time to rehydrate himself. He couldn't face eating breakfast yet. A cup of tea and a cool shower cleared the muzziness in his head. The last phase of his recovery relied upon the coffee machine's ability to produce a strong espresso.

It was a sunny morning, so Keating drank his shot of caffeine in the garden. He sat reading the free local paper that the paper girl had pushed through the door earlier, until he fell asleep.

It was 2.30pm before he woke up. A walk to the Hat Maker's Arms for a carvery lunch was the final highlight of the weekend. Keen to appear at his best for tomorrow's meeting, he decided on a rare night of abstinence. Mr Kilburn would surely want to see him after the meeting to thank him for his diligence.

Chapter 3

Steven and Sarah did not sleep well on the Sunday night because Steven's restlessness kept them both awake. The Watcher's visit before midnight was brief. There was no carnal activity to interest him that evening.

The dreaded Monday morning had arrived. It was a bright June morning, and the dawn chorus heralded the daylight hours. Steven lay there mulling over what today might bring. His thoughts, again, were not positive. It was about 7am when one of Sarah's eyes opened. She looked across at Steven. He was lying on his back, staring up at the ceiling. The meeting at Kilburn's was at 10am. He'd need to leave at about 9.15am.

Sarah was also apprehensive, but hid this feeling when she forced her other eye open and swung her legs over the edge of the bed. She stretched her arms out towards the ceiling whilst mouthing a noisy yawn. She looked over at Steven.

'How about I make us both a nice cooked breakfast whilst you jump in the shower?'

Steven thought briefly. 'Thanks darling, but do you know, I really don't feel I could eat much this morning,' - and then compromised - 'perhaps I could manage some toast and a strong coffee.'

'Coming right up!'

She went down to prepare breakfast for them both.

Conversation over breakfast was slow. Steven did his best to eat as much as he could, wanting to please Sarah.

'Right! I must get ready, thanks for brekkers love.' He went upstairs to prepare himself for the day.

When he reappeared, he was suited and booted. Sarah loved to see him in his suit. He always looked immaculately dressed. She loved him for it. He always smelt good too, Issey Miyake today, if she wasn't mistaken. A little after 9.10am and Steven was ready to leave. Sarah adjusted his smart red tie, even though it didn't need it. They had a long, lingering kiss in the hallway. Sarah leaned back, grabbing both of his hands, 'Don't worry love, whatever happens, I still love you and I'm sure everything's going to be fine.' On that encouraging note, Steven left and climbed into his ageing Nissan Primera for the journey to work.

He pulled up to the entrance of Kilburn's car park at about 9.50am. Steven could recall very little of the drive in, not even the suicidal tendencies of several birds daring to swoop low in front of the car as it travelled down the lower Harpenden Road.

He parked the car and made his way inside the building. His security pass had been suspended. He approached the reception desk.

Samantha was working there this morning. She looked up as he arrived at the desk.

'Hello Mr Cooper, it's nice to see you back.'

'Hi Sam, it's good to be back. Can you let me in, please? I don't have a pass with me.'

'Of course.' Without hesitation, she reached over and pushed a button with a perfectly manicured finger. The turnstile gate clicked, allowing Steven to push through. 'Thanks Sam.'

'No problem, Mr Cooper, have a nice day.'

Steven turned immediately right and walked down the corridor towards the HR department. As he approached, a familiar guffaw echoed down the corridor, Keating! There he was, sharing a joke with someone from Accounts. He stood with a small audience gathered around the water dispenser, sipping water from one of those silly conical paper cups. Steven felt sick in the pit of his stomach at the sight. *What is he doing here? Ready to spill more poison to discredit me?* The group dispersed as Steven got nearer. Keating walked off towards an emergency exit further down the corridor. This exit was commonly used by employees wishing to pop out for a smoke. Steven watched him disappear through the door.

He knocked on the door marked Human Resources before pushing it open.

Inside, the HR lady was sitting at her desk. Nafesa was a bubbly personality with smiling eyes. She was very efficient and ideally suited in her position as PA to Carlton Wills- Cromby, the Director of HR.

Nafesa looked up as Steven appeared in the doorway.

'Good morning, Steven. Come in, I'll let Carlton know you're here.'

'Morning Nafesa, thanks.' Steven entered the office.

She pressed a button on her desk phone. Wills-Cromby's familiar voice sounded, 'Yes, Nafesa?'

'Mr Cooper has arrived for your ten o'clock meeting.'

'Ah, good, thank you. Give me two minutes and I'll be right out.'

Nafesa gestured towards a comfortable seat against the opposite wall.

'Take a seat while we wait. He won't be long.' Steven sat down just as the office door opened again and in walked Keating.

Avoiding eye contact with Steven, he went straight over to the PA's desk.

'Hello my darling, and how are *you* today?'

Steven saw Nafesa's smile slip at the over-familiar greeting from this creepy individual!

Keating wasn't a pleasant person to be around at the best of times. Today was no different. The odour of a heavy smoker quickly permeated the room. He was what Steven termed a dirty smoker, his breath and clothes always stank of the over indulgences of his habit. Nafesa wrinkled her nose in disgust.

'Please take a seat Mr Keating.' She then quickly diverted her attention to something apparently more interesting on her computer monitor. Keating took the hint and moved away.

Steven's hand instinctively patted his trouser pocket as his smartphone buzzed. Glad of the distraction, he took it out and used his fingerprint to access its contents. He was pleased to see a WhatsApp message from Sarah.

Love You Darling - good luck xxxxxx.

The door to the inner sanctum opened. Steven's stomach churned as the eccentrically dressed Director of HR emerged. He bent down to whisper something in Nafesa's ear. Steven thought he heard mention of Kenny. *This could be bad news,* he thought. When they called Kenny to HR, it was normally his job to supervise a desk clearance operation before escorting unfortunate, sacked employees off the premises. Kenny was an ideal choice for security. He was over 6 feet tall and powerfully built. He was, in fact, a gentle giant. He could be intimidating if he needed to be though.

Nafesa picked up the phone to make the call as Wills-Cromby straightened and pulled down the bottom of his brightly coloured waistcoat. He twiddled with his matching bow tie before turning to the two waiting men.

'Good morning, gentlemen.' He gestured his hand towards the door marked Conference Room. 'Thank you for being on time. We'll meet in here. Please go in and take a seat.'

The meeting room was opulently furnished with a large oval light oak table. There were ten comfortable chairs arranged around it and a conference phone in the centre of the table. The wall at one end of the room supported a large monitor. The opposite wall had an interactive smart board.

The colourful director followed in. He turned around and asked Nafesa to join them when she had finished her call. He sat opposite them, placing a large folder on the table in front of him. Steven strained to hear what was being said outside. Yes, Kenny's name was mentioned again. More stomach churning took place.

Wills-Cromby put on his half glasses. The colourful arms on the spectacles complemented the matching bow tie and waistcoat ensemble. Looking very judge-like, he peered over the top of the spectacles balanced near the tip of his nose before opening the folder.

On top was an ominous-looking sealed white envelope. Steven couldn't read the writing on it from his position, but it was obviously a person's name, judging by the spacing of the characters. Steven heard the phone go down outside. Nafesa entered the room. She shut the door and took her seat at the end of the oval table below the giant TV screen. Wills-Cromby looked up from his folder first at Steven, then he glanced over at Keating.

'I've asked Nafesa to take written minutes for our records. We need to show that we have followed proper procedures.' The director studied some written notes for a few seconds.

'Do you both understand?'

Steven and Keating nodded in unison.

'Also, can we confirm that you both know the purpose of this meeting?'

The two men nodded again.

'For the record,' - Wills-Cromby nodded at Nafesa to be sure she minuted this bit - 'it is to discuss the outcomes of our investigation into an allegation made against you, Steven, and to take whatever action is deemed necessary.'

Nafesa skilfully and efficiently noted this down in shorthand. She also recorded the responses made by Steven and Keating.

'Before I present our findings, have either of you got any questions? Would either of you like to say anything?' Both shook their heads.

'OK,' the director began. 'You are both aware of the serious allegation. It required a thorough investigation before we could decide what action we should take.'

He peered over his glasses at the two men opposite.

'We've concluded that investigation and I have to say it revealed some very interesting results.'

Keating adjusted his seating position and cleared his throat as if he was about to speak but didn't.

Wills-Cromby reiterated the allegation.

'Our R & D boys discovered some software and components in a competitor's product, identical to those in our own sampler module. Tim's initial investigation has implicated you, Steven.'

He peered over his spectacles once more. 'So, gentlemen, is that your understanding of the facts?'

Steven nodded and Keating finally spoke. 'Yes, that's what we discovered.'

'Do you wish to comment, Steven?' the director asked. Steven cleared his throat.

'Just, I've always been loyal. I categorically deny giving information to any outsiders.'

Keating made a 'humph' noise, trying to ridicule Steven's plea of innocence. He then had eye contact with the director, expecting to see a positive acknowledgement, but Wills-Cromby remained impartial.

'Until yesterday, we had little evidence to disprove this…'
'But…' Keating interjected.

The director quickly showed Keating the palm of his hand, cutting him short. He then carried on with his deliberations.

'It all came down to an analysis of email and phone records.' He cleared his throat.

'We found an incriminating email trail in your email history, Steven, which didn't look good for you. We also found one telephone call made from your desk phone, the timing of which ties in with these emails and attachments. The emails blatantly discuss the sampler module design in some detail.'

Keating relaxed. His efforts to get rid of Steven seemed back on track.

Steven protested. 'I don't understand this! I promise you; I have contacted nobody from Shaw's by phone or email.'

'Bear with me, Steven. I understand your frustrations. Let me finish.'

Keating looked smugly at Steven.

Wills-Cromby continued, 'The email trail was interesting. A record of every email sent and received is logged on a server with a unique journal number. When we examined the log, we noticed some journal numbers were missing. Strange, we thought.'

Keating started wringing his hands.

'I had our IT Administrator restore the email backup files around the date of the missing journal numbers.'

Keating became the subject of a sharp stare from the director. He was now looking nervous.

'I think *you* can shed some light on these missing emails, Tim.' The stare continued. Keating looked like a rat caught in a trap.

'No, I, I don't know what you mean… What about the phone call he made?'

'Ah yes, the phone call. That was initially a mystery. We decided anybody could have made that call.' The director paused and then continued. 'One thing *is* for certain, Steven didn't make it! Neither did he send the suspect emails!'

Keating ridiculed the very suggestion, 'Pah! How could you know that?'

Steven relaxed a little as he listened to the discussion between the two men.

'Because Steven was working in Nyon in Switzerland that week!'

Keating's mouth dropped. 'Well, who sent the emails? Who made the calls?'

'We've proof of that too,' came the reply. The director looked through the pile of papers in his folder before producing and referring to a single page report. 'We analysed the security pass records. I'm sure you know we keep a record of who accesses which areas with their pass. Records show everybody except *you*, Tim, had left the office before the call in question took place. You also accessed Steven's email account and sent those emails from his desktop computer. Then, to cover your tracks and to make sure Steven wouldn't see them, you deleted them from the sent box. A few minutes later, records show you left the office for the night.'

'That's ridiculous. How could I have possibly accessed Cooper's email account?'

'Initially, we also wondered how that was possible,' the director mused. 'The answer came from the IT boys. Luckily, one of them remembered that you, Tim, had requested access to Steven's account two weeks previously. Apparently, you said that Steven was uncontactable and that you needed urgent access to some test results stored on his computer. As Steven's line manager, the IT Helpdesk granted you the access you requested.'

Keating was still catching flies when asked to explain this damning evidence. He was apparently speechless as he saw his world crumbling.

Wills-Cromby took off his glasses and looked directly at Keating as if passing sentence. 'This is an act of gross misconduct; therefore, I dismiss you from this employment with immediate effect.'

The letter Steven had noticed earlier was passed across the table to Keating. Struggling to speak, Keating, shakily, protested, 'It's not true. It was him!' pointing an accusing finger at Steven.

Wills-Cromby turned to Nafesa, 'Call Kenny in please, Nafesa.'

Nafesa opened the door. The man-mountain frame of Kenny entered the room.

'Kenny, please escort Mr Keating to his desk. Allow him 20 supervised minutes to clear it then escort him off the premises - thank you.'

Kenny turned to Keating, who now looked close to tears. Kenny gestured a hand towards the door. 'Come with me please, sir.'

Keating jumped from his seat and lunged at Steven. 'You'll pay for this!'

Steven leaned back to avoid contact. Kenny quickly restrained Keating. and wagged his left index finger in

Keating pointed and wagged his left index finger in Steven's face.

'You're a dead man walking!' He moved his outstretched index finger closer to Steven's face and followed up with, 'Pow!' sharply pulling his hand back as if from the recoil of a gun.

He's lost it, thought Steven.

Wills-Cromby held a finger up. 'Just one more thing.'

Keating turned to him, breathless and with watery eyes, 'What now?'

'Please put your company car keys and security pass on the table.'

Kenny still had hold of Keating's arm. Keating attempted another lunge forward, this time towards Wills-Cromby, who didn't flinch. Kenny still had a firm grip when Keating ripped his pass from the lanyard around his neck. He threw it onto the table. He then reached into his pocket and removed a bunch of keys. His hand shaking, he removed the Beemer keys and threw them towards the director. They skidded across the shiny surface and tipped over the edge onto the floor, landing at the director's feet.

'Take him away now please, Kenny.'

Kenny jostled the protesting man towards the door. 'I'll sue for unfair dismissal!' Kenny unceremoniously pushed him out of the office. Things fell quiet again as the outer office door closed. Nafesa took her seat at the table once more.

Wills-Cromby sighed and shook his head slowly whilst he neatly reassembled and stacked the papers in the folder before closing it and sliding it aside. He looked at Steven. 'Coffee?' Taken aback by this sudden change in the man's persona

Steven struggled to find the words. 'Erm... yes please, sir.'

'Carlton, please,' was the reply. Carlton then turned to his PA. 'Thank you, Nafesa. Type those minutes up and place them on file, also, we'd better send a copy to Mr Kilburn, just to keep him in the loop. But please bring us some coffee. I'm sure Steven could use some.'

Nafesa assembled her notes and left to make the coffee.

'We need to talk. George and I want to say how sorry we are. It was a nasty business. Your HR record keeps its blemish-free status. It's been a difficult few weeks, I expect.'

Steven didn't need to think long. 'It was stressful! I have a lovely, beautiful wife who has supported me throughout the process, but she shared my anxieties too. I know it's rude, but would you mind if I sent her a quick message? I'd like to put her mind at rest.'

'Of course not, old chap. Go ahead, call her if you like I'll check the progress of the coffee.'

Carlton rose from his seat whilst Steven reached for his mobile. He decided against calling as she would want to hear all the details, it would take too long to relay everything that had happened, so he sent a quick message instead.

Don't worry, everything has turned out fine. I am innocent! Will explain all when I get home. Love you, S xxx.

The HR Director returned to take his seat. Nafesa followed in with a tray of fresh coffee and proper cups and saucers. Steven felt honoured that the best china was brought out for him. He confirmed how he liked his coffee. Nafesa quickly poured the freshly brewed coffee before leaving them both alone to talk.

'OK...' Carlton began. 'We now need to replace Keating, don't we? I've made George, erm, Mr Kilburn that is, fully aware of this morning's events. He knows of Keating's demise. We've discussed the vacant position and we both unanimously agree that we would like to appoint you as the new Head of Product Development.'

Steven looked stunned, not believing what he was hearing. He quickly put his coffee cup down in case he dropped it.

'Don't give me an answer now, you'll probably want time to think about it and discuss it with your lovely wife and that's fine.' He paused. 'There's something else I need to tell you. In two weeks, we are picking up a major project with Médecins Sans Frontières in Portugal. We'd like you to head up the project team.'

The director lifted his cup to take a generous gulp of his coffee whilst looking for a reaction from Steven.

'Erm, yes, I'd welcome, positively welcome the promotion, thank you.'

'I should add that it comes with all the usual benefits like private health insurance, the bonus scheme and' - Carlton picked the car keys up from the floor - 'a car... This one is only six months into its lease. Would you take this one over. It's a Series 5 BMW, I think? We'll have it valeted for you. What do you think?'

'Yes... Yes, of course, no problem.'

'OK, we have a bit of paperwork to do. I'll get Nafesa to prepare a formal offer for you in writing. I'll have the car delivered to your house. We'll post the keys through your letter box if you're not there. George, I know, will be very pleased that you are accepting the position. We're sorry you have had an awful few weeks. George and I have agreed that your start date in the new position will be exactly two weeks from today. Go home. Tell your wife what's happened. See if you can get a late booking somewhere in the sun.

Oh, and the other thing is that Keating won't be getting his bonus now, so we are diverting £1500 of it to your bank account to pay for your break. Think of it as compensation. For what he put you through.'

'Thanks very much. I really thought you were going to sack me. I can't take it all in. I appreciate your diligence in rooting out the evidence to find the truth and thank you for the job offer and thanks to you and Mr Kilburn for the company's generosity.'

Carlton held his hand up, showing Steven his broad palm. 'No need. We're glad the facts were established, and the right person got his comeuppance. We could then do the right thing by you.'

The director finished his coffee and looked at his watch. 'You must excuse me. I have another meeting in five minutes. Stay, finish your coffee, phone your wife if you need to.' He reached across the table to shake Steven's hand. 'We'll see you in two weeks' time. Enjoy your break. Be ready for some hard work on an exciting project when you return.'

'I will. Thank you once again.'

'Good, good,' said the director, giving Steven's hand an enthusiastic shake. He then gathered up his folder and left the conference room. Steven sat down again to ponder what had just happened.

* * *

Less than 30 minutes later, Keating sat in a quiet corner of the Rat hidden from sight from the rest of the bar, only revealing his presence to refill his glass with his favourite IPA brew. Whilst deep in thought, his bloodshot, red-rimmed eyes stared ahead.

To rub salt in his wounds, he overheard two of his ex- co-workers, over lunch, talking about the events of the morning and gleefully speculating what work life will be like under their new manager, Steven Cooper. Keating's vengeful thoughts focused on plotting various schemes of retribution against the man he hated. He remained festering until late afternoon. It was time to catch the last bus home.

* * *

Steven's mind was still replaying the morning's events as he turned into his drive at the end of his journey. Sarah saw the car draw up outside; she ran to the door to greet her man. Steven ran into her arms for a long, passionate kiss. She pulled him into the lounge, where Steven told her the good news.

'That's great news. I knew you'd be ok. How exciting, we can go on holiday too.' Before the end of the afternoon, they had booked a last-minute ten-day break to Majorca, leaving from London Luton Airport the following day.

Sarah popped around to see Karyn. Over a cup of tea, she relayed the news to her friend. Karyn was so pleased and yes, she would look after the house and water the plants whilst Steven and Sarah enjoyed their holiday.

Sarah finished her tea. 'Must dash now, got to work out what to pack,'

The ladies hugged. 'You have the lovely time.' Karyn lightly kissed her friend on the cheek.

'Mark's being busy in the Man Cave. He is coming in soon, I expect. I'll tell him the time of the aeroplane. He'll drive to the airport with you both tomorrow.'

Excited, Sarah said goodbye and went home to prepare for their unexpected holiday.

The Watcher had already received the news; he was sure that he would witness an evening of celebratory passion at the Cooper's and wasn't disappointed.

Chapter 4
September 2017

Steven had been in his new position at Kilburn's for three months now. Some normality had returned to the Coopers' lives. There had been some odd occurrences, though. The Coopers received junk mail daily, more than you would expect. Anything from companies offering funeral plans to sex shop catalogues turned up. Added to this, somebody was instructing local fast- food chains and restaurants to deliver pizzas, Chinese and Indian meals to their house. Steven suspected Keating' s hand in this. It was just the sort of childish thing he'd do.

It was Saturday morning on 16th September. Sarah had popped into town. Steven was relaxing at home listening to more Seasick Steve. The letter box rattled as the postman pushed through today s delivery This time, amongst what had become the usual ' drivel . of junk mail, was a more formal looking letter addressed to Steven and marked *Private and Confidential*. Steven pulled the flap of the envelope open. Inside was a single sheet of A4 paper folded into four Steven unfolded the paper As he did so, a small amount of . white powder spilled . from the missive onto the kitchen table and floor.

'What the...' Steven then stared at the chilling message on the sheet of paper.

DIE NOW!

This malicious arrival shook Steven up. Thoughts raced through his mind. *What should he do now? What is the powder? Anthrax? Or something noxious?* He washed his hands with plenty of soap and water. He then reached for his mobile and dialled 999. The call handler asked several questions to establish what the emergency was. When the details were clear, she called all three emergency services, including a Chemical Spillage Unit.

The first help to arrive was nine long minutes later. A police car with its siren blaring pulled up outside. Steven opened the door to the police officer. He told the officer not to enter. He explained what had happened and his fears.

After checking there were no injuries and no immediate medical emergency, the officer told Steven to wait inside for further instructions. A cacophony of sirens disturbed the peace once more. An ambulance and a Chemical Spillage Unit arrived together.

Steven stood inside, looking out, watching the police officer brief a paramedic and an officer from the fire service.

The team from the fire brigade swung into action. They erected a decontamination tent at the rear of the fire department vehicle. Steven watched a figure, looking like something from a science fiction film, emerging from the tent.

The approaching figure carried something that looked like a picnic cool box. The person approached the front door. The door was pushed open, the emergency worker stepped into the hallway. Steven appeared at the lounge door. The tall figure, made even taller by the helmet that topped off his personal protection equipment, addressed Steven.

'Good morning, sir, Steven, isn't it? Do you mind if I call you Steven?'

'Erm… yes, that's fine.'

'Right, Steven, first thing laddie, are you ok?'

'Shaken with all of this, but yes, I'm fine.'

'Any reactions, rashes or dryness in the throat?'

'No nothing.'

'Good, that's an encouraging sign.'

He was doing his best to put Steven's mind at rest. The officer pressed an area on the front of his outfit. A blast of white noise emitted from his radio.

'This is Jackson with a status report, over.'

Accompanied by some static, the two men heard, 'Go ahead.'

'Mr Cooper is fine. There are no visible signs of injuries, rashes or breathing difficulties, over.'

The authoritative voice continued. 'Good, is the spillage contained within one area? Over.'

Steven responded, 'Yes, it's in the kitchen there,' nodding towards the closed kitchen door.

'That's great. You've contained the problem. Well done!'

A voice came over the radio once more. 'How much of this stuff is there? What does it look like?'

Jackson looked at Steven for an answer.

'Very little. No more than a dessert spoonful I'd say. It's a fine white powder.'

'Did you touch it?'

'Yeah, some fell on my hand as I opened the envelope.'

'Show me.' He held his hand out for the officer to examine.
'I washed my hands afterwards.'

'Good, good.' Jackson studied the hands. 'There are no obvious signs of trauma.' The officer produced a pair of latex gloves. 'Keep your hands away from your face and mouth, the gloves will help.'

To avoid contamination, Jackson held each glove open so Steven could just slide each hand in.

A conversation between the officer and incident commander outside ensued. The officer relayed his actions to the commander.

'OK sir, you must stay here.' Jackson entered the kitchen to collect a sample of the powder. He secured a small quantity inside the cool box, ready to carry out for analysis in the on-board laboratory.

Steven looked outside. An inflatable tunnel now stretched from the tent to his front door. A few minutes later, the kitchen door opened. The suited officer transported the mysterious cargo through the tunnel. Once inside the strange tent, a torrent of water erupted within to decontaminate the officer.

Steven's mobile phone rang.

'Hello Mr Cooper, it's Chief Fire Officer Taylor here. Are you still OK?'

'Nervous, but yes, I'm fine, thanks.'

'Good. You're doing well in there. Keep it up. Whatever you do, you must not leave the property; we'll get you out safely when and if we need to. The chances are that this substance is harmless, but we cannot take any chances. It's being analysed in our mobile lab; we should be able to identify it soon. Meanwhile, Mr Cooper, please stay inside with the door closed.
Is that clear?'

'Yes, no problem.'

'Questions?'

'No, I'm OK, thank you.'

'If there's any change in your situation, you must call me straight away. Do you understand?'

'Yup.'

'OK, keep calm whilst we work to identify this substance. We'll be in contact again as soon as we know, try not to worry though.'

The call ended. Steven felt alone, but a little reassured. He sat down to wait for news.

Meanwhile, The Watcher stood in the small gathering in the street, observing the activities outside Steven's house. It satisfied him that everything was on track for future developments he had planned for Steven Cooper.

Chapter 5

'Hydrated magnesium silicate?' Steven repeated as the fire commander looked on.

'Yes,' he said. 'You'll know this better as talcum powder... it's harmless. Somebody's idea of a joke, I expect.'

Steven now felt embarrassed he'd overreacted!

'Well, it's in poor taste! I can only apologise for wasting your time.'

The officer shook his head. 'No, no, sir, you did the right thing in calling us. You cannot be too careful this day and age.'

Steven seemed anxious. 'I was so worried about the powder; I'd forgotten about the message. Do you think my life's in danger?'

'Sorry sir, I didn't mean to sound alarmist, but you need to talk to the police about that. They're outside talking to my officer at the moment. They'll want to speak to you next, I'm sure.'

'Yes, listen, thank you for everything you have done today, and please thank your men as well, especially Mr Jackson.'

'I will, thanks. The ambulance has already left; nobody needed medical treatment. We'll finish packing our equipment and be on our way too.'

Steven held his hand out. The commander shook it and said, 'Enjoy the rest of your day, Mr Cooper.' Steven watched the commander walk up the garden path before closing the door.

Sarah arrived home just as the last of the decontamination equipment was being put away. She panicked to see the scene outside her house. She parked the Primera in the road and ran into the house.

'Steven! Where are you?'

Her husband emerged from the kitchen, dustpan and brush in hand.

'What's happening? Why's the fire brigade here? Who are those people outside? Has there been a fire?'

The dustpan and brush dropped to the floor as Steven put his arms around his panicked wife. 'It's a long story,' he said, 'but don't worry, everything is fine and no, there hasn't been a fire.'

Sarah took a step back and looked at her husband.

'Why didn't you call me? What's happened?'

Just then, the doorbell rang. Steven looked towards the front door.

'Look love, this is the police.'

Sarah looked shocked at the mention. 'The police?'

'Yes,' said Steven 'They want to speak to me, I think you'd better sit in on this for the full story.'

Still mystified, Sarah watched as her husband answered the door to a short, balding man.

'Good afternoon, Mr Cooper?' Steven nodded to the visitor. 'I'm Detective Chief Inspector Grant, Bedfordshire Police. I need to ask you about the events of this afternoon.'
He held his warrant card up. Steven read the name DCI Norman Grant below the younger-looking picture of the officer. 'Sure.' Steven said. 'Come in.'

The detective stepped in, shaking Steven's hand, then smiled and nodded at Sarah. Steven introduced her. 'Oh, this is my wife, Sarah.'

'Detective Chief Inspector Grant, pleased to meet you, Mrs Cooper.'

Sarah also shook the detective's hand.

'I'll make us some tea,' she said.

'Excellent,' said Grant. 'Milk one sugar, please.' Steven ushered the DCI into the lounge.

Grant began with some formal paperwork to record names, address, and details of the incident. He reassured Steven that his actions were justifiable. They continued the conversation as Sarah walked in with the tea. Her arrival was timed badly. The detective was mid-sentence:
'...after all, we mustn't forget this threat to your life.'

Sarah froze, still holding the tea tray as she stared at the two men. The teacups rattled on their saucers.

'What the hell has happened?' she asked.

Grant gestured towards a vacant armchair. 'Sit down, Mrs Cooper, please don't worry. We're here to help and investigate what happened. We'll find out who's responsible.'

Steven took the tray and placed it on the large, solid oak coffee table. Sarah's hand was shaking as she started pouring from the large teapot. She needed chocolate and helped herself to a large chocolate digestive before falling back into the armchair to listen. The detective leant forward to take an item from his jacket pocket.

'I hope you don't mind, but I would like to record this interview on my recorder.'

'No, that's fine,' said Steven.

Sarah sat, listening to Steven's account of the morning's events.

The interview moved onto the next stage. 'Who's behind this, do you think?'

'Well, yes, there's one name that comes to mind. Tim Keating. He tried to get me sacked from my job several months ago. He manufactured some evidence to give my employer the impression that I had been selling company secrets to a competitor. Fortunately, my employer saw through his subterfuge. He ended up getting the sack himself. I clearly remember the last words he spoke to me. He said, *'you're a dead man walking'!*'

'I see. Where can we find this Keating fellow?'

'I'm not sure,' said Steven. 'I knew where he lived when he was still with his wife, but it's my understanding that he moved out of the marital home.'

A pause for thought then, 'He might be known to you guys though.'

'Oh, why's that?' the DCI asked.

'I don't know the details, but I heard rumours that police removed him from his home because of a domestic incident.'

'Could be useful in tracking him down.'

'Otherwise you might need to contact Carlton Wills-Cromby, he's the HR Director at Kilburn's. You'll need to wait till Monday to do that though.'

'No problem, thank you. That's very helpful. Can you think of anything else? Or anybody else that might be of interest to us?'

Steven thought, 'I don't think so.' He turned to Sarah.

'Can you think of anything, love?'

'No, nothing comes to mind.'

The detective picked up his recording device. 'This is DCI Grant ending the interview with Mr and Mrs Steven Cooper at' - he looked at his watch - '15.12 on Saturday 16th September 2017.' He switched the device off.

'Thank you for the tea, Mrs Cooper.'

'You're welcome Chief Inspector.'

The detective rose to leave. 'I hope you don't have any more problems. I'll ask uniform to increase patrols in the area. Just a precaution you understand. Somebody will call you later today or tomorrow with a crime number. SOCO will drop by later today to take your fingerprints, Mr Cooper.' Steven looked up. 'Fingerprints?'

'Don't worry, it's just so we can eliminate your fingerprints from the envelope. We would be interested in any prints inside the envelope and its contents, you understand. An officer will call within the next few days with a transcript of our interview, a statement, for you to sign. Oh, and let us know if any more suspicious packages arrive.' 'Oh, OK. I understand.' The detective departed.

The Watcher had been a virtual attendee at the meeting. He was feeling very pleased with the outcome, things were going just as he'd planned.

Chapter 6

Two weeks prior to the curious events of the white powder incident, the four neighbours sat enjoying an early evening glass of wine in the cool garden shade of Mark's cabin.

They talked. Conversation was just general chitchat when suddenly, Sarah remembered a juicy bit of gossip she'd forgotten to share.

'Oh, yes… guess who I keep seeing?'

Mark was first with a witty suggestion. 'The Queen?'

They all laughed, 'No, don't be so silly.'

The next suggestion was from Steven. 'Lord Lucan riding Shergar?'

They laughed again. Karyn only laughed because everybody else did. She didn't know who Lord Lucan or Shergar were!

Sarah shook her head, 'Nope, I see this person in the park as I'm walking to the charity shop.'

Steven couldn't stand the suspense. 'Who then?' 'Your old boss, Keating!'

'Oh, him,' Steven said disdainfully.

'Yeah, but that's not all. He looks like a tramp now. And he's usually well on his way to being drunk, even at 10am in the morning! I see him sharing a park bench with a group of alcoholics. They're all drinking and smoking. He fits in well, looking like one of them now. I'm sure he's probably homeless, jobless, and penniless too.'

'Are you sure it's him?'

'Oh yes, he's got that very distinctive nose. I remember him from the Christmas do last year. And he's been there every day since I first saw him.'

Steven mused. 'Oh, how the mighty fall.'

Karyn chipped in with one of her unique turns of phrase, 'Sounds like he now gets his just deservings.' The others laughed at her comment.

Lively conversation continued, talking about nicer topics until the light faded.

Steven and Sarah thanked their hosts for a lovely get-together before departing. Both tired from a busy week, they quickly retired to bed.

There was nothing for the Watcher to see this evening.

Chapter 7

Keating's alternative lifestyle was a far cry from the one he'd been accustomed to. Most of his meagre Jobseekers Allowance was spent on cigarettes and alcohol. Divorce proceedings meant his bank account was frozen. He could no longer afford his rented flat and was forced to move into a grim bedsit in a not-so- nice area of town.

Each day was spent socialising with like-minded individuals in the local park. The circle of friends could all tell their own sad story. They'd given up on mainstream life, preferring instead to numb their senses with cheap alcohol from the supermarket.

His mobile phone no longer worked because of unpaid bills. With no phone, he couldn't continue the vendetta against Cooper. The animosity against the man he hated still festered inside. These feelings were slightly tempered as each day ended with him close to oblivion. Life for Tim Keating couldn't be much worse, but soon it would be.

It was a balmy Friday morning. The usual gathering of alcoholics occupied the park benches, all of them in a party mood. The alcohol slowly numbed the pain of their circumstances as time went by.

Cigarettes being smoked by the group were the product of foraging. They collected tobacco from the detritus of discarded dog-ends in the park. The precious harvest was sparingly rolled into cigarette papers, providing a cheap nicotine fix.

They enjoyed some laughs as the alcohol took effect. The activities attracted looks of disdain from passers-by rushing to fulfil their hectic lives.

Occasionally, strangers drifted through and joined the party. Some stayed for hours, others for days, and some even became regular members of the group.

Drifters were welcomed as long as they provided their own alcohol and smokes. They were especially popular if they shared whatever they brought to the party.

Today was one of those days. An extra member joined the get-together. He was welcome, providing beer and cigarettes, which flowed freely. Some of the makeshift roll-ups included the added ingredient of cannabis, also supplied by their new best friend. Nobody asked where he had got these welcome treats.

They remained non-judgemental and cared not about the origin of the treats.

By midday, the merry band was slurring their speech. At worst, some seemed close to a comatose state. The unknown visitor remained alert, as he'd only pretended to consume the copious amounts of alcohol and narcotics that the others had indulged in.

The visitor paid discreet attention to Tim Keating, watching and waiting for an opportune moment. *It wouldn't be long now*, he thought. Within the hour, the effects of smoking weed and drinking alcohol took over. Keating's head nodded until his chin was resting on his chest.

The Watcher seized this opportunity. He took care not to disturb the sleeping alcoholic, secreting a small plastic bag containing some white powder into a back pocket of Keating's grubby jeans.

Satisfied that the incriminating evidence had been planted, he walked away with the apparent gait of an intoxicated person towards the public conveniences behind the bandstand.

Twenty minutes later, none of the motley crew recognised the smartly dressed man walking past as their unexpected benefactor from this morning.

Chapter 8

Norman Grant was back in his cramped office. He sat in a high-backed leather chair at his desk. Opposite the desk were two ageing wooden chairs, one of which was occupied by Detective Inspector Jane Patterson. Patterson was new to the team, her first posting as a DI in the force. She was a slightly built brunette with sharp features. The 25-year-old had a First-Class Honours Degree in Criminology. She was keen to forge a suitable career in the police force for herself.

She sat attentively whilst DCI Grant briefed her on the incident he had attended earlier that day. They listened together to the recorded interview. Jane made the occasional note in her notebook as the interview progressed. The recording ended.

Her new boss was sceptical about these young, fast-tracked officers. He wanted to see how she performed.

'Ok Jane, what do you think about this case? Has any crime been committed? If so, who committed it and what should we do about it?'

'It's an interesting case. I believe a crime has been committed. Though whether the CPS would decide to prosecute, I'm unsure.' She paused, 'At the moment we have no proof that this erm' - she quickly consulted her notes - 'Keating is the perpetrator. We should track him down and get his version of the story, if there is one.'

Grant nodded an impressed nod. 'Good, and if we're to believe all the facts before us at the moment, what's he guilty of?'

'This amounts to harassment, stalking if you like. The Protection of Freedoms Act 2012 created two new offences in the previous act, one of which covers alarm or distress towards the victim. Sorry sir, I can't remember the exact section and paragraph details of the act.'

'Good call lass, well done! Next step?'

'I understand SOCO are looking at the envelope and its contents?'

Grant nodded.

'Then we wait for the results whilst we track down our suspect. Armed with what evidence we can get from SOCO, we'll pick him up for a little chat.'

'OK, that's a good start. I want you to take this case on. You OK with that?'

'Of course, sir, thank you,' was the eager reply.

'Good, keep me posted at all stages. When you go out to see our suspect, make sure you take someone from uniform with you.'

'Yes sir! Thank you.'

'Now, take my recording and get someone from Admin Support to type up a transcript. We need to get Mr Cooper to sign it afterwards. Then start some enquiries to locate this Keaton fellow.'

'Keating,' she corrected.

'Erm, yes, Keating,' confirmed the DCI.

Jane quickly jotted down her to-do list. She rose to leave. 'Thank you, sir!'

Chapter 9

The day after the white powder incident, Steven was jogging along the lanes bordering the golf club. Unable to think about anything else, he replayed yesterday's events through his mind again and again.

He thought how things could have turned out differently if the powder was indeed something dangerous. Keating had a sick and vindictive mind, that's for sure. It was a police matter now. Steven was sure the police would speak to him. At the very least, they would *fire a shot across his bows*. Hopefully, this would deter him from any more stupidity.

Steven paused, marking time at the entrance to the golf club car park. He searched for some music on his smartphone, intending to drive the thoughts of yesterday out of his head. Happy with Pink Floyd's *Dark Side of the Moon*, he jogged steadily through the car park and out into the leafy lane beyond, his troubled mind left behind.

Further down the lane Steven's pace of jog had nicely synchronised to the music he was enjoying. He continued past the abandoned pillbox at the side of the road. As he passed this point, he was totally unaware of a bead of red laser light dancing around on the back of his head.

The Watcher was practising focusing the laser light onto his intended target. Today wasn't the day for the next stage of the plan, but being a meticulous planner, he was entirely satisfied with the dummy run.

* * *

Nothing like some brisk exercise to get those endorphins going, Steven thought as he arrived back home.

'I'm home, love!' he called as he came through the back door.

'Did you have a nice run?' echoed from the lounge.

Steven poked his head into the lounge. 'Yeah, it's a lovely morning out there.'

Conscious he might be smelly after his vigorous exercise, he jumped into the shower to freshen up. Halfway through Steven felt the familiar form of Sarah's nakedness behind him. They enjoyed the rest of the shower together before moving into the bedroom.

The Watcher would have been disappointed to learn that he had missed the couple's afternoon activities.

Steven jumped out of bed to go downstairs to make them both a cup of tea. They sat up in bed enjoying the fresh brew and talked, once again, about the events of the day before. Steven expressed surprise that a uniformed officer should call a little after 9pm the previous evening to get a signature on the typed- up statement and then a forensics officer shortly afterwards to take Steven's fingerprints for elimination purposes.

'Do you think we're in danger?'

'No. The police promised extra patrols in the area which is a comfort. I'm sure they'll be keeping a close eye on us. It's not as if we don't know who is doing this, is it?'

'No, that's true. It's just a bit worrying to think what he might do next.'

'The police'll soon pick him up. I'll bet the letter he sent is covered in his tell tale prints and possibly some DNA, you'll see.'

Sarah felt a little better after Steven's comforting words.

'Goodness! It's nearly four o'clock,' she said. They both laughed.

'Hungry?'

Steven nodded, 'Tell you what, let's take a late lunch at the pub, then we can have a quiet night in later with a glass of wine and a DVD.'

This is what they agreed to do to bring the weekend, memorable for lots of reasons, to a close.

Chapter 10

Jane Patterson arrived at the office at 9am Monday morning. On the desk was an A4 sealed jiffy bag addressed to her. The package was from the Forensics Department, who had efficiently investigated and prepared a report for the evidence collected from Saturday's incident. She eagerly opened the package and began read the report. The report highlighted key points for consideration:

> Two sets of fingerprints; one Mr Cooper's and the other unknown.
>
> No DNA present on the envelope or contents.
>
> Text was created by an everyday laser printer - owned by millions in the UK alone.

Not much to go on, she thought, but, remembering the interview with Mr Cooper, she recalled that the prime suspect was known to police for a domestic disturbance. Were Keating's fingerprints recorded? she mused, probably not for this minor offence. A quick check of the police database confirmed this.

As a first step Mr Keating needed to be brought in for fingerprinting. Armed with the last known address, the marital home, Jane started her hunt. Mrs Keating was helpful, but even she didn't know where her estranged husband now lived. She thought he was not working and was probably on the dole.

Jane emailed the DWP requesting an address for Mr Keating. She was now waiting for a response.

* * *

Two days later, DCI Grant was attending another unrelated investigation when he felt his smartphone buzzing in his pocket. It could be important, so he checked to find an email from the DWP. It didn't contain the information requested *for security reasons,* but the email contained a link to a password-protected site with the requested information. A text message followed on his phone with a password to be used to access the site. He forwarded the email and text message to Jane with a reiterated warning not to go looking for this Keating fellow without backup.

***

That afternoon, Jane and a uniformed PC named Joe Chandler arrived outside the address given by the DWP. The uniformed officer manoeuvred the patrol car into a narrow gap between an abandoned Ford Fiesta and an old tatty BMW. The officers got out of the car.

Jane looked at the faded nameplate by the main entrance to check the address. 'Hall Place, this is it.'

The tired looking three-storey building stretched in front of them. Window frames were long overdue for a repaint. Window panes were covered in years' worth of grime. Jane, who was a self-confessed person with OCD regarding cleanliness in her own home, looked distastefully at the scene before her. The scruffy net curtains hanging in the window next to the entrance were in tatters. They were probably white when new, but now heavily stained yellow by the excesses of tobacco smoke. It was part of her job to visit places like this. She grimaced.

The front door of the building was ajar. Next to the door was a vandalised panel of buttons. Some had names against them. Some plastic fronts to the buttons had been defaced with heat from a Zippo or something similar. These were melted and distorted. The officers entered the premises. Jane's nose wrinkled at the unpleasant smell of stale urine and tobacco smoke within.

They both observed evidence of drug taking under the stairwell on the right, mostly pieces of tin foil tainted brown and black from its illicit use. On the left, was room 101, a scruffy door and frame. Various botched repairs evidenced damage of it being broken down more than once. The officers walked along to the end of the corridor. Here there was a lift. The door was open, and it had been this way for a very long time. In the gloom, on the floor of the lift, was what looked like a bundle of rags. Upon closer inspection, Jane realised that within the rags was a person sleeping. On either side of the lift was a corridor leading to the other rooms on this ground floor. Because rooms on this floor started with a one, they assumed that room 211 would be on the first floor. The officers turned to ascend the steps.

The walls of the stairwell were daubed with many obscenities and so-called tags from those who rated themselves as a bit of an artist. The stairs turned on to a landing halfway up to reveal more of the same. Once on the first floor, a corridor replicated that on the floor below. Four holes in the plastered wall suggested there was once a sign attached to show which way to go. Jane turned to the left, whilst her colleague turned to the right.

Joe spoke first. 'This side starts at 215.' He turned to look at the door opposite. 'Hang on, the door number is missing on this one.' He moved further down the dark corridor. 'This one's 233, so I think the last one is 234. 211 must be on your side.'

Joe walked back towards the DI and joined her in the search for room 211.

A few doors down the gloomy corridor, lit only by a flickering fluorescent tube, a blue door with the number 211 came into view. The PC banged loudly on the door and, for good measure, also rattled the metal letter box cover. They both tilted their heads towards the door, listening intently for any signs of life within.

There was nothing to be heard apart from the annoying ticking sound of the strobing light in the corridor.

'Try again, Joe.'

He once again banged on the door, harder this time. Both listened, once again, nothing! Then, the sound of bolts sliding across from the door behind them. They turned to see who would appear. The door to room 203 opened, restrained by a door chain, the face of a tall unkempt man appeared in the gap. Fresh, unpleasant smells wafted from the room to further irritate Jane's nose. The face spoke with a voice that could only belong to a heavy smoker.

'Hey man, wot's goin' on down wit all dat noise?'

'Sorry we disturbed you, sir.' Jane held up her warrant card to the gap in the door.

'I'm Detective Inspector Jane Patterson from Bedfordshire Police.'

The man squinted his eyes to better read the identification being shown.

Jane gestured towards the door opposite. 'Do you know the person who lives here?'

'Yeah, I seen 'im abaht… why wot's 'e dun?'

Jane dodged the question. 'We just need some help with a local investigation, that's all.'

'Well, 'e ain't in I 'erd 'im go aht this mornin' 'e allas does you know… I 'ears the door slammin' 'baht the same time every day' …'e dun't come back till artur tea normally.'

Joe moved closer to the gap in the door. 'Do you know his name?'

'Nah mate, we don't do names 'ere.'

'Do you know where he goes during the day?' asked Jane.

'Dunno if 'e goes t'same place every day but saw 'im once wiya bunch o' mates by the old bandstand in the park dahn the road.'

Jane was ready to leave. 'Thank you, sir. You've been very helpful. Enjoy the rest of your day.'

'Yeah right,' he rasped as the door abruptly slammed shut. The officers looked at each other.

Fairly new to the area, Jane wondered where the park was.

'It's just down the road,' her colleague indicated with a wave of his arm.

They both turned and walked out to get air.

There was only one park with a bandstand in the town, conveniently located 200 metres down the road. The officers parked the patrol car in a designated parking bay for police vehicles outside the park gates. On the opposite side of the gates was an ice-cream van doing a roaring trade on this hot day. They entered the park on foot and followed a winding footpath that curled towards the old bandstand. As they got nearer to the bandstand, a bunch of scruffy-looking men occupying two park benches came into sight. All were decidedly worse for wear because of the amount of alcohol each had consumed throughout the day. A local byelaw stated that consuming alcohol in this public place was illegal. Despite this, none of the motley crew made any attempt to hide their liquor at the sight of an approaching uniformed officer.

Jane paused for a moment and shared a picture of Keating with her colleague. 'This is our man; his mugshot was taken within the last year.'

Chandler viewed the picture, picking out the most striking feature of their quarry, his bulbous nose.

They approached the men. The comedian amongst them slurred:

' 'Ello, 'ello, 'ello what do we 'ave 'ere then?'

The group laughed in unison. The officers smiled.

Jane spoke, 'Good afternoon, gentlemen.'

'Gentlemen?' the comedian piped up once more. The others guffawed again. 'Long time since we was called one 'o them… ain't it, lads?'

A couple mumbled in agreement, though neither officer really understood what they had said. Jane produced her warrant card and introduced herself. 'And this is Police Constable Chandler. We were hoping you could help us to locate a Mr Tim Keating.'

One of the group looked up suddenly at the mention of the name. Joe and Jane studied his face; apart from the scruffy greying beard it now sported, this was their man. Jane addressed the suspect. 'Mr Keating?' 'What?' he barked.

'We need you to accompany us to the police station, where we would like to interview you about an incident that occurred a few days ago.'

The scruffy man looked confused. One of his fellow drinkers let out a rasping laugh between his lips at the suggestion. Their suspect looked angered. 'Not guilty! Sorry, can't help you. Goodbye.'

He took another swig from his can of lager.

'I'm sorry, Mr Keating, but it is essential that you attend. A refusal to come quietly will mean I will have to arrest you,' Jane firmly stated.

'Try it!' was the confrontational reply.

His pals, even the comedian, fell quiet, waiting to see what would happen next. The officers shared a glance between them. Jane gently nodded at Joe to confirm the arrest should take place.

Both officers took a step forward. Joe reached out for Keating's arm as Jane said, 'Timothy Keating, I am arresting you on suspicion of stalking.'

Joe grabbed his arm to pull him to his feet. Keating reacted violently. He lunged at the PC, drew his head back and brought it forward quickly, so that his forehead contacted the bridge of Joe's nose with a loud crack. Joe reeled back, clutching his bloody nose.

The others sitting on the bench rose, still holding their precious cans, and stood back to watch the ensuing foray. Joe was on his knees now, blood dripping from his nose onto the ground.

Keating sneered and turned towards Jane. He towered above her and made a grab for her. She quickly countered his move, grabbed his right arm and turned her body. She jabbed an elbow into her attacker's midriff. She then expertly threw the enraged man to the ground. Still holding his arm, she twisted it hard up his back, causing him to yelp in pain. She then knelt on him, keeping him pinned to the ground. She reached over for her handbag and used her spare hand to retrieve her shiny new handcuffs. She expertly slapped one cuff onto the arm she was holding before grabbing his other wrist and pulling it firmly behind his back so she could attach the other cuff.

The prisoner lay on the ground, obviously in discomfort after the blow to the stomach.

Jane looked over at the recovering PC. 'Are you OK?'

He was now rising to his feet. Jane passed him a tissue. He wiped blood from his nose. 'Yeah, I'll be fine.'

She pulled Joe's hand away from the source of the blood to examine the injury. Bleeding from the slight cut had almost stopped.

'Doesn't look too bad. You might have a bit of a black eye later though.'

'Thanks!' He dabbed the bridge of his nose again. 'Remind me to take you out with me on my next arrest, won't you?'

Jane hid her amusement as Keating was pulled to his feet and then pushed to a sitting position on the bench. The audience had dispersed, no longer amused by the altercation involving their acquaintance.

'Call it in Joe. Get some transport to pick him up. It's too risky to take him in the car.'

Jane looked at Keating. 'I'm further arresting you for two counts of assault on a police officer.' Jane read Keating his rights.

Keating grunted, feeling humiliated to have been beaten by this mere slip of a girl.

Back at the station, Keating stood, swaying slightly in front of the custody desk. The custody sergeant decided the prisoner was not fit to be interviewed. He would need to sober up first. The sergeant authorised his detention until he could take part in an interview.

'Empty your pockets, please.'

Keating placed a few screwed up supermarket receipts and a small amount of loose change on the custody desk. The sergeant nodded towards another uniformed officer and informed Keating that PC Watts would now search him to make sure his pockets were empty.

'Is there anything in your possession that is likely to cause me harm?' Watts asked.

Now resigned to his predicament, Keating shook his head from side to side. The constable conducted his search, finally looking in the back pockets of Keating's scruffy jeans. Watts took out the small resealable plastic bag of white powder he found there and placed it on the custody desk with Keating's other belongings. The sergeant picked up the bag and gave it a little shake.

Looking at Keating, he said, 'Take drugs, do we?'

Keating looked at the bag. 'Never seen it before. It's not mine; one of your lot must've planted it.'

'I've heard that one before,' said the sergeant. following up with, 'You're further arrested on suspicion of possessing a quantity of Class A drugs.'

They bagged up the prisoner's belongings. When the formal paperwork had been completed, both parties signed it. They led Keating away, kicking and screaming, to his cell. The sergeant sent the white powder to the forensics laboratory for analysis.

Chapter 11

In a clearing within a secluded copse, a small beam of laser light danced around the unlikely adornment hanging from a light tree branch. Some fifty metres away, a marksman concentrated on his aim. The darkness of the target absorbed the laser light, making it a little difficult to see. When he was sure that his weapon was on target, he squeezed the trigger.

With a reassuring click, the missile travelled at an impressive 300 feet per second. A short half a second passed before the bolt penetrated its target with ease. The Watcher carried his hunter's crossbow by his side to inspect the damage caused.

The impaled target bobbed gently on the tree branch. Tape secured a coconut shell to the front of a watermelon; the hard shell would simulate a person's skull. He'd read somewhere that a watermelon makes a good substitution for human flesh. Clean entry and exit holes were visible on the target. Juice from the exit hole was still dripping to the ground. The bolt was embedded in the main trunk of the tree.

Internet research suggested that more damage was possible with a simple modification to the tip of the bolt. He replenished the target and returned to the launch site. A fresh bolt pulled from his rucksack had a split tip modification. He placed the bolt into the launch groove of the crossbow. Once again, the deadly missile smashed into its target and the result this time was more explosive.

The coconut shell had shattered. The entry hole in the watermelon was larger. There was no exit hole, so The Watcher used his knife to cut into the fleshy fruit to examine internal damage. The bolt had done its job. Shards of the shaft had split and splintered, curling outwards to cause more internal damage to the watermelon.

The damage this could inflict inside a person's skull would certainly cause instant death. The evil hitman packed up his equipment with the satisfaction that he now had a greater potential to kill.

Chapter 12

The Coopers were away on one of Steven's business trips. Trips had become more frequent and now often spanned Monday through to Friday. This was a longer trip than normal, as the couple had added both before and after weekends to the stay.

It was Monday, three days into the trip, and events were unfolding back home.

Karyn was busying herself around the house on some household chores. Keen to get some exercise, Mark left to walk into town.

The vacuum cleaner efficiently ploughed a path through the generous carpet pile in the couple's bedroom. Karyn tutted when she saw a pair of Mark's trousers draped over the dressing table chair. He does this, she thought, and shook her head. *'That man, he just can't be bothering to hang himself up in the wardrobe!'*

She picked up the trousers, an item dropped out of a pocket. She examined it thoughtfully, recognising it as the key to the mysterious cabin. Karyn had only set foot in this space on the day they moved in. Mark then forbade entry to anybody.

For all she knew, he might be seeing another woman in there.

Just what is in there? she wondered. Enough time had elapsed for him to have arrived at the mall. She was tempted to look inside before he got back. He'd never know. *But wait, the cabin's in view from some upstairs windows in Sarah's house. What if they saw me? What if they mentioned it in conversation with Mark?*

The Coopers knew that the cabin was out of bounds. Then she remembered, they were in Portugal. A splendid opportunity to take a covert peek at Mark's little empire.

Karyn turned the key in the cabin door lock. She pulled the heavy wooden door open and entered, peering through the darkness. She switched the light on, using the pull switch just inside the door. Fluorescent lighting clicked and strobed before settling down to illuminate the interior. Karyn froze as she surveyed what was before her. The face in the large poster on the wall opposite the door looked familiar; an

icy shiver trickled down her spine. After a sharp intake of breath, 'It's Sarah!'

She knew the nature of Mark's work, so the monitors and computers she saw fitted in, but there were other things she could not understand. She saw strange paraphernalia scattered around the cabin on shelves and desks. The empty eye sockets of a bleached skull placed on a shelf seemed to observe her as she surveyed the room. She saw large robes hanging on hooks. The place gave her the shivers. An enormous spider emerging from the eye socket of the spooky skull was all she needed to persuade her to leave.

* * *

Mark strolled through the shopping mall, stopping occasionally to look in shop windows, clothes mainly. He arrived at his favourite coffee shop and purchased a flat white before taking a daily paper from the paper rack near the door. He sat down to enjoy his coffee and catch up on what had been happening in the world. Halfway through reading a worrying article about North Korea, Mark felt his smartphone buzz in his pocket. The notification was strange as it buzzed three times, suggesting a sense of urgency. *Probably three text messages coming in together,* he thought. He reached into his pocket for his phone.

A message had arrived. Mark opened his email application and looked at the worrying notification that had arrived in his inbox. An intruder alert: the silent alarm had gone off in his very private domain. *Could be a false alarm,* he thought (and hoped). Mark opened the applications on his smartphone that allowed him to access real-time images streamed to the Internet by a monitoring camera in the cabin.

The coffee shop Wi-Fi service was slow; it took over two minutes for the image to load. What he saw incensed him. His secret life was at risk of being exposed. 'The stupid bitch!'

He threw the paper down, left the coffee he had hardly touched, and fled from the coffee shop.

Karyn, shocked and spooked by what she saw, quickly switched off the light before securing the door once more. She returned the key back to the trouser pocket and sat on the bed for a think. Who was this man she lived with and thought she knew? Just what was he into?

Trying to make sense of the eclectic mix of items she saw in the cabin, she finally convinced herself that these were probably props he'd used in a filming assignment somewhere.

Karyn didn't see or hear the taxi draw up outside. The first sign that her partner was home was when she heard his key rattling in the door. She had a sharp intake of breath whilst wondering why he was back so soon.

He was angry. 'Karyn! Where are you?'

A quick recce in the downstairs rooms led him to assume she was upstairs. Mark bounded up the stairs two at a time and burst into the bedroom to find her sitting in tears on the bed. The confrontation began.

Chapter 13

DI Patterson picked up the brown manila envelope on her desk. Addressed to her, she opened it to inspect another report from Tracy Hamilton. Jane skimmed the report.

The suspected Class A drug was, in fact, talcum powder. *Interesting*, thought Jane.

The report discussed another recent case that involved talcum powder. The scientist compared samples from the two cases for similarity. The tests evidenced they were from the same manufacturer.

No fingerprint evidence was present on or in the polythene bag.

Jane took the lift down to the custody suite. A quick check on the board showed Keating in cell M4. She walked along the corridor looking for M4. Passing the cell next door to Keating's, she could hear somebody weeping bitterly within. She arrived at his door, recognising his scruffy, scuffed shoes outside.

The prisoner's bloodshot eyes looked up as Jane slid the viewing window across. 'Who's there?'

She stood almost on tiptoe to look inside. The dishevelled man was sitting on the sleeping platform, a half-eaten bowl of cereal on the floor next to him.

'It's Detective Inspector Patterson here. I just wanted to make sure you were fit enough to be interviewed this morning.'

'Of course I am. What am I here for? I've done nothing I tell you, nothing!'

The viewing window slammed shut. Keating's protests echoed down the corridor. 'I want a solicitor. I'm an innocent man. I'm gonna sue you idiots for wrongful arrest! DO YOU HEAR? I am innocent!'

Obviously, Jane thought, *he's forgotten that he assaulted two police officers.*

Back in her office, Jane revisited the evidence so far and decided on a strategy for the interview. The assaults were an aside; they would charge him for those and go before the judge. She was looking into the feasibility of being able to charge her suspect for an harassment or stalking offence.

Jane and her colleague, DC Ashok Patel, interviewed Keating. The duty solicitor sat next to his client. Most questions were responded to with 'No comment.'

Jane tapped a well-manicured finger on the small bag of white powder on the table between them. 'Can you explain how this found its way into your pocket?'

That question did provoke an outburst from Keating. 'How the hell should I know? What is it? I've never even seen it before! One of your lot must've planted it! That's all I can say or think!'

The two officers then asked questions about the stalking and harassment towards Mr Cooper. Keating denied this also, but he smirked when asked about the phantom deliveries from fast-food restaurants and arrivals of taxis at the Cooper's home.

The interview was going nowhere. It was obvious to Jane he was lying about some things. She wasn't so sure about the white powder, though.

She concluded the interview with a reminder of the assaults on the two arresting officers. Despite Keating's denials, they told him he would be charged for these. The only bit of good news was that he was no longer suspected of possessing a Class A drug.

This tiny crumb of good news invoked a Humph!!! from Keating.

A copy of the interview tape was passed to the solicitor. The prisoner was returned to his cell.

Jane reviewed the case with DCI Grant. After discussion, they both doubted that there was enough evidence to charge him with a stalking offence. If it reached the courts, sentencing would be minimal and probably suspended. Maybe the experience Keating had just endured might be enough to prevent further harassment towards the Coopers. They decided that a caution would be an appropriate alternative to prosecution. The one caveat to this would be that the suspect must admit the offence. The DCI suggested another chat with Keating to see if he would accept a caution. Jane keenly volunteered to carry out this task.

Patterson entered Keating's cell. He swung his legs over the side of the sleeping platform whilst Jane explained the options.

'If you come clean and admit your guilt, we'll settle this with a caution. If you still maintain innocence and we take it to the CPS, it may lead to prosecution. If the case goes to a court of law, you will get a fair hearing and may still be found innocent. I think you should talk to your solicitor.'

'I'm tellin' you I ain't done nothin',' he remonstrated. After a few moments of silence, his head bowed in thought, he continued in a subdued tone. 'I want to speak with my solicitor.'

Jane arranged the meeting and left the two men alone to discuss the options.

Later that day, Jane and a colleague prepared a fresh tape in the interview room recorder. Keating and his solicitor sat opposite, waiting for the interview to begin. Jane introduced all four members present before starting the interview. Thinking a caution would be the lesser of the two evils, Keating confessed to something he didn't do. The duty solicitor read out a prepared statement that formed Keating's admission.

Back in front of the custody sergeant, they formally charged Keating on two counts of assaulting a police officer. They bailed him to appear in a Magistrate's Court within 28 days. They dealt the stalking offence with a caution. Conditions were that Keating should not contact nor approach Mr Cooper nor his family. After reluctantly signing various bits of paper at the request of the custody sergeant, Keating roughly stuffed copies of the documents in his pocket before being allowed to leave the police station.

Chapter 14

The following Sunday night, EZY2022 touched down at Luton airport five minutes early. With only cabin bags to collect, the couple quickly cleared immigration and customs. A short taxi ride later, they arrived home at 1.15am in the morning. Both were tired after a week away.

Steven had left by the time Sarah woke up. Once showered and dressed, she started unpacking their bags before setting the washing machine going. Whilst sitting down to a well-earned cup of coffee, she noticed the plant on the kitchen windowsill was looking sorry for itself. The long, green, shiny leaves drooped down the side of the pot; the tips lying flat on the shelf. *Strange*, she thought. Two potted plants in the conservatory had suffered the same fate. *Had Karyn neglected to water the plants?* She remembered last night finding a week's worth of post behind the front door. Perhaps Karyn hadn't been well.

Sarah tended to the sad-looking selection of plants around the house. Some had fared better than others. She hoped that the casualties of neglect would survive.

Later that day, Sarah popped round to number 35. She was hoping her friend was OK. Nobody answered the door. Their drive was empty, so the enigma of the plants would remain a mystery for now.

Back in her kitchen, Sarah waded through the mountain of post. With the paper shredder on standby, she quickly despatched all the junk mail. There were also two bills, a bank statement, and one envelope addressed to Steven from the police force. She suspected it was something to do with the events surrounding Keating. She texted her husband to tell him that the formallooking letter had arrived. She ended her text with... *shall I open it?*

Steven read the text message and smiled to himself. Knowing she was eager to read the letter, he replied:

No, don't worry yourself with it. I'll open it when I get home.

Sarah read the reply and briefly considered steaming it open before another text from Steven arrived.

Oh, go on then :0).

Seconds later, the envelope was in tatters on the table, and Sarah read the letter.

Dear Mr Cooper,

My department has investigated the incident reported on 16th September 2017. Based on information from you, we arrested the prime suspect, Mr Timothy Keating. After interview, Mr Keating has made a full confession, admitting placing spoof orders for taxis and at fast-food restaurants etc. Mr Keating has also confirmed that he was behind the delivery of the white powder to your property. These were minor offences that lacked sufficient evidence to present to the CPS for prosecution. This has therefore been dealt with by issuance of a simple caution. Mr Keating has been instructed not to contact you or your family again.

This is the end of the investigation; no further action will be taken, and the case is now closed. However, should further contact or harassment from Mr Keating occur, please report these again to us quoting the Crime Reference Number at the top of this letter.

She sent Steven a paraphrased version of the letter by text. He replied to say he hoped that was the end.

***

That evening Sarah expressed her concerns about her friend next door. 'I've seen no sign of either of them today. Perhaps they've gone away. Karyn never mentioned it though.'

No sooner had she finished her wonderings when the doorbell rang. Steven went to answer the door.

Sarah listened carefully to the voices in the hall. She overheard:

'Come in, mate.'

Steven ushered the visitor into the lounge.

Sarah jumped out of her chair, surprised to see her neighbour. 'Mark!'

Sarah studied Mark. His face and demeanour suggested that all was not well. Mark sat down in the armchair by the window, his friends looking on with concern.

Steven spoke first. 'What on earth's the matter? Is Karyn OK?'

Mark lifted his bowed head and looked at them both. 'She's fine, but, she's left me!'

Sarah looked across at Steven, then back to Mark, speechless at first. 'When? How? Where's she gone?'

Mark appeared visibly upset. He explained the blazing row they'd had last Monday. 'You must have heard us arguing before.'

'Well, yes, we had, but neither of us reckoned it would come to this,' said Sarah.

Mark gave a little laugh. 'You never really know what goes on behind closed doors, do you?'

Steven poured two glasses of Southern Comfort. He waved the bottle at Sarah, but she declined his offer.

Knowing that her friend had no family in the UK, Sarah enquired, 'Where's she gone, do you know?'

'It's been brewing for a while. Over the past few months she'd been skyping with her family in Ukraine. She missed them, especially with one or two new-born nephews and nieces arriving. We rowed on Monday, next day she told me she was going back home. Shortly after that, a taxi arrived to take her to the airport. She... she just left!'

'What, just like that?'

'Yup. Just like that!'

'We were friends. I'm surprised she didn't say goodbye before she left. Has she been in touch since?'

Mark slowly shook his head.

'I don't think she will. It's well and truly over, I'm afraid!' Steven and Sarah looked on at Mark, a pitiful sight before them. Sarah sensed a man-to-man talk might be what Mark needed. 'I need a cup of tea.'

'Look mate, I'm really sorry to hear your news. Is there anything I or we, can do?'

'I'm OK. I probably knew it would end like this one day... it comes as a bit of a shock when it does though. Look, I appreciate your concern, you and Sarah are good neighbours and friends.'

'Well, if ever you want to talk, or have some company, we're here for you.'

Mark took another sip from his glass, which prompted Steven to do the same.

'We lived as a married couple but were never married, you know.'

'I didn't know that.'

'Probably just as well. It makes life easier at times like these, don't you think?'

'I suppose so.'

'Yeah, no lengthy, messy divorce proceedings for me.' The effects of the Southern Comfort were kicking in.

'Won't she come looking for some recompense with the house and stuff?'

'She can try. I'm not selling up though! That's my business premises in the back garden. It would be too much of an upheaval to move all of my equipment.'

Steven looked on thoughtfully whilst he listened to his friend.

'Still, we'll cross that bridge when and if it comes.' Mark drained his glass.

'Another?'

'Well, perhaps a small one. Thank you.'

Whilst pouring another, Steven wondered how the inevitable would not happen. Surely Karyn would want a slice of what they both worked towards whilst they were together. He passed the refreshed glass to Mark.

'Why do you think she might not want a piece of the estate?'

'Her family in Ukraine are property owners, including two hotels, so they're quite wealthy. I reckon she might just want to forget we ever happened.'

Steven doubted his friend's optimism.

Sarah returned as Mark was draining his second glass.

'Enough of my troubles and woes, I must leave you two in peace.'

He rose from his armchair and bade his friends goodnight.

Sarah was the first to speak. 'Well, I didn't see that one coming!'

'All very strange. Did Karyn ever mention she might leave him?'

'Never mentioned it! I feel a little hurt, really. I thought we were best friends. Surely you would confide in your best friend if things were that serious, wouldn't you?'

'Yes, I believe you would. Well, what's happened has happened, all we can do is support him where we can. Maybe I'll go up the pub with him later in the week. We need to keep an eye on him though, we don't want him doing something silly do we?'

This worried Sarah. 'You don't think he would, do you?'

'No, no, I'm sure he'll be fine. It's just me finding an excuse to go to the pub,' he added with a smirk. Sarah gave him a playful punch on the arm in response.

'You don't normally need an excuse to go to the pub.'

The playful banter ended with Sarah stretching her arms up and, after an enormous yawn, she said, 'I need sleep. It's up to bed for me... Night, love.'

She gave Steven a goodnight kiss.

'Night love. I'll be up shortly when I've finished my drink.'

Both still tired from their recent trip to Portugal, there would be no entertainment for The Watcher tonight.

Chapter 15

The Watcher was a key member in the online chat room. A very private chat room on the Dark Web. Nobody taking part used their real name for these meetings.

The regular video conferences focused on arrangements for the *Main Event*. Society brothers and sisters in the room eagerly wanted to know how plans were progressing for this important occasion. Those present directed most of the questions to The Watcher. He was the principal organiser, The Master.

One question was asked regarded the c*atering arrangements,* another member asked about their s*pecial guest*.

The catering arrangements referred to something entirely different from food and drink. It was explained that the special guest would not understand they were even going to this event until they were there. All attendees to the virtual meeting knew what the various cryptic terms referred to. It was necessary to communicate in these terms, as security was paramount.

The Watcher assured members he had identified the perfect venue for the event. Apart from stating that the venue was in a central location, the exact details would remain a secret until days before the meeting was due to take place. He assured them that plans for the special guest were on track.

The discussion continued excitedly for over an hour. At the end of the meeting, the members agreed a new security password, date and time for the next meeting. The Watcher reminded members to follow the strict procedure of logging out of the meeting and told them to remove any evidence of accessing the sinister side of the Internet from their computers.

The meeting closed.

Chapter 16

April 2018

The lives of Steven and Sarah had at last returned to normality. There were no more occurrences of Keating's shenanigans.

Steven did hear through the grapevine that his old arch enemy had appeared in court on some assault charges and had received a 42 day prison sentence.

Mark continued living as normal next door. He and Steven regularly went to the pub for a mid-week drink. Steven enquired once about Karyn.

'Has Karyn been in touch at all?'

'Nope, nothing at all, and I really don't expect to hear from her,' was the short reply.

Mark quickly changed the subject. Both men often talked about their work. Steven's project in Portugal was going well. Mark was still secretive about what he actually did but would sometimes let slip he was working on a wildlife film, the occasional TV advert or his favourite, an investigative journalism programme for TV. He divulged no real details about his work though.

Steven once asked, 'How do you get these jobs?'

'Through an agency,' was all he would say.

Steven and Sarah continued to enjoy their frequent trips to Portugal. Whilst spending weekends at home, Steven would go jogging on a Sunday morning. He told Sarah that it would cancel out the indulgences of over-eating whilst in Portugal.

On more than one occasion, unnoticed by Steven, the small red dot of laser light would dance mischievously on the back of his head as he jogged along the lane between the concrete pillbox and the now defunct horse-riding school.

* * *

On one bright spring Sunday morning, Steven jogged steadily along the lane. Once past the old pillbox, the playful red spot bobbed around on its target once more. The Watcher focused steadily whilst his finger applied steady pressure to the trigger of the high-powered crossbow. The weapon released a modified bolt. One intended to inflict maximum damage.

The missile obediently flew along the path of the laser light until it hit its target. It entered the back of Steven's neck just at the base of his skull. Steven Cooper was dead before his body came crashing to the ground.

The Watcher emerged from the old wartime outpost. He moved quickly, running towards the gateway for the old stable block. He stopped briefly at Steven's body on the way. Very little blood spilt, which was what he was hoping. With latex gloves on, the murderer searched for and located Steven's mobile phone. He smeared some blood from Steven's head onto the phone and then pressed it into his lifeless right hand, smearing bloody hand and fingerprints all over it. He held the phone carefully between his gloved thumb and index finger and then threw the phone into the undergrowth at the side of the road.

The murderer ran into the stables to retrieve his concealed vehicle. He parked next to his victim's body and ran to swing open the back doors of the van. He grabbed the body bag and placed it next to the fresh corpse. Already unzipped, he rolled the body into the bag and zipped it up again. The side handles on the bag were used to haul the heavy load up into the rear of the vehicle. A quick check of the area revealed nothing incriminating, so with the doors shut he reversed the van and drove back through the stables. He negotiated the rutted and bumpy track that led into a nearby housing estate.

Careful not to draw any attention, The Watcher drove the practised route through the new housing estate to where he joined the main A6 road.

Chapter 17

Sarah was relaxing at home on Sunday morning, listening to some music and reading a book. The sun was streaming through the vertical blinds at the front room window, and Sarah's mind wandered from her book for a few moments. *What a wonderful morning Steven had for his run,* she thought. Whilst she was no athlete, she had a notion that one day she might buy one of those handy fold-up bicycles and join Steven on his run. This morning would have been ideal for such an event. He'd be back in about an hour. She'd mention it on his return. The current CD track finished, a new one started and served as a prompt to continue reading her novel.

She was dozing in the chair by the time the CD player went quiet. Her book sliding off her lap woke her with a start. The clock showed a quarter to twelve. *Where's Steven?* she thought. She assumed she hadn't heard him arrive back because she was asleep. He's probably upstairs in the shower or getting changed, she reckoned.

In the hallway, she called up the stairs.

'Hi love, just making some coffee. Do you want one?'

She inclined her head, straining to hear his reply... Nothing. Total silence. Curious, she climbed the stairs to look for him. After searching all the rooms, the mystery as to his whereabouts deepened. She lifted the lid to the laundry basket, hoping to see his shorts and tee shirt within. It was empty! She double-checked the en-suite shower room, expecting his running outfit to be lying on the floor. The floor was clear! Sarah called his name again as she descended the stairs.

'Steven...! Where are you, love?'

Becoming slightly concerned, she moved her search to the garden, then the garage. He left over four hours ago now. He's never been gone this long before. Thoughts raced through her mind. *Something's happened. An accident? A fall? Surely not taken ill?* She ran into the kitchen to find her phone. No messages or missed calls. She quickly dialled Steven's number. She counted the number of rings in her head, one, two, three... she got to the eighth ring before the phone was answered. She knew what was coming next, Steven's voicemail message. Sarah waited for the tone before speaking.

'Where are you, love? I'm getting worried you haven't returned yet. Call me when you get this. Love you!' She then ended the call.

Still worried that something was wrong, she turned her ring volume up full. She kept the phone by her side and re-dialled and texted several times for the next anxious hour of no news.

Sarah racked her brain to think where he might be. *Could he be next door?* she thought. She reassured herself, further thinking, *Yes, I'll bet that's where he is, sharing a few beers no doubt.*

She grabbed her phone and house keys and walked around to her neighbour's house. The ostentatious bell chime finished its rendition. Sarah listened for Mark's approach to answer the door, there was no sign of life within.

Probably in the garden, she thought. She followed the pathway to the tall wooden garden gate at the side of the house. It was closed but not locked. She pushed the gate open and hurried into the garden. Mark was there, on his knees, tending to one of his flower borders. Sarah called over, 'Hi Mark!' Startled, Mark looked up.

'Hello Sarah, just tidying up my borders on this lovely day.' Her neighbour's smile quickly faded as the expression on Sarah's face showed all was not well. With an already damp tissue, she wiped the tears rolling down her cheeks. Mark ran forward to comfort her. He put his arm around her. 'Hey sweetie, what's this all about?'

Between sobs and gasps, Sarah told Mark of her concerns for Steven.

'Have you tried his mobile?' was the first helpful suggestion.

'Yes, of course I have. Sorry. Yes, loads of times. His voicemail answers, I left a message, and I sent text messages as well… Nothing. No response… Just… nothing.'

Mark led Sarah over to the steps to his cabin and beckoned her to sit next to him on the top step.

'Right! Let's have a think, there will be some rational explanation for his delay. Do you reckon he could have bumped into someone he knows?'

'Possible, but why doesn't he answer his phone?'

'Perhaps he's run out of battery?'

'No, that wouldn't happen. He charges it up every night on the docking station.'

Sarah scotched other suggestions put forward by her helpful neighbour.

'It's a lovely day. Perhaps he popped into the pub for a cool pint of beer.'

'No, he wouldn't go to the pub in his running gear. Even if he took another route today, he wouldn't be this long without calling me.'

An elongated pause before Sarah gasped. 'What if he's had an accident? Or perhaps he's fallen, or… Oh God, what if he's been hit by a car?'

Her emotions took over once more. Mark put a comforting arm around her shoulders. 'Hey, come on love, I'm sure he's fine… Wait there.'

He got up from the step and walked into the house. He reappeared a minute later with his mobile phone in his hand, probing the screen with his fingers. He sat back down with the phone to his ear. After a few seconds, Sarah heard half of the conversation.

'Yes, hello, I am trying to locate a friend of mine who may have attended A & E earlier today.' A pause, then 'OK… Thanks… Ah yes, hello, can you tell me if a Mr Steven Cooper has attended your department this morning?'

Mark spelt the surname out. There was another pause whilst the person at the other end searched records. At last, the answer.

'OK, thanks for your help.'

The call ended. He turned to his distraught neighbour.

'Good news. He's not in the hospital.'

Small comfort, for she still didn't know where he was. Mark could see the distress his neighbour was in.

'Tell you what, let's jump in my van and trace his steps! Do you know the route he takes?'

'Yes, more or less.'

'Lets go then!'

They both got up and walked down the garden. Mark grabbed his keys and locked up the house. Sarah checked her house one more time to see if Steven had arrived home.

She locked up her empty house and jumped into Mark's van.

'OK, where to?'

'He starts off running down Bedford Road towards the old converted barns.'

'Yes, I know them.'

They quickly joined the Bedford Road (A6). Sarah studied the track alongside the road for any sign of her husband. As they approached some converted barns, Sarah gave more directions.

'He turns right here and runs along the lane to South Beds Golf Club.'

Mark turned right and continued down the lane behind the barns. Again, Sarah kept out a keen eye. The van pulled onto a verge just before the entrance to the golf club car park. They couldn't enter the car park as the barrier was down.

Sarah pointed across the car park.

'He crosses the car park. There must be a pedestrian exit at the opposite end.'

They got out of the van and ventured over to the far corner of the car park. They could see no obvious exit, but then Mark found a well-trodden gap that led onto another lane. Not an official exit, more of a gap in the fence. He called Sarah over. They looked down the deserted lane. Grass and weeds sprouting through the crown of the tarmacked lane was evidence that suggested it had long been closed off to the major thoroughfare of traffic.

Both investigated the first 50 metres of the overgrown track before Mark suggested they return to his van.

'I think it will be easier to search the lane from the other end. I know a way through. Providing the lane has not become overgrown with hedgerow we should be able to get through to the old stable yard.'

They retraced their steps back to the main road.

Mark searched out the side road that led to the old stables and turned into it. A tired-looking, redundant road sign appeared through the hedgerow, warning that horse riders may be ahead.

This confirmed that they were following the right track for the stables. The road condition was not too bad and the van easily negotiated its way to the stable entrance.

Two gnarled and grey wooden posts flanked the entrance to the stable yard. The gate that once bridged the gap was long gone. The van drove between the posts. At the opposite end of the yard was a similar opening. The old five-bar gate was still attached and open, its base entangled by years' worth of undergrowth, rendering it inoperable.

Mark drove through the yard exit and turned left.

'This is the track that leads to the club car park.'

Both maintained their vigilance as the van slowly made its way to the area they had searched just 20 minutes earlier. The lane was narrow, but Mark turned the van round in seven goes. They returned to the stables.

Mark gestured his hand to show up ahead and to the left.

'There's an old pillbox over there. It might be worth investigating, just in case he went behind for a pee or something and has slipped.'

Sarah was willing, anything that might help find her loving husband.

Mark stopped the van between the pillbox on the left and the yard entrance on the right. 'There's the pillbox,' he gestured.

Sarah jumped out and picked her way through to the deserted, dilapidated, concrete monolith. Back at the van she shook her head solemnly whilst climbing back in. Mark drove back into the yard and parked beside the stable wall.

'We'll search around. I'll check out the area beyond the pillbox.' He pointed towards a group of trees nearby. 'You look in the copse over there.'

They both walked back to the lane. Mark turned to the left and Sarah headed towards the copse on the right. After a five-minute recce, the two met again at the yard entrance.

Sarah's bottom lip quivered.

'Where can he be?' she stifled another cry.

'I don't know. Try his mobile again.'

Sarah shakily hit the redial button on her mobile. Fifteen seconds later, they both heard a mobile phone ring. The ring tone was familiar to Sarah. She recognised it as Steven's.

They ran towards the direction of the ringing phone. There it was next to the road in the undergrowth, still ringing. Sarah picked up the phone. She noticed something smeared across the screen. *What was that? Mud?* She looked closer, shocked to see what she thought might be blood.

An anguished cry of 'Oh Noooo!' came from Sarah as she sank to her knees, staring incredulously at the phone. She bowed forward, then suddenly she scrambled to her feet, realising Steven might be close by, 'Quick, he's here somewhere and hurt, help me find him.'

They intensified their search of the local area. Sarah shouted out, constantly listening for a response from her husband. There was no reply to her anguished cries.

Armed with fresh evidence Steven was probably hurt, Mark called the hospital to check once more. Still no news of a Mr Cooper.

There was only one course of action left. Sarah dialled 999 on her mobile. The couple sat in the van waiting whilst Mark comforted his worried neighbour.

Twenty minutes passed before a large police vehicle entered the yard and pulled up in front of the van. The passenger door opened. A large, uniformed police officer, made even bigger with his protective over-clothing, emerged from the vehicle. Sarah, eager not to waste any time in the search for her husband, jumped out of the van and ran over to the officer. She struggled to explain all at once what had happened.

A short while later, Sarah was calmer and able to explain to the policeman that her husband was missing. It wasn't until she showed him Steven's blood-smeared mobile phone that he really took notice of what she was telling him. The driver of the patrol car had a similar conversation with Mark.

Both officers, convinced something untoward had happened, called in a helicopter for a thorough aerial search.

Later that day, low on fuel, the helicopter returned to base after a fruitless search. The incident was upgraded, and more police personnel arrived at the old stable yard. They cordoned the area off as a potential crime scene. A female family liaison officer arrived and eventually persuaded Sarah to let her take her home whilst a police investigation and search began.

They allowed Mark to leave after being interviewed by a detective.

Chapter 18

The evil murderer felt confident he had disposed of the body in what he considered a safe place. He sat down in front of his computer, thinking, *They'll never find it there,* as he reviewed his earlier actions.

He later needed to find out what was happening with the police investigation. A priority for now though, was to join the pre-arranged Dark Web chat room meeting. He desired to report the fact that he had achieved a significant step forward today. His followers would receive the news well.

Members quickly joined the meeting. The Watcher addressed those assembled. 'I have exciting news to tell you,' he began. 'Many of you know that securing the guest for our special evening was going to be complicated. Today, I have separated her from her partner. I now have plenty of time to prepare her for our celebration.'

A general hubbub of approval echoed through the group before they asked questions.

'Impressive. How have you achieved this at such an early stage?' asked one.

With some irritation, the reply came, 'It's important not to discuss details. I cannot discuss or divulge my actions.' Someone asked, 'What did you do with the body?'

Their leader had a short temper. 'Body? What body?'

'Oh, I just assumed…'

'Well, don't! You only need to know that I'm dealing with the problem. Nobody needs to know my methods.'

Another member addressed the group with a supportive message. 'Secrecy is the key everybody. Our Master here is doing a great job. We have over 12 months to wait for the *Main Event* to take place. There's a lot to do between now and then. It has to be perfect. Without our special guest, the event will lose its impact and possibly not take place at all. We must let our respected friend do what he has to do without questioning his ways.'

Members unanimously agreed that they must trust their leader and allow him to get the job done without questions.

The meeting continued for another half hour. At the close, everybody closed their Dark Web sessions securely.

The Watcher waited until the final attendee disappeared from the screen. It was time to see if there was any news.

He opened another application on his PC. After a brief delay, his monitor displayed images from the covert cameras positioned in the Coopers' house. Sarah was sitting in the lounge, a family liaison officer was introducing herself. He eavesdropped in to their conversation. The discussion clarified that the investigation had made no progress.

The next few weeks would require The Watcher to be cautious and mindful of police inquiries. Resting his elbows on the desk, he closed his eyes and steepled his index fingers. He held this pose whilst re-running the day's events in his mind. *Have I forgotten anything?* He concluded his tracks were covered well, but he must keep his cool in case the police came knocking on his door.

Chapter 19

Vanessa, the Family Liaison Officer, was a kind-faced individual in her thirties. The brunette officer had impeccable make-up and eyeliner that gave her eyes an almost oriental appearance. She had long slender fingers with nails expertly coated in a rich red nail varnish that matched the colour of her lipstick perfectly. When she spoke, she had a calming voice, ideal when dealing with people involved in traumatic situations.

Back at the house, Sarah searched for her keys. She was shaking so much she could hardly locate the keyhole in the door. Vanessa took over and opened the door for her. She gently guided Sarah over the threshold and ushered her into the lounge.

Sarah sat on the capacious sofa in the lounge, wringing her hands and shivering, even though the house was warm. Vanessa left the room for a moment to find her way around the kitchen. Her minder recognised that Sarah was suffering from shock. She knew that at times like these, hot sweet tea seemed to help. The friendly officer arrived back in the lounge carrying a tray with tea and some Bourbon biscuits she had found in the cupboard. She placed the tray on the large coffee table before sitting at the opposite end of the sofa. 'I'll be mother.'

She poured a mug of tea with milk and a generous spoonful of sugar for Sarah before pouring herself a mug of tea with milk. She reached for her handbag to retrieve an artificial sweetener dispenser. The dispenser clicked twice to release two tiny white pills that plopped into her tea. Once stirred, she picked her mug up and encouraged Sarah to do the same.

'Come on, have some tea. It'll do you good.'

Both ladies took a sip of the hot tea together. Sarah spoke first.

'What's happening? Are we being kept up to date on developments?'

'Don't worry' - Vanessa reached into her bag and took out her mobile phone. 'If there's any news, the officer in charge will call me.' She placed the phone on the coffee table. 'Tell me about Steven. How did you two meet? How long have you been together?'

Sarah gave the officer more than a potted history of their life together. She even smiled at one point whilst recalling an amusing incident from one of their holidays. Vanessa's soft voice was reassuring. She knew exactly what to say to comfort Sarah and to get her talking.

'It would be useful at some point if we could have a photo of Steven.'

Sarah looked over at the picture frame next to the TV. Vanessa looked to see what had caught her attention.

'Is that him?' Vanessa asked.

Sarah held back her tears and nodded.

'He looks lovely,' said the officer. 'Very handsome.' Another smile from Sarah.

'He is,' she managed.

'Is there someone I can call for you?' Sarah sobbed again.

'What about family, or a friend?'

Sarah blew her nose into an already sodden tissue.

She regained her composure, 'No, there's nobody. The only family I have is Uncle Angus. He lives in a residential home in Scotland. He's frail and elderly. I don't want to worry him.'

'How about a friend?'

'We lead a busy life. There was a neighbour next door, but they separated. She left him and returned to Ukraine.' She let out an enormous sigh. 'Steven is my best friend!'

Vanessa sat closer to her and gave her a comforting hug.

The powerful beat of the police helicopter passed overhead. Sarah looked up, her head tracking the invisible position of the craft as it proceeded.

Vanessa looked pensive for a moment.

'Sarah,' she said, 'I have to ask you this, it's a routine question, it doesn't mean we think anything is amiss yet, but we need to make a thorough investigation into his disappearance. Can you think of anybody who might have cause to harm Steven?'

Sarah froze, eyes open wide she stared at the enquiring officer for a moment before saying, 'Tim Keating!'

Vanessa wrote the name down. Sarah explained some of the history with Keating.

'I see. This is certainly somebody we need to find and talk to.' She added a couple more notes. After pausing for a moment, she asked, 'The phone we found,' looking enquiringly at Sarah. Sarah looked up. 'What about it? It's Steven's phone.'

'Oh, I'm sure it is. It's just that it was smeared with something.'

Sarah cut in. 'It was blood, wasn't it?'

'We can't confirm that. We've sent it for forensic examination. Even if it is blood, it may not be Steven's.'

Sarah was feeling irritated. 'Well, whose blood do you think it is?' she snapped.

'Sorry, this must be difficult for you.'

Sarah mellowed, 'No, Sorry, I didn't mean to snap back at you. You're very kind, and I know you are trying to help.'

'That's OK. It's a stressful time for you. Look, we have to give the investigation its best chance. We need to check the suspect smear on the phone and confirm who it belonged to.'

'Belonged?'

Vanessa realised an awful choice of words.

'Sorry, I mean belongs.'

'What do you need?' asked Sarah. 'We need some of Steven's DNA.'

Sarah looked puzzled. Shaking her head, she asked, 'Where from?'

'The bathroom might be a good place to start,' said Vanessa. 'Maybe a comb, hairbrush or his toothbrush?'

'He has a comb near the TV in the bedroom and he uses the blue toothbrush in the bathroom. Shall I get them?'

'No, wait, I'll call this in and get them picked up. It minimises contamination if we don't move them about too much.'

Vanessa retreated to the kitchen to call DI Patterson with the information she had gathered. Whilst talking to her colleague, the doorbell rang. The caring officer moved quickly to answer it but, hopeful of some good news, Sarah beat her to the door. It was her neighbour.

'Hello love,' he said.

Sarah opened the door fully and motioned her head to invite him in. Vanessa, thankful it wasn't the press at the door, returned to the kitchen to continue her call.

'How are things?' said Mark. 'Any news?'

Sarah, close to tears again, shook her head. 'No, nothing,' she said.

'I feel so helpless,' said Mark. 'Is there anything I can do?' Sarah's tears flowed.

'Oh, Mark,' she sobbed. 'I'm not sure that anybody can do more than they already are.'

Mark offered the box of tissues from the coffee table. She pulled three tissues from the box. She patted her face and dried her eyes with them before scrunching them up in her tightly balled fist. Vanessa entered the room again.

Mark introduced himself to her.

'I live next door.'

Vanessa nodded an understanding. An awkward silence passed between them before Mark said, 'Look, if you, you know… need anything, then just call me. Same goes if there's any news.'

He gave his distraught neighbour a hug and a light kiss on her forehead before leaving.

Alone again, Vanessa asked, 'Is there anything I can do for you?'

Sarah shook her head. 'No thanks. Is there any news?'

'None yet. Enquiries are continuing.'

The doorbell rang. Vanessa was already standing, so she got there first. Sarah stood in the doorway between the lounge and the hallway with a look of hope on her face.

The door opened to reveal a uniformed officer on the doorstep. He introduced himself, 'PC Thompkins ma'am, I've come to collect some DNA samples.'

'Ah yes we were expecting you. Please come in.' Vanessa stood aside to let the officer in.

'Sarah, this is PC Thompkins. Can we collect Steven's comb and toothbrush now? If you'd show us the way.'

Sarah muttered quietly, 'Yes, hello constable, follow me.'

They trundled up the stairs and into the bathroom. Sarah nodded towards the cup containing two toothbrushes on a glass shelf above the basin.

'Steven's is the blue one.'

The uniformed officer produced a pair of thin rubber gloves from his pocket and pulled them on. He unfolded the evidence bag and using fingertips he removed the blue toothbrush from the cup and dropped it into the bag.

'Is there anything else?' he enquired.

'Yes, there's a comb in the bedroom he uses.'

They left the bathroom, and Sarah led the way into the bedroom.

'There's the comb, by the TV.'

The officer placed the first sealed evidence bag on the bed and produced another empty bag from his pocket. Using fingertips again, he placed the brown nylon comb into the fresh bag.

'Brilliant!' he said. 'I'll take these straight back to the station for examination.'

The uniformed officer left with the items whilst Sarah and Vanessa returned to the lounge to sit and wait for news.

Chapter 20

Detective Chief Inspector Norman Grant was the officer overseeing the investigation of the mysterious disappearance of Steven Cooper. A missing person of this age would not normally receive such a prompt investigatory response. It would only normally take place if the adult was vulnerable. The presence of a blood smeared mobile phone gave the investigation the early impetus it needed.

DI Jane Patterson approached her superior.

'Sir, do you remember the *white powder* incident a few months back?'

The DCI nodded, 'Yes I do. It's the same people isn't it?'

Jane nodded. 'Yeah.'

'We need to pick that Kipling chap up, don't we?'

'Keating,' said Jane.

'What?'

'Keating,' she repeated. 'That was his name, Keating.'

'Oh yes, now I remember. Call it in will you? Get uniform to pick him up. I don't think there is much more we can do here tonight. We'll have a quick look round for anything obvious then leave it to SOCO and the search team. We'll interview our suspect back at the station.'

Jane pressed the speed dial button on her mobile to get through to the CID office. She spoke to a colleague and arranged for Timothy Keating to be brought in for questioning.

The stable yard was filling up with police vehicles, including one from the next county. Eighteen uniformed officers had arrived to conduct a thorough fingertip search for clues of Steven's whereabouts. An Incident Support vehicle was next to arrive with a delivery of some powerful arc lights. These were quickly assembled to illuminate the locality before the sun disappeared below the horizon.

Whilst Grant and his willing subordinate continued their cursory look around, a police helicopter arrived overhead and joined in the search. Before leaving, the two CID officers had a quick conversation with a scientific officer from SOCO and the uniformed sergeant coordinating the search. There was nothing to report.

Back at the station they learned that uniform had wasted no time. Keating was waiting in an interview room.

Patterson sat opposite Grant in his office. They were discussing a strategy for Keating's interview. Jane recapped the latest information.

'I've given the phone to forensics. Mrs Cooper confirmed it was her husband's phone. We must know if the blood smear is his, too.'

'Yes,' said Grant. 'We need something to compare DNA with, don't we?'

Jane agreed. 'I spoke to the family liaison officer. She's with Mrs Cooper now. She will look in the bathroom for a comb or brush that Mr Cooper used. Hopefully, we can get some hair follicles for comparison. Oh, and interestingly, when she was asked if there was anybody who might want to do her husband harm, she immediately cited our friend Keating.'

Chief Inspector Grant was deep in thought as he digested this information.

Jane continued, speaking hypothetically this time. 'You know, sir, I don't think Keating can be guilty of what looks most likely to be an abduction.'

'Oh? Why's that? Tell me your thoughts.'

'Well, let's just suppose he is involved for a moment. I think if Mr Cooper was injured, perhaps a fall, or something, then he would still be local to the area where his phone was discovered.'

The Chief Inspector nodded slowly as he listened to the young detective's hypothesis.

'I think the ground search team, or thermal imaging on the helicopter would have found something by now. Don't you?'

'Go on.'

'Well, it looks likely that Mr Cooper is no longer in the immediate locality, so, if he has been abducted then the abductor must have used a vehicle to remove him, don't you think?'

'You're right. Unless our extended search reveals he's still in the area.'

'I saw Keating's circumstances when we arrested him last time. He lived in a dirty hovel. Now, unless his circumstances have drastically changed, I'll bet that the man has little or no money. He certainly doesn't have a car, nor could he afford to run one. Most of his money goes on tobacco and alcohol. Thinking about it, I reckon he was probably innocent of sending the talcum powder to the Coopers as well.'

'Why's that? I thought we had a confession.'

'We did, sir, but I suspect he would have said anything just to get out of here. After all, we didn't prosecute, we let him off with a caution.'

'So what makes you think he may have been innocent?'

'I recall the envelope and its contents. It was printed, probably on a computer. I'm sure he doesn't own a computer or a printer.'

The DCI offered the suggestion of a typewriter.

'I thought about that too. The typeface on the envelope and page inside was different in size and font. Typewriters normally don't do this unless they are very expensive.'

'Didn't we find him in possession of some powder though?'

'We did. His claim was that the arresting officers planted it. He said he'd never seen it before. I don't think he's stupid. Don't you think he'd have discarded left over powder instead of carrying it around in a convenient form for us to find? What if someone did plant it?'

Grant agreed. 'That all sounds feasible.'

For a thorough and proper investigation, the two officers agreed that an interview was still necessary. They had nothing else to go on; and were not even certain a crime had been committed yet. The decision was that at this stage an informal chat with the suspect was the way forward.

Grant and Patterson went down to the interview room for a nice, friendly chat with their prime suspect. Despite their friendly approach, Keating was less than helpful and intoxicated. The interview would have to wait until the morning when he had sobered up. Despite his objections, they detained him for the night.

Chapter 21

Sarah and Vanessa spoke freely, unaware they had an uninvited guest eavesdropping on their conversation. The voyeur was saddened that Sarah was going through this nightmare, for he loved her. Sarah looked pale and drawn in the images being broadcast back to The Watcher's den. The suffering was necessary though, and The Watcher knew that the anguished pain would soon subside when he could finally get to her when she was alone. He would then use his special gift to quell her anxiety. One day, she would be his.

The Watcher stayed with the conversation until late. He listened as Vanessa said, 'Tomorrow's likely to be a long day for you, I think you should try to get some sleep.'

'I won't be able to sleep.'

'It'll be difficult. At least lie down, get some rest.'

'But what if they find him?'

'I'll be first to hear any news. With your permission, I'll crash out here on your sofa with my phone by my side. If there's any news, I'll come up and tell you straight away.'

Vanessa got up from her seat and helped Sarah from hers before ushering her towards the stairs.

The Watcher observed his lovely Sarah lying fully clothed on the bed. Sad to see her crying. She frequently reached over to the bedside table, grabbing another tissue to absorb the salty product of her despair. Her eyes finally closed just after midnight. The house fell quiet; The Watcher abandoned his vigil.

Sarah woke with a start the following morning. Sleep was only made possible through mental exhaustion. She quickly recalled the nightmare she was living. *What's happening? Have they found Steven?* Lots of unanswered questions. She reached for her mobile phone and called Luton Police Station.

'Can I speak to Detective Chief Inspector Grant please?'

Chapter 22

DCI Grant and his young DI rendezvoused in the CID office at 7am on Monday morning. A review of the investigation took place with the CID team and the uniformed sergeant who coordinated the search yesterday. There wasn't much to report. Eagle 1, the call sign for the helicopter, continued the search for an hour after they'd abandoned the ground search for the night. They spotted nothing of any significance from the air.

Jane opened the report from Forensics. There was a 99.9% match between the DNA from the dried blood sample and DNA from Steven's personal items. This was good enough to confirm that Steven had sustained an injury.

The night shift CID team had been busy reviewing CCTV footage from the golf club car park. They identified Steven jogging through on Sunday morning. He disappeared through the gap at the back of the car park leading to the lane. They viewed the footage until a male and female appeared to look around suspiciously and investigate this corner of the car park. Jane identified the couple as Steven's wife and her next-door neighbour. After that, nothing else of significance appeared in the footage.

The DCI spoke to the uniformed sergeant. 'Is there anything left to search in the area?'

'Yes, sir, I'm getting a team together now. We need to get some divers into the field drainage gullies and there is a body of water over there. Call it a large pond if you like. That also needs investigating. My men picked up and bagged anything they found during the ground search. Forensics is examining these items. Nothing of significance stands out, just litter really.'

A ringing phone interrupted his report. A colleague picked it up. 'Just a minute,' he was heard to say. He looked over at the DCI.

'It's Mrs Cooper, sir, asking for any news.'

The DCI bit down on his bottom lip. What could he tell this poor distraught lady?

'OK. Pass me the phone.'

The team listened to the half of the conversation they could hear.

'Yes Mrs Cooper, we've had a team working on this all night. No, we've no leads yet. Yes, we have one suspect in custody so far. On this occasion we don't think he had anything to do with your husband's disappearance, we will be talking to him later this morning. I know what you're saying, Mrs Cooper, but he wasn't in a fit state to answer questions last night. Please trust me and my team to do the right thing. We can't tie this suspect into any involvement in the case.' This was followed by a period of silence. 'I'm sorry this has upset you Mrs Cooper, we're doing everything we can to find your husband.

Is Vanessa there?'

After a brief pause, Grant spoke again. 'Hi Vanessa, Mrs Cooper called me on her mobile. Waiting for news has got to her. There is nothing to report apart from a DNA match to confirm beyond reasonable doubt that Mr Cooper's blood was on that phone. Today, we'll search some flooded drainage ditches and a pond using divers. Don't tell Mrs Cooper that. Just say we're continuing our search. She's upset so I'll let you comfort her, but tell her we'll call round to speak to her later today. Meanwhile, just call in any information you can tactfully gather that you think might be useful. OK, thanks, speak to you later, bye.' The DCI put the phone down and turned to the team.

'OK ladies and gentlemen, split yourselves up into sub teams. Sergeant, thank you for your help so far. Yes, carry on organising the diving team.'

The sergeant nodded and turned to leave the room. The DCI focused on his CID team.

'I want Mr Cooper's bank account monitored. Somebody needs to get the phone back from Forensics, go through his calls, messages, social media messages, see what you can find. I want someone to contact his place of work.'

'Kilburn's,' one of the team chipped in.

The DCI looked at him and said, 'Good, I want you to go along to Kilburn's and find out how things were there. Was Mr Cooper under stress? Or any other reason that might need looking into. Check his emails, speak to his colleagues, bring his office computer in for Forensics to go through, search his desk and so on... Oh, and someone check incoming and outgoing calls on his home phone. DI Patterson and I will visit his home today. We'll have a good look around and bring anything that

needs further investigation to the team... Questions?'

Silence.

'OK team, let's do this. We will meet for an update here at 5pm this evening.'

The meeting disbanded into smaller groups to discuss and decide who would do what.

A uniformed officer brought Keating to Interview Room 2. Grant and Patterson beckoned for him to sit down next to the duty solicitor also present in the room.

He was a little more chatty this morning.

'I'm gonna sue for wrongful arrest,' he said

'Just to be clear,' Grant began, 'You're not under arrest at the moment. We just wanted a little chat about your movements yesterday.'

'Why was I thrown in a cell last night then?' he remonstrated.

'Sorry we had to do that, but you were heavily intoxicated, so we hung on to you for your own safety. You were unsteady on your feet. We couldn't forgive ourselves if we sent you on your way and you had a fall or were in collision with a car.'

'Pah!' was all he said to that.

'Look, Mr Keating, we just want a friendly chat with you - we need your help with one of our investigations. All we need is no more than ten minutes of your time. You can then be on your way.'

The suspect calmed down. 'OK, what do you wanna know?' Grant looked to Jane as a prompt for her to begin the questioning.

'We would like to know where you were yesterday between the hours of 10am and 3pm?'

Keating looked over to the solicitor who leaned over to instruct his client.

Jane overheard the instruction. 'You do not have to answer. Just say no comment.'

Keating looked up at the two officers.

Nah, I got nothing to hide. I was where I normally am, wiv me mates in the park. I got nothing else to do. Why're you asking anyway?'

'It's just that your name has been mentioned in some enquiries we are making at the moment.'

'Who? What enquiries?'

'When did you last see Mr Steven Cooper?'

The mention of that name was like lighting the blue touch paper on a volatile firework. Keating exploded.

'Oh no, not 'im again. That man has ruined my life! I ain't seen 'im fer ages! Nor do I want to! Can I go now?'

Jane looked at her boss. Satisfied that this wasn't their man, Grant said, 'Yes Mr Keating, you can go. Thank you for your help. An officer outside the door will escort you out.'

Keating and the solicitor rose from their chairs and left the room.

Chapter 23

The Watcher made an early start. The family liaison officer was sleeping in the lounge. He listened in, slightly amused that she was snoring. Sarah was awake, and sitting on the edge of her bed, her head bowed. He couldn't see her face from this camera angle. He watched whilst browsing the local news on the Internet, just to see if the media had got hold of the story. No mention yet, but the heavy police presence at the back of the golf club would surely attract some interest before long.

Sarah reached for her mobile phone. The Watcher listened. He heard her ask for DCI Grant. It was hard hearing half the conversation, but one or two facts came to light. Annoyingly, his plan to frame Keating seemed to have failed. It also sounded like the police were scratching around for leads. Sarah, looking distraught, left the room with her phone still in her hand. The Watcher diverted his attentions to the now awake liaison officer downstairs.

Sarah entered the lounge, holding the phone at arm's length.

'Chief Inspector Grant would like to talk to you.' She passed the phone to Vanessa; the conversation continued briefly before the call ended.

The Watcher was sad to see Sarah looking so distressed. She was a pretty girl, but her facial features at the moment detracted from her full beauty. Her eyes were red and puffy. One even looked bruised but it was down to some smudged eye make-up from the day before. Normally, Sarah would have a strict regime before bed, removing make-up and applying moisturiser to her perfectly smooth, beautiful skin. Last night was different. Her routine seemed unimportant; she had other things to think about that were important. Sarah turned to speak to Vanessa again. The Watcher saw her blotchy cheeks and neck. He knew that time would heal these temporary imperfections in her natural beauty before she would be his.

Vanessa sat Sarah down, gave her a tissue, and offered to make some breakfast.

'What do you normally have for breakfast?'

Nothing for me. I'm not hungry. I don't think I could keep anything down at the moment… You help yourself to something though. Before you go, what did he say? I need to know.'

'Oh, the DCI? I think he probably told you as much as he could. He asked me to tell you that the search is continuing. That's all we have for now. Will you have some tea if I make it?' Sarah dabbed her eyes and nodded.

'I really would like you to eat something. How about a slice of toast?'

Sarah turned her nose up. Then, 'OK, I'll try, thanks.'

The Watcher observed Vanessa as she left the room to make tea and breakfast. Sarah remained seated in the lounge, reaching for more tissues as she did so.

So sad was her observer that a tiny tear appeared in the corner of his eye. He muttered to himself. 'I am so sorry you have to go through this my darling, but soon I'll make it right.'

Vanessa reappeared carrying a tray with tea and hot toast thickly spread with butter and strawberry jam along with a bowl of breakfast cereal for herself. Sarah took a couple of sips of the sweetened tea. Vanessa pushed the small plate of toast towards her.

'Here, just try some.'

She looked over at her fractious charge, thinking how awful she looked, brought on by worry and lack of sleep.

'After breakfast, I'm going to call your doctor. I'll get him to make a house call. I think you need something to get you through this.'

'Really. There's no need.'

'We'll let the doctor decide that.'

To show that she was fine, Sarah reluctantly picked up half a slice of toast and took a tiny bite. She chewed for ages before being able to swallow and then took more tea. With encouragement from Vanessa, she ate most of the toast and finished the tea just as the doorbell rang.

Both looked towards the front window. The caller was out of sight and there were no cars outside. Vanessa felt it was too early for the DCI to call and immediately suspected someone from the press. *Just how do these people get hold of their information?* she wondered. She rose from her chair.

'Wait there, I'll deal with whoever it is!' Sarah strained to hear who was at the door.

Vanessa took an immediate dislike to the cocky individual on the doorstep. He had piggy eyes and a ridiculous wispy beard thing sprouting from the end of his chin. His left earlobe was stretched to capacity with an earlobe plug and he had an indecipherable tattoo on the left side of his neck.

'Hello love.'

'First, I'm not your love. Who are you? And what do you want?'

Some of his confidence gone, he became more subservient.

'Sorry, dear.' He shoved an ID card attached to a lanyard around his neck forward so Vanessa could read it. Just in case she couldn't read he recited, 'Barry Burnett, Reporter for the Luton Tribune.'

'What do you want?'

'They've asked me to report on the police activities at the back of the old stables. My enquiries led me to this address. I would like to ask a few questions about the incident.'

Vanessa suspected he knew nothing and was trying to second guess what might have happened, to give the impression that he knew more about the events of yesterday than he really did. She was ready for this intrusion. 'Incident?'

The reporter was now on his back foot. He really didn't know what had happened and was now being invited to expand on the *incident*.

'Yes, I understand there has been some kind of accident down there?'

Vanessa now had confirmation; he knew *nothing*. How he related things to this address though she did not understand. He must have a mate or contact in the force who had passed some details on, for a fee no doubt. Vanessa put him out of his misery, though he would hardly be satisfied with her prepared statement and was sure to want more details.

'All I can say is that Bedfordshire Police are investigating a report of a missing person. A search is being conducted in the missing person's last known location.'

The reporter, hungry for more information, fired the first of many questions he would want to ask. 'Who is…'

Vanessa cut him short. 'This is all we can say at the moment. We have no further comment to make.'

The reporter, predictably unhappy with this brief statement, tried to ask more questions as Vanessa showed him her palm whilst shutting the door.

The cheeky reporter jammed his foot in the doorway to stop it closing.

'If you don't remove your foot now, I'll call the police!' Vanessa scolded.

The reporter wisely pulled his foot back.

'Thank you, bye-bye.'

The door closed. The reporter turned away from the house and replayed Vanessa's statement on his digital recorder as he walked up the garden path.

Back in the lounge, Vanessa told Sarah that the press had got hold of the story and may become a nuisance.

'Let me answer any phone calls, and I'll answer the door as well.'

Sarah was in agreement, thinking she would not cope with intrusions from the press.

Chapter 24

Police Sergeant Tom Fuller briefed the Police Diving Division on the areas to be searched. Acting Police Sergeant Kit Carson led the diving team.

Carson surveyed the drainage gully running alongside the field.

'I doubt they'll have disposed of a body in the gully, it's too shallow, for one.'

'I think you're right. We'll look though. I'll get some of my team to pull back the overgrown areas to give you better access.'

'Thanks, that'll be a great help. Whilst your boys do that I'll get my lads onto the lake.'

The two sergeants directed their teams to work.

Four hours later, the search of the lake ended. The divers recovered an eclectic mix of items from the stagnant pool. This included the apparently mandatory shopping trolley and bicycle. The most bizarre item appeared, at first glance, to be a harp. They later identified this unusual item as the frame from a baby grand piano. They found no human remains or anything suspicious.

The team had a break before embarking on the less popular job of searching the drainage gully. They worked systematically along the 100 metres of muddy gully. No shopping trolley this time, but the bike was there. They found a potentially suspicious item, a rusty blade, thought to be off a scythe. Fuller examined it and bagged it up, ready for a forensic examination. They found nothing else of interest.

Tom Fuller called Grant's mobile. An answering service answered the call, so he left a message to give an interim report on findings.

'I'm now standing my teams down,' he concluded.

The search teams packed up their gear and left the site. The area remained cordoned off with *Police Line - Do Not Cross* tape. Two occupants in a single police patrol car stayed to make sure nobody entered the suspected crime scene.

Chapter 25

Back at the house, it was becoming obvious that word was getting round. Vanessa was fielding phone calls and visitors to the door, mostly representatives from the press. There was a chilling irony to the cold call about an accident somebody in the household might have had. The only welcome callers were DCI Grant and DI Patterson.

The DCI introduced his inspector to Sarah and thanked Vanessa for looking after her. 'Why don't you take a break for a few hours? Jane here will stay until you return.'

Vanessa was grateful for the opportunity. She departed, needing a freshen up and change of clothes in her overnight bag.

'Is there any news?' was Sarah's first question to the police officers now seated in the lounge.

The Watcher was keenly listening in to see what progress had been made.

'I am sorry Mrs Cooper, but so far we have drawn a blank. We are pursuing several leads and Forensics continue to examine items found in the vicinity of where your husband's phone was found.'

Sarah was keen to know more. 'What lines of enquiry?'

Grant was feeling uncomfortable as he knew that most lines were superficial and not based on any concrete evidence, there just wasn't any!

'Well,' he began, 'We are examining his phone to see what calls and messages were made and received.'

Sarah studied the DCI intently, waiting for more. He continued.

'We are monitoring Steven's bank account to see if there is any activity. We have a team at erm...' 'Kilburn's,' Jane prompted.

'Yes, Kilburn's. We are questioning staff and colleagues there. We are also examining his work computer, emails and telephone records. We are looking at CCTV images from the golf club car park. We have posted a notice at the golf club reception asking for information. Forensics are looking at a range of items found around the area of interest.'

Grant was sorry he didn't have more positive news. Sarah stared at the DCI for several seconds.

'You haven't really got anything have you Chief Inspector?'

'Well, I wouldn't say we have nothing. My team is working hard on several lines of enquiry and forensics can take some time. Hopefully, we'll have more news tomorrow.'

Sarah was weeping again. Jane grabbed some tissues from the box on the coffee table, sat next to Sarah, and put her arm around her shoulders.

'Mrs Cooper,' the Chief Inspector began, 'I know this is difficult for you, but we need to ask you some questions. Do you think you are up to it?'

Sarah gave her nose a good blow and shook her head. 'No, that's fine. Sorry, yes, please ask your questions.' The inspector set up his recorder.

'Just so we forget nothing that's said, I hope you don't mind, but I would like to record our conversation.'

'No, I don't mind. Go ahead.'

The DCI placed the recorder on the coffee table and began his questioning.

He initially enquired about Steven's state of mind.

'How was he coping at work?'

'Fine, he loved his job.'

'What is your marital relationship like?'

'I don't know what you are trying to imply inspector but we are both very happily married.'

'Forgive me Mrs Cooper. I don't mean to upset you, but they are questions I must ask.'

Other enquiries included: Did the couple have any financial problems? Was there anybody, apart from Keating, that might have a grudge against Steven or someone who might want to harm him? Were there any family feuds?

None of the answers to the questions were useful in the investigation. They appeared to be the perfect couple enjoying life together.

Grant switched off his recorder.

'Thank you, Mrs Cooper, that was very useful. There's one more thing we need to do.' Sarah looked over at the DCI. 'We need to look around the house. Do you mind?'

'No, of course not. Help yourself.'

The Watcher was delighted with the apparent lack of progress and evidence in the investigation. Knowing the detectives would visit all rooms in the house, he directed his focus to the Coopers' bedroom. The Watcher smiled to himself as he heard a conversation between the two detectives in the bedroom.

The young female detective conceded to her DCI, 'There's nothing here.'

The DCI nodded in agreement. 'I don't think I have ever known a case like this with so little to go on, a genuine mystery.' The Watcher's smile turned into a broad grin. *They really do not know*, he thought to himself. Satisfied that they had no reason to suspect him, he abandoned his eavesdropping activities for now.

The detectives returned to the lounge. Sarah sat morosely, staring into space. Movement of the opening door snapped her out of it.

'Mrs Cooper,' the DCI began. 'We found a computer in the back bedroom. We need to take this for a forensic examination.'

Sarah nodded, 'Steven mostly used that for online shopping and banking. Yes, take anything you need. You'll find his work laptop in a bag in the cupboard under the stairs.'

Grant nodded and turned to Jane. An unseen and unheard message passed between them. The DI turned and went to the hallway to retrieve the laptop.

'I have to leave now, but Jane here will keep you company until Vanessa returns. Do you have questions or anything to tell me before I leave?'

The DCI studied Sarah, looking for signs that she might be hiding something. Grant knew that all too often the guilty party in a violent crime is known to the victim and regularly it turns out to be a family member. There was no betraying body language that would identify Sarah as being involved in her husband's disappearance.

She looked up at the inspector, dabbing tears from her face.

'No, nothing, thank you.'

Grant gently touched her shoulder.

'Don't worry Mrs Cooper, my team and I are working very hard to get to the bottom of this mystery. If there are any developments, I will call in and speak to Jane here or Vanessa if she's back. Meanwhile, if you think of anything that might be of interest to us, please let us know.'

Sarah took the business card offered by the DCI and nodded, unable to speak. She placed the card on the table and reached for another tissue to mop up her anguish.

Jane heard her superior drive off as she sat down. She put a comforting arm around Sarah. They sat like this for several minutes until Sarah's distraught sobbing subsided.

The doorbell rang again. Vanessa had warned Jane that the press was sniffing around. She went to answer the door, prepared to deal with an unwanted intrusion.

Sarah strained to hear the conversation at the door and was surprised to hear the door close with a male voice engaged in a hushed conversation in the hallway. The lounge door opened and in walked a tall silver-haired man. Jane studied his features. Despite being a man in his sixties, he had kept his good looks. She figured he had probably broken a few hearts in his time. He was the epitome of a TV soap heartthrob doctor. Doctor Barker looked at Sarah and said,

'Hello Mrs Cooper, sorry to hear what's happened. Let's see what we can do for you.'

Jane, respecting privacy, left the doctor and his patient. She went to the kitchen to wash up and make tea.

Chapter 26

The Watcher tuned in to the activities in the Coopers' lounge once more. Who was at the door? Police? Press? He had to know. He listened to the conversation.

'…It's natural to feel this way Mrs Cooper, you've had a great shock and only time or some good news regarding the whereabouts of your husband is going to make you feel better.'

Sarah was crying once more. Doctor Barker produced a blood pressure monitor from his briefcase and slid the cuff up Sarah's arm. The machine buzzed until the cuff gave a sigh when the process was complete.

'Hmm, 130 over 90, a little high, probably because you are feeling stressed, not sleeping well, I expect?'

Sarah responded with a shake of the head.

'Are you eating? It's important you eat enough and keep your fluids up, you know.'

Sarah nodded this time. 'I did eat a little breakfast, but felt sick afterwards,' she said.

The doctor retrieved a prescription pad from his bag.

'Are you, or do you think you might be pregnant, Mrs Cooper?'

'No,' was the quick reply.

'I'm prescribing some Fluoxetine capsules. Initially, take one in the morning after breakfast. You can take another after lunch if you need to.' He paused. 'I'm also going to give you something to stop the nausea. These are gastroresistant tablets, you should take one about 30 minutes before you eat.'

Doctor Barker scribbled something illegible to the untrained eye. The top page of the pad was torn off in a practised move and handed to his patient. He studied the poor distraught woman before him.

'I hope you get some positive news soon, Mrs Cooper. If you need me, I'm happy to do further home visits. Call the surgery to arrange one.'

Sarah uttered her thanks as he repacked his bag and bade her farewell before leaving.

Jane returned from the kitchen, carrying a tray of tea and biscuits. She was pleased to see the prescription on the table.

'Ah, good, he's given you something. We need to get these picked up for you, don't we?'

Jane sat down just as the front doorbell sounded again. Sarah poured some tea whilst Jane answered the door. Hoping this caller had some positive news, she listened, recognising the voice of her neighbour, Mark.

Mark entered the room holding a bunch of flowers. Jane scooped up the flowers before returning to the kitchen to find a vase.

'Hello, love, how are things? Any word yet?'

Sarah welled up again. 'No, nothing. It seems the police don't know, and the prime suspect is no longer a suspect.'

Mark observed her red-rimmed teary eyes looking up at him.

'I'm sorry to hear that. Let's hope that no news is good news, shall we?'

With a concerned look, he sat down beside her and put his arm around her for a comforting hug. The tears rolling down her face dripped onto the his polo shirt, forming a dark patch on his shoulder. They both remained in their embrace until Jane came back with the flowers arranged in a vase.

Sarah sniffed and, whilst trying to smile, she thanked Mark for the lovely gesture.

'From the garden,' he said.

'Would you like some tea?' Jane asked.

'I'd love a cup,' said Mark.

Jane retrieved another cup from the kitchen and the three sat drinking tea and eating biscuits for the next half hour.

Mark looked at his watch. 'Goodness, is that the time? I must go, I've work to do, I'm afraid. Is there anything I can do? Or anything you need?' he enquired as he stood up.

Jane reached for the prescription and gestured it towards the neighbour.

'Can you pick this up from the pharmacy for us? Do you mind?' she asked.

'Of course not,' he took the form from the detective.

'You'll need some money,' said Sarah, reaching for her purse in the coffee table drawer. She pulled a £20 note from the side pocket and gave it to her kind neighbour.

'Stay there, both of you. I'll see myself out.'

Jane decided now would be a good time to press Sarah for more information. She poured more tea.

'Has Steven ever gone missing before?'

'No, *never.* He is the most dependable, reliable person you could ever hope to meet!' She was a little annoyed that the detective might even consider Steven had intentionally gone missing.

Jane said, 'Sorry, I'm not suggesting for one minute he's disappeared on purpose.'

Sarah dabbed her nose with a tissue saying, 'He really is Mr Perfect, you know.'

'Do you think he might have contacted a friend or family member?'

'He doesn't really have mates to speak of. There's Mark next door, of course. The two of them visit the pub once or twice a week providing he isn't working away. He occasionally meets with colleagues at work, normally a birthday or leaving do. We always go everywhere together. He's got no living relatives that I know of. Our wedding was a tiny affair. The only relative to attend was my Uncle Angus. He lives in Scotland. Poor Uncle, he now has mobility problems and lives in a residential home. So, the answer to your question is no, I can't believe he would have injured himself and then gone somewhere without contacting me or getting help, would he?'

'I agree, but he could have amnesia after falling and banging his head.'

Sarah became upset again.

'I'm sorry. I didn't mean to upset you.' Jane backed off from asking more questions for now.

The melodious chimes of the doorbell interrupted their conversation. Jane rose from her seat and went to answer the door. Sarah cocked her head, straining to hear who it was.

Jane returned to the room holding the medication and change from the £20 note.

Chapter 27

Sarah's situation remained the same for the next two weeks. The medication was helping. She finally informed Uncle Angus on a phone call. The old man was very concerned: 'Can I help? I've money if you need some, anything, just ask.'

Vanessa did not need to stay with Sarah now. She visited once or twice a week instead, intending to provide updates, but there was often nothing to report.

* * *

DCI Grant called the team together for an evening briefing. Each member of the team confirmed what they had been investigating and the outcome. It frustrated Grant that each line of enquiry had drawn a blank. The investigations had been thorough. They had even viewed CCTV images from the petrol station on the main road. Steven would have passed the petrol station on the last leg of his run home. There was nothing on that fateful Sunday. They viewed footage from the previous weekend. On that occasion, they could see Steven jogging past the fuel station, so it was likely that he would also have appeared on camera the day of his disappearance.

The press were like baying dogs. It was decided to update them at a press conference. The very day of the press conference, a story featured on the front page of the local evening paper. The headline read: *Have you seen this man?* Boldly printed above was a photograph of Steven. A column of text next to the image concisely detailed information from the conference.

There was one response to the newspaper article. An elderly lady called, sure that the man in the picture had delivered her weekly groceries. The police quickly established that this was not the case.

At another evening meeting later that week, Grant threw a question out to his team. 'Any ideas? Where do we go from here?'

The only response was from Jane: 'What about a TV appeal?'

Grant, looking thoughtful, was silent for a few moments before saying, 'I think that's a good idea Jane, I'll talk to the super about it.'

The meeting disbanded. Grant went to his office to call Superintendent Dickerson.

A few minutes later, Grant reappeared at his door. Jane was sitting at her desk nearby.

'We're on. Dickerson will arrange a meeting for the press that an Anglia TV news team will attend.' 'Great news!' said Jane.

'That's not all though.'

Jane looked to her superior, waiting to hear what else his boss had said.

'He wants Mrs Cooper to speak at the appeal and for a profiler to be present.'

Jane knew what this meant. All too often, murder victims knew the person responsible for the crime against them. A profiler analyses body language and dialogue at the appeal. This process could reveal that Sarah knows more than she's letting on. Jane screwed her face up.

'Do you think she's hiding something?'

'No, I don't. It'll be an ordeal for her, but he's the boss, and that's how he's told us to proceed. I need you to speak to Mrs Cooper. Put a positive spin on the idea, emphasise how it will help the investigation. Make her understand that her involvement is essential. Hopefully, you can persuade her. Tell her she can bring a friend if she likes. Perhaps she will ask that chappie living next door.'

'Mark,' Jane chipped in.

'Yes, that's him. See what you can do.' Grant checked his watch, 'It's late now. Visit her tomorrow morning. Get her agreement first, then we'll arrange a date and time.'

'Ok sir, will do.'

She logged off from her computer for the evening. She needed to devise a strategy on the way home.

* * *

Meanwhile, The Watcher was busy on the Dark Web, meeting his international coven of brothers and sisters. Nobody used their real name on this forum.

The attendee known as Elias Phinn asked about the so called *catering arrangements*.

Their leader assured, 'A delivery will arrive in good time for the event.'

Elias nodded before asking, 'What's in the shipment?'

A flash of annoyance appeared across The Watcher's face. Some brothers well knew his volatile temper.

Toby Bryant sensed an awkward moment, 'We don't need details at the moment.' The Watcher calmed down.

'No, Toby. It's OK. I will have sufficient cocaine and cannabis to satisfy the numbers expected. I'll have some heroin too for our more adventurous guests.'

The members nodded in agreement.

'I need a volunteer to take orders from delegates. This way, we can prepare pre-paid orders.'

Another committee member, Carston Dean, spoke out, 'I'm happy to coordinate this.'

'Good, thank you, brother. I suggest you approach all the brothers and sisters now. The sooner we know requirements, the better it will be. I have arranged a minimum quantity but can ask for more if needed.'

Dean was happy to please The Master. 'Leave it with me.'

'One other thing,' The Watcher added, 'I'll need some help nearer the time preparing these orders.'

All the committee members agreed to assist. If nothing else, it would be an opportunity to have a face-to-face weekend meeting and, they hoped, a chance to see the venue and meet their intended *special guest*.

Elias asked if the attendance of the *special guest* was definite.

'Everything is going to plan. I now have her on her own. The police investigation is leading to nothing. Nearer the time, I'll use my special powers to impose my will.'

Several of the brothers found this amusing. They knew how powerful the mind of their leader, Igor Torpitz, could be. The covert meeting concluded with a reminder for delegates to close their sessions securely.

The Watcher reflected on the meeting and chuckled as he realised he had morphed back into his old drug dealing ways as Micky Lawson. It was time, he decided, to check on his quarry, curious to see if any developments had occurred.

Sarah looked lost and asleep in the king-size bed she once shared with Steven. The bedroom activities, with her departed husband were now no more. The Watcher's lecherous voyeurism was now restricted to the occasional glimpse of her whilst dressing or undressing. One day, though, she would be his.

Chapter 28

Jane stood patiently at the door of number 34 Chatsworth Close, waiting for it to be answered. It was early, around 8.30am, not too early she hoped. She needed to speak to Sarah about yesterday evening's developments. She was on the verge of pressing the doorbell button again when, at last, she saw movement through the glass panels of the modern-looking wood effect front door.

Jane fully understood the cautiousness afforded by Sarah as she fitted the door chain within before cracking open the door. The local press had been a nuisance in recent days but seem to have given up of late. No developments meant no news for their publications.

'Who is it?' came the soft voice from within.

'Hello Sarah, it's Detective Inspector Patterson, Jane. Can I come in to talk with you, please?'

Hopeful the DI had some news, Sarah removed the safety chain before inviting the young detective in. Still attired in her PJ's Sarah apologised for the time taken to answer the door.

'It's the medication given to me by the doctor. I don't wake up as early as I used to.'

'That's ok Sarah, at least you're getting some sleep now.'

Jane studied her for a moment, obviously she was still traumatised. She looked tired, pale, and drawn. She was wringing her hands in anticipation of what Jane wanted to see her about. *Has there been a development?*

'What's happened? Is there any news?'

'I'm sorry, Sarah, but no there've been no further developments. I do need to talk to you though.'

Sarah's face dropped, showing disappointment. She bit her bottom lip whilst stifling back more tears.

Jane wanted to take a softly softly approach to her request.

'I've plenty of time so, how about I make some tea? And some breakfast for you? If you like, whilst you perhaps shower and wake up properly before we talk.'

'You're very kind, thank you.'

'I've a couple of calls to make on my mobile. You go upstairs and get ready. I'll have some tea and toast ready for you in 20 minutes.'

The officer sat down and pulled out her phone to make a couple of private calls whilst Sarah went upstairs to get showered and dressed.

Sarah reappeared just as two slices of toast popped up in the toaster. Jane, already familiar with the kitchen and where things were kept, produced a plate, knife, butter and jam from various cupboards and the fridge. Sarah sat at the kitchen table and, whilst spreading butter and conserve on her toast, the detective placed a mug of hot sweet tea in front of her.

'Thank you.'

Jane studied Sarah once more, thinking she looked better already. *Amazing what a shower can do* she thought. Sarah took a sip of her tea and cut her buttered toast into triangles.

'What is it you want to talk to me about?' she asked, before biting into a slice of toast.

Jane cleared her throat and took a sip of her tea before beginning.

'Despite the considerable resources we've dedicated to the investigation, we've got nothing, no clues, no leads. We've come to a dead end. The requests for information in the local papers were fruitless. A Facebook campaign has also drawn a blank. I'll admit, we're running out of options.'

Sarah swallowed the first bite of her breakfast.

'How can that be? People don't just disappear without a trace, do they?'

'No, they don't normally. We've been very frustrated by the lack of progress! Checks on your husband's bank account show there's been no activity since he disappeared, no witnesses have come forward, we've reached an impasse.'

'So, what happens now? Do we just forget it ever happened? Is this going to be one of those cold cases now?'

'No, of course not. DCI Grant has suggested we make a TV appeal. It seems likely that somebody out there knows something of what happened to your husband. A TV appeal will reach a wider audience. It'll probably go out at a peak viewing time. What do you think?'

Sarah had seen similar things like this on TV. She didn't need to think long before agreeing that this was a good, next logical step.

'There's one thing you need to agree to though.'

She looked over the top of her mug before placing it back down onto the table. 'What's that?'

'We want *you* to make that appeal.'

Sarah froze. She couldn't possibly, could she?

Seeing seeds of doubt germinating in Sarah's mind, the detective quickly added, 'Don't worry, you won't be facing the media alone. We'll be at your side. All you would have to do is read a prepared statement to the cameras. The press will be there as well. They're likely to have questions afterwards. We'll help and support you throughout.'

Silence, as Sarah just stared, her eyes going watery once more. Eventually…

'I… I don't know, I don't know if I could.'

Jane took another sip of tea whilst waiting for a further response. None came. Sarah just sat motionless, thinking. Jane eventually broke the silence.

'Look, I know it's a big ask. Just think about it. I'll call back later today to hear your decision.' Sarah nodded tentatively and carried on eating breakfast and drinking tea, as if the conversation had never taken place.

'A silly question, but how have you been coping? Have you been out?'

'It's like I am living a nightmare. No, I haven't been out. I don't know what I'd do without Mark next door. He calls round most days, bless him. He gets my bits of shopping and he's even prepared meals for me. A nice man.'

'I'm glad somebody's looking after you. Does Vanessa call you?'

'Yes, she has been a great help and comfort as well.' Then, 'He's dead, isn't he?'

Jane was taken aback by this.

'We don't know that yet. There's still hope.'

'Oh, come on,' she said, with a *do you expect me to believe that* attitude. 'He'd very little money on him when he left. He's not drawn any out of the bank since he disappeared. What else am I to believe?'

Jane had no comforting words to offer. After all, her thoughts concurred with Sarah's.

'Well, we haven't given up on him yet. It's still possible that there's an explanation for his disappearance.'

'Like what?'

'Ok, let's suppose he had a fall, and he hit his head. He might have amnesia. Who knows? He may have made it back to the main road, got on a bus and ended up confused and in a hospital in another town.'

Both ladies thought it unlikely, but Sarah thought yes, something like this might have happened.

'I'll do it!'

Jane looked up at Sarah, 'Sorry?'

'Yes, I'll do the appeal. Just tell me what I need to do and say, I'll do it.'

'That's brilliant,' said Jane.

'When will it be?'

'It's yet to be decided, but soon, I mean, in the next couple of days.'

'OK. It won't be easy as I don't enjoy speaking in front of people. I have a fluttering in my stomach just thinking about it. I'll do it for Steven though.'

Jane, pleased that she had persuaded Sarah to do this, was now keen to go back to the DCI so that arrangements could be made for the appeal.

Sarah was left sitting alone at the kitchen table, weeping once again.

Later that day, Mark called round just to see how she was. He offered to make them both a drink, but Sarah made them both coffee. Mark took this as a sign that she was pulling herself together. They sat in the lounge talking.

'How are you today?'

'Oh, you know, one day at a time, it doesn't get any easier. It's the not knowing.'

Mark nodded an understanding.

'The police called round again earlier.'

'Oh, any developments?'

'None!' said Sarah 'They want me to take part in a TV appeal for information.'

'Are you going to do it?'

'Yes, I'm not looking forward to it though. It will be the first time I've ventured out since the day he disappeared you know. I can't just sit here day in day out. I need to be more proactive I decided. This way I can try to help bring the investigation forward. I won't feel so damned helpless then.'

Mark agreed it was a good thing to do.

'What will you say?'

'I just have to read out a prepared statement and then maybe answer some questions from the press.'

The Watcher was now aware of this development. Initially worried, but he decided it would be ok. The police were *grasping at straws* he thought. They know nothing and an appeal was likely to reveal the same. He must be vigilant to find out when the appeal would take place. He wouldn't want to miss it.

* * *

Two days later, a familiar vehicle pulled up outside Sarah's house. Jane Patterson emerged and walked down the garden path. Sarah promptly opened the door. The ladies went into the lounge unaware that their conversation would be overheard by a third virtual member in the room.

Jane revealed the TV appeal would take place in two days' time. Anglia TV news cameras would be there along with members of the press from local papers in Herts, Beds and Bucks. The location would be in the hall of a local community centre.

'I've a prepared statement for you.'

Sarah took the single page from the detective and sat down whilst reading it. Obviously distressed by its contents, she thought that yes, she could read it at the appeal.

'I'll pick you up. Vanessa will be there too. Don't worry, you'll be fine.'

Sarah was nervous and didn't seem convinced.

Chapter 29

The community centre was prepared for the appeal. DI Patterson surveyed the scene. All was professionally laid out; banners with contact numbers behind the blue cloth-covered top table with the police logo displayed clearly at the front. All cables were safely covered, and a production team were busy checking equipment, Just then Vanessa came in with Sarah. Jane ushered them into the kitchen, out of the way to wait until proceedings began. Vanessa and Jane stood by Sarah's side making reassuring comments as they waited. Chief Inspector Grant was in the main hall talking to a tall, smartly-dressed man with a Van Dyke style beard. The man looked pensive whilst he gently stroked his beard.

Yesterday, Sarah had practised reading out the words on her script several times, Jane had helped her get this right.

Jane tried to take Sarah's mind off the pending ordeal, 'Are you ok, Sarah?' 'Very nervous.'

'You'll be fine,' Vanessa chipped in.

Sarah noticed another man enter the room. He went straight over to the Eastern News team for a quick chat before announcing to the room in a loud voice:

'Ladies, gentlemen, could you please take your seats at the top table, we need to carry out a quick sound check to make sure you'll all be clearly heard during the recording.'

Sarah noticed the clock on the wall at the back of the hall, just ten minutes to go before the appeal starts at 2pm.

At 2pm the cameras started rolling, Chief Inspector Grant began.

'At the moment, the investigation is being treated as a *Missing Persons* enquiry. We believe Mr Cooper may be injured and possibly in need of medical help. His last known whereabouts was on the bridleway behind the old stables. The last sighting we had of him was on CCTV from the South Beds Golf Club security cameras. He jogged across the car park and through an opening onto the bridleway. Next to me here I have

Mrs Cooper who would like to add to the appeal.'

The profiler shifted his balance and again stroked his beard. He focused on her body language whilst she read out the prepared statement.

It was an emotional plea, twice her voice wavered, and she stopped speaking, trying to keep it together. Jane put a comforting arm around her shoulders and then Sarah continued until the statement was finished. She just got the last words out before weeping profusely. Jane produced tissues to replace those already sodden with the torrent of tears.

Chief Inspector Grant took over once again.

'We appeal to anybody who has information leading to the whereabouts of Mr Cooper. Crimestoppers UK are offering a reward for information that subsequently leads to finding Mr Cooper. Thank you. We'll take some questions now.'

Multiple members of the press immediately started firing questions at the panel.

The floor manager armed himself with the boom mic as Grant showed the palm of his hand to the audience.

'Please! One question at a time.' He pointed to a lady sitting in the front row, 'You first.'

She began, 'Chandra Abdulla, from the Three Counties Echo. Chief Inspector, what leads you to think that Mr Cooper might be injured?'

The inspector replied, 'I'm sorry, but I can't reveal details at the moment, as this may jeopardise the investigation.' She quickly came back with. 'Was he assaulted or…?'

The inspector cut her off mid-question. He pointed to a wispy bearded reporter, 'You next.'

'Barry Burnett, Luton Tribune' he announced. 'As is often the case in investigations like this, a member of the family or person known to the victim has committed the crime. Have police exhausted enquiries on this front or do you have a prime suspect?'

Sarah reacted badly to the cruel question and reached for more tissues to stem the fresh torrent from her eyes.

'We don't yet know that a crime has been committed so there are no prime suspects. I can confirm that one person so far has been eliminated from enquiries.'

A few more questions were asked. Sarah did well to respond to a couple before the Chief Inspector called time, 'Thank you ladies and gentlemen, no more questions now.'

The Chief Inspector and Jane rose from their seats to retire back to the kitchen area. Jane helped the distraught Sarah to her feet and guided her out.

The ordeal was over. Sarah sat, drinking a glass of water whilst being comforted by Vanessa.

As members of the media departed, the inspector walked over to speak with the profiler, Simon Jones.

'Well, what did you think?'

Jones stroked his tidy beard before beginning.

'She showed all the right signs. She's genuinely distraught and did you notice in the couple of questions she responded to, how she spoke of her husband in present tense rather than past? For example, my husband *is*, rather than *was*. This would suggest that she thinks he's still alive.'

Grant nodded.

'There were no give-away signs to suggest she was being untruthful. Sometimes people give out micro gestures to belie what they're saying. A small shake of the head whilst stating a positive fact could mean that they don't believe what they are saying, because it's a lie. There were no tell-tale shoulder shrugs or leg tremors. From what you tell me, they appeared as the perfect suburban couple, never a cross word and all that. We deduce that she either knows he's still alive or refuses to believe he's dead. I think the latter is true. There's nothing in her body language or what she said to make me believe anything different. I hope that helps Chief Inspector, I will of course write a formal report and send it in before the end of the week.'

The men shook hands, and the profiler departed. Grant was satisfied that Mrs Cooper was genuine. He thought this would be the case. The one thought he did have but wasn't yet willing to share with her, was that Steven Cooper was probably dead. If the results of the appeal were negative, he would be looking to change the status of Mr Cooper to '*missing, presumed dead*'.

Chapter 30

'And now for the news and weather in your area,' the evening news anchor announced. The familiar Eastern News graphics, currently being sponsored by *'Warmwell Home Improvements '* played, whilst the studio changeover took place.

Mark sat watching the news. A couple of local politics stories and some historical scandal at a children's home preceded the report he was waiting for.

'Police in Bedfordshire launched an appeal today for information connected to the disappearance of a Luton man. Our local correspondent takes up the story.'

The person Sarah would recognise as the floor manager at the appeal laid out the basic facts before handing over to what he called an emotional appeal by Mrs Cooper.

Next door, Sarah could not bear to watch. She hated having her picture taken, so to see herself on TV in the wretched state she considered herself to be in, was too much.

* * *

Fifteen miles away in a town called Stevenage, Malcolm Knight was seated in front of his television about to eat a TV dinner. Malcolm lived in a one bedroom flat that could be kindly described as cluttered. Piles of books everywhere, the carpet between the hallway and kitchen had lost its pile long ago and in places was now shiny. The kitchen bin was overflowing and had the odour of rotting leftover food.

Housekeeping was not his strength. He'd not yet taken his first mouthful before his attention was diverted to the appeal being broadcast on the local news.

The distraught Sarah ended the appeal with; 'Somebody out there must know where Steven, my husband, is. So please, I urge you to contact Bedfordshire Police or Crimestoppers UK with any information that may help their enquiry.'

In his own mind, Malcolm knew exactly what the cause of Steven Cooper's mysterious disappearance would be. What's more, he thought he had the evidence to prove it.

Malcolm showed a high order of intelligence in things he was passionate about and believed in. His Asperger's meant his social skills were lacking though. He found it difficult in new situations and found it hard to approach others: would he have the courage to call the number which he had already memorised from the end of the appeal?

Chapter 31

Sarah sat at home. The TV was on but she wasn't paying attention to the programme about antiques. She used to enjoy watching these with Steven, but lately she'd lost interest. It was only on now because the evening news was on the other channel. She really didn't want to watch the appeal. She thought she looked ghastly and expected the TV cameras to be less than complimentary in transforming her image for broadcast. A short while later, her caring neighbour rang the doorbell.

'Come in.' She beckoned him towards the lounge. Mark walked in and sat down. He could see that she was feeling down so he tried to lighten her mood.

'I love watching these programmes. My favourite bit is the auction at the end.'

Sarah managed a thin-lipped smile.

'How are you? I saw the appeal.'

'I hated it. It was an ordeal I would never want to repeat.'

'Of course, I understand. Let's hope somebody sees it and can help move the enquiry along.'

'Shall I make some tea?' Sarah asked.

'I'd love some. I'm always ready for a cuppa.'

Sarah rose and went to the kitchen. A couple of minutes later, as Mark could hear no activity in the kitchen, he went to investigate. She stood, head bowed, weeping into some paper kitchen towel. Mark hurried forward to embrace his distraught neighbour.

'Hey, come on,' he said, 'Let's look on the positive side and hope that today's efforts help solve this mystery.'

He put his hand under her chin and lifted her head towards his, their faces were just a couple of inches away from each other. He looked into her eyes, *God, she was beautiful.* 'Look at me.'

She looked into his eyes. His stare was intense, more intense than normal. 'Listen to me. You're going to dry your eyes and then you will sit down. I will make the tea and bring it to you. Do you understand?'

She nodded and felt strangely compelled to obey. The already damp tissue was used to dry her eyes on the way back to the lounge.

Minutes later, her neighbour returned carrying a tray of tea and biscuits. 'I hope you don't mind, love, I found some biscuits in the cupboard.'

'No, of course not. Thank you.'

There was currently no sign of the upset witnessed in the kitchen. She even managed a smile.

They sat talking, at times recalling a few stories involving Steven for the rest of the evening. It was 11pm when Mark drained the dregs of his Southern Comfort. Sarah took a tiny sip from the glass of wine she'd hardly touched.

'I must let you get some sleep.' He stood up to leave, Sarah also stood up. He took her hands in his, facing each other, he stared deeply into her eyes. Sarah was drawn to return the stare.

'When I leave, you will take your medication and then you will go to bed for a great night's sleep.' He then turned to leave, 'I'll see myself out.'

The front door clicked shut. Sarah obediently took her medication and retired to bed.

Chapter 32

A few days had passed with no news or response to the appeal. Sarah's mind was in turmoil. The following day, she answered the door to a sombre-looking Chief Inspector.

'What is it? Has there been some news?'

'Can I come in?'

Sarah stood aside and motioned for him to go into the lounge.

'Sit down please Mrs Cooper.'

Concerned, Sarah sat down, not taking her eyes off the inspector.

He cleared his throat, 'I'm sorry to report that we've found a body.'

Sarah stared into space, her eyes filling up with tears, surely, she cannot have many more tears to shed! She dabbed her eyes.

'Is it, is it, Steven?'

'All I can say at the moment is that it is a male of about 40 years old. Yes, we think so but I cannot confirm this until somebody has identified the body.'

Another short period of silence. 'I'm sorry Mrs Cooper, I have to ask you to accompany me to the morgue for the purposes of identification.'

More tears, the inspector passed the box of tissues to the distraught lady.

'Now?'

'If you don't mind Mrs Cooper, I can wait whilst you get ready. Take your time.'

The journey to the morgue was in silence. Sarah was escorted straight through to the Chapel of Rest. 'Take a seat Mrs Cooper. I'll arrange for the viewing.'

A few minutes later, the inspector returned. 'Are you ready?'

Visibly shaking, she couldn't speak, she just nodded. The door to the inner chapel was opened and Sarah entered the dimly lit room.

A smartly-dressed attendant stood by the body, which was covered in a white sheet. Sarah stood looking down at the head of the shrouded body. The inspector stood nearby and gently nodded at the attendant.

He reached forward and uncovered the head and shoulders of the body.

'Oh, my God!' shouted Sarah, 'Yes, this is him!' She looked at his perfect form laying there. Many thoughts ran through her mind. *How did he die?* No obvious injuries. She touched his face, cold as ice. But wait, as she stared at the body before her, it was obvious something was wrong. *Why is he wearing his suit? The one he wears for work.*

The attendant gently covered the body again. Sarah emitted a guttural cry, 'Nooo!' It was this that woke her up from the cruel nightmare she'd just experienced. She rose from her bed, damp with perspiration and tears. She just made it to the bathroom before she was violently sick.

Chapter 33

The Watcher was again meeting members of the coven on the Dark Web. He was not talking to the brothers and sisters at the moment, but was completing the catering arrangements for the Main Event. The Watcher was keen on this idea as he would earn a six or seven-figure sum for the service.

A key element of the Main Event would involve heavy consumption of a large amount of narcotics. The merchandise will be transported by road from Turkey across Europe to a small airstrip just outside the French town of Hazebrouck. Here, the shipment will be transferred to a waiting aircraft. A light aircraft, with its valuable payload will make a night-time, low-level flight over the English Channel to deliver the goods to a disused Kentish airfield.

The Watcher was delighted at the quantity ordered by the delegates, as they were paying a premium. He stood to make a substantial profit. The most risky part of the operation will be the collection in Kent and transportation by road to be stored, prior to the event taking place.

The goods would be delivered a few days before the event, scheduled for 30th April 2019, the eve of the feast of Saint Walpurga.

Once again, he was careful to close his Dark Web session securely so that no trace of his interaction would exist.

Chapter 34

Three weeks had passed since the TV appeal. A few calls had come through on the appeals line, but nothing of significance. A couple of *put downs* with no message and a message from one lady who thought she recognised the missing man. Her message stated he caught the same train towards London at Luton Parkway railway station early each morning. This sighting was investigated, just in case, but was predictably a case of mistaken identity. A call was also received from a public call box, which appeared to be a bunch of kids larking about. The investigating team were disappointed and frustrated that the investigation was not moving on.

At the case review meeting, the team were scratching around for ideas. A phone started ringing in the office, it was an internal call, identifiable by the type of ring tone. DC Patel was closest to the phone, so picked it up and had a brief conversation. He replaced the handset on the cradle.

'Sir! That was the front desk on the phone. There's a Mr Malcolm Knight down there, say's he knows what happened to Mr Cooper.'

At last, a glimmer of hope for the team.

'Well, let's talk to him. Jane, I want you in on this.'

The detectives left the room together to investigate this apparent lucky break.

'I'll commandeer Interview Room 4. Jane, will you pick up Mr Keightly from reception?'

'Knight,' corrected his DI.

'Sorry?'

'It's Mr Knight.'

'Oh, yes, that's him, I'll wait in here.' He entered interview room 4.

Jane continued to reception, smiling to herself. Her boss was a great man and had the respect of all his team. His career was eventful, and he had several commendations and a George Medal for Gallantry, awarded after his actions to apprehend a terrorist whilst he served in the Met. She smiled because he could never seem to remember a name, a fundamental requirement for a policeman she would have thought. Still, he'd lots of other good qualities and was a good boss to work for.

A green light illuminated on the access control panel next to the reception door as Jane swiped her NFC card over the sensor. She pushed the reception door open.

To the right was the reception desk, to the left, against the wall was a row of plastic chairs mounted on a metal frame which was secured to the floor. Two of the chairs were occupied, neither occupant was what Jane expected to see.

Closest to her was a female, early twenties, Jane would guess. Tattoos everywhere and a copious amount of piercings adorned her face. Jane noticed the needle tracks on her arms and reckoned she was a seasoned drug user. She certainly wasn't Mr Knight.

The other person sat close to the reception entrance. He was probably in his forties. Despite the warm temperatures at the moment, he wore a large woollen bobble hat. *Strange*, Jane thought. He needed a shave, and a wash, by the looks of him. His tee shirt, which was probably once white, was grey, particularly around the armpits and sported a variety of food stains from previous meals and beverages. His trousers were scruffy, the front of them bearing several dubious stains. The back of his baggy trouser bottoms were frayed, having been trodden into the ground with the heel of his scuffed brown shoes. At his side was a shopping bag. Jane's first impression was that he was a homeless person.

'Mr Knight?' she called out.

The scruffy man turned and acknowledged her call.

'Would you like to come with me, sir?'

The man grabbed his shopping bag, got up from his seat and shuffled over towards Jane. She could now understand how his trouser bottoms had become so frayed. She held the door open as he passed through. Predictably, his personal hygiene was not good. Reluctant to shake the man's hand, Jane introduced herself before he reached her.

'I'm Detective Inspector Patterson.'

The man may have said something, she wasn't sure; it sounded more like a grunt.

She covered her nose as he walked past in anticipation of an unpleasant odour. He paused on the other side of the door. 'Straight down, sir, we're in Interview Room 4.'

The man proceeded down the corridor until he arrived at the fourth door on the right. Jane followed at a distance. The door was ajar, 'Go straight in sir.'

The Chief Inspector was seated inside, he rose from his seat as the man entered and offered his hand.

'Mr Knight?'

'Yes, that's me.' He grabbed the offered hand. The visitor's handshake was unpleasant, clammy and limp.

'I'm Chief Inspector Grant, please, take a seat.'

The nervous visitor sat across the table from the DCI and Jane took a seat next to her superior.

'Thank you for coming in Mr Knight. I understand you know something about the disappearance of Mr Cooper?'

'Yes, and I have photographic evidence as well,' he patted his shopping bag.

'Really? This sounds interesting. Do you mind if I record the interview?'

He looked unsure.

'Don't worry, it's just in case we forget something that was said, you understand?'

'OK, I agree.'

The inspector switched on his digital recorder, the red light confirmed that a recording was taking place.

'This is Chief Inspector Grant, with Detective Inspector Patterson interviewing with?' The inspector looked over at Knight, intending it as an invitation for him to say his name, he just stared back unaware what was being asked of him. 'Could you please state your name for the tape?'

'Oh yes, of course.'

It was obvious Mr Knight was not entirely comfortable using this technology. He almost rose from his seat and leaned across the table to be closer to the recorder, 'My name is Malcolm Knight.'

'Thank you. The recorder's very sensitive, there's no need to move closer, just sit there and relax whilst you tell us in your own words what you know.'

Knight looked hesitant. The detectives waited patiently for him to begin.

'I'm sorry, I get nervous around people.'

The detectives realised their interviewee might have some mental health issues by some of his actions and things he said. They took a very *gently gently* approach to encourage him to tell them what he knew.

Grant broke the ice, 'It's OK. Take your time, would you like some water?'

'Yes, please.'

Jane rose from her seat and went out to get a cup of water from the water machine. She also brought more water for her and the chief inspector.

The interview began again.

'For several weeks, I've been observing some suspicious activity' - he took a sip of water - 'I have some photographs. Nobody would believe me otherwise.' 'And what was this activity?' Grant asked.

'This might sound silly, but it was lights.'

'Lights?'

'Yes, in the area that Mr Cooper disappeared.'

'So, was this at night?'

'Yes, always at night.'

'What was the source of these lights? Was it a torch? A vehicle?'

'Oh no, not a torch, but more of a... a vehicle.'

'You have pictures?'

'Yes,' he opened his bag, removed some A4 sized papers and handed them to the detectives.

Baffled, the two studied the images, mainly black pages with splodges of white.

The DCI frowned, 'I'm not sure what I am looking at here. Where were the pictures taken?'

'I live in Stevenage; this is to the east of Luton.'

The detectives both looked puzzled, unsure of where this was going.

'I've taken these pictures over a period of several weeks, looking skyward to the west. This puts these sightings in the general area we are interested in.'

'Skyward? Sightings? What are these?'

'Let me show you something.'

The man took his bobble hat off and turned it out onto the table to show that it was lined with what looked like silver tin foil.

Jane looked on, still not understanding what was going on. The Chief Inspector leaned forward, shut his eyes and pinched the bridge of his nose between his thumb and index finger. A few moments later, he looked up. The man tried to explain.

'I hunt for UFOs, the silver foil in my hat protects me from extra-terrestrial interference. I believe that your missing man may have been abducted by aliens. I believe these images to be of alien spaceship activity over north Luton.'

The officers could not believe what they had just heard. Even more convinced that Mr Knight might have some mental health issues, they decided to let him down gently.

'May I keep these pictures?'

Pleased that he'd apparently been taken seriously, the man's mood brightened,

'Oh yes, of course, I have more.'

'I think we have enough here. Listen, thank you for taking the time to come in with this information, very useful. I'll add these to the case notes. Thank you once again.'

Not wanting to waste any more time on this, the Chief Inspector switched off his recorder and tidied the papers in his case folder.

'Jane here will show you out.'

Grant rose from his seat, and forgetting his first handshake experience, held out his hand again. Before he could withdraw the gesture, Mr Knight shook it heartily. Nobody had taken him seriously before. He passed a piece of pre-prepared paper with his contact details on, should the detectives wish to talk to him again.

Jane held the door open and gestured, 'This way, sir.'

He followed Jane down the corridor to the reception door. He passed through the door, and Jane once more avoided his handshake.

Back in the office Grant relayed the news from their *star witness* to the team. It was met with a cacophony of laughter. The laughter reignited when one detective shouted. 'Probably the latest flight taking off from Luton!'

Chapter 35

Sarah had weekly conversations with Uncle Angus, *I must visit him again soon,* she thought. Uncle Angus was worried about her finances?

Money hadn't been a problem till now. Kilburn's were still paying Steven's salary. However, a couple of weeks ago an ominous-looking letter arrived from Kilburn's. It caused concern. Steven's salary payments would stop at the end of the year. The car was also to be re-called. The only bit of good news was that she would be eligible to receive a lump sum pay-out from Steven's pension contributions.

Sarah did manage to visit her uncle prior to Christmas 2018. Uncle Angus conducted a thorough interrogation.

'How much do you still owe on the house?'

'The last statement said £95,000.'

The thought of it worried her, she struggled to hold back her tears. 'I need to pop to the loo,' she held it together until she was in the privacy of the bathroom. She wept tears of concern for a good few minutes until she pulled herself together. She washed her face, dabbed her eyes and re-applied her eye make-up. After a last check in the bathroom mirror, she re-joined her uncle in the lounge, sat down and smiled at him. She wasn't fooling anybody though; Uncle Angus could still sense her distress. He slid a piece of paper across the coffee table.

'This is for you my dear.'

With a puzzled look, Sarah turned the paper over to reveal a cheque for £100,000. Initially speechless, she looked at her uncle, mouth and eyes wide open with surprise.

'Pay your mortgage off, I won't be around long enough to spend all I have. One day, when I'm gone, it'll be yours anyway, so you might as well have some of it now.'

Finally, Sarah found her voice, 'Uncle, I couldn't possibly…'

Her generous benefactor held his hand up, 'No buts. Just take it and have one less thing to worry about.'

She once again produced floods of tears, this time the tears were a mix of sadness and happiness. She flung her arms around her kind uncle, hugged him tightly, and kissed him on the side of his face.

'Thank you, uncle. Thank you so much.'

* * *

Grant and his team were frustrated that the investigation had drawn a blank. All lines of enquiry were fruitless. The case had now been relegated to the *Cold Case Pile*. There had been no movement on Mr Cooper's finances since his disappearance, the team now considered him to be missing, presumed dead.

He gazed thoughtfully through his office window, thinking what an unusual case this was. *People don't just disappear, do they?* There was apparently no known motive for the disappearance, no body. Perhaps that UFO nut was correct, perhaps Mr Cooper *had* been abducted by aliens. Grant laughed to himself, what was he thinking? There has to be another explanation, but for now, it'll remain a mystery.

* * *

Christmas Day 2018 arrived and Sarah was feeling down. She didn't know why she had accepted an invitation to lunch from her good neighbour, as she felt she wouldn't be good company.

She called Uncle Angus for a chat in the morning. Angus was delighted to receive delivery of the finest bottle of cask aged malt whisky he had ever had. Sarah had arranged the surprise delivery with the care home supervisor. The special gift was handed over to her dear uncle that morning.

They discussed their plans and activities for the rest of the day. The highlight of uncle's day would be a game of Bingo after lunch and of course, a glass of whisky before bed.

Apart from lunch with her neighbour, Sarah didn't know what else she would be doing, most likely watching TV or listening to her well-played Motown Greatest Hits CD. No matter what it was, Steven would never be far from her thoughts.

At 12.30pm, Sarah was wrapped up warmly, standing on her next-door neighbour's doorstep. Today's doorbell chime was Jingle Bells. The door opened to reveal Mark wearing a Christmas jumper and Santa hat.

Sarah grinned at the silly look on his face. She stepped across the threshold. 'Where did you get that jumper?'

'You wouldn't believe it, but I bought it at your old charity shop in the week. Only £4.99.'

'You were diddled, I'd take it back if I were you.'

Mark pretended to look hurt. Then they both burst out laughing.

Mark put a hand on each of her shoulders and gave her a light kiss on each cheek. 'Merry Christmas. I hope you're hungry.'

Her host took her coat and then beckoned her into the lounge.

'Sit down. Dinner's not ready yet, so we can have a drink whilst we wait.'

In contrast to the one or two degrees of temperature outside, the lounge was what Sarah would describe as toasty. A woodburning stove in the corner, transformed the room to positively tropical temperatures.

Mark poured a large glass of sparkling wine for each of them. He passed a glass to Sarah and then sat in the armchair opposite his guest.

'Cheers,' he held up his glass. Sarah did the same, and they both took a sip of the nicely chilled wine.

Sarah looked at the small row of Christmas cards on Mark's sideboard. They were neatly arranged under a small Christmas tree festooned with an array of multicoloured flashing LED lights.

'Your tree's lovely.'

'I wasn't going to bother this year, but I was rooting around in the loft a couple of weeks ago and found it in a box. I thought why not? So I got it down and set it up. It brightens the place up, don't you think?'

Sarah looked morose.

'Since Steven's gone, I can't think of things like that at home. It doesn't seem right. It's times like this that I find difficult. I miss him so much.'

'I'm sure you do my dear, have you heard any more from the police?'

'Nothing! I don't suppose, after all this time, that they're spending too much time on the investigation now.' A tear appeared in the corner of her eye.

Mark sensed it was time for a change of subject. He picked up a remote control and pressed a button. Music started playing. Sarah didn't recognise the artist, but it was good.

'You relax my dear. I'm going to carry on preparing dinner in the kitchen.'

He refilled her glass before leaving the room.

The food did smell good. The music went on to another equally enjoyable track.

Mark popped in regularly to check on his guest, making sure she was well supplied with wine. By the time lunch was announced, she was feeling a little tipsy.

She looked wide-eyed at the enormous plate of food before her. 'I'll never eat all of this.'

'Tuck in, but leave room for pudding!'

'Oh my gosh, pudding as well!!!'

Despite her doubts, she did the meal justice and ate a small pudding. She leaned back in her chair to relieve some of the pressure on her full stomach.

'I'm stuffed! I don't think I can move.'

The two of them sat at the dinner table, looking across at each other. Mark gave her that stare again, the one where she couldn't blink or look away.

'A couple of years ago, an aunt of mine sadly passed away. She left me a property out in the Hampshire countryside. I sometimes go there to stay. It's not big, two small bedrooms. You need a break. In a couple of months, you're going to stay there for a long weekend. It's what you need. What do you say about that?'

Still transfixed on her neighbour she responded with a simple, 'Yes.'

Mark blinked and the visual bond between them was broken. Strangely, the conversation between them continued as if that moment had never happened.

Sarah retired to the lounge with coffee. Her host refused all offers of help to clear up. She sat listening to the music and tried not to drift off to sleep with the excesses of food and alcohol.

Mark reappeared. They sat talking until the early evening darkness arrived, and Sarah decided to thank her host for a lovely meal and return home.

Prepared for the sub-zero temperature outside, Sarah stood in the hallway, ready to leave. Mark turned towards her and once again their eyes were locked with each other.

'Go home, get warm, have a glass of wine and go to bed,' he looked away, and the link was broken.

An icy blast penetrated Mark's hallway as he opened the door. Sarah stepped forward to leave.

'Thank you for your company and a lovely meal today.'
'T'was a pleasure.' He stepped aside to allow his visitor to leave. She hurried back to her house and disappeared inside. Once home, Sarah sat in her warm lounge drinking a glass of wine. She then went to bed for an early night.

Chapter 36

Sarah had not been home long before The Watcher was already carrying out his covert observation. He watched her sitting in her lounge, sipping a glass of wine. He could hear the dialogue from a Christmas film playing on the TV, but she didn't appear to be watching it. She sat motionless, just staring ahead.

She finished her wine. The TV went silent. The lounge went dark. The Watcher diverted his attention to bedroom surveillance. She appeared and removed her clothing. The Watcher feasted on her naked spectacle before she pulled on her PJ's. Soon, she will be his.

With his quarry tucked up in bed, he turned his attentions to the Dark Web, wondering if any of the brothers or sisters were online. He followed the procedure to make a secure, untraceable connection to the Walpurga chat room.

One elder, Tarquin Masala, was present. The men discussed progress. Tarquin addressed his Master by his coven name, Igor Torpitz.

'I've been thinking about you, Igor. I know the brothers and sisters are all looking forward to our celebration. How are the arrangements coming together?'

'Very well, I'm pleased to say. Orders have exceeded expectations and payments have been coming in daily.'

'When's the shipment due?'

'When the time is right, the shipment will cross the Turkish border, but not before payment has been made.'

'How will you make payment? An online payment has the potential to leave a trail, we don't want that, do we?'

'Tarquin, my dear, and ever cautious friend, you don't need to worry. Payment will be made with Bitcoin to an untraceable account that will be active only for a brief time until money is transferred out again.'

Tarquin never ceased to be amazed at his Master's organisational skills. He'd thought of everything.

'How about our special guest, The Queen of Pentacles?'

'When the time's right, she'll be ready. She's unaware that I've already started imposing my will upon her. She's been a willing subject so far, so I'm confident that she'll not let us down.'

The conversation ended. Igor reminded his loyal friend to close his Dark Web session down securely.

Chapter 37

Sarah continued her lonely existence, missing Steven, especially on Valentine's Day. He always bought roses and they always went out for a romantic meal on that day. The ever lustful Watcher got to know and always tuned into the bedroom activity on that evening. He would watch the couple end their romantic day in ecstasy. There would be no loving embraces this year though.

The trips to the mall coffee shop became a regular occurrence for the neighbours on a Wednesday afternoon. Sometimes Sarah would pop into the charity shop just to say hello. Depression meant that she was not inclined to work there again though.

It was one bright Wednesday afternoon in March; the UK was enjoying an unusually good spell of weather. Sarah and Mark were walking through the park to the Mall wearing clothes more suited for a summer's day. It was beautiful.

'I spoke with Uncle Angus on Monday.'

'How is he?' Mark enquired.

'He's fine. It's funny you know.'

'What is?'

'Well, poor uncle doesn't go out much, so he only sees life in his residential home. I suppose in total there are about ten residents there. You would think that uncle would not have much to say, but, when he gets going, he could talk for England. I sometimes find it hard to get a word in edgeways.'

'What does he find to talk about?'

'All sorts,' said Sarah. 'He often talks about things that happened years ago. He made me laugh the other day. He asked if I remembered things from the war days. How old do you think I am, uncle? He thought for a few moments and then remembered I wasn't even born then!'

Mark laughed and admitted he used to have an aunt that did the same.

'He did say something interesting though.'

'Oh, what was that?'

'One carer at his home has a flat nearby that has become available for rent. She was telling Uncle Angus all about it and is thinking of maybe selling it later this year. She doesn't want to take on a long-term tenant at the moment, so the flat sits there vacant. Uncle Angus has suggested I move into the flat for a while to see how I like it up there. He's even offered to pay the rent for a few months. He said, if I like it, why don't I consider finding a house in the locality and selling up here? Property is considerably cheaper in Scotland, so he reckons I could afford a small mansion. Not that I would want anything too big of course, maybe a three bedroom detached property. I could then see more of Uncle Angus.'

Mark was a bit taken aback by this news. The way Sarah was talking seemed like she'd already decided.

'I don't know what to say, are you going?'

'I thought I might spend a couple of months up there. A sort of holiday, just to see if I like it. It might do me good. There are a lot of painful memories for me here, maybe I need a break from it all.'

They walked the rest of the way to the mall in silence, both deep in thought.

Chapter 38

Mark was alarmed and slightly panicked upon hearing his quarry might be leaving the area. The pending event was deemed *special* and needed to be celebrated to the full. Without his *special guest,* the celebration would lose its impact.

Some of the coven elders had now viewed images of Sarah. It was wholeheartedly agreed that she had a striking resemblance to the eighth-century abbess, Saint Walpurga. It was deemed no coincidence that she was brought close to the Master, a powerful message that couldn't be ignored.

Walpurgisnacht would be an excellent opportunity to recognise the pagan celebration of fertility rites. It was therefore Mark's intention to consummate the marriage to his bride on this special night.

Mark was in his cabin. He studied the antique etching of Saint Walpurga above his desk whilst drumming his fingers on the desktop. He was trying to think of a way to disrupt his neighbour's sudden change in plan. Coven members would be disappointed if the planned event was cancelled. He also stood to lose a large profit. Worst of all, he would lose the person he coveted and loved. There was still a good amount of time to avert disaster, but he would need to keep hold of her for a longer period than expected. It was time to call upon a higher authority.

He reached forward to the ceramic container on the back of his desk. The ceramic pot was in the form of a macabre-looking skull. The crown of the skull was a lid that lifted off. Mark aptly called the caricature *Charlie*. The relevance of the name revealed by the contents of the container. He removed a plastic bag of white powder from the vessel.

Two generous lines of cocaine were carefully prepared on the desktop. The narcotic was noisily consumed through a paper tube up his nostrils. Effects of the drug were soon evident and with bloodshot eyes, pinpoint pupils and white smudges visible on his top lip, it was time to seek guidance from his master.

A rug covering the floor was pulled back, revealing a five-pointed star crudely drawn beneath it. Five black candles were lit and placed, one at every point of the pentagram. After removing all his clothing, he covered his naked body with a
monk's habit and sat cross-legged in the centre of the magical symbol.

By the light of the flickering candles, he looked up to the etching on the wall. His arms were held wide, as if expecting a welcome embrace from someone above. This position was assumed for several minutes until he launched into a Latin incantation to summon the daemones 'ignis (demons of fire). Flames on the surrounding candles flickered and flared, brighter and higher when his demonic prayers were being answered.

When the chants were finished, he pulled the hood of the habit over his bowed head and rested his wrists on his crossed legs, as if in meditation. There he stayed for several hours, sitting in silence, waiting for guidance from the demonic presence he had summoned to the room.

Dawn was approaching by the time the rituals had finished. All five candles extinguished simultaneously as the demons of fire suddenly departed the room. Only thin wisps of smoke rose from the wicks to show that they had been recently burning. He emerged from his deep meditational state. A sinister plan had formed in his mind. He knew exactly what his next move would be. One thing was for sure, Sarah would not be going to Scotland.

Chapter 39

The neighbours were on their regular Wednesday afternoon stroll to the Mall. Discussions turned to the charity shop that Sarah used to work at.

'You'd be amazed at some things people brought into the shop to be sold for charity.'

Mark was intrigued. 'Like what?'

'False teeth, a box of out-of-date cornflakes, a World War II gas mask. Oh, and other erm, shall we say *unmentionable things*.'

'What are they?'

'Personal items. I'm too embarrassed to name them. People bring boxes of stuff in from lofts and house clearances of deceased relatives without always realising what's in the boxes.'

Mark didn't press the subject, he could only guess what some of these items might be.

'I think you should pop into the shop today.'

'What for?'

'Well, don't you want to say goodbye if you plan on going to Scotland?'

'I suppose It depends who's in the shop. Since I left, a couple of new volunteers have taken over. If it's somebody I know, I might pop in and say hello.'

'I'll come too' said Mark. After a pause he then made the tongue-in-cheek comment, 'I'll have a browse round the shop to see if any unmentionable things are for sale.'

Sarah was amused.

'Don't bother, you won't see any, they normally go straight into the bin outside. The shop has a reputation to maintain you know!'

They approached the main concourse to the Mall.

As they reached the shop, Sarah recognised Polly Jameson rearranging the window display. Polly looked up and saw her old colleague immediately. Sarah waved, Polly beckoned her in as she climbed out of the window display area.

Polly was a buxom lady in her forties. She always reminded Sarah of a dinner lady she once had at school.

'Come in my dear, how lovely to see you.' She embraced Sarah and gave her a big hug. She looked over at Mark.

'Oh, this is Mark, my next-door neighbour. We often pop down here on a Wednesday for a coffee.'

'Lovely to see you, my dear.'

'Nice to meet you too. Why don't you two have a natter whilst I have a browse?' He looked at Sarah and saw a faint smile flicker across her face. 'You can give Polly your news.'

'News?' said Polly.

'Yes, sadly, she's thinking of leaving us!'

'Pray come and tell me all about it.' Polly ushered Sarah into the back storeroom for their natter.

The ladies, still chatting, emerged from the storeroom about 15 minutes later. Polly was thrilled for Sarah and thought the move might be just what she needed.

'I know it's just a trial period but you might like it up there, you know, make new friends and of course you get to see more of your dear old uncle. You could get a lovely house in exchange for where you live now. How exciting, you will write, won't you?'

Finally, in a rare lull in the conversation, Sarah and Mark said their goodbyes and left the charity shop in need of a coffee.

Chapter 40

'Yes, uncle, I'm getting ready to come up to see you. I hope the carer's flat's still available.' She paused, with the house phone pressed close to her ear intently listening to her uncle's reply.

'There's no problem with the flat my dear. Margaret's pleased to have it occupied for a wee let whilst she decides what she wants to do with it. How long will you come up for do you think?'

Sarah thought for a moment. 'I was thinking five or six weeks, how does that sound?'

'Perfect, I'm really looking forward to seeing you lass.'

'Me too, uncle, me too.'

'Do you have a date when you might come? Margaret will need to know. You'll like her, I've told her all about you and she cannae wait to meet you.' Angus really did sound excited.

'I was thinking late March and then I'd return early May. It's a long way but I'll drive up, of course, the car will be handy whilst I'm up there.' She made a mental note to have the car serviced in the next week. 'It'll be too far to do the drive in one go, I'll probably stop off and spend a night in a budget hotel in Durham or Newcastle or somewhere like that.'

'That's a good idea. I'll speak to Margaret tomorrow and give her the news. There's no need to bring anything with you as the flat's fully furnished. Oh, bedding, I suppose, and towels, you know, stuff like that.'

Sarah was getting quite excited at the prospect. There was nothing really to keep her here. She thought she would miss Mark; she didn't know what she'd have done without his kindness and support since Steven's disappearance.

The elderly uncle said his goodbyes and the telephone call ended.

Her plotting neighbour had eavesdropped on the telephone call. He could glean from the half of the conversation he had heard, that Sarah was planning to leave for Scotland in a few weeks' time. The exact date of her plan would be needed. He wouldn't want to get caught out.

So far, he'd been successful in hiding his true identity and his evil intentions from his unsuspecting neighbour. That would soon have to change, as his revised plan was implemented. He'd need to use his special powers to impose his will upon her before it was too late to do anything about it.

Mark, in his friendly neighbour persona, stood patiently waiting for Sarah to answer her door. It took a little longer than normal before the door opened.

'Sorry Mark, I was in the toilet, come in won't you?'

'How are you love?'

'Oh, you know, one day at a time.'

Mark felt she seemed a little happier of late. Sarah went to the kitchen to make some tea. Mark never refused a cup of tea on his visits and followed her.

'How are plans going?'

'Scotland you mean?'

'Yeah, do you have a date yet?'

'I leave on the 21st.' She stirred the tea 'I'm staying up there for about 6 weeks until say… beginning of May I think. That's the plan, anyway. If I really don't like it up there, I can always cut the trip short and come home sooner.'

'Sounds exciting,' though the tone of his voice didn't concur with the feeling he had inside.

Sarah happily agreed and hadn't noticed her neighbour's gloomy response. A sudden thought struck her.

'Oh. I need to get the Primera serviced before I go, it's long overdue. Do you have any idea where I can go? I don't think there's a Nissan dealer in the town now.'

This enquiry from Sarah germinated the beginnings of an idea in Mark's mind. 'Yes actually, I use a garage in Barton Le Clay, he's very good. Probably not the cheapest but I trust him. If you like, I'll take it down for you early next week and get it serviced.'

'Would you? That would be so helpful, I've so much to do before I leave.'

'No problem, I'll call him later and book it in for you.'

Sarah was thankful that Mark was going to do this. She didn't enjoy going to garages.

'Do you know the way to your uncle's place?'

'No, not yet. I was going to get to grips with the satnav in the car. I've used it before, but that was a while ago.'

'Give me your uncle's postcode and I'll program the satnav for you when I take it in for its service.'

Again, Sarah appreciated Mark's kindness. She never really understood the satnav, Steven always used to program it when he was around.

'I might need a crash course on how to use it before I go.'

Mark found this funny, 'Don't worry, you'll be fully trained before you go.'

They spent an hour chatting over tea and biscuits. The evening darkness was drawing in when Mark returned home.

Chapter 41

Later the same evening, the brothers and sisters were attending a meeting on the Dark Web. The chatter amongst those present was lively. Their leader called the meeting to order: The followers were eager to know that everything was going to plan, there were a lot of questions and an air of growing excitement in anticipation of the fast-approaching event.

'One at a time, please! I'll choose who to speak next.'

The Watcher answered the usual questions relating to the event. Some needed to be reassured about the shipment of narcotics, a common question at these meetings. Igor supposed it was because many attendees would be coming from abroad and they didn't want to get caught carrying their own supply through customs. Reassurance was given that there would be more than enough. As well as satisfying orders placed, he had arranged a contingency supply. After all, he wouldn't want to miss the opportunity to maximise profits from the sale of the illicit contraband. The number of attendees was discussed: 212 so far. This was nearly double the number from previous events and only confirmed the importance placed on this year's special occasion. It was thought the number would increase. Igor confirmed there was a capacity at the location for up to 500. He informed members that payment to attend the event was also payable in advance using cryptocurrency.

The exact location of the event was still a closely guarded secret that would only be revealed shortly before the event. Visitors from all over Europe were expected. Society elders were the only members who currently knew the event location.

Igor clarified that he would need help from a small team of members in the weeks and days leading up to the event. The opportunity was also taken to form some sub committees to administer things like car parking, registration and the selling of merchandise.

All questions answered and everybody content, a last reminder was given to everybody to close down their Dark Web session securely.

Chapter 42

Sarah was busy gathering everything she needed for her extended trip to Scotland. The weather lately hadn't been good; April showers seemed to have descended upon the UK early this year. This inclement weather was making it difficult to get those final bits of washing dry. A warm airing cupboard was a saviour though. It was currently crammed full of damp laundry; it was doing the job. *Only a couple of days to go* she thought. Whilst Steven was never very far from her mind, she hummed to tunes on the radio. It had been a long time since she'd had anything to look forward to.

She used the pole to release the latch on the swing down loft door. This would be an experience! Steven was always the one to go up into the loft, she'd never been up there. She needed to go up to retrieve a suitcase. Nervously, she climbed the aluminium ladder. Her head emerged through the hatchway, and she found a pull switch cord to activate the stroboscopic flashing of a fluorescent light tube.

Still standing on the ladder, she immediately burst into tears as the first thing her eyes focused on was a plastic container with a lid. On the side, it was clearly labelled *Wedding Photos*. Oh, how she missed him! She produced a tissue ball from the sleeve of her cardigan.

Nervously, she stepped onto the bare wooden loft flooring. Wishing to avoid any more things to remind her of her loss, she quickly grabbed the suitcase and was soon relieved to be back down safely. Something was rattling around inside as she carried the case to the bedroom. She placed it on the bed and released the two catches on the front of the luggage. When the lid was lifted, there was another painful reminder of the loss of her handsome man. The familiar aromas of the toiletries in Steven's travel wash bag wafted into her nostrils. He kept this in his suitcase to use on his frequent trips abroad. Through streaming eyes, she removed the wash bag and placed it in a bedside table drawer. She sat on the bed for a few moments. Her thoughts were interrupted by a weather bulletin on the radio:

'The Met Office has issued an amber weather warning for the East of England over the next week. Storm Jezebel is expected to bring gales, snow and low temperatures. The storm is expected to bring severe disruption to travel in the UK and winds likely to cause structural damage along the East coast. Heavy snowfall will affect Norfolk, Suffolk, Essex and Kent.'

Sarah listened to the full report. *Would it affect me?* She picked up her iPad from the bedside table and studied the local weather predictions for the next few days. Local weather initially seemed ok, but temperatures were dropping significantly towards the end of the week. She was due to travel in a couple of days, so she'd be in Scotland by that time. A prudent thought reminded her to take some warm clothing with her. Her preparations were disturbed by the front doorbell ringing. Sarah quickly popped down the stairs to answer the door to her neighbour Mark.

'Hello love, you ok? I've come to pick up your car for its service.'

Sarah didn't let on that it had slipped her mind.

'Oh, yes, of course.'

She found her jacket hanging on a hook in the hallway and retrieved the car keys from the pocket.

'Thanks Mark.'

'No problem, do you have your uncle's postcode?'

'Oh yes, the satnav. Step inside a minute. I'll get it for you, I think it's in the Contacts list on my iPad.'

Mark waited in the hall whilst she ran upstairs to get her iPad. She was browsing through it as she descended the stairs.

'Ah, yes here it is.' She wrote Uncle Angus's postcode and address on a Post-it note on the hall table. She peeled the top page off and gave it to her neighbour. 'You'll have to show me how to use it later.'

He stepped back outside.

'Don't worry, you'll be fine with it after my mini tutorial. I'll have the car back later this afternoon.'

'Thank's again.' She watched as he climbed into the car. Back inside, she busied herself again preparing what she had to take on her trip.

Chapter 43

Mark sat waiting in the reception area of the garage. His mind was occupied with his plans to stop Sarah getting to Scotland. *Have I missed anything?* There were still a few weeks before the Main Event, so he would need to keep her concealed before then. This would be the unpleasant bit, he thought. Sarah would know he wasn't the person she thought he was. She would most likely have changed her opinion of him long before she could fulfil her ultimate act of devotion towards him. He would need to use his special powers to control her mind. He already knew that her mind was receptive to this, and she had unknowingly been hypnotised to perform simple tasks, like Christmas Day evening, when he commanded her back to the house. He would, of course, miss his voyeuristic activities whilst waiting for the special day when she would become his.

His thoughts were interrupted.

'Mr Stewart?' a rather greasy looking individual dressed in what was once a white boiler suit called, as he entered the reception area. He was wiping his oily hands on some blue paper towel as he scanned the individuals sat in reception.

'That's me,' said Mark.

'All done for you, sir.'

The mechanic reached for the invoice that was sticking out of his breast pocket.

'This is the bad bit.'

He summarised the work he'd completed whilst advising that the front tyres would need changing in about another 5000 miles.

'…and all of that comes to just £397 and 67p,' he ended.

Nearly 400 quid thought Mark. Why do people always try to make it seem like a trivial amount, *just* this much or *only* this much.

'Shirley at the desk'll take your payment, keys are in the car.' He handed over the paperwork. 'Thank you, sir, enjoy the rest of your day.'

Mark found the car parked in one of the MOT parking bays. He climbed in and switched on the ignition. Ignoring the Post-it note in his jeans pocket, Mark set about programming the route that Sarah would take in two days' time. It wasn't the address that Sarah had supplied him with, but an address somewhere in Hampshire. Mark saved the plotted route and labelled it *Uncle Angus*.

The Primera was old, but Mark thought how well it performed during his drive back. The engine was super smooth and certainly quieter than his van. Despite its age, the vehicle was well equipped, one of the first production cars to have inbuilt satellite navigation as standard, a car before its time. He needed to make sure Sarah had enough fuel in the car for the trip, so he called into the supermarket petrol station and filled the car up. He entered the close and reverse parked it in Sarah's driveway - partly to make loading the car more convenient and partly to see how useful the reversing camera was on the car. *Impressive*, he thought. Mark reckoned the car would not be moved again, so he purposely made sure the car was in the field of vision of his CCTV security camera.

Sarah quickly answered the door to see her car keys being dangled right in front of her face.

'All done, I filled her up with fuel as well.'

'Oh thanks ever so much Mark, that has saved me so much time.' She took the key, 'Now then, how much do I owe you?'

'That's the sad news,' joked Mark. 'Here's the bill for the service and a receipt for the fuel.' He handed the paperwork to Sarah.

'Ouch,' she said. 'Heaven knows how much that would have been if I'd taken it to a main dealer. Step inside. Would a cheque be OK?'

'Of course,' said Mark as he stepped into the hallway. Sarah scribbled the cheque and handed it to him.

'Thank you.'

'No, it's me that should be thanking you.' She opened one of the kitchen cupboard doors in the corner unit by the sink. She peered into the gloomy interior before reaching in. When her hand reappeared, it was holding a litre bottle of blended whisky. 'Here,' she said. 'This is for you as a thank you.'

'Well, that's very kind,' he did feel a little guilty, if only she knew what plotting and subterfuge had taken place. He took the bottle and held it firmly by the neck. He leaned forward with puckered lips. Sarah, a little taken aback, flushed a little as she offered her cheek to receive the cheeky kiss.

'Ah, nearly forgot,' Mark said as he was about to leave,

'I have programmed your route to Scotland in.'

'Thank you, I never really got the hang of that.'

'When you're ready to leave I'll come out and set it up for you.'

'Brilliant! Thank you, I don't know what I would have done without you these past months.'

Mark moved back towards the front door, 'Well then, I'll let you get on with your preparations.' He stepped out and lifted the bottle whilst walking towards his house, 'Thanks once again for this.'

'Just don't drink it all at once!' Sarah shouted after him.

She closed the front door firmly before returning to the kitchen. She stood for a few moments, absently reading the garage invoice whilst thinking she was another step closer to leaving for her trip.

Chapter 44

The evil neighbour would enter the riskiest part of his plan on Sarah's day of departure. It would only be a short time before she was totally under the control of his will.

He reached for the drawer in the right-hand side of his desk. The drawer opened to reveal a black leather clad box inside. The occultist removed the box from the drawer and placed it, with the two brass catches toward him, on the desk. He released the catches on the front of the box and raised the lid open to reveal a deep-purple crushed velvet interior. The soft plush base was perfectly moulded around a dagger. Its polished, stainless-steel blade was double-edged and capped with an ornate handle cast from silver. Embossed on the butt of the handle was a pentagram image. Small grotesque images akin to gargoyles decorated the handle grip, these small grotesques surrounded a larger engraving of a horned figure depicting the devil. Latin transcript was etched upon the 10 inch blade.

With wondrous eyes, he gently removed the dagger from its case. He regretted running his finger along one side of the blade, drawing blood from a small cut in the process. *Optimum sacrificium* (ideal for the sacrifice), he thought to himself. He polished the dagger with a soft cloth and, satisfied that it was in good shape, he returned it to its case and placed it back in the drawer.

He leaned back in his chair quietly thinking for a while, going over and over what he'd planned for the few weeks before the celebrations. He felt confident that his meticulous planning had left nothing to chance. Yes, Sarah's failure to arrive in Scotland would be noticed, and no doubt investigated but, he had it covered. Nobody would suspect him of being behind it all.

He waited patiently watching the live video link expecting Sarah to retire to bed soon. She's later than usual, he thought, but then she was probably still preparing everything she needed for her trip.

He looked along his row of DVD recordings and found what he was looking for, a recording dated before Steven's death. The drawer on the DVD player accepted the disk and quietly retreated into the player. A wall mounted flat screen TV turned itself on after receiving a signal from the device. He prepared to watch his favourite recording of Steven and Sarah enjoying some deeply intimate moments together. This must have been the last time the lovers had embraced like this before Steven's death.

His attention was suddenly diverted to movement on the live video stream on his PC monitor. He watched as Sarah prepared herself for bed. *Soon, very soon, she will be mine.*

Chapter 45

It was the day of her departure and Sarah was up early, showered, and not really looking forward to the long drive ahead of her.

Since Steven had gone, she had no real interest in her house plants, most of them had died due to lack of watering. She had two left: one of them, a beautiful orchid with flowers that looked like butterflies; the other, she thought was called a Coleus, a non-flowering plant with variegated leaves. Both seemed hardy as they had survived the recent neglect.

She approached Mark's front door with her survivors in a box. The storm wasn't due for a few days, but the wind was picking up and the temperature had dropped from the previous day. She stood waiting for Mark to come to the door, a cold draught whipping around the corner of the house made her wish she had slipped on a coat before venturing out.

Mark came to the door to see his neighbour standing with shoulders hunched against the icy blast.

'Come in,' he stepped aside to let her into his hallway.

'Ooh, it's cold out there, and the storm still has a few days before it gets here.'

Mark quickly shut the door, 'Let's not let all the heat escape. Are you ready to leave yet?'

Sarah slightly lifted her box to present it to Mark.

'Almost, I've still got these plants, they've resisted all of my efforts to kill them off. If I leave them, they'll almost certainly die, so I wondered if you would take them on? They don't need a lot of attention.'

Mark took the box from her, 'I haven't got the greenest of fingers, but I'll have a go. How are preparations going? What time do you expect to leave?'

'I'm packed, just need to load up the car. I'm thinking I might leave at about mid-day.'

'Sounds good. Do you have time for a cuppa?'

'Why not?'

They sat enjoying coffee and biscuits for the next hour. 'I'll miss our Wednesday afternoon trips to town.'

'You might not miss this week's trip, I think the storm may be upon us later in the week.' Mark laughed and agreed.

It was 10.30am when Mark offered some help, 'Let me come round and help you load up your car, then we can go through your satnav training.'

That's exactly what they did.

Mark had lost count of the number of trips from the house to Sarah's car.

'Blimey! How long did you say you were going for?' 'Nearly finished, just the kitchen sink to go in,' she joked.

It was a little after midday when she was seated in the driver's seat and Mark was temporarily installed in the passenger seat. He helpfully ran through a checklist.

'Doors locked? Water off? Heating turned down? - best leave it ticking over on low. Got your bag, purse, money?'

The checklist complete, he was ready to run through the satnav with her. Now was the time to impose his will upon her. He turned towards her and looked into her eyes.

'Listen carefully. You will follow the directions given without deviation, do you understand?'

Sarah stared back unblinkingly and nodded slowly, 'Yes.'

Mark entered the pre-programmed route that was labelled Uncle Angus on the sat nav.

'Now, give me your phone.'

She obediently handed her smartphone over.

Mark attempted to switch the phone on. it needed a passcode.

'What's your passcode?'

Still staring ahead blankly, she revealed the key to unlock the phone; '7… 8…3… 8…3…6.'

Mark practised entering the passcode. The phone successfully unlocked. He slipped the phone into his pocket and smirked.

'You're now ready to leave, what are you going to do?'

'I'm going to follow the directions given without deviation.'
'Good.'

The visual bond between them was broken. Mark leaned across, gave her a kiss on the cheek.

'You must leave now bye.'

Sarah nodded again, still silent, as if in a trance.

Mark got out of the car and Sarah departed, unaware where she was really going. He watched her drive off, waving as she disappeared around the corner. This stage of the plan was a success.

Chapter 46

Back in the house Mark powered down Sarah's smartphone before applying a Post-it note, that simply read 783836, to the screen. He then placed the phone into a jiffy bag. He sealed the jiffy bag up and checked the address, a PO box in Durham. *Perfect*, he thought.

Mark had also prepared to leave home. He reversed his van down the side of his house. Satisfied that his activities were not being recorded on his CCTV, he opened the rear doors of the van and transferred an overnight bag from the back kitchen door. He placed the jiffy bag on the passenger seat before setting intruder alarms and locking the house up. He departed in his van.

First stop was the local post office. He paid cash for an early next day delivery. Back in the car, Mark punched a number into his mobile phone. The call was answered on the third ring. 'It's me, just listen. The package will arrive tomorrow before 9am. As agreed, you need to collect it and do the necessary.' The person at the other end hardly had time to respond before he ended the call.

Such was the power of Mark's mind, Sarah did not know that she was under his control and diligently obeyed her satnav's instructions. She unquestionably headed for the A1 at Hitchin and turned north. It was not until she reached the Alconbury exit on the A1 that the route took an unusual deviation. Her satnav directed her off the A1 onto the A14. She continued this route until just before reaching Huntingdon. Here she was directed left onto the A141, only to re-join the southbound A1. Regardless, she continued to follow the directions given, unaware she was now travelling away from her intended destination.

Mark was taking the more direct route to their destination. He was confident that the detour he had arranged on Sarah's route would buy him the time needed so that he would arrive first. His devious plan had the added bonus that any search for his neighbour would be confused with the little route deviation he had programmed into her satnav. The CCTV camera outside his house would clearly show him waving her off so any suspicions would not be on him.

The journey to Hampshire took Mark a little under two hours to complete. He approached MacDonald Lane, a small private road on the left, marked by a *No Through Road* sign. Mark pulled into it, its curve meaning that any activities just a few metres into this secluded cul-de-sac were hidden from the main road. It was narrow, only wide enough for single file traffic. Grass growing through the crown of the gravelled road surface was evidence that traffic rarely came down here. Rabbits, normally undisturbed, quickly scurried out of the road, back into the undergrowth as Mark's van slowly proceeded to the end of the lane.

Two hidden entrances appeared at the very end. On the left was an entrance to a dwelling. A rotting post standing at a jaunty angle barely supported a weathered sign, *The Vicarage*. Opposite this was another entrance, the sign for this entrance was long ago consumed by the copious amount of foliage, a mix of brambles and ivy. Had the sign been visible, it would have read *Saint Hugh's Church*. The foliage around the entrance had also captured a wooden arch with an apex covered in ivy. There was just room to pass a vehicle between the structure supporting the roof.

Mark had occasionally tended the house on the left since the passing of his aunt. Whilst also overgrown, the house was more accessible and showed more recent habitation. Grass lawns each side of a paved footpath led up to the double fronted, two- storey house. The gardens had once been well-tended, but the lawns were long overdue for cutting. The front door of the house was set in a porch of similar wooden construction to the entrance of the churchyard. Apart from a climbing rose on one side of the entrance, the surrounding vegetation had not yet arrested the porch and the door was easily accessible.

He reversed and parked the van in the entrance of the churchyard, effectively blocking access to the church. This would leave anybody coming down the lane with only one option at the end, which would be to turn into the vicarage entrance.

Mark retrieved his overnight bag and left the van where it was. Lots to do before his Sarah arrived.

Meanwhile, Sarah was heading westbound along the M3. She was still unaware that her route would not take her to see her beloved uncle, such was the power of Mark's mind, one of his more special powers, admired, respected and sometimes feared by brothers and sisters of the fellowship.

Mark busied himself in the basement of the vicarage, preparing for his special guest's arrival. In the galley kitchen, cupboards, fridge and freezer contents were fully stocked and checked. The bed was made. The bathroom was stocked with toiletries. Cooking would take place on a small Belling cooker, and food from the freezer could be re-heated in the microwave. An electric kettle, tea, coffee, sugar, long life milk, it was all there.

Proud of what he'd achieved he sat upstairs in the opulently furnished lounge to await Sarah's arrival.

The crunching sound of car wheels turning into the driveway awoke Mark from his nap in the chair. Sarah had arrived, she might be a little confused, so he needed to go out to greet her.

Upon first sight, Sarah fell in love with the accommodation she thought her uncle had arranged. The car stopped on the gravelled area in front of the overgrown lawns. Thinking that the journey hadn't been that bad, she fumbled about in the centre console to retrieve her mobile phone. *Strange*, she thought, *it wasn't there*. A follow up notion, of course, it was probably in her handbag. She grabbed her bag from the passenger seat and got out of the car.

She had to do a double-take as the sound of the vicarage door opening drew her attention. Expecting to see her new landlady, she was surprised and confused at seeing her Luton neighbour instead.

'Mark! What are you doing here?'

She approached the front door of the property.

'I came to welcome you to your temporary home.'

'But...'

Mark put his index finger to her lips and looked deeply into her eyes, 'Just follow me inside and make yourself at home.' She instantly obeyed.

After a quick tour of the property, he settled his visitor into the luxurious surroundings of the lounge and served his quarry some tea and biscuits.

'I think you'll be very comfortable here.'

'Well, yes, it's lovely. I expected nothing like this. I don't understand though, have you been talking to Uncle Angus?'

'Of course,' Mark lied. 'We both knew you'd like this.'

'When can I visit him?'

'Soon, my dear, soon, probably tomorrow. Just relax after your long journey.'

Sarah accepted every line of deceit being fed to her by Mark and fell quiet whilst she tried to make some sense of the situation. She had questions in her mind, but no answers would come. Convinced she was now in Scotland, she accepted that all would be well and she would see her dear uncle tomorrow.

Her thought process was broken when Mark suddenly grabbed her keys from the coffee table. 'Let me fetch your bags.'

Twenty minutes later, he surveyed the mountain of baggage now sitting on the hallway floor.

'Goodness, you have packed a lot.'

'I'm sure I'll have forgotten something,' she said.

It was now late afternoon. Mark rose from his seat, 'I'm going to prepare us some dinner.' He walked over and looked intensely into Sarah's eyes. It was time to reinforce his control over her. 'You sit back, relax, soon you will sleep.' He stepped back, the invisible bond between them was suddenly broken.

Subconsciously, she knew that things weren't right but Mark's powerful influence meant she couldn't bring any coherent thoughts to the front of her mind that would make sense of it all. Sarah then drifted off to sleep in the chair.

Chapter 47

Mark made the final preparations for dinner. The table was laid, a bottle of chilled Prosecco was waiting to be enjoyed. He had prepared a steak dinner, cooked just how Sarah liked. French fries and peas accompanied a small ramekin of teriyaki sauce on each plate. A strong flavoured sauce to mask the fact that Sarah's ramekin was specially prepared with the additional dissolved ingredient of Rohypnol.

'Sarah,' he called softly, but loud enough to wake her from her nap.

'Dinner's ready, come on love.'

Sarah rose from her chair to approach the table.

'Mmm, smells good.'

Her host poured a generous glass of wine for them both. He held his glass aloft, 'Cheers, I hope you'll be very happy here.'

Sarah reciprocated and lightly chinked her glass to his. After a sip of wine, they both started eating. Mark poured his sauce over his steak.

'You'll like this I think. When I was at uni, I shared digs with another student on a catering course. He was training to be a chef and cooked some fantastic meals for us. He showed me how to make this sauce.'

'What's in it?'

Mark hovered his knife over his empty sauce container whilst listing the ingredients, 'Water, brown sugar, soy sauce, honey, garlic and ginger, thickened with some cornflour.'

Sarah doused her steak with the sauce and ate her dinner.

He watched closely as she ate some sauce covered steak, 'Nice?'

Not wanting to speak with her mouth full, Sarah responded with a complimentary nod of her head.

When they had both finished eating, an overwhelming tiredness came over her. Mark observed her carefully. To prevent her from falling he rose from his seat and assisted her back to the safety of an armchair. Less that a minute later, she lost consciousness and drifted into a drug-induced slumber.

Her whole body was now relaxed. Mark smiled to himself as the relaxation of the soft tissues in Sarah's throat emitted a light snorting noise as she exhaled. For several minutes he observed her, looking forward to the night of the celebrations when she would be his.

It was now time to implement the next stage of his devious plan. The beautiful oak staircase in the hallway almost acted as an archway for the large, heavy door beneath. One could be forgiven, thinking that this door was access to a simple cupboard under the stairs. Mark turned the key to hear the satisfying click of the deadbolt sliding out of the mortice. He grasped the brass knob and twisted it to release the door. The door creaked as it was pushed open. The darkness within still did not immediately reveal the secrets beyond.

Mark reached inside to locate the string of the pull cord switch. He tugged the cord, the gloom was immediately illuminated to reveal a bare wooden platform beyond the door threshold. The platform formed a landing at the top of wooden stairs that led down into the cellar.

He stepped back into the hallway. One by one, he retrieved Sarah's bags and took them down into the subterranean room. He removed her iPad and was satisfied there were no other devices.

Back in the lounge, Sarah was still unconscious in the chair. Mark assessed the best approach he could take to move her. Initial attempts to move her were thwarted, she was a deadweight and her body was totally floppy. Eventually, he slid his hands under her armpits. He pulled her tightly toward him and clasped his hands behind her. He enjoyed the experience of her vulnerability and being close to her. His head was buried into the side of her neck, he inhaled deeply. She smelt good. He resisted the urge to take advantage of her comatose state as he decided that he must wait until the night of the celebrations.

He lifted her from the chair and stooped down to flop the top half of her body over his shoulder, he could then lift her in a fireman's lift. *Her slight frame is not heavy at all*, he thought. She was easily carried towards the cellar door. Even an unfortunate bump on the head from the door frame did not wake her. Carefully, he made his way down the stairs and then, as gently as he could, he lowered her onto the bed and pulled a blanket over her, she would sleep for several hours. Satisfied that she was now securely captive, he made his way back to the top of the stairs. At the side of the door opening, a rope was loosely tied in a figure of eight fashion around a toggle, screwed to the wall. He released the rope and looked up to the ceiling where it was routed through a pulley and then back down to the foot of the staircase. He pulled the rope and the bottom half of the staircase rotated upwards, its fulcrum being sturdy hinges on the inner and outer string of the stairs. When the bottom half of the staircase was horizontal and out of reach, Mark secured the rope to the wall toggle.

The heavy entrance door was closed. The sound of a key turning in the lock was confirmation that Sarah was now effectively a prisoner in the cellar.

Pleased with the day's work, the evil occultist retired to the lounge. Just ten minutes had passed when the glass-topped occasional table exhibited two white lines of powder. They were soon consumed nasally using a rolled-up banknote. Mark closed his eyes and sat in the comfortable armchair to enjoy the effects.

Chapter 48

Angus Kirkpatrick was thinking excitedly about the pending arrival of his beautiful niece. He secretly hoped she would make the move permanent as he loved having her around. She was, after all, the only remaining relative he had left. Poor Sarah had been through a lot recently, He was of the opinion that she needed a fresh start. He made a mental note that he shouldn't give her added pressure for her to stay; that might be counterproductive.

'Good night, Angus!' a voice called through his open bedroom door.

'Night, Margaret! Sarah should be with us tomorrow. I think she's staying in a hotel tonight. Durham. She said it breaks the journey up for her. She's coming straight here. Are you working tomorrow?'

'Yes, I'll be here. Depending what time she arrives, I might have to ask if I can pop out for an hour or maybe finish a wee bit early. Then I can take her over to the property and get her settled in.'

'Sounds perfect.'

Margaret blew him a playful kiss, 'Must dash, I need to buy something for dinner on the way home before they close.'

The old man waved a dismissive hand. 'Away with ye, I'll see ye tomorrow.'

With that, Margaret scurried down the corridor, heading for the front door of the home.

Angus wiled away the rest of the evening watching a bit of TV. Before he knew it, the ten o'clock news was on. The newscaster finished his bulletin.

'…and now, over to Annette Campbell for the weather.' The camera panned over to the familiar face of the weather forecaster waiting expectantly by a weather map. 'It's not looking good towards the end of the week, is it Annette?'

'No, we need to batten down our hatches over the next day or so.' She waved her hand over a swirl of weather in the Atlantic. 'Storm Jezebel is on the way and the Met Office have issued severe gale warnings in the South and East of England.'

Angus listened to the report and studied the graphics that showed the worst affected areas. Scotland didn't seem too bad actually. Satisfied that Sarah's journey would not be affected, with the bonus that being in the north, she would apparently miss the storm anyway, Angus switched off his TV and prepared to retire to bed.

Chapter 49

At 9.30am the following day, the brother known as Elias Phinn stood looking at his reflection in a Durham clothes shop window. He checked to see that his wig and glasses still looked OK; he didn't want to be recognisable on any CCTV footage when he retrieved the package. Satisfied that the disguise was suitable, he walked along the road and entered the town's main post office.

He reappeared on the street. With the package tucked under his arm, both hands stuffed into his fleece jacket pockets and with shoulders hunched, he hurried back to the multi-storey car park to his car.

Elias pulled on a pair of gloves and opened the package. He carefully laid Sarah's phone on the passenger seat whilst he checked a text message on his own phone. The message contained instructions given by his fellowship leader Igor
Torpitz;

Use the passcode supplied to open the device then snd a txt msg to uncle (in the contacts list. Msg should read; Hi uncle, looking forward to seeing you later today luv S xx. P.S. Delete this msg when you have finished.

Elias followed these directions. He checked the settings on the phone; it had an almost full charge, good! He changed it to silent mode then, still with his disguise, in a quiet area of the shopping centre, he sat on a marble ledge that surrounded an indoor planting area. After a couple of minutes looking round, satisfied that he wasn't being observed, he discreetly buried the phone in some earth around a sturdy palm tree. Mission accomplished, he returned to his vehicle.

Elias did not know why he was asked to do these things, but he trusted (and feared) The Master and knew not to ask questions.

Chapter 50

Sarah had slept for almost 13 hours before she regained consciousness. She tried to lift her head from the pillow, a movement that caused a severe ache to shoot behind her eyes. Still not aware of her surroundings, she lay for a good half hour trying to work out the events of last night that would cause her to have such a severe hangover.

Her mind was a blank. She half opened one eye and focused on a bottle of water next to the bed. With a leaden arm, she struggled to reach it and barely had the strength to break the seal and open the bottle. It was one of those sports cap bottles, so she was quite happy that she didn't have to sit up to drink from the bottle to rehydrate herself.

The cool liquid did its job, her mouth was no longer dry. She opened both eyes; it took a couple of moments staring at the bare wooden ceiling boards before she wondered where she was. She realised something wasn't right and suddenly jerked up to a sitting position.

Daylight flooded through the only window in the cellar. The non-opening window was at a height of about 2.5 metres. It was wide, but not very deep. Sarah could hear the wind picking up outside. Treetops swaying in the breeze and a cloudy sky were visible through the window. Still bewildered, Sarah looked around. She saw a closed door so decided to investigate. Shakily, she got up from the bed and, holding on to anything she could, she made for the door, expecting it to be an exit from the room. Beyond the door, she found a well-appointed bathroom. Turning away quickly she almost lost her balance. Clearly, she could see that she was in some sort of bedsit. There was a galley kitchen with a small countertop oven, hot plate, toaster, microwave oven, sink and a large fridge freezer which was well stocked of all she could need. There were even two cases of wine stacked in the corner on the floor. She carefully rose from examining the cupboard under the sink and had to support herself for a moment whilst a dizzy spell passed. When she opened her eyes again, she saw the elevated stairs. She could see the door up high and there was no way to access it. It was only then that her thoughts gathered, and she realised that she was a prisoner.

She looked around quickly for any other means of an exit. Of course, there were none. She did however see an envelope propped up against an empty wine glass on the occasional table. She grabbed it; the envelope read *Sarah*. Ripping it apart she retrieved the message within.

    Dear Sarah,
    I am sorry that I had to do this to you, but when you said you were going to Scotland, I had no choice. There is a very special event coming up soon and you are going to be my special guest. This event has been planned for a long time; I was shocked to hear that you would likely be away.
    You will be here for a few weeks, I hope you will be very happy during your stay. I've thought of everything you need. Your bags are on the floor waiting for you. In the kitchen, there's enough food and wine for you to enjoy.
    Please don't attempt to escape, you may harm yourself in the process and I can tell you now, it's impossible. The heavy door at the top of the stairs is too high to reach, and it is also locked. You will see a window, also too high to reach and doesn't open anyway. Your location is remote and no amount of calling, screaming or banging will attract any attention. I advise you not to bother trying, just relax.
    I wouldn't want you to be bored here, so I've supplied some books and magazines, a radio, a TV and, if you look in the TV cabinet you will find a pile of DVDs to watch. Your medication, enough to last you, is in the bathroom cabinet.
    Nobody knows you are here. I don't want you to get your hopes up of a rescue, you will not be found, I've covered my tracks well.
    I'll be keeping an eye on you, so don't worry. Please make yourself at home my love, Mark.

    Suddenly, the man who had helped her through her troubled times, one whom she regarded as a good friend, was the person she most hated on earth. She scrunched the letter up before ripping it into bits and discarding the shreds onto the floor. Her shoulders shook as she sobbed uncontrollably into her hands. It was several minutes before a thought struck her. *My phone! Where's my phone?* She randomly scattered a TV controller and the wine glass onto the floor whilst searching the occasional table. The broken glass crunched underfoot as she dashed to the bedside table. The phone wasn't there either. *Her bag, where was her handbag?* She frantically looked around the room. She rummaged in the depths hoping to find it. Unsuccessful in her attempts, she resorted to emptying the contents onto the bed. She didn't know why, but she started laughing hysterically. Steven always used to say she had everything but the kitchen sink in her bag. The phone wasn't there, she sank to her knees next to the bed as the laughing turned into inconsolable sobbing once more.

Her head was pounding partly from the effects of being drugged the previous night and partly because of the stress she was feeling. She heard a noise from above. She stopped her crying, did she imagine it? She listened intently. No, there it was again, faint footsteps above.

'HELP!' she screamed at the top of her voice. 'HELP! Let me out!!!'

She fell quiet again, listening to see if there was any response from above. Yes, footsteps again, they seemed louder this time, perhaps they were getting closer. Was it her captor, or somebody coming to her aid. The noises faded again.

'HELP!'

She ran to the kitchen, pulled open some cupboards and found a saucepan under the sink. She ran back into the main room and with all her might started banging the saucepan on the wooden clad wall.

'HELP ME! PLEASE HELP ME!'

Her head felt as if it might explode at any moment. The frantic activity and noise she was creating wasn't helping her pain. She paused a couple of times to listen for any signs from above, there were none.

Finally, she turned to lean on the wall, her hands fell to her side, she dropped the now battered saucepan to the floor. Exhausted, she slid her back down the wall to a sitting position and cried her eyes out.

Chapter 51

Mark became The Watcher once more. The events of yesterday had gone well. The abduction of his innocent neighbour was successful, and he'd covered his tracks too. He sat down with his laptop to view images from the camera installed in the cellar below.

Sarah was laying virtually in the same position he left her in last night. He was sure she'd be coming around shortly. Soon he would be travelling back to Luton, but before he left, he wanted to be sure his abductee was awake and OK.

Whilst waiting, he went out and moved Sarah's car so that it was not visible from the lane. He packed the few things he'd brought with him for the overnight stay into his car and returned to check on her.

She'd moved her position and was laying motionless on the bed with her forearm covering her eyes. He watched carefully, zooming in to watch what her reactions would be when she'd fully regained consciousness.

Mark watched Sarah's painfully slow movements as she had a drink and expertly zoomed in from camera to camera as she explored her surroundings.

'Read the letter my dear,' he quietly willed in the hope she would soon notice the envelope on the table.

He'd need to visit her before he leaves to re-impose his will upon her, but he wanted to be sure she was in a better state of recovery from last night's intake of Rohypnol.

The camera was at ceiling height above the door. At one point, she was looking up to the top of the stairway. It was almost as if she was looking straight into his eyes. Had she seen the camera? He didn't think so. She turned and spotted the envelope. He watched intently to see what her reaction would be.

The gravity of her situation dawned. In a fit of desperation and annoyance, she ripped the letter apart and threw it aside. A period of sobbing followed.

Mark was saddened to see this, he meant her no harm after all. She was beautiful but the excessive upset she experienced had caused her eyes to become swollen and her face reddened. That, along with yesterday's eye makeup becoming diluted with her salty tears, had aptly caused her appearance to personify one who might be possessed. He paused his observations to make some tea. He returned to his laptop just as the banging started. Curious as to what the noise was he resumed his covert observation.

'Silly girl, you might need that pan to cook some dinner.' He shook his head and tutted a couple of times knowing that she was wasting her time. He watched her slide down the wall to the floor when her efforts to attract attention were exhausted and there she sat, crying again.

She remained in this position for over an hour. *Possibly asleep*, Mark thought. It would soon be time to enter the cellar. He looked up at the screen to see if there was any movement, just in time to witness Sarah's next move. An action that shocked him, causing him to make a dash for the cellar door. She must be stopped. Now!

Chapter 52

Angus was introduced to the digital age late in life; he never really understood any of this technology stuff. Somebody once told him he was a *Digital Migrant*, whatever one of those was. He studied his mobile phone wondering why he had a flashing green light. It wasn't a battery problem; he knew that if it flashed red it was time to recharge the battery. What could a green light mean? He was puzzled.

It was late afternoon, Elizabeth, today's duty carer entered his room to collect his lunch tray.

'Hello Angus,'

'Hello my dear.'

The kindly carer smiled at him. 'Another cup of tea?'

'Yes please, and, while you're here, do you know what this means?' He showed her the mystery green flashing light on his phone.

Elizabeth pulled a face, 'Ooh dear, I think you might be asking the wrong person here,' she quipped. 'Let's see,' she took the phone from him to examine it. She held the phone at a distance, screwing her eyes up, she realised that she couldn't really see it. She patted the pocket of her tabard, feeling for her glasses. 'Ah, these'll help,' she placed the pair of bejewelled glasses on her nose.

Typical of an elderly person's mobile, there was no security, the small screen lit up as she pulled the clamshell phone open. She pulled her glasses down her nose and peered over the top of them, trying to make sense of the flashing green light.

'Ah here it is, you've been sent a wee text message.'

'A text message? Nobody sends me text messages. What does it say, can you read it?'

Elizabeth pressed buttons again. 'Hang on a wee minute. Here we go,' she paused, while still peering over the top of her glasses. Once focused, she read the message.

'Hi uncle, looking forward to seeing you later today love S kiss kiss.'

'Ah, that's from Sarah, she's coming to Scotland for a few weeks. She's staying in Margaret's let for a while.'

'That's lovely Angus, I'll bet you're looking forward to that - I seem to remember she's a sweet wee thing.'

'Yes, she's a lovely lass alright. The only family I have left you know. She's had a bad couple of years back home. Her husband went missing. Despite an extensive police investigation, the mystery of his disappearance was never solved. She needs a break, poor girl, I'm secretly hoping she moves up here for good. You know, make a new start of it.'

'What time do you expect her to arrive?'

'Any time now, she's travelling up from Durham. Does it say what time that message arrived?'

Once again, she looked over the top of her glasses. She studied the screen and pushed some more buttons.

'Och, here we go. It arrived this morning, at 10.18am.'

Angus looked at the clock, just after 3.30pm, a little over five hours ago. He didn't think that Durham was that far, maybe a steady three hour drive, but no more. He looked out of the window at the empty visitor's parking space.

'Perhaps she had a couple of stops en route, she'll be here soon I expect.'

Elizabeth cleared away the remains of lunch.

'Yes, I'm sure the lass would take a break on such a long drive. I'll be back soon with your tea soon, love.'

'Thank you, dear,' Angus acknowledged as she left.

Once again, he looked at the clock pensively, a little concerned and worried that his niece had still not arrived.

As each hour passed, he became increasingly concerned. He opened the clamshell once more. There were no more flashing green lights. His mildly arthritic fingers negotiated the menus to find Sarah's mobile number. He pressed the call button. After six rings, the phone was answered. He listened to a message;

The person you are calling is unable to take your call.

Disappointed, he ended the call.

Probably driving still, he thought to himself.

Chapter 53

After sitting motionless with her back against the wall for what seemed like an eternity, Sarah finally lifted her head. What should or could she do now? The idea came to her whilst she looked at the broken shards of the wine glass on the floor. She moved onto all fours and crawled towards the broken pieces.

The stem of the glass was fairly complete with only the bowl shattered. She picked up the stem and returned to her position by the wall. There was no other option. The stem of the wine glass was firmly held in her right hand. She stretched her left arm out. With eyes closed, she firmly applied the sharp edge over her skin drawing blood in the process. At that moment, she was fully committed and intended to end it all, there and then. It was only the noise of the key turning in the door above that stopped her completing her deadly mission.

Despite the meticulous planning on Mark's part, he'd forgotten one thing. Sarah was still suffering from depression. He'd underestimated the effects that this might have. There was only one way to put an end to her darkest thoughts.

Sarah looked up as the door opened to see a figure silhouetted against the hallway light. She couldn't see features, but knew by the size, shape and stance of the figure that it was her neighbour. Throwing the stem of the wine glass aside she got up from her sitting position to confront her captor.

'What's the meaning of all this!!!!' With her fists clenched, she breathlessly waited for his response.

He looked down at her in silence before he spoke. 'Calm down my dear. Things are not as bad as you think.'

'Where am I? How did I get here? What is all this nonsense in the letter? What event?'

'So many questions, slow down, in fact, calm down, relax and I will explain.'

His voice was calm, which caused Sarah to relax, just a little, evident by her breathing slowing down. It was time to impose his will upon her once more. He pulled the cord of the light switch next to the doorway and the cellar was bathed in light. Sarah could now see his face. 'Now look at me.'

Sarah obediently looked up at him. His gaze was intense. She couldn't look away.

'Listen to me carefully!'

She relaxed some more, her arms hung loosely by her side.

His voice penetrated her mind, 'You'll forget everything about visiting your uncle, you live here now. Do you understand?'

She slowly nodded.

'Life will be as normal whilst you are here eating, sleeping and entertaining yourself with TV, radio and books. Do you understand?'

She acknowledged her understanding.

'You'll not try to escape, you will be happy whilst you are here. Do you understand?' Mark smiled as she nodded once more. Sarah stood still as he untied the rope supporting the lower half of the stairway.

With the stairs lowered, he descended, keeping a watchful eye on his beautiful prize in case she had faked acceptance of his hypnotic suggestions. It was fine, she was calm.

He stepped off the bottom step, 'Hi Sarah, how are you today?'

'Fine thanks.' It was as if they had met for the first time today. She leant forward to give him a light embrace.

'Hey, what happened here?' he held her left wrist to look at the cut. The bleeding had almost stopped, he was glad it wasn't serious.

She also looked at the minor cut, 'I don't know how that happened.'

He looked down at the floor. 'Oh dear, what a mess!'

She looked down at the broken glass, the battered saucepan and several items that were once in her handbag. She looked puzzled, 'Oh, I don't remember. Maybe I accidentally cut myself on that glass - I don't remember dropping it though.' She went to get down on her knees to pick up the scattered items from her bag.

Mark held her arm lightly and addressed her softly, 'No, don't worry love, I'll clear this up for you. Why don't you get yourself some clean clothes, go in the bathroom and take a shower, freshen yourself up? Put a dressing on that wrist, there's a first aid box in the bathroom cabinet.' He leant over and hauled her bags onto the end of the bed.

Without question, she unzipped the larger bag and selected an outfit. Mark pointed out her make up and toilet bag.

'Do you need these?'

'Oh yes, thank you.'

The bathroom door closed. Mark cleared up the broken glass from the floor.

Aware that Sarah hadn't eaten since yesterday, he prepared a microwave meal from the freezer for them both. Spaghetti Carbonara seemed perfect to be washed down with some Prosecco.

The bathroom door opened, 'Mmmm, something smells good.'

He tried some humour, 'Is it me?'

'No, silly, I meant the food!'

He looked at her, there was no sign of the earlier distress, she was beautiful once more.

They sat down to eat. Conversation between them flowed well.

Mark refilled Sarah's glass, 'I must get back home later this evening.' He observed her reaction.

'Ah OK.'

'Is there anything you need?'

She sipped from her replenished glass. 'No, I think I've everything I need.'

'Good, what will you do for the rest of your evening?'

She went to speak and then suddenly stopped as if something had dawned upon her.

'...Do you know, I don't even know what day it is? Or what's on TV tonight?'

'It's Friday.'

She gave a puzzled look, 'Is it? Days just seem to fly by lately.'

He looked at his watch, 'Yup, it's the 22nd.'

'Then, to answer your question, I'll watch the next part of that drama on BBC 1 tonight.'

'Right, I must go now,' he again looked for a reaction.

'OK, when will I see you again?'

Sometimes, the power of his mind surprised Mark himself.

'I'll come back and see you in a few days.'

'Oh, that'll be nice.'

She seemed totally unaware that a couple of hours ago she totally despised the man sitting opposite her.

Mark rose from the table and said his goodbyes. He'd stayed a little longer than expected but felt happy that all was well with his captive.

At the top of the stairs, he pulled on the rope holding the lower part of the stairs. Sarah looked on as the bottom half of the stairway elevated.

'I'll pull these up for you. You'll have more room.'

She reflected his charming smile. 'A good idea, thanks.'

'You have a light switch there. by the bed.'

She moved over to the bed and flicked the switch to further illuminate the room. Mark pulled the cord on the pull switch to turn the main light off.

'Bye, my dear.'

She was preoccupied with looking around for the TV remote, but gave a dismissive wave to bid him farewell. She didn't hear the key turning in the cellar door.

Chapter 54

It was 8.45pm at the residential home, still no sign of Sarah. Angus really was panicking now. Margaret popped in to see Angus looking for news.

'Any sign of her yet?' she enquired.

'Not yet. I must admit I'm getting a wee bit worried that something bad has happened to her.'

'Are you sure it was today she was arriving? Maybe the date she gave you was when she was leaving home.'

'No, she sent a text message to confirm she was on her way. I've tried calling her phone umpteen times. It's the same woman that answers, an operator I think. She says that Sarah cannot take the call.'

Margaret suppressed a grin at the fact that dear old Angus thought the recorded message he was hearing was actually a person.

It was a little after 9pm now. Margaret made an excuse to leave the room and make them both a cup of cocoa. During her absence, she went to the office and dialled the non-emergency number for the police.

Eventually the phone was answered by a call dispatcher.

'How may I help you?'

The dispatcher patiently listened to Margaret's enquiry, she ended with the question. 'I wondered if there'd been any road traffic accidents today somewhere between Durham and Edinburgh?'

The call dispatcher searched for incidents in the locality. There were three today that required police attendance but none of them were serious and the name Sarah Cooper was not involved in any of them. She would have to pass the enquiry onto other forces in England for incidents south of the border to Durham. The dispatcher took some details and promised to either call back or send a text message to her mobile phone with any information.

The dispatcher sensed that Margaret was worried and offered a plausible reason, 'Maybe her car has broken down. If that's so, she would probably have needed to make lots of calls to get it fixed or recovered. She may have run out of battery power in the process.'

'Yes, I expect something like that's happened. OK, thank you for checking.'

'No problem, madam. I hope you get positive news soon. Have a good evening.'

The call ended and Margaret resumed making cocoa.

Margaret returned to Angus with his hot drink. They sat talking for a while. She didn't want to alarm him so didn't tell him she'd called the police. She did relay, as her own thoughts, what the call dispatcher had said about the car breaking down.

'Goodness, it's half-past nine, I need to go home now.'

'Of course, thank you for staying for a chat, like you say,

I'm sure there's a very plausible reason for her non-arrival today.'

Her phone buzzed in her pocket as she leaned over to give Angus a parting embrace, 'Bye Angus, try not to worry. I'm sure she'll be here tomorrow.' Once outside the room, she examined the phone. A message had arrived from Police Scotland: I can confirm that there have been no reported road traffic incidents requiring police attendance involving Mrs Cooper today between Durham and Edinburgh.

The care worker, feeling she had done all she could to solve the mystery, left for the night.

Uncle Angus prepared himself for a fitful night's sleep.

Chapter 55

A pleasant morning greeted the next day in Luton. Mark had arrived home a little after midnight, so slept in a little. He lay in bed thinking about how things had turned out yesterday. He concluded that the plan couldn't have worked better.

It was mid-morning by the time he'd risen and taken a shower. He took some coffee and toast out to his office in the garden. Once sat at the large wooden desk, he logged onto his sophisticated surveillance system.

Initial views of the cellar in Hampshire showed no sign of his captive. He panned the camera around using the cursor keys on his keyboard. He zoomed into areas in the kitchen before focusing on the bathroom door, which was ajar. No movement within was apparent. Escape was impossible, where could she be?

A few minutes later, he breathed a sigh of relief. Sarah finally appeared from the bathroom with her head swathed in a towel; she'd been washing her hair. As well as feeling relief, he was also happy that she appeared to have accepted her captivity with no concerns and was living life as if things were normal.

He sat back, eating toast and sipping coffee whilst watching her slender body clad only in underwear. She vigorously rubbed her hair dry on the towel and made frequent trips back to the bathroom to further pamper herself. In the final visit, the camera picked up her reflection in the mirror; she was brushing her hair before skilfully tying it up in a bun. She emerged, dressed and looking ready to face the rest of the day.

Mark checked the time on his watch and did a mental calculation on what time it would be in Turkey. *Now was a good time to make contact,* he thought. He sent a text message to a mobile number to arrange an online meeting with his supplier.

* * *

Tariq Abdhulla was sitting by the pool in his luxury apartment located just outside Istanbul. His mobile phone vibrated loudly on the mosaic-tiled table next to his lounger. He adjusted his position to see what the notification was. The grossly overweight man licked his thick top lip as he tried to make out who was trying to contact him. Too late, the screen blacked out before he had the chance. His left hand reached out and grasped the phone. He stabbed at the screen with a sausage- sized index finger on his right hand. The screen illuminated in response; he pushed his sunglasses up to the top of his forehead and screwed his eyes up, straining to read the message in the bright afternoon sunlight.

Reluctantly, he launched his enormous frame out of the lounger, grunting as he did so. He walked into the cool lounge area of his apartment and puffing under the exertion, he slumped down into an oversized armchair. Now he could clearly see the screen. A scar on his top lip made it appear that he had a permanent sneer. The sneer became more prominent as he read the message, exposing the crooked yellowing teeth surrounding his large gold incisor:

WLTM 13.45 BST.

He knew that the message was from his UK customer wanting to check the progress of the shipment. With beads of sweat glistening on his greasy forehead, he once again attacked the jewel-encrusted phone with his stubby fingers. He located a number from his contacts list and initiated a call. He put the phone to his ear.

Seconds later, a conversation in Kurmanji began, 'Ser chava ser sera... Mohamed' (*Good Day Mohamed*).' The dialogue continued in their native tongue. Tariq asked his courier to check the progress of the shipment. The smile on his face confirmed that all was well; the shipment was on track. The call ended with another prod from the oversized index finger.

The Turk grunted as he exerted himself back out of the chair. He would return to his poolside resting place until it was time to meet his UK customer on the Dark Web.

Chapter 56

Angus Kirkpatrick lay awake listening to the dawn chorus, still concerned that he had heard nothing from his niece. His thoughts were disturbed by a gentle knock on his door.

'Come in,' the old man called, eager to see if it was somebody with some good news.

The door opened, and Margaret entered the room with a cup of tea. 'Any news?'

'Nae lass. Nothing yet. I was hoping you might have some for me, where can she be?'

Margaret placed the tea on the bedside table. 'What time is it?' Angus asked.

'A little after 7.30am'

'What do you think we should do Margaret? We've heard absolutely nothing. I'm worried that she may have been in some sort of accident. I think we should contact the police or hospitals or something. I don't know, what do you think?'

Margaret confessed that she had done just that last night.

'They sent me a message just as I was away for the night.'

'What did they say?'

'No reports of any incidents involving Sarah.'

Angus reached for his mobile phone. then he rested his spectacles on the end of his nose whilst he studied the tiny screen. First, looking to see if there were any messages or missed calls, then he navigated through the menus to call his niece once more. Sadly, he heard the now familiar message;

This number is currently unavailable - please try again later. He couldn't even leave a message.

'There's nae answer still.' He flipped his clamshell phone shut.

'Och, I'm sure 'tis a mystery that'll be solved later today, you'll see.'

'I do hope so, I cannae think straight right now, I need tae get up and have some brekky before I decide what I can do.'

'Of course, I'll leave ye tae wake up proper. I'll prepare your breakfast now, we can talk after.'

The kindly carer smiled and left Angus to prepare himself for the day ahead.

Chapter 57

Mark diligently closed down his Dark Web session. The news from Turkey was good. It was now time to check on his captive. He started an application on his PC to access the camera surveilling the Hampshire cellar. Panning round, he found Sarah sitting sideways in the armchair, her legs dangled over the arm whilst she was calmly reading a book. He could see the light from the TV screen flickering across her face. She occasionally looked up at the cellar window. He panned around to see what might be attracting her attention. She was watching the treetops swaying wildly in the breeze. Clearly, the storm was well established in Hampshire.

Luton, so far, was only subject to gusty blasts, the worst was yet to come according to the local weather forecast.

His observations were interrupted by an alarm beeping on his smartwatch. It was time to access the Dark Web for a scheduled meeting. Fellowship brothers and sisters will welcome a positive progress report for sure. Everything was falling into place, so his mood tonight would be more tolerant.

The meeting began with excited chatter. He called everybody to order. Proceedings began with a discussion on expected numbers. All members of the sect were invited. Each member could bring up to three guests. Acceptances (including guests) numbered over 300. A few latecomers were predicted. The tally was mostly for couples. There were also some groups of three or four and a handful of singletons. As the event would span a couple of days, attendees would have to come prepared to sleep in their own accommodation. Camper vans, caravans and tents were expected to be used. Igor assured those assembled at the meeting that the area around the venue would comfortably accommodate these. The lucrativeness of the event was confirmed by the premium each person was prepared to pay to attend. Pure profit for Igor.

A common question raised was about Sarah. Today was no exception. 'What of our special guest?'

'She's already close to the venue and under my influence. I'll prepare her and transfer her to the venue in time for the event.'

Another member enquired about the shipment of narcotics. 'Earlier today I spoke with our supplier. Things are going to plan. I've increased our order. I will need some help from some of you when delivery is due. We can discuss these arrangements another time.' He neglected to mention the extra special prices he'd negotiated. His eye was on the increased profit he would gain from the sale of these drugs.

The general feeling of the delegates was one of satisfaction. Questions dried up, and the meeting drew to a close.

Whilst leaning back in his chair, he made a mental calculation on his likely windfall - it would be a seven-figure payday!

The wind still buffeted his sturdy garden office. For the second time today, he decided to look in on his captive prize. Sarah was now watching TV and drinking wine. She showed no concern for her situation. It was just as if she was sitting and relaxing in her own home.

It was time for worship. The occultist revealed the crudely drawn pentagram on the floor. He placed a large black candle at each point of the symbolic star. He donned a monastic gown made of a rough material to cover his naked body. He then consumed a generous white line of cocaine. With the hood pulled over his head he sat cross-legged in the centre of the pentagram. The effects of the cocaine kicked in. He raised his arms and began his Latin incantations. The candles burned more intensely and flames grew in height in response to the occultist's call to his fire demons.

The storm outside the cabin was gathering strength and ferocity. As if on cue the chanting finished with an instantaneous lightning strike and clap of thunder. A power cut caused the computer screen to go blank. The cabin was left eerily lit only by the candles. Their flames had returned to their lazy flickering form. The etching of Saint Walpurga seemed to dance in their gentle glow. The occultist had long finished his chanting to summon the fire demons. He now sat in quiet meditation.

The night was surrendering to a new dawn by the time his rituals were complete. It was still blustery outside, but the worst of the storm had gone.

Today would be busy. There was lots to do in preparation. Pleased to be relieved from the discomforts of his ceremonial garb, he dressed himself again. He securely locked the office before walking back towards the house.

There was a muffled beeping coming from Sarah's house. He recognised it as the house alarm, probably upset by the earlier power failure, he presumed. It would probably sort itself out when the batteries run down. Once inside his own house, he was pleased that power had been restored and was now ready to spend a couple of hours in bed.

Chapter 58

The 101 call centre lady was not the most patient of operatives when dealing with Uncle Angus's call. The old man just wanted to report his niece's disappearance straight away, but the surly lady taking his call seemed uninterested, insisting she had to take some details first.

Angus was becoming frustrated, but persevered regardless.

'Full name?' the operator began.

'Angus Kirkpatrick.'

'Address?'

Angus was confused by the question, he only knew the name of the retirement home, not the address. After all, he never needed to have the address or to memorise it. His watery eyes looked at Margaret, who was sitting by his side, straining to hear both sides of the conversation. She had heard the lady's request and held up her index finger whilst mouthing; *one moment*, to Angus.

'One moment please, we're just finding that out.'

'No problem, Mr Kirkpatrick.'

Angus didn't think she sounded like she meant it though. There was a lot of background noise and talking. He thought for a moment that she'd moved onto the next call.

Margaret reappeared and placed a brochure for the retirement home in front of him, pointing out its address.

'Hello, are you still there?'

'Yes, go ahead Mr Kirkpatrick.'

Ah, she hadn't abandoned him. Angus read out the address from the brochure.

'Telephone number?'

This was also on the brochure, so he provided this information too.

Finally, he got to explain his reason for calling. 'It's my niece, she's gone missing and I want to report it.' The questions got harder as Angus tried to provide all the information requested. Some of it, he had to look up, Sarah's home address and telephone number, for example.

'Her date of birth?'

Angus, his head slightly shaking from side to side, couldn't remember this.

'Roughly, how old would you say?'

The old man thought for a moment, '...mid-forties, I would say.'

More confusion followed when he tried to explain Sarah's itinerary, he initially got the days wrong. Luckily, Margaret was able to put him right. Next, he was asked questions about her car.

'It's grey,' he thought for a moment, '...It's a few years old, I can't remember the make and model... or registration... Wait! I think it was a Nissan.'

Margaret overheard the next question, 'A Nissan what?'

Poor Angus was struggling to remember. The call handler ran through a few Nissan models.

'Micra?'

'No.'

'A Juke?'

'No.'

'Was it a big car?'

'Quite big.'

'Like a four-wheel drive?'

'Oh no, it was a large saloon I seem to remember.'

'An Almera or a Primera?'

'Yes, that was it, a Primera, I'm sure.'

The call continued. Margaret was a great help, prompting him until, eventually, the call handler was satisfied with the information given.

'I'll log this as a missing persons report. This will be picked up by the appropriate team and somebody will call you within the next 24 hours. Is there anything else I can help you with?'

'24 hours? But we haven't heard from her for nearly two days now, can't something be done sooner?'

The call handler explained that investigations would likely begin before that.

'Meanwhile, if she turns up, or you think of anything else we should know, please call back and quote your reference number.' She asked once again, 'Is there anything else I can help you with?'

'No,' replied Angus.

'Thank you for calling 101 today.'

Margaret was still by his side. 'How did you get on?'

'She didnae seem to have any sense of urgency about her, which was a worry.'

She patted the back of his hand gently. 'I'm sure they're working on the case right now. Don't forget, she takes lots of calls everyday, so the lass has been trained to be calm.'

'Aye, I suppose so,' the intonations in his voice and furrowed brow belied his true thoughts.

Chapter 59

Mark was busy preparing his van as the shipment was due tonight; he needed space to load it. He made a quick call to his chosen helpers, Elias and Toby, to confirm that they would both be at the pickup point.

Elias had the furthest to travel from Durham, so would be coming down by train. Mark noted down the time of his train and picked him up at Dartford railway station. Toby lived in Basingstoke so would travel independently to the pickup point.

* * *

It was 10pm, Central European Time as Pierre Lamont sat in his air traffic control tower at a small aerodrome in Northern France. The controller was monitoring local air traffic, particularly light aircraft. There was nothing unusual here, just a few aircraft on a descending course, probably for Paris CDG. A couple of *high flyers*, who knows where they might be destined for?

There was the occasional shadow of something close to the ground, but Pierre was used to seeing this, more often than not, just a large lorry on the motorway. It aroused no suspicions for the experienced air traffic controller.

* * *

Antonio DaSilva, the pilot of the Piper Cub, was careful to remain at a low altitude over land. Here was his best chance to avoid detection. For the short hop across the English Channel, he would drop to about 1000 feet. Fortunately, Storm Jezebel, which had ravaged the UK had moved north east and was currently threatening Northern Europe, otherwise the delivery would not go ahead tonight.

Chosen for its short takeoff and landing capabilities, the Piper Cub was ideally suited for these covert deliveries. DaSilva was a very experienced pilot but a good landing in a field depended on the organisation of the people in the UK.

* * *

It was a clear night, Mark and Elias arrived at the field about an hour before the delivery was due. Toby arrived 15 minutes later to find them busy unloading bundles of cables.

It was the ingenuity of Mark who had marked a makeshift runway using strings of cheap decorative LED lights; the sort used to decorate garden patios or Christmas trees. Mark knew the pilot would perform a *Short Field Landing*, difficult at the best of times, but in the dark it was described as *scary* and *not for the fainthearted and lily livered*. There were enough bundles of lights to make two 200 metre strips. There would be gaps, but it would be enough to give the pilot a notional sign of the boundaries of the landing area. The lights would be powered by large heavy duty car batteries. Mark indicated where the cables should be stretched out on the short grass in the field. They were secured and kept tight and straight with metal tent pegs. A quick test was carried out to make sure they were all working. It was all systems go.

Elias spoke, 'How will we know when it's our plane overhead?'

'He has our GPS position, he'll circle the field twice, which will be our signal to turn on the landing lights. We don't want to arouse too much suspicion, so we must turn the lights off as soon as he's safely down.'

Toby was impressed by the simplicity of the arrangement. The men stood chatting by their vehicles, positioned close to the end of the landing strip, waiting for the delivery to arrive.

'When will we meet her?' Toby asked.

'It'll be too late to see her tonight. We'll see her on camera in the morning, you probably won't meet her in person until the actual day.'

'How much does she know?'

'Almost nothing, she certainly has no inclination that she'll be my bride.'

Elias patted his Master on the shoulder, 'I don't know how you do it.'

Mark suddenly cocked his head to the side and held up an index finger, 'Listen!'

They fell silent, straining to hear. Some distant traffic was evident, but, yes, there was a faint drone of a light aircraft. Could this be their delivery?

It was time to move to the end of the makeshift runway, ready to switch on the landing lights. The aircraft came closer until it was overhead. Initially, it appeared not to be the one expected, as it overflew the field. They watched the dark shadow in the sky fly past. The aircraft displayed no navigational lights
or stroboscopic positional lights. For this reason, Mark was convinced this was their delivery.

* * *

Antonio checked his GPS, the landing area was coming up ahead. Being cautious, he planned to overfly the location first. Not that he expected to see too much with the naked eye in the darkness beyond. He reached into the seat next to him to find a pair of night vision goggles. He used the goggles to look out of the port side of the aircraft; he could make out three figures and two vehicles in the field. They hadn't been there long as the goggles picked up heat still radiating from the front of each vehicle. Satisfied that this is what he expected to see, the skilled pilot banked his aircraft around to head back to the field, hoping he would soon see some sign of where he should land.

The aircraft reappeared overhead and circled the field. This was it. Mark gave the order to switch on the lights. Elias and Toby connected the loose crocodile clip to the spare terminal on each battery, the LED lights came to life and marked two clear lines across the field.

Antonio saw the landing strip come to life and prepared to land. He pointed the little aircraft to fly south of the field then banked around 180 degrees ready to line his approach up between the improvised landing lights.

The three watched the aircraft manoeuvre round for a safe landing in the field. The Piper Cub came to a standstill at the end of the runway, its engine was cut and the landing lights were switched off.

DaSilva jumped out of his cockpit and Igor moved forward to greet him. The pilot was of swarthy Mediterranean appearance. His English was very good, as you would expect from a pilot used to conversing with air traffic controllers.

'We must hurry, I don't want to be here any longer than I have to be.'

They removed the valuable cargo packed into the fuselage of the aircraft. Packages of drugs were loaded into the rear of Mark's van, leaving some room to repack the landing lights and batteries. The rest of the packages were loaded into the back of Toby's van. Twenty minutes later the aircraft was ready to depart.

The Piper Cub tail rudder manoeuvred the craft to face south again. Antonio gave a thumbs up, and the landing lights were rekindled. The engine revved up; the aeroplane lurched forward and proceeded down the runway.

The trio held their breath as they watched the plane struggling to get airborne. Hedges, bordering the field were getting closer.

Antonio was expert at these short field take-offs. He knew that with clever use of his flaps he would avoid too much drag on the ground and achieve a take-off in the shortest horizontal distance. He rotated just in time, remaining cool and calm. The aircraft soared above the hedgerow bordering the field, missing it by little more than 3 metres.

Chapter 60

The police call handler redeemed herself somewhat after ending her call with the distraught elderly gentleman. She escalated the report and routed it through to Durham Police, marked *Urgent*.

Janice Thomas, a civilian police employee at Durham Police Headquarters, picked up the report almost immediately. She read the report carefully and started a preliminary investigation herself. She accessed DVLA records to get the registration number of the MISPER's car. She searched the incident database for any reports in the last two days involving a car of that registration. The search returned no results.

She then searched the database for any incident involving a *Sarah Cooper*. The search again was fruitless. If Sarah had been involved in an incident, she could be an unidentified person in hospital. She searched the database once more. There were two matches. She quickly discounted the first in Kincardineshire. Another, closer to home had occurred in Sunderland.

Eager to find out more, Janice opened the report. A female had been admitted to Sunderland Royal. She read on. The lady, elderly and confused, was found wandering in Sunderland town centre in her nightclothes. Clearly not Mrs Cooper.

The limited investigative possibilities available to her were exhausted. It was time to pass the report up the line to CID upstairs. She updated the record to document the results of her enquiries and passed the report on.

Detective Constable Justin Page received notification of an email. The email was categorised as MISPER. Page knew that a quarter of a million individuals go missing in the UK each year. Mostly, there's an identifiable reason as to why they've gone missing. He wondered which category this one would fall in. An abusive relationship? Mental health issues? An abduction? Or, perhaps this one had been involved in an accident and is lying in a ditch somewhere, waiting to be discovered.

He read through the report. His first action was to involve the traffic division. He updated the report. Within minutes, every patrol car in the UK, equipped with ANPR, would be on the lookout for Sarah's car. He knew it was also worth trying the phone numbers that Mr Kirkpatrick had supplied.

The automated voice on the mobile line apologised that this number was currently unavailable. Sarah's home phone number rang and rang. After 15 rings, the detective gave up.

He studied the online report for any more potential lines of enquiry. It stated that Mrs Cooper was booked into overnight accommodation somewhere in the Durham area. The exact location was unknown though. *Researching that one would be like looking for a needle in a haystack,* he thought.

The last known communication was a text message sent to Mr Kirkpatrick. It apparently came from the Durham area. Justin made a mental note that this should be checked out with the mobile phone company in the morning. The only other thing that could be followed up for now was Sarah's address.

He added to the report, requesting a Bedfordshire Police patrol car to call round Sarah's home address. He also requested they enquire at neighbouring houses, if there was no answer.

The detective read through his comments on the incident report. He corrected a couple of typos before finally clicking on the Submit button at the bottom of the screen.

The formal investigation into the disappearance of Sarah Cooper had begun. Page leaned back in his office chair, stretching his arms upwards and yawning. His shift was over, he would let the actions he had started simmer until tomorrow.

'Night all!' he called out as he headed for the door.

Colleagues bade him farewell before refocusing on their individual tasks.

Chapter 61

The three occultists were pleased with the previous night's work. They slept in a little the following morning. Both vehicles still contained their illicit loads. For security, they were backed into the driveway of the vicarage, well out of sight of the main road.

Igor and Toby were up and dressed first, Elias appeared later in his dressing gown, just in time for a breakfast of toast and eggs.

Downstairs, Sarah was aware of movements above. Still under the powerful influence of her captor's mind, she just assumed the noises came from the people in the flat upstairs.

Over breakfast, Elias and Toby said they were keen to see their leader's intended bride. He was reluctant to allow a face-to-face meeting, but agreed to show them surveillance images on his laptop instead. The visitors looked over his shoulder as he accessed the surveillance camera. The men moved closer to the screen for a better view. Toby was the first to speak.

'She's perfect!'

Igor grinned with pride.

Elias, who also had the etching of Saint Walpurga at his makeshift home temple, stroked his chin. 'The likeness is uncanny. That she moved in next door to you means that this was surely meant to be. She's looking so relaxed too, how have you achieved this?'

Igor closed the lid down on his laptop. 'Yes, I agree. I've imposed my will upon her. It has worked well, she doesn't know that she is my prisoner. We won't disturb her for now though.'

Today's plan was for Igor and Toby to transport the narcotics to the venue. Both men were due to return home later. Elias would stay until after the event.

Elias sat relaxing and enjoying a cup of coffee in the vicarage lounge. He heard the others depart for the venue to unload their cargoes. The last of his coffee drained, he decided it was time for a shower. He picked his cup up and walked to the kitchen area to deposit it. On the way down the hallway, he walked past the mysterious door under the stairs.

I wonder, he thought, observing the key in the solid oak door, *could this be where our lady is being held?* Eager to find out, and for a face-to-face meeting, he reached for the key.

Sarah looked up, startled at the sound of a key turning in the door at the top of the stairs. She didn't normally have visitors.

The big oak door creaked open. A dark figure appeared in the shadows above, looking down. The face was difficult to see. She strained her eyes to see more clearly. From where she was, the mysterious figure appeared short and plump. It was a man; he stood there with his arms crossed in front of him. Sarah could make out a huge ring with a large stone on one finger of his left hand. The figure lifted his head a little to reveal his bulging eyes. A lizard-like tongue flicked out and licked a pair of thick fleshy lips. The figure standing there in a dressing gown was nothing short of grotesque.

Sarah was frightened. 'Who are you?'

Initially, there was no reply from the mysterious visitor. Then, his shoulders started shrugging in time with a snorting laugh that forced sharp exhalations of air from the nostrils of his large, hooked nose. The bridge of the nose reached to eyebrow level, the balding head seemed to extend this extraordinary proboscis. The shrugging suddenly stopped.

'Hello, my dear, how nice to meet you.'

The creepiness of the voice freaked her out. She threw the book onto the coffee table and jumped to her feet.

'Who are you? What do you want?'

'I'm sorry my dear, how rude of me. My name is Elias Phinn, and you must be the lovely Sarah.'

'Yes, but who are you?'

'I'm a... shall we say, friend or colleague of Igor's.'

'Igor! Who's Igor?' Sarah was confused.

'Why are you here? Why am I here? Where am I?'

Her upset and confusion was causing her captor's powerful influence to fade. Again, the evil-looking figure above started shrugging with that snorting laugh.

'Where are you? You're currently in Hampshire.'

'Hampshire?' she shrieked. 'What am I doing here?'

'Why, you're here for the wedding. Hasn't Igor told you my dear?'

'Igor? Wedding? What wedding?'

'Your wedding to the Master of course.'

'What? My wedding? The Master? What do you mean?'

'Your wedding to The Master.'

Sarah was becoming distraught and enraged, she hadn't a clue what was going on, so many questions in her head. She screamed at her tormentor, 'Let me out of here now! Where's my uncle?'

It was just then, as she was looking up at the fat little man on the landing, she saw a hand reach in from behind. The hand grabbed the slimy character by the throat. His eyes bulging, he was dragged back through the doorway.

Sarah screamed with fright. There were sounds of a scuffle up top. Some choking sounds and at one point she thought she heard the words '*Please Master, no, forgive me.*' Then, all went quiet.

Mark appeared at the top of the stairs. Sarah immediately bombarded him with questions.

'Who was that? Wedding, what wedding? Why am I here? Where's my uncle? Who's Igor?'

It was the last question that alarmed him most, just how much had that idiot Elias revealed?

Mark held his hand up, 'Calm down my dear, everything is fine, just look at me and I'll explain.'

Wiping tears away and still giving involuntary sighs as she sobbed, Sarah made the mistake of looking up at her captor again. He stared down into her eyes. She couldn't look away. Her captor's calming voice once again drilled into her innermost thoughts, she was quickly back under his influence. He told her to forget the visit from Elias. She became calm once more.

The evil occultist started his visit again.

'Hi Sarah, just thought I'd pop in to make sure you're OK.'
'Oh, hi Mark, yes everything's fine,' she confirmed happily.

'Do you need anything?'

'Erm, no, I don't think so,'

'I'll pop back in a couple of days and see you again,'

'That'll be good.'

Mark waved goodbye and stepped back into the hallway, locking the door behind him. This time, he removed the key and put it in his pocket.

Elias was still writhing in pain on the hallway floor. For good measure, Mark kicked him hard in the kidneys. His victim shrieked in pain.

'Don't you ever disobey me again!' He stepped over his cowering follower.

'I won't Master, I won't, I've learned my lesson.'

Igor gathered his things together. Elias, bruised and battered, pulled himself up to a sitting position still winded and smarting from the beating he had received.

Igor appeared in the hallway with his packed overnight bag, ready to leave. Before opening the front door, he turned to scowl at Elias. The look was a warning, Elias knew not to engage direct eye contact, else he too would fall under his power.

'Remember!' he began whilst pointing an accusing finger, 'Don't you ever disobey me again, you idiot!'

Elias whimpered, his watery eyes reflecting the pain he was in. He flinched, fearful that more violence was headed his way.

'I'm leaving now, I'll be back in a few days. Any repeat of this morning's debacle, I tell you, I will inflict so much pain on your pathetic fat body that you will wish death visits you sooner rather than later. Do you understand?'

Elias was a quivering wreck now, 'Yes Master, yes,' he gasped. 'I'm sorry, it was a mistake. It won't happen again.' He clutched the edges of his dressing gown and gripped them tightly around his throat, as if these actions offered some protection.

Igor departed. Elias felt safe once more.

Chapter 62

It took two full days following Detective Page's request for a marked police car to pull up outside Sarah's house. Both occupants looked down the drive at the house. There were no apparent signs of life. Windows were shut, no car in the drive, the grassed front garden would need a cut in the next few days, but growth was not excessive.

PCSO Dave Mitchell, the burly passenger, got out of the car.

'I'll knock and look round,' he said as he closed the car door.

He listened as he pressed the bell push. He heard the classic bing bong resound inside. With his head bowed and still listening intently, the PCSO tried to detect any faint sounds of movement. There were none. PC Pamela Pitt locked up the patrol car and wandered down the pathway to join Dave.

'Let's look around,' she suggested.

It was getting dark now, so the absence of any lights illuminated inside would further suggest an empty house. The officers shone their torches through the letterbox, and any windows they had access to, whilst peering in to see if there was anything suspicious.

'I'll try the neighbour,' said Pamela.

Mark's van was parked in the drive, lights were on in the house. The young PC knocked the door. A few moments later, the door was opened. Mark put on his *surprised look,* as if a visit from the police was unexpected.

'Hello sir,' Pamela began. 'Sorry to bother you this evening, but we've had a report to suggest one of your neighbours may be missing.'

'Oh, who?'

'Can you tell me who lives at number 34?' 'Yes, Mrs Cooper, Sarah, is she OK?'

'That's what we are trying to establish sir. When did you last see Mrs Cooper?'

'Oh, about five or six days ago I think.' Mark thought for a moment, then added, 'Yes, it was the day before the storm. There was a massive clap of thunder that evening and I think it has taken the electrics out next door as I noticed the security light over the front door doesn't work now. I don't think she's been back since then. I didn't expect to see her anyway.'

'Why's that, sir?'

'She's gone to Scotland to stay for a few weeks, close to where her uncle lives. Edinburgh, I believe. He's in a home you see.'

'Ah, OK, I understand. Did you speak to her?'

'Oh yes, I was helping her get the car packed up. She even got me to program her satnav for the journey.'

'When exactly was this, sir?'

'Erm, tell you what, why don't you step in? I think I have it on my security camera. It'll be timed and dated.'

The PCSO rattled Sarah's back gate, it was secure. He looked over as Pamela beckoned to him. They entered the obliging neighbour's house to view the footage of Sarah's departure.

The recording was reaching the end when it showed Mark getting into the passenger seat of Sarah's car. 'Ah,' said Mark, 'this is where I got into the car to set up the satnav for her. It was her husband's car originally, she never really understood all the gadgets on it.'

'And where's her husband now?' asked Pamela.

'Nobody knows, he disappeared a couple of years ago. She's had a rough couple of years, poor girl. I think the idea of going to Scotland was for a fresh start. Are you saying she didn't get there?'

Pamela paused, making a quick note of the video time check as Sarah's car pulled off the drive. 'No, she didn't arrive as expected, Mr?'

'Stewart, Mark Stewart.' He held out his hand for a handshake with each officer 'I do hope she's OK.'

'I'm sure there'll be a perfectly good explanation,' the PCSO chipped in.

'Do you know if she was going anywhere else?' Pamela asked.

Mark frowned thoughtfully, 'I think she planned to do the journey in two parts, stopping off in a hotel on the way.'

'Do you know where and which hotel?'

'I think she mentioned Durham. I wouldn't know which hotel though. You might like to speak to the lady in the Age UK charity shop in the Mall,' he volunteered, 'Polly, I think her name was. She had quite a chat with her recently. They were discussing her trip to Scotland. Maybe she has more information.'

'What was the address you put into the satnav?'

'Oh dear, I can't remember that. It was a postcode. I think it was DH something... Sorry.'

Pamela made a note of this information.

'That's ok sir. Thank you for your time, we must get back to the station to file our report now. Meanwhile, if she turns up, will you give us a call please?'

'Yes, of course, officer.'

Mark opened the door and Dave did a *Ladies first* gesture before following his colleague out.

'Good night, officers,' Mark said as he closed the front door. He leaned back on the door, smiling to himself. Apart from a tricky question about the satnav there were no suspicions towards him. Time to celebrate in the office.

Chapter 63

Angus sat in his favourite armchair. There was torment in his eyes as he stared ahead, playing various scenarios through in his head as to what may have become of Sarah. It was a good day and a half since he reported his niece missing. He'd heard no news. At this time of day, he would normally be listening to the afternoon play on Radio 4, but not today. The only sound in the elderly gentleman's room was a ticking clock. The clock whirred, about to strike the chime for 2.30pm. The two bongs from the clock were closely followed by a knock on his room door.

'Come in!' Angus shouted.

'Hello Angus, dear,' said Margaret, her head appeared around the door. 'I've a policeman here to see you,' she pushed the door open further and a uniformed policeman entered the room.

The uncle's eyes lit up a little, 'Is there news?'

'No sir, nothing yet,' the bearded constable said, then he continued, 'I'm Police Constable Fraser. I would just like a few words with you regarding your report of a missing person.'

'Oh,' said a disappointed Angus. 'Yes, of course, please sit down constable. My name is Angus Kirkpatrick.' The two men shook hands.

'Shall I bring some tea?' asked Margaret.

'Good idea,' said Angus. 'You'll have time for a wee cup of tea won't you, constable?'

Feeling that he didn't really have a choice, Fraser nodded, 'That'll be lovely.'

Angus launched into the interview with the question that had been troubling him most, 'What do you think's happened to her, constable?'

Fraser leaned over so that he could pull his notebook and pencil from his pocket. 'Hopefully, nothing too serious, we'll soon find out,' he replied leafing through the notebook to find the first blank page.

'Now then,' the policeman began, 'Let's start from the beginning. If you don't mind, I'll take down a few notes as we go. Is that OK?'

'Yes, of course. When you say from the beginning how far back should I go?'

'Well, how about you briefly fill me in on when Sarah decided to come to see you. I don't need too much detail here but, I'd like a more detailed account as we progress. For example, when you last heard from her before she left and when you last heard from her after she'd started her journey. Take your time Angus, can I call you Angus?'

'Yes, yes, that's OK, I've been called a lot worse.'

The glimmer of humour was a sign that the old man was feeling a little better that the police now seemed to be doing something. He began slowly explaining Sarah's decision to come to Scotland. He got to where he said that Sarah lived in a large house alone and that she had no ties down south anymore.

'Is she married, or does she have a partner?'

'That's what makes me worry about her disappearance even more.'

'What do you mean?'

A knock at the door and in walks Margaret with a tray of tea and a plate of Scottish shortbread. She placed the tray on the occasional table.

'Thank you, Margaret, you're a wee angel,' Angus said.

'I'll leave you to pour,' she said with a smile and left the room, closing the door for privacy.

Angus poured the tea, 'How do you like it?' he asked.

'White, no sugar please, erm, you were saying Angus?'

'Oh yes, I was about to tell you. A couple of years ago, Steven went missing and no trace of him was ever found.'

'Steven?'

'Sarah's husband. He went out jogging one morning and naebody has seen him since. The only thing that was found was his mobile phone by the side of the road. There was a TV appeal and everything. So, officer, you see why I'm concerned. This is so out of character for Sarah. She's a lovely girl and all I've got left in the way of family.'

The old man's eyes started watering. He picked up a paper napkin from the tea tray and started dabbing them.

'I'm sorry Angus. I can see why you're anxious, I didn't know about this and will need to find out more. Do you have any details?'

'Details?'

'Yes. Dates, investigating officer, stuff like that.'

'I cannae be specific. All I can say is that it was a couple of years ago.'

'Not to worry, I'm sure I can find details in police records. I'll look it up when I get back to the station.' He made a note.

'Can we continue talking about Sarah's visit?'

'Aye, of course, though there's not much I can tell ye.' Angus gave as much detail as he could.

The constable made frequent notes and asked the occasional question for clarification. 'And do you know the name of the hotel or guest house she stayed in when she got to Durham?'

'I don't, I did have a wee text message from her on the morning of the day she was due to arrive.'

' Can I see that?'

'Aye, of course.'

PC Fraser waited patiently whilst the old man wrestled with the technology. After a few wrongly pressed buttons he finally got there. 'Ah, here it is.' He handed the phone over to the policeman.

The message was short, Fraser made note of its contents and also the number of the mobile phone that sent it.

The men drank some tea and helped themselves to a biscuit each.

'Is there anything else you think I might need to know?' the policeman asked.

'I dinnae think so. I fear that I've nae been of much help at all, have I?'

'You've been fine,' the constable assured and gulped down some more tea. He reached into his breast pocket and pulled out a business card. He turned it over and wrote something on the back. 'Here. These are my contact details. If you hear from Sarah or think of anything else we might need to know, please call this number.' He pointed to the telephone number on the front of the card. 'On the back,' he turned the card over, 'is your crime reference number.'

'Crime?' exclaimed Angus. 'Has a crime been committed?'

'We hope not, don't worry, it is just a number we use to reference your case. Everything that's reported to us will receive a crime number.'

Fraser stood up. 'Thank you for your time Mr Kirkpatrick. I hope we find something out soon, and that we can give you good news. Often, in cases like these, there's a perfectly good explanation for the disappearance and everything turns out well. We'll be in touch soon I expect.'

Angus took the constable's offered hand and shook it.

'Thank you constable.'

The PC departed. As he walked down the corridors of the large residential home, he had a bad feeling. What a strange coincidence that her husband had disappeared previously. He remembered what his old sergeant used to say before he retired, 'There's nae such thing as coincidence, laddie!'

Later that day, back at the station, Fraser was on the telephone, relaying the details of his visit to DC Page in Durham

It was the bit about the previous disappearance of the MISPER's husband a couple of years ago that convinced the detective to ramp the importance of the case up a gear.

The DC prepared to end the call, 'Thanks for that, you've been a great help. Do me one more favour and update the online case notes please.'

The constable north of the border agreed to do this. The call ended.

The young detective stretched back in his office chair, thinking for a few moments, *perhaps there's more to this case than meets the eye.* It was time to research the disappearance of Steven Cooper.

Chapter 64

Sarah had calmed down after Mark's intervention. As commanded by him, in his thought transference process, she had forgotten the incident with that idiot Elias. She was unaware that she was frequently under video surveillance whilst she busied herself watching TV, reading, cooking and pampering herself with the generous range of toiletries supplied in the bathroom.

She would have been mortified to know that she was being lustfully observed in various states of undress as well.

The Watcher was a patient man and would wait to consummate the marriage to his bride during the Walpurgis celebrations.

* * *

The Dark Web was active again. The fellowship brothers and sisters were very excited about the approaching event. They had lots of questions for their leader.

'When should we arrive?' was the first enquiry.

'Any time the day before is ideal, though I understand some of our overseas visitors would like to arrive a day or two earlier, and that's also OK.' Questions continued.

'Where will we collect our orders?'

'It's all arranged, the orders will be prepared and ready to pick up at the main house.' The brothers and sisters were warned, 'Most of you've pre-paid. Cash payments only will be accepted at the event. We want nothing traceable.'

The brothers and sisters agreed this was a sensible precaution.

So, it was all arranged, Mark's incredible organisational skills had left nothing to chance. Any awkward question that may have thrown a spanner in the works was answered confidently. The Dark Web session was closed down securely, all members confident that the event will be a great success.

Time for a celebratory line of Charlie thought Mark. Once again, the satanist prepared his area, revealing the pentagram, lighting the black candles and donning his monastic habit. The rituals began.

It was the early hours of the morning, the incantations long finished, before Mark awoke, still sitting cross-legged within his protective geometric star. His arms were still outstretched with wrists resting on his knees, palms facing upwards.

There were preparations to do today before returning to the vicarage tomorrow.

An oak wooden trunk was dragged from a cupboard in the corner. This would contain paraphernalia required for the ceremony. Mark removed the padlock from the hasp and staple to liberate the heavy lid. The substantial hinges creaked as the lid was raised. With flared nostrils and wide eyes, he inspected his ceremonial outfit, neatly arranged inside the trunk. The sight of it excited him immensely. He gently lifted the outfit to inspect its finery.

He carefully returned the outfit to the trunk before adding the treasured sacrificial dagger in its case. He removed his habit and laid the boiled wool garment into the trunk with the other items. The black candles, now extinguished, were packed into a cardboard box and also added to the trunk. This is all he would need from his secret place of devil worship. He securely locked the trunk and carried it to the house ready for loading into his van in the morning.

Excited about the upcoming event and still affected by the powerful stimulant of the previous evening, overnight sleep was fitful.

Chapter 65

DC Ashok Patel was sitting at his desk in Luton Police Station when an email pinged into his inbox.

The young officer looked up from his paperwork to see if it might be anything important or interesting. The email was from one of the desk sergeants. He opened the email and read it.

Subject: This MISPER report might be of interest to you

Hi, We had a request from Durham Police to visit the address of this MISPER. The address sounded familiar. It bothered me I couldn't exactly remember where from. I searched on the database and it turns out the address was known to us. It belongs to the Coopers; you may remember, the husband disappeared without trace a couple of years ago, his whereabouts remain a mystery. You're not going to believe it, but Mrs Cooper has now been reported missing. Too many coincidences here, I think. Incident report attached.

Kind Regards, Sgt. Boyce.

Hell, yes, he was interested. He opened the attachment and called out, 'Jane! You're gonna want to see this.'

Jane came over to his desk, 'What've you got?'

'You remember that case a couple of years back with the Coopers?'

'Yes, I still think about it today.'

'Well, you're not going to believe this, but' - he hurriedly skim-read the first few lines of the report before confirming - 'yes, it's her!'

'What is?'

'Mrs Cooper has now gone missing!'

'No... Are you sure? Let me see.' She squatted down next to her colleague's desk to read the report. 'Oh my God! You're right, it is her!'

They continued to read the full report in silence.

Jane stood up, holding her hand to her face in thought, she was the first to break the silence.

'We need to speak to the boss. This needs investigating.'

Ashok nodded in agreement, still staring at the report on his screen.

'We must keep an open mind, but the disappearance may be linked to Mr Cooper's.' She paused. 'We don't know what her mental state is, she may just want to be on her own for a while.' Another pause. 'The unthinkable might be that she has done something silly to end it all.'

'It's too late to do anything this evening. I'll forward this email to the DCI. I'll request a meeting in the morning,' said Ashok.

'Good idea. Meanwhile, I'll contact Records to get the old case notes sent up.'

The officers busied themselves with their individual tasks to prepare for tomorrow.

Chapter 66

Mary and Margaret were busy in the kitchen of the residential home.

Mary was loading the dishwasher, 'Any news on Angus's niece?'

'Och no, my dear. I'm getting really worried about the poor man.' She paused, trying to avoid cutting her fingers whilst slicing a tricky shaped carrot that seemed to have a mind of its own. 'He's hardly eaten anything these past couple of days you know. Niamh said she noticed a lot of food left on his plate when she collected it after lunch.'

Niamh entered the kitchen and heard some of the conversation. 'That's right, I didn't think he was his normal chatty self either. He normally says something like *Hello my dear, how lovely to see ye today*,' she mimicked. 'There was none of that!'

Margaret nodded, 'Aye, he's worried alright. There's been no word from the lass herself or from the police. 'Tis a mystery without doubt, that's for sure.'

Mary set the dishwasher going, 'I really hope there's a perfectly good reason for her disappearance and that the wee lass is OK.' She thought for a moment, and tried to brighten the mood. 'Perhaps she's been taken unwell and is resting in a hospital somewhere.'

Margaret finished the carrots and moved on to make some tea. 'Let's hope we hear some good news very soon. Hopefully dinner tonight might cheer him up a little. It's his favourite, steak and kidney pudding with carrots and tatties.'

* * *

Angus sat in silence. The only noises in the room came from the ticking clock and the grinding of his teeth, a habit he had when he was feeling anxious. He continued to replay scenarios in his mind that might explain the disappearance of his beautiful niece.

He imagined her being involved in a serious car accident, perhaps she was seriously injured, laying in a hospital somewhere… or, worse still, perhaps the accident was fatal! Thinking this scenario through, he decided that this was unlikely as surely the police will have her car and be able to identify her through its ownership. No, this couldn't be the case.

Another scenario came to mind: what if her car had left the road and plunged into deep water somewhere? The car could be hidden underwater… her body could still be trapped inside. This scenario was the most plausible and would explain her disappearance and losing the vehicle. The old man was saddened at this. Each time he replayed this in his mind, the sadness he felt became visible as tears welled up in his eyes.

There was another unthinkable possibility, supposing she'd been abducted by somebody? A rapist perhaps! Little could he know how near to the truth this was.

After mulling over his torment, he eventually dismissed each scenario only to invent other equally abhorrent possibilities. His current thoughts were disturbed by a knock at the door. The old man called his visitor in. He hoped it was somebody with good news.

The door creaked open and in walked Margaret, carrying a tea tray.

'I've brought you a nice cup of tea.'

Angus was always ready for a cup of tea. 'Och, you're a wee angel. Thank you, my dear.'

'As a special treat, I've baked a sponge cake. I know how much you like my sponge cakes, so I've added a wee piece on a plate for you.'

The cake could in no way be described as *wee* as it was huge! It was Margaret's covert attempt at getting the poor old man to eat something.

'Och, you spoil me.'

Margaret glimpsed one of his increasingly rare, lighter moments. She'd stopped asking if there was any news. When she did ask, he quickly became morose again. She was sure if there was any news, good or bad, the dear old man would share it with her. She sat for a while chatting and decided to relay an amusing story about Hamish Campbell, the local farmer, and his escaped cows.

'Aye, it was the early hours of the morning. The police had to close the road whilst his prize winning herd was rounded up.' Margaret changed her voice and mimicked the old farmer: *'I tell ye, the po lees have nae a clue aboot rounding up heeland coos. They was running down the lane a flapping their arms as if they was trying to take off like a bird you know.'* Margaret was pleased to see a smile on the old man's face.

'How did he get the cows back in the field?'

'He told the police to block off the road to keep the cows penned in, then he went back to the farm to fetch his quad bike. He

199

soon rounded them up and got them back in the field. A rambler had left the gate open, would you believe?'

Angus tutted and shook his head, 'A city dweller no doubt!'

Margaret was happy to see Angus eating the sponge cake as they talked. She finished her cup of tea before getting up to leave.

'I must get on preparing this evening's meal. It's your favourite tonight, steak and kidney pudding!'

'Lovely! Thank you Margaret, t'was a real tonic, having a chat with ye. It's brightened my day up no end!'

Margaret gave a little wave as she disappeared behind the door to get back to her duties.

Angus returned to his pondering once more.

Chapter 67

Next morning, Chief Inspector Grant arrived to his office early. He reviewed his emails and voicemail messages. One ominous message was left by Chief Superintendent Dickerson. Grant listened as his hands-free phone replayed his superior's message. *'Norman, it's Tom here, as soon as you get in tomorrow morning, I want to see you in my office.'*

Grant knew his boss was in already, he had seen his car in the car park. After quickly skimming through his emails and wondering what his two officers were excited about, he prepared himself to see Dickerson.

He walked down the corridor, straightening his tie and running his hand through his hair, just to tidy it up a little. Dickerson's outer office was empty, his secretary normally started later. His office door was closed, Grant knocked loudly twice and listened for a response. 'Come!' resounded from within.

Grant entered. 'You wanted to see me, sir.'

'Ah yes Grant, come in, sit down please.' Normally, when Dickerson addressed him as *Grant*, it was bad news.

The senior officer was in the middle of writing something on a pad when the inspector entered. Grant sat down whilst Dickerson resumed his writing with what looked like an expensive pen; *probably a Mont Blanc or something*, the inspector thought.

Dickerson didn't look up, 'Won't keep you a minute.'

Grant sat in front of his desk. 'OK sir, take your time.'

The superintendent finished his writing and screwed the top back onto his precious pen. 'Now then Grant, I met the district commander yesterday,' the superintendent frowned over the top of his glasses at the chief inspector. 'To put it mildly, he's not happy.'
Grant already had a suspicion why this might be, but
thought it best to play ignorant and said, 'Oh sir, why's that?'

Dickerson lightly slapped the palm of his right hand onto the desk. 'Clear-up rates! Apparently, we're not solving enough crimes!' Then he mellowed slightly, 'Oh, I know it's not all down to you old chap, and I'll be having a similar conversation with other teams. We've got to address this though. What I need from you is a report showing your current caseloads. I need to know how close you are to making arrests and the likelihood of the CPS taking the case further. I need this before the end of today, do you understand?'

'Yes sir, I'll get on it right away.' Grant knew there'd be no point defending his corner when Dickerson was on the warpath like this. Sometimes he hated the job, for all his efforts and the hard work of his detectives it was often a thankless task. When being boiled in the pot by superiors like this, there was never any mention or acknowledgement that the department was severely underfunded by the government. Despite this, forces throughout the UK were still expected to meet government targets. Otherwise, arses would be kicked. He was confident that he had a great team and would shield them as much as he could from this latest criticism from the commander.

Grant entered the outer office and noticed Patterson and Patel poring over something on a computer monitor. They both looked up as he headed for his office door.

Jane spoke up before he disappeared behind his closed office door. 'Sir! Can we speak to you?'

Grant showed them the palm of his hand, 'Not right now, I'm busy. I do want to speak to the whole team at 8.30am this morning though - make sure everybody knows as they arrive.' The DCI disappeared into his office and closed the door.

The 2 colleagues looked at each other, 'I wonder what's going on?' said Ashok.

Jane shrugged, 'He doesn't seem very happy, does he?'

They both returned to review the information in the cold case files concerning the disappearance of Steven Cooper.

A little after 8.30am, the whole team was assembled in the outer office, speculating what the meeting may be about. The grim-faced Chief Inspector emerged from his office to address them. Despite the grilling he'd had earlier from Dickerson, he remained polite as he began speaking.

'Morning everybody, I know you're all up to your eyes in it, but thank you for sparing the time for this meeting. I won't keep you from other important business for long. I do have some admin business that I need you all to complete this morning. Superintendent Dickerson has requested an audit of your caseloads,' A groan from those assembled sounded. 'I know, not very exciting work but necessary none-the- less. I'm interested in cases approaching closure and need to know when we can make some arrests. Sorry folks, but I need this by 2pm today,' Another groan. 'DCs, pass your information to your DIs, DIs I would like you to send me a spreadsheet via email. I've emailed a spreadsheet template to you all prior to this meeting, which shows the information I require. Any questions?' None were forthcoming. 'Thank you ladies and gentlemen, let's get on with it.' Grant turned and walked back to his office, closing his door behind him. It was office protocol that he was not to be disturbed when the door was closed.

The enthusiasm of detectives Patel and Patterson to investigate what might be a new lead in a cold case were dampened as these new priorities were imposed upon them.

The meeting with Chief Inspector Grant would have to wait.

The investigation teams dutifully provided the requested information by the 2pm deadline. They then returned to their individual caseloads. The door to the inspector's office remained closed for the rest of the afternoon.

It was almost 7pm when Jane noticed the Chief Inspector lean back in his chair and stretch his arms above his head. This suggested that he'd finally collated his information and may be at an impasse. She was eager to see if the office door would open. Frustrated and impatient, she watched him make a couple of phone calls, only then did he get up from his seat and open the office door.

Jane jumped up and tapped Ashok on the shoulder to draw his attention to the opportunity to meet with the inspector.

The eager officers approached his office and tapped lightly on the open door.

Grant looked up. 'Come in, take a seat. Sorry we couldn't meet earlier. The s*uper* was on the warpath. What've you two got for me?'

Jane began, 'A MISPER has been brought to our attention. A female. She went missing, somewhere between Durham and Edinburgh.'

'And why would that concern us?'

'The MISPER is Mrs Cooper, Sarah Cooper, wife of Steven Cooper.'

'Steven Cooper,' he repeated. 'Why is that name familiar to me?'

Ashok filled him in on the details of Steven's disappearance a couple of years ago.

'Ah yes, I remember now, we had that nutter in, claiming he'd been abducted by aliens, didn't we?'

'Yes, that's the one. We think this needs further investigation. We'd both like to look into it.'

The DCI knew what these two keen officers wanted to do. Tired at the day's activity, he removed his spectacles, closed his eyes and pinched the bridge of his nose with his right hand. His detectives exchanged anxious glances whilst Grant pondered the request. After about a minute's consideration, he placed his glasses back on and prepared to address the detectives.

'Look, you say she went missing somewhere up north?' They nodded, 'Yes, sir.'

'And it's being investigated by Durham Police?' They nodded again.

'Well sorry, but with caseloads and clear-up rates being what they are, we can't take this on. That is not unless our colleagues up north come back with information that shows a link that needs investigation down here.'

Jane and Ashok looked disappointed, Grant acknowledged this. 'I know it's not what you wanted to hear. Give me some good results over the next few days and we might reconsider, but meanwhile, I'm sorry, we can't get involved. Drop it. I don't mean to be rude but unless there's something else, I need to prepare for a meeting with the s*uper* tomorrow. No doubt he'll want to discuss our caseloads after he's reviewed the spreadsheet.'

Jane stood, preparing to leave. 'Of course, sir, we understand, thank you.'

Grant smiled politely at his enthusiastic team members. Ashok followed Jane out of the office. 'Pull the door up please, Ash,' he requested as they filed through the door.

Back at their desks, Jane was first to speak. 'He's grumpy today, isn't he?'

'I suppose the s*uper* gave him a roasting earlier. I'm sure he'll be back to his normal self in a couple of days when all this has blown over'

The disappointed detectives fell silent.

Jane was deep in thought wondering what her next move would, or should be. Tonight, on the way home, she would call round to number 34 Chatsworth Close - just for a look.

Chapter 68

Mark had returned to the vicarage, ready to make the final preparations. Elias was still wary of him, so stayed well out of his way, spending most of the time in his room.

With his bag unpacked, he sat down with a glass of wine to watch some TV.

A pathetic game show was just finishing, its contestants putting on a brave face at the amount of money they could have won but didn't. The host signed off, 'Don't forget to tune in same time tomorrow folks!' before showing off the pearly white veneers lining the front of his mouth. Cue the repetitive music and credits. *How can people watch this rubbish*? he thought. Five minutes of adverts and a trailer for a new period drama starting tonight preceded the news.

The news reports started. Another government minister has resigned over new trade deal disagreements following the ongoing saga and fallout of BREXIT. More unrest in the Middle East whilst Syria, supported by Russia, continues to attack rebel forces holding out in various towns.

It was the same old stuff and Mark soon lost interest in the broadcast until he heard the news anchor report: 'Police in Durham have appealed for information following the disappearance of a Bedfordshire woman. The woman named Sarah Cooper, was last heard of in the Durham area on Friday morning and thought to be travelling towards Edinburgh. She was driving a silver grey Nissan Primera, registration ZY03AHY. We go over to Nigel Wren, our correspondent in Durham. Hello Nigel, what can you tell us about this mystery?'

'Police here are investigating the disappearance of Mrs Cooper. There has been no sign of her or her car since she left her home in Luton. It is understood that she sent a text message to a relative on Friday morning. The location of her phone suggested she was in Durham, expecting to arrive in Edinburgh later that day. Police would like to hear from any hotel or guest house in the area who might have accommodated Mrs Cooper on Thursday evening. They also would like to establish the whereabouts of Mrs Cooper's vehicle. If anybody has information that might be of interest they are asked to call Crimestoppers on 0800 555 111. Back to you in the studio.' 'Thank you Nigel, and now we go over to Matthew Farmer in our weather studio...'

Mark's attention drifted off the news report, deep in thought, whilst he was considering what effect the last news report might have on his prisoner downstairs.

Returning from his racing mind, he reached for his laptop computer. He would have to view her reactions on the surveillance camera.

* * *

Meanwhile, some 70 miles away, Malcolm Knight was eating a TV dinner whilst the report of Sarah's disappearance was broadcast. Malcolm had an incredible memory for names and recalled Sarah's from her TV appeal for her missing husband. *Surely this is the same person,* Malcolm thought. He regularly had private conversations with himself, this was one such occasion. 'Ah well, It looks like they've taken another.' As a precaution, he checked the silver foil protection inside his hat.

* * *

Mark waited impatiently for his computer to boot up. He was listening intently for any sounds that might be coming from the cellar. Eventually, his operating system decided it was time to allow access. Mark quickly accessed the internet to find the streamed video feed coming from the camera in the cellar. He breathed a sigh of relief when he saw Sarah busy cooking in the tiny kitchenette. The TV was off.

The scheming occultist leaned back in his armchair his hands clasped together, with his index fingertips pressed together and pointing upwards. He hadn't factored in the possibility that Sarah might feature in TV news reports, it wouldn't be good if she saw one and recognised the report to be about her. After several minutes deep in thought, he decided he must drop in on Sarah and apply some more of his will upon her.

Sarah finished preparing her meal and brought it to a comfy chair. She, too, was about to enjoy a TV dinner. She reached over to the TV remote controller and aimed it at the TV. The news had finished and the first of the evening's soaps had begun. As the introductory music to the programme was ending, she looked up at the cellar door, alerted by the noise of a key turning in the lock. Had she been in her right frame of mind, she might have been pleased to hear the door opening, perhaps she was to be released. But no, such was the power of her controlling master that she saw this intrusion as an irritation, just as her favourite soap was about to start.

Mark appeared on the platform at the top of the stairs.

'Hello my dear, how have you been?'

'Mark, what a lovely surprise to see you.'

'I said I'd pop in to see you soon, didn't I?'

'Yes, you did.'

He unhitched the rope securing the stairs and controlled its release through the pulley above. The foot of the stairs settled on the floor below with a thud. He descended the stairs.

Sarah put her TV dinner to the side, ready to get up to greet her visitor.

'No, don't get up. Finish your dinner before it gets cold.'

Her guest approached, bent down, and gave her a gentle peck on the cheek.

'I'll make us a cup of tea whilst you eat, shall I?'

'Um, yes, that'll be nice,' came Sarah's slightly muffled reply, whilst chewing a mouthful of lasagne.

He smiled a charming smile at her before walking into the kitchenette to make the tea. She was coming to the end of her meal, when he returned to sit opposite her. He placed a mug of tea, made just as she liked it, next to her empty dinner plate. 'So, how've you been?'

'Good,' she nodded slowly.

'That's good to hear, you look well anyway.'

The two of them took sips of tea during what appeared to be an awkward moment when neither really knew what to say to each other. Sarah's conversation topics would be limited, as being imprisoned like she was, there were no recent life experiences or news that she could share with visitors. Mark realised conversations were going to be difficult, so he set about what he had come to do.

He looked and stared intently at her beautiful face. She placed her tea back down and looked directly at him. Hypnotism was becoming easier with his unsuspecting victim. Their eyes met, and she could no longer look away, he'd now captured her mind as well.

His voice was deep and penetrating. 'Listen to me carefully.'

'Yes.'

'I want you to forget who you are because I am going to give you a new name, a special name, do you understand?'

'Yes.'

'From now, you'll forget your name. When you hear the name Sarah, Sarah Cooper or Mrs Cooper, you'll think that this is referring to somebody else. Do you understand?'

'Yes.'

'You will not recognise images of yourself. Do you understand?'

'Yes.'

'You will not remember owning a car. Do you understand?'

'Yes.'

'From now your name will be Walpurga, you will answer to this name. Do you understand?'

'Yes.'

'What is your name?'

After a pause that nearly had him thinking it had failed, she finally responded, 'Wal… erm Walpurga.'

Excellent, he thought. If she should now see or hear any media reports mentioning her name or details about her car, she wouldn't recognise them as being about her.

He released her from his captivating gaze and took his phone out. He switched the camera on and aimed the lens at his bride to be. 'Smile!'

She tilted her head to strike a pose. Mark took the picture as she did so.

They continued chatting, finding some common ground on the latest *fly on the wall* production being shown nightly on Channel 4. Eventually, he looked at his watch.

'Goodness, is that the time? Well Sarah, I must go now, but I'll come back and see you in a couple of days.'

She looked puzzled, 'Sarah?'

Mark looked up from his time piece

'What?'

'You said Sarah.'

'Did I? Sorry love. I've a client called Sarah. I was talking to her earlier on the phone, her name must be sticking in my mind.' He pulled his phone out of his pocket once more. 'Here,' he said, 'I've a picture of her.'

He showed the image he'd taken less than an hour ago onto his screen. He turned the phone towards Sarah.

Sarah examined the picture, 'She's beautiful. What does she do?'

Thinking quickly, Mark replied, 'Erm, she's a researcher, doing some research for my latest documentary film.' Cutting the conversation short, he was satisfied his prisoner didn't recognise her own picture, he quickly followed with, 'I really must go now.' He rose from his chair and leaned over to give her a peck on the cheek. She responded by angling her head to receive his farewell gesture.

Mark started ascending the wooden stairs. He pulled on the rope to elevate the stairs again. He secured them by tying the rope around the toggle on the wall. He turned and looked down at her. 'Bye my dear, I'll see you soon,' he waved.

Sarah waved back, and Mark disappeared through the door. When the key turning in the lock fell silent, she returned to what had become her normality, focusing on the TV, checking when her favourite programmes would be on tonight.

Chapter 69

It was dark when Jane parked her car outside number 34 Chatsworth Close. She sat for a few minutes studying the house. It was in total darkness. There was an outside light next to the front door, but this was not illuminated. *Perhaps it's on a motion detector,* she thought.

Eventually, she got out of her little car and walked down the front garden path. She fully expected the outside security light to announce her arrival, but it didn't. She tried the front door; it was securely locked. She pushed her hand through the letterbox and touched what felt like a leaflet, teetering within, before it fell to the floor. Not sure what she expected to see, she used her hand to cut out interfering light from a streetlamp and peered through the front room window. Nothing, just an inky blackness. She walked round the side of the house and tried the gate. This was locked or bolted on the other side and wouldn't open. A good shake of the wooden structure confirmed it was sturdy enough to climb. She grasped the top of the gate and hoisted herself up to cock a leg over. She paused astride the gate.

Note to self... Next time, wear trousers! She was thankfully alone, otherwise Ash might have got quite an eyeful if he were there.

She jumped down from the top of the gate and proceeded around the back of the house. The back door and the patio door were also securely locked. She'd an overwhelming urge to gain access to the inside of the property. Illegal as she knew it would be without a warrant, a plan formulated in her mind.

* * *

John Patterson was totally focused on shooting the grotesque creatures that seemed to appear, fully armed, from nowhere. It was a case of shoot or be shot. Of course, he'd been shot many times before and would become frustrated that he had to start again on that level of the game. Tonight would be one of those frustrating nights, as he was startled out of his imaginary pixelated world by the ringing of his business mobile phone. Business was slack, he couldn't afford to ignore it.

'Hello, John Patterson, Master Locksmith speaking,' he looked on in dismay as the interruption caused his avatar to be destroyed by some gun toting monster.

'Hi John,' was the voice on the other end, 'It's Jane.'

'Oh sis,' he remonstrated. 'You just got me killed!'

She knew, of course, that his sad demise was in a virtual world on his beloved Xbox. 'Oh sorry bruv,' she tried to sound sympathetic, but the comment was bordering on sarcastic.

'No matter. How's you?'

'I'm OK but I need your help.'

'What's up?'

'I'm locked out of a property that I need access to, for an investigation I'm involved with.'

He responded with a drawn out, 'Yeees,' unsure of where this was going.

'You know, on the side of your van you advertise a 24/7 service?'

'Yeees.'

'Well, I wondered if you would come out now and get me in?'

'Do you have a warrant to access it?'

'Erm, no, I want to do it on the QT.'

'But that's breaking and entering. It's illegal, you do know that surely?'

'Yes, of course I know. Look, I wouldn't ask if it wasn't important. A woman's life might be at stake here.'

'Wow, that's a bit dramatic. I don't know, I could get into trouble for this myself.'

'Nobody need know you were involved... I promise. Oh please John, just this once?'

'What if a neighbour sees me and calls the police or something?'

'They won't, the garden's very private and backs onto woodland. I'm pretty sure the next-door neighbour is out anyway... Please John, help me.'

Finally, he surrendered and agreed to help. 'OK. You'd better come and visit me if I get put inside for this! What's the address?'

Jane avoided a repeat of her un-ladylike negotiation of the gate by sliding the bolt across to exit the back garden. She returned to her car to wait for her dear brother to arrive.

* * *

Jane held the torch steady whilst her brother performed his magic on the conservatory door lock in the back garden. Still nervous about this illegal entry to a property, he wore rubber gloves to avoid leaving any of his fingerprints around the door lock.

'I don't like this sis.'

'Don't worry, nobody'll know it was you that opened the door.'

'I can't believe I am helping my sister, a police officer, to break into a house. When it's opened, I'm off back home.'

She was amused at his discomfort with the situation. At last, the patio door lock surrendered with a satisfying click. John rotated the door handle and slid the heavy door aside.

'Right, that's me outta here now. I haven't broken the lock, I opened it as if with a key. You must remember to lock it from the inside before you leave. Nobody'll know that this door has been opened.'

'You're an angel,' she leaned forward to give her brother a peck on the cheek as he was packing up his tools. 'Thanks a million, I'll buy you some beers and bring them round later this week.'

'OK. See you in a couple of days. Providing you're not in a police cell charged with breaking and entering.'

'Go on then, off you go, nobody will ever know what you did - thanks John.'

With that, he picked up his tools and quickly hurried around to the front of the house. Jane heard the clattery engine of his van start before she set foot across the threshold of the conservatory doorway.

It took a minute or so for her eyes to adjust to the darkness within. She made out the internal door opening and figured there would be a light switch next to it. She felt her way around some wicker furniture, banging her shin on the edge of a glass-topped wicker coffee table on the way.

'Ouch!'

She reached the doorway and found a light switch. Flicking it down, she expected her eyes to be bathed in glaring light. But there was nothing, just darkness. In the excitement of her covert operation, she'd forgotten the torch in her pocket.

I bet the power was tripped by a lightning strike in last week's storm, she thought. Electrics wasn't her forte but she was hoping the main circuit breaker was tripped during the storm. *This should be easy to fix.*

She found the main fuse box in a cupboard under the stairway. Shining the torch at the array of circuit breakers, one, the largest in the box with a red trip switch, was in the down position. All the others were up. She pulled the clear plastic cover down and gently pushed the trip switch up. The hallway was immediately bathed in light from the outside porch light and some clicking noises came from the boiler in the kitchen area.

She drew the curtains in the lounge before she then felt happy to turn the light on. She stood for a moment, what was she looking for?

In the hallway, she'd noticed a pile of post below the letter box. She picked up the pile on the floor. She studied the letters carefully. Most were circulars, a bank statement, a utility bill, a couple that she couldn't identify from the envelopes but, one caught her attention.

She examined the envelope carefully. It was official- looking: a brown envelope with Mrs Cooper's name and address clearly showing through the opaque window. It was what was on the back of the envelope that drew her attention: *Hampshire Constabulary*. She shook the envelope to adjust the position of its contents to see if it revealed any clues through the window. Nothing obvious came into view. She really needed to access the contents of this envelope. Then, her attentions was diverted by a noise.

Beep Beep! Her phone? She removed her phone from her pocket and checked its status. No, everything was normal. She focused on the envelope once more, readjusting its contents, holding it up close to the light, but still it revealed no clue as to the contents. If she tore it open, it would give the fact away that somebody had entered the house. A bright idea occurred to her. She leapt up from the sofa and rushed towards the kitchen. As she passed through the door, there it was again, *Beep Beep!* This time, she knew it wasn't her phone. She paused briefly, but decided that the investigation of the envelope would take priority.

After a search through the kitchen cupboards, she found a cereal bowl. She filled the bowl with water and then placed it in the microwave oven with the envelope resting on top. She closed the oven door and programmed the microwave for three minutes on high power.

Whilst that was cooking, she returned to the lounge. She sat listening for the mystery sound again. After a couple of minutes, there it was: *Beep Beep!* This time she had a good idea which direction the noise came from, somewhere near the TV.

The microwave pinged, her envelope should be ready. She opened the microwave door and was pleased to see that the gummed edge of the envelope had wrinkled. A knife was used to gently ease the flap of the envelope open.

She carefully removed the letter from the Hampshire Constabulary, which revealed a *Notice of Intended Prosecution*. Jane read the letter carefully to reveal the fact that Sarah's Primera had been caught speeding on the A30 in Hampshire. Just about to reseal the envelope with the residual gum, she thought for a moment, *what was the date of the offence?*

She reread the letter, then opened her phone to check the calendar… The offence was committed on the day, and at a time she was allegedly in the north east of the country.

This is getting interesting she thought. She re-sealed the letter and made sure the address was showing again through the window. She stood with both arms spread out and palms flat on the kitchen worktop. What on earth was she to do next? Her pondering was disturbed again by that beeping noise coming from the lounge. *What is that?*

She searched around the TV area expecting to find a mobile phone that had run out of battery. There was no phone, then she heard the beeping again, clearly coming from within the TV. Puzzled, she examined the set closely. She grabbed the power cable and gave it a tug, the end appeared from behind the TV stand. The TV was not plugged in. Whatever was making this noise was powered by battery. She plugged the TV in, the red standby light on the front illuminated. She waited for a good few minutes, listening. There were no more mystery beeps emanating from the TV. She took a cursory look around the room for anything else that warranted investigation. She noticed a notepad next to the phone. There was no writingon the top page, but she could make out some indentations from the page before. She picked up the phone and dialled 1471. It was called earlier in the day, the caller withheld their number. Probably an ambulance-chasing nuisance call, offering to get compensation for an alleged accident.

Still, the TV didn't beep - could this suggest that whatever was inside was now charging its batteries on the restored power?

She recognised the picture on the sideboard. It was Sarah's husband, the same picture that was used in the appeal for information following his disappearance. Jane picked it up and examined it closer. *God, he was handsome,* she thought.

Things weren't right here. She wondered if she was on the verge of making a breakthrough to solve the disappearances of this charming married couple.

Still no more beeps from the TV. The rooms upstairs needed investigating now. She crept up the stairs into the darkness above. On the landing, she flicked the light switch, which provided some light at the thresholds of all four bedroom doors. The smallest bedroom was first. It was a box room really, used as a dumping ground for an assortment of things. There was a desk against the back wall, piled high with books, papers, folders, and a pile of blankets. She wondered if this used to be Mr Cooper's office. Nothing of interest here though. She found an empty suitcase in the master bedroom, presumably Mrs Cooper didn't need this for her trip. There was evidence that clothes were missing from the wardrobe and the ensuite shower room was devoid of toiletries. She switched off all the upstairs lights and made her way back downstairs.

Back in the lounge, she looked quizzically again at the TV, desperate to figure out why it was beeping earlier. This was a Samsung smart TV so it would link up with a router for access to the internet. She had never heard of one that used mobile phone technology though. She made a note of the model number promising herself she would check online later. She then remembered, in one of the kitchen drawers, there was a Phillips screwdriver. Perhaps she could slip the back off of the TV now and look inside.

She retrieved the screwdriver. She unplugged the TV again and gently turned it around ready to attack the screws securing the back cover. Disappointment. The screws were not compatible with the screwdriver. She shone the torch to examine the screw heads. They were not cross head screws but more of a six-pointed star configuration. *Tamper-proof*, she thought, the likes of which she had never seen before. Defeated, she returned the TV to its normal position.

The beeping had not returned, even with the TV unplugged. Probably a sign that the battery within had accepted some charge during the half hour it had been plugged in. This was one mystery she would not solve tonight. It was time to go.

She bolted the gate again and locked the patio door from the inside. The dish and knife in the kitchen was cleared away. All internal lights were switched off, only the outside security light remained illuminated. Lounge curtains were opened once more. The light streaming through the front door was just enough for her to return to the fuse box under the stairs. She flicked the big red trip switch down again. Once more, the house was in complete darkness.

A final check to make sure she had all of her belongings. The post was again scattered onto the hall floor beneath the letterbox. Thankful for a more dignified exit than entry, she carefully stepped over the post to leave through the front door. There was some serious thinking to do this evening. *How could I persuade Grant to investigate the mysteries of the house without revealing how I came by the information?*

Chapter 70

The Investigation team at Durham CID was having a case review meeting following the TV appeal. DC Page was taking the lead.

'OK, we need to share information to see where we are with this. A person just cannot disappear without a trace, can they?'

Detective Sergeant Davis was curious. 'Did anything at all come from the TV appeal?'

'Nothing sarge, just the usual time wasters and even a garbled message about alien abduction.'

The team laughed at the unlikely explanation.

'Any joy on the hotels?' Justin looked around at the team to see which members had been following this lead. Tom Scott, a young DC, put his hand up.

'Me and Tamsin have been ringing round.'

Tamsin looked up. 'I've one possibility, there was a booking at a budget hotel off Junction 62 of the A1M. The person I spoke to on the phone confirmed they had a booking for a room on the night in question, but the customer was a *no show*.'

'And was the reservation for Mrs Cooper?'

'I can't confirm that yet, the receptionist was covering the evening shift and wouldn't give out any details because of data protection.'

Justin tutted and shook his head. Sometimes a policeman could be forgiven for thinking that a lot of these laws to uphold political correctness and privacy were made just to frustrate their investigations.

'Where do we go from here? Do we need to get a warrant?'

The two DCs started talking at the same time, then Tom gestured to Tamsin to carry on.

'Tom and I are going to see the hotel manager tomorrow morning. We hope our warrant cards might persuade him or her to reveal the identity of the *no show*.'

'Good! Keep on it, Tamsin. If they still won't play ball, we will have to get a warrant, if only to eliminate the lead from our enquiries.'

Tamsin nodded in agreement, 'Yes, of course.'

'Anybody else got anything to add? Hospitals? Traffic?'

Cory Cummings was next to report, 'I got Katy in admin to call round local hospitals.'

'Any joy on that?'

'No, nobody matching our MISPER description.'

'How about traffic?' Justin looked around to see who would respond.

Cummings' hand went up, 'Me again. Erm, Sergeant Pike was looking after traffic today.'

'And what did Pikey have to say?'

'His boys have been looking for the past couple of days for the vehicle. All ANPR capable vehicles have been set to alert if the target vehicle is seen. The search has turned up absolutely nothing.'

'Maybe she's not currently mobile,' Cory offered as an explanation, 'she may be in a car park somewhere.' 'Or at the bottom of a river,' was another suggestion.

'Yes, that may well be the case. OK Cory, get Pikey's guys to check multi-storey car parks and any hotels with underground car parks, especially the hotel that Tom and Tamsin have found. Just ask him to keep at it, will you?'

Cummings noted something down in his notebook, 'Yup, will do.'

The meeting was drawing to a close, Justin made a final check. 'Has anybody else got anything to add or say?'

Cory spoke up. 'All the local enquiries have so far drawn a blank. I think we have to consider the fact that she never actually arrived in Durham. Maybe we should widen the enquiry and start investigating further south.'

Page nodded in agreement. 'Yeah, it's looking that way. The only evidence we have that she was ever in Durham was the message sent from her mobile phone to her relative. I looked into that myself and the phone company confirmed that the mobile phone was certainly in the Durham area the morning the message was sent.'

'Yes, but,' everybody looked towards Cory, '...supposing the phone was not in her possession. Just suppose she met someone in... I don't know... a service station or a cafe on the way. Someone who befriended her. Maybe he or she found out some stuff about her, then knew she was due to visit her uncle. Maybe this person attacked her, left her for dead somewhere, stole her phone. It would probably be easy to find *uncle* in her contacts list, so this mystery person, to cover their tracks, sent the text message. There's been no further contact from the phone, so maybe the perpetrator then threw the phone in a river or something.'

Page shared his thoughts on that one, 'Of course, there could be many reasons for the disappearance, but Cory's theory is plausible. OK, let's tie up these local loose ends we have by this time tomorrow. If we've got no further, we'll take Cory's suggestion and widen the search. Has anybody else got anything to say?' The room remained silent this time. 'OK folks, have a good evening. We'll meet again same time tomorrow night.'

The meeting disbanded. Some, eager to get home, grabbed their coats while others remained, either in conversation or busy on their computers.

Chapter 71

The following morning, Igor was waiting patiently for Toby to arrive. It was planned that the three men would attend the venue today to prepare pre-paid orders for the event. Drugs would be bagged up ready for guests.

Igor had already been paid handsomely for the orders placed by members of the fellowship. He was especially pleased with himself for buying direct from the supplier in Turkey, cutting out the middleman. Such was the profit for this lucrative venture that extra supplies were afforded. These would either be sold during the event, further increasing the profit, and anything left after that would be kept for personal use.

Whilst waiting, Igor accessed the Dark Web, posting final instructions for the attendees. It was clarified that there would be no catering on site, delegates would need to cater for themselves. Limited toilet and bathroom facilities would be available in the big house, but caravaners and those in camper vans were requested to use their own facilities. This would leave the facilities in the big house for those who were camping in tents. The location of the venue, a closely guarded secret until now, was revealed at this meeting.

Elias entered the room, feeling a little nervous around his Master due to the recent kicking he received.

'When's Toby due to arrive?'

'I'm expecting him any time now. We'll be at the venue all day so you can make yourself useful in the kitchen whilst we wait. Prepare some bread, cheese and ham to take for lunch.'

Elias obediently made for the kitchen and set about putting some supplies together. 'Shall we take some wine?' he called out.

'Yes, why not?' was Igor's reply from the lounge.

Elias had just finished when the wheels of a vehicle crackled on the stony drive outside.

Igor looked up, pleased to see the top of Toby's van go past the window. He left his chair and made for the front door, ready to greet his other partner in crime.

The front door was opened and a jolly-looking Toby advanced up the garden path to the door, his right hand already being offered for a handshake.

'Igor my friend!'

They shook hands. 'Come in, good to see you.'

Out of his two acolytes, Igor preferred Toby. He was a tall man with one of those faces that always seemed to be smiling. In his fifties, he had a ruddy complexion and grey hair surrounding the bald crown of his head. He had eyebrows that had gone awry long ago; almost meeting in the middle with the ends each twirled to a point at their outside edge. A bit *mad professorish* Igor always thought.

Elias appeared, framed in the doorway to the lounge.

'Elias!' Toby's voice boomed, 'Hello again.' He reached out and shook hands.

'Hi Toby, I hope you're ready for some hard work. It looks like we've lots to do in preparation.'

'Of course, old chap...' He turned to Igor, 'And how's our special guest?'

'Oh, she's fine, I'll not disturb her for now though.' They sat down to a cup of coffee, talking about what needed to be done over the next few days.

'I take my hat off to you Igor, your organisational skills have been excellent, it seems you've thought of everything.' Toby's compliment was accepted with a slow nod. 'We do our best, we do our best.'

Igor drained the last dregs of coffee from his cup. 'Gentlemen, we must go. My van's pretty full Toby, so you'll also need to bring your van. Elias, you'll come with me.'

Elias responded as positively as he could, not being too pleased at the prospect of sitting next to his leader, but not wanting to show it.

The trio worked quickly to load the vehicles. Toby followed Igor's van as they set off on the short journey to the venue.

They were driving past a six foot high brick wall on the left-hand side of the road when Igor spoke.

'It's just the other side of this wall.'

The van started slowing as an opening appeared ahead. Igor pulled into the opening and stopped close to a pair of substantial iron gates. The top of the gates were tipped with flaking gold paint. *They probably looked good in their day,* Elias thought. Alongside the van was a pillar with a numeric keypad on the top. Igor reached across to the keypad and entered a code to open the gates. He spoke as he pressed each digit of the code, '6 - 6 - 6'. Elias realised the significance of this number.

The gates opened slowly and the vehicles drove through. Up ahead, at the end of a long drive, a large baronial hall came into view. Flanked by two turrets, the imposing building seemed amply large enough for the event.

'It used to be owned by somebody in the music business. He died from taking an overdose one night. The place has been empty ever since. It's hired out now and then for Murder Mystery weekends. The landlords think we're making a film here.'

Elias was impressed, 'This is perfect.'

'Wait till you see inside,' Igor boasted.

The vehicles pulled up outside the imposing entrance to the hall. Igor retrieved a very large key from the glove box of his van. 'Come on, we've lots to do.'

They ascended the big stone steps leading up to the large oak doors fronting the entrance. Igor slid the large key into the fancy escutcheon around the keyhole. With some considerable effort, he turned it. The old lock issued a reassuring clunk. He grabbed the large verdigris covered brass doorknob, twisted it, and pushed. The heavy door creaked open, allowing access to a high-ceilinged hallway.

The hallway was divided by a large staircase up to the first floor. At the top, a landing ran from left to right with double door entrances to upper rooms.

Igor's voice echoed off the polished parquet flooring. 'What do you think?'

Elias looked up at a stained-glass lantern roof in the centre of the capacious hallway. 'It's huge!' Igor turned on his heel.

'Come!' He walked to the double doors on the lefthand side of the hallway. He twisted the two brass handles and gently pushed. The doors swung open in silence to reveal the large room beyond.

'This, is the Great Hall,' he announced.

The hall was about 18 metres long and 10 metres wide. Halfway down on the inner wall was a huge Georgian fireplace. Displayed above it was one of many giant paintings around the room, all ornately framed in ostentatious gold frames.

At the side of the room, Elias recognised the packages they had recently collected from the remote Kentish field.

Igor noticed the direction of his gaze and also looked across.

'Yes,' he said. 'I've a list of who has ordered what. We need to bag up these orders ready for our partygoers to pick up when they arrive. I've found some old trestle tables in the stables - I thought we could erect these in the hallway. I'll need both of you to help later, setting up a giant screen.' He surveyed the room. 'We need to erect it in front of the fireplace here.' He walked towards the fireplace as he spoke, stopping in front of it with his arms outstretched. 'This is perfect.' He spun round to face his followers. 'Right, let's get the trestle tables in first.' Igor headed for the door, Elias and Toby followed.

It took some effort to bring them in. They were substantial, not meant to fall apart at any rate. Toby found some old curtains, also in the stable, packed in a large crate. *Black velvet, ideal for the occasion,* he thought. These were used as cloths to cover the gnarled wooden planked surface of the tables.

The shipment of narcotics was brought through to the hallway. Then, guided by Igor's printout, they packed the orders in individual self-seal plastic bags. The bags were named and organised in shallow plastic crates in alphabetical order. The task took over two hours to complete.

'Come, help me bring in the equipment from my van.' Toby quickly took a long, cool swig of bottled water before following him. He listened to his leader's unpacking instructions.

'This structure here needs to go in first, it will form a framework to support that large monitor at the back there,' he pointed to the largest TV monitor that Elias had ever seen.

They set about moving the framework in to the hall. Igor produced a toolbag with the tools and wrenches to assemble the support. The top half of the framework was on a hinged cantilever, allowing it to lean back and touch the floor.

With the supporting frame assembled, it was time to attach the huge monitor. It took the three of them to struggle with the enormous item. Igor then had to lie on his back to attach the screen to the framework whilst the others supported the item until he said it was safe to let go. Once attached, the cantilever was gently pushed so that the monitor rose into the air. In its elevated position the monitor could be clearly seen from all points in the hall.

It was now dark outside, so they *called it a day*, and locked the building up for the night before returning to the vicarage for dinner.

Chapter 72

Jane was first in the office, engrossed and studying her PC monitor when her DC came through the door. He breezed past his superior, 'Morning!'

She didn't look up, preoccupied. 'Um, morning Ash.'

He walked over to her desk and observed what was so interesting on her screen.

'Ah, thinking of buying a new telly are you?'

'No, I'm just doing a bit of research on a case I'm working on.'

He looked puzzled. 'Oh, what case is that then?'

She quickly looked up and around the office. They were alone. Should she reveal what she found out last night?

Ash stood, still waiting for an answer. She looked around again to make sure they were still alone. 'Look Ash, not here, let's go somewhere private where we can talk.'

'This is very mysterious. I'm intrigued, come on, you look like you need some coffee. I'll buy you one in Orlando's round the corner.'

She grabbed her coat and bag and they set off to the cafe in Rosamund Street.

* * *

Ashok placed a steaming hot mug of coffee in front of her and sat opposite her in a booth far away from anybody else. 'Ok, what's all this about then?'

'Um… um… some information's come my way.'

'Information, what information?'

She patted her colleague's arm, 'Shhh, keep your voice down.'

His tone quietened, 'Sorry, what information?'

'It's about Mrs Cooper.'

'Oh God, you're not on that one again are you? You know what the boss said, we've gotta drop it!'

'I know, I know, but it's bothering me, so I decided to carry out some erm… shall we say, undercover investigations of my own.'

He grasped the bridge of his nose between his thumb and forefinger.

'I'm not going to like this, am I?'

'Erm, you might not. Look Ash, I trust you, what I'm about to tell you, you must promise not to reveal to anybody.' He stared at her for a few moments.

'Well?'

'Well, what?'

'Do you promise?'

'You've done something silly, haven't you? Yes, I promise.'

'Mrs Cooper has received a speeding ticket. It was issued on the day before she was reported as a MISPER and the offence was committed in Hampshire. That's what? 300 miles away from where she was reported to be?'

'How on earth did you find that out?'

'I gained access to Mrs Cooper's house last night and um… opened some of her post.'

'You did what?' Ash interjected incredulously.

Jane looked around quickly, 'Shhh, keep it down will you!'

'Sorry.' He composed himself. 'That's not all is it? Where do TVs feature in this story?'

'Whilst I was investigating the speeding ticket, the TV started beeping.'

'Beeping you say?'

'Yes, you know, like a mobile phone beeps when it's running out of battery.'

He looked puzzled.

'I took down the model number of the TV to Google it this morning, just to double-check it didn't have its own mobile phone installed for whatever reason.'

'Why would it?'

'I don't know, but it was a smart TV, and I wondered if software updates or something were transferred using mobile phone technology.'

'I've never heard of that before.'

'No, and my research this morning showed that they don't have mobile phone technology installed. I even asked a technician in an online chat session.'

The young DC looked thoughtful. 'What do we do now?' Jane liked the use of *we* in that question.

'I don't know. Obviously, I can't tell the boss. He'd be furious that I'm wasting time on an investigation he's told me to drop. And, worse than that, I've broken the law, illegally entering a property. I could lose my job.'

Ash nodded in agreement. 'Just how did you gain entry?'

'That bit of information is classified, you don't need to know.'

They sat in silence, thinking, and finishing their coffees.

'You said you opened some post last night. Have you left evidence of that…like an envelope that's been tampered with?'

'No, I've covered my tracks, the NIP is securely sealed back in the envelope and back on the hall floor with the other post, under the letterbox.'

'Did you damage anything to gain access to the house?'

'No, the patio door was opened as if with a key. It's all locked up again. You'd never know it had been opened.'

He looked thoughtful and then slowly started nodding to himself.

'What…? What are you thinking?'

The nodding turned into a faint smirk. 'I've a plan.'

'A plan? Tell me, what is it?'

His smile broadened, enjoying the fact that he was making his colleague slightly anxious. 'Leave it to me. I'm not going to tell you what I'm going to do. I promise I won't drop you in it. I almost guarantee that the boss will call us into his office over the next few days and ask us to investigate this further.'

'What are you going to do? You're worrying me now, tell me.'

'No. It's best you don't know the plan. I'm sure it'll work though.'

She gave up trying to find out what it was and decided she would just have to trust him.

The work colleagues finished their coffees and returned to the station to carry out official work.

Chapter 73

The next morning, the Main Event organisers were back at the venue.

The trio stood in the Great Hall looking up at the giant TV screen. Neither of the followers yet knew the purpose of this.

Igor broke the silence. 'The formal proceedings won't be happening here.'

His followers turned to him, looking somewhat puzzled.

'What do you mean?' Toby asked.

'Follow me.'

They followed their leader through the huge building. They passed through a Dickensian-looking kitchen and exited through a rear door onto a terrace. The grounds beyond were impressive. Elias studied a pair of victorian statues flanking the terrace. He looked away from the milky white statues to survey a huge grassy area bordered by trees on all sides. In the middle distance was a large rectangular lake, two swans gracefully powered themselves across it, leaving faint ripples in their wake. Beyond the lake was a building, fronted by a pair of arched doors.

Igor made his way down the terrace steps, 'Come.'

The occultists walked down the side of the lake, turning at the end towards the mysterious building. A set of stone steps led up to the arched doors. On the left-hand door was a large cast iron handle in the form of a ring. Igor grasped the handle and twisted it. The interior of the building was brightly lit with morning sunshine, streaming through colourful stained glass windows.

Toby looked around. 'Oh! It's a church!'

'A chapel,' Igor corrected.

'This, gentlemen, is where the ceremony will take place. Today, we need to erect cameras here and link them back to the TV monitor in the main house. I've all the equipment we need in my van, so let's get busy.'

Elias stepped outside and stood at the top of the chapel steps. He noticed another building, hidden on their approach by trees. He pointed towards it. 'What's that place over there?'

Igor joined him. 'Oh. That's a folly. Used as a crypt.'

'A folly?'

'Yes, wealthy landowners used to build these buildings just to confirm their affluence to others. Come you two, let's get to work'

Igor descended the steps and headed back towards the main house.

Toby and Elias did all the donkey work hauling cables to link the main house with the chapel, whilst Igor worked on the technical bits, erecting lights and cameras, linked to a PC in the chapel. He skilfully configured his software control the cameras. He checked the camera angles and made adjustments until he was happy with the results. All that was left to do was to check that images from the chapel were streamed to the large TV screen in the Great Hall.

It was mid-afternoon before the CCTV system was fully working and tested. They sat and ate a late lunch.

Toby finished first, 'I noticed you have some large boards in your van.'

'Yes, that's our next job.'

'What are they for?'

Their leader was very mysterious, 'You'll see, you'll see very soon.'

Toby was still inquisitive, 'Tell me, what's the plan, how are you going to transport our special guest to the event?'

'I've thought a lot about this. I need her in a different mindset and feel it's better to sedate her first. She must be dressed appropriately before we leave, I'll do that myself. I'll then need the help of you both to help bring her up from the cellar. At the venue, we'll carry her in to the chapel and prepare her.'

Elias was aware some blood-letting would be necessary during the formalities in the chapel. 'Have you brought the sacrificial dagger?'

'Oh yes, I have it safely stored in its case. The sedative will have worn off by the time we start the ceremony, which is good because I want her to be compos mentis throughout.' Elias noticed his leader's nostrils flare at the very thought.

'Soon, gentlemen, we'll welcome Brother Tarquin Masala to the vicarage. Tarquin will take care of the front-of-house. He will choose other brothers or sisters to control entry and administer the narcotic orders. I'll need both of you present in the chapel during proceedings.'

The disciples nodded, Toby being the more enthusiastic of the duo. Elias had quickly developed an inner hate for his evil Master. He was finding it increasingly difficult to become enthusiastic. Abandoning the project now would be dangerous, as he knew Igor would hunt him down to inflict a punishment worse than death itself.

* * *

Sarah carried on life in the comfortable cellar. Her days were occupied reading and watching TV. Normal wants and needs, like going out for a walk or shopping, were suppressed. The TV news reports troubled her. Police were issuing regular appeals for information on the whereabouts of a Sarah Cooper. She hoped the poor woman would be found safe and well. Despite images being shown in each report, she didn't recognise herself.

She didn't know the horrors that were to come, as the occultists upstairs plotted and discussed the important part she would play in the upcoming satanic celebration.

There were only three people in the world who knew where she was, none of those were likely to come to her rescue. One of them knew only too well the consequences of interfering. It seemed her final destiny was sealed and inevitable.

Chapter 74

Two days had passed since Jane confessed her illicit actions to her faithful colleague. This unofficial case was never far from the back of her mind and she occasionally worried that Ash knew what she'd done and wondered what he was planning to do.

Chief Inspector Grant's office door opened. He waved some papers in his left hand. He peered over the top of his spectacles as if reading some information from the paperwork. 'Jane, Ash, will you come in here for a moment, please?'

The officers glanced at each other as they rose from their desks. Jane thought she detected a wink and a smirk from her colleague.

'Sit down, please.'

Grant was still studying the papers in his hand and paused whilst he continued reading. Finally, 'I've received this fax. It's from our friends up north and about that MISPER you were talking about the other day, Mrs erm…' He looked back at the fax in his hand.

Jane prompted, 'Cooper, sir?'

'What?'

'Cooper, Mrs Cooper.'

'Oh yes, that's right. Well, they did a TV appeal asking for more information related to her disappearance, a Crimestoppers thing, and they have received some information from an anonymous source. You'd better read this, both of you.' He passed the fax across the table.

Durham Constabulary.

Dear colleagues,

Whilst investigating the disappearance of Mrs Sarah Cooper we have received some information that needs investigation. The information was left by an anonymous caller. The call was made from a public telephone in Luton Shopping Mall. A transcript of the call:

'I'm calling regarding the disappearance of the Cooper woman. She ain't up north but's gone down south. I suggest you check any recent speeding offences she's committed as proof of what I say. Also, you need to check her house out.

There's somethin' funny goin' on there too.'

I researched the speeding ticket claim, which is confirmed.

A copy of a NIP relating to this, issued against the MISPER's vehicle will follow. As you will observe, the offence was committed on the A30 in Hampshire on the day she was allegedly up here in this area.

Not sure what the reference is about regarding the house, but would suggest this needs checking out too.

Kind Regards

DC. Justin Page.

Durham CID.

Brilliant! Jane thought as she read the fax.

Grant eyed the two of them suspiciously. He had been in this game too long not to recognise a set-up.

'Right, we've some investigating to do.'

They both nodded. Ash pretended not to know more than he did, 'There must be somebody else involved in this. Where would they find out about the speeding fine? It must be somebody who knows Mrs Cooper or was with her when the offence was committed.'

The DCI nodded, 'quite... quite.'

Jane was eager, 'Shall we look into it, sir?'

The superior officer stroked his bristly chin. 'I want you to issue an ANPR alert to Hampshire Constabulary, get them to keep an eye out for Mrs Cooper's vehicle. If it's still driving about we should soon find it this way.' He thought some more before conceding, 'Alright, I'll give you 24 hours to come up with something. We'll review the case this time tomorrow to decide how we proceed.'

Ash spoke up first, 'We'll need a warrant to enter the house, sir.'

'OK, do the paperwork and bring it to me for signing. Remember, 24 hours is all you have. Off you go, both of you.'

They quickly left the office and gathered around Jane's PC, searching for the online paperwork to request a search warrant for 34 Chatsworth Close.

Chapter 75

Igor gestured towards some of the van's contents, 'These boards are heavy. They need to go down to the chapel for assembling. It's too far to carry them so I'll drive the van over there first.'

All three jumped into the van and Igor carefully negotiated the vehicle around the side of the house to access the grounds at the back. He slowly drove alongside the lake leaving a silvery trail of track marks in the morning dew. It was a bright, fresh morning, and Toby had the passenger window open, breathing in the sharp fresh air.

Igor parked the van in front of the chapel steps. They alighted promptly. Igor pulled back the sliding door at the side. He removed the securing straps from around the sturdy boards to prepare for their transportation.

'We need to unpack them here and move them into the chapel one at a time. When they're all in there, we'll assemble them.'

Toby picked up a battery-driven driver and small toolbox from the compartment above the driver's cab of the vehicle.

'Yes, we'll need those,' Igor confirmed.

Toby took these items in, leaving the double arched doors of the chapel open as he went.

Elias helped to remove the boards until they rested, unsecured, on the side of the van. They transported them one by one into the chapel.

Toby set one of the heavy boards down at the front of the chapel. 'What are these for?'

'This, gentlemen, will be my altar.'

Under Igor's instruction, the boards were fixed and secured together. Once assembled, the elevated, flat surface revealed a sharply painted pentagram. Four points of the pentagram had a sturdy metal eyelet secured to the base. The two fellows assisted their Master in the final positioning of the makeshift altar. Igor frequently checked and rechecked camera angles as they did so. This structure would be the focal platform for their very special guest.

Igor was pleased with the end result.

The occultists returned in the van to the vicarage. Igor escorted them back into the lounge.

'Wait here, I've a special treat for you both.'

His disciples sat waiting patiently. Igor reappeared with a small plastic bag full of white powder. He expertly cut three white lines of powder on the glass-topped coffee table and gestured to Toby to help himself to a line.

Toby did so with no hesitation, quickly snorting the narcotic through his right nostril whilst blocking the left with his finger. As he rose from the deed, Elias noticed some of the white powder smudged under his nose on his top lip.

Igor then invited Elias to take the second line. He was hesitant, cocaine wasn't something he'd ever taken before, preferring something more herbal. Such was his fear of the Master though that he copied Toby's method and snorted the powerful narcotic. He lifted his head, coughing and spluttering after doing so.

Igor then took the third line and also devoured the dregs left over from the other two lines. With a deep breath, he rose from his fix. 'Come, follow me.' He led his acolytes into an upstairs room.

The room was dark inside. This was probably just as well, as the pupils of the three devil worshipers were rapidly dilating. There was no furniture in the room. The focal point was a large white pentagram painted on the floor. Each point of the sinister star was punctuated with a well burned down, black candle. The previously melted wax of each candle, hardened in solidified pools at the base.

Igor handed each man a monastic habit.

'Here, put these on.' The men stripped their clothes off and pulled on the robes, securing the scratchy garments with a rough jute tie. Igor lit the candles. Each man pulled the hoods over their heads and sat cross-legged, heads bowed, with their backs against each other, inside the protective barrier of the pentagram.

A couple of minutes of silence passed before Igor raised his outstretched arms above his head and began his Latin incantations. Elias could understood that he was calling upon the fire demons. The brightness of the candlelight burned an image that remained visible when each man closed their eyes. The brightness intensified as the chanting reached its climax. Igor fell silent at last and the three worshippers sat in quiet meditation for an indeterminable amount of time, watching the hallucinatory images that conjured up in their minds, a combination of burned retinas and the effects of the illicit white powder. Elias, being a first timer, suffered additional discomforts, breaking out in shivers and cold sweats, a reaction to the horrific images in his mind.

Chapter 76

Jane shivered on this bright fresh morning, pulling the collar up on her coat to keep out the cold. Ash, warrant in hand, stood next to her at the front door of 34 Chatsworth Close. Both officers stood with their backs to the front door waiting for the locksmith to arrive. Jane didn't dare ask her brother again, besides, the police had preferred suppliers for this sort of thing.

'I don't know why we didn't just get uniform to come along with *The Big Red Key*,' said Jane, referring to the handheld battering ram, frequently used in police raids to gain quick access to houses suspected of harbouring drugs, weapons or violent suspects.

Her DC doubted the DCI would have appreciated the repair bill for such an entry.

It was the first time the two had been alone and able to talk since their meeting with the DCI.

'I didn't get the chance to thank you for what you did. It was clever of you. I loved your phrasing in the call's transcript.' Ashok denied any knowledge with a smirk.

She gave him a sharp elbow dig in the ribs. 'Yeah, right! You did good though, thanks.'

Just then a van pulled into the close, cruising along checking house numbers on its way. It finally stopped outside number 34.

The locksmith was an elderly ruddy-faced individual. He hobbled down the path to meet the officers, with a toolbox in his hand. He placed the toolbox on the ground and held out his right hand.

'Jack Jackson, Master Locksmith.'

Jane and Ashok introduced themselves, each accepting the offered handshake.

'Now then, officers, I understand you require access to this property?'

In unison they nodded. 'Yes.'

'Well, we've a bit of paperwork to do. First, have you got a warrant?'

Ashok produced the warrant. The locksmith checked the details before taking a quick snap of it using the camera on his mobile phone.

'Good.' He produced a pad of order forms from his toolbox.

The suspense of these formalities was frustrating. Jackson carefully filled out the order form and then requested a signature.

Ashok grabbed the offered pen and quickly scribbled a signature at the bottom. He tried to pass the pad back, but the *jobsworthy* locksmith wasn't finished with the formalities yet.

'Erm, and print below, please.'

Ashok printed his name below the illegible squiggle.

Finally, satisfied that all was in order, the locksmith began the task of opening the door.

Jane observed the operation performed on the door lock, which was destroyed in the process. She thought her brother would have done a much better job of gaining entry. At last, the door surrendered, and it swung open, giving the officers access. The locksmith replaced the damaged lock, whilst the eager police officers started their investigation inside the house.

Jane picked up the post from the hall floor and hurried through to the kitchen. More post had arrived in the last day or so. She retrieved the one of most interest; the speeding ticket.

'Here, this is the speeding ticket.' She handed the loosely-sealed envelope to her colleague, who opened it to inspect the contents.

'Yup, it's just the same as we saw in the boss's office - definitely happened in Hampshire.'

'That's not all.' Jane pulled her colleague towards the lounge. 'Sit down for a minute,' she pushed him down onto the sofa, 'Listen!' she held a finger up, nodding her head towards the TV.

They remained silent for a couple of minutes. There was no noise coming from within it today. They'd need something in order to start a forensic examination of the TV. Jane plugged the device in for a while. She checked to see that the power was getting to the TV.

'Oh, I forgot,' she walked quickly towards the hallway. 'The power's off, it was off the other night.' She disappeared under the stairwell, 'Probably down to the storm last week!' She turned the main switch back on.

Ash watched the red power light illuminate on the front of the TV. The boiler in the kitchen started making clicking noises, and compressors in the fridge and freezer kicked in.

Jackson reappeared in the hallway holding a pair of keys attached to a ring. He gave them to Jane. 'That's me done, folks. I'm off to my next job now.'

Jane thanked him and the tradesman departed.

Jane stood looking at the TV. 'We probably need to let whatever is making the beeping noise get a bit of charge before we listen again. Let's look around the rest of the house to see if there is anything else of interest.'

For the next half hour, they examined every room looking for anything that might be out of the ordinary. There was nothing to arouse any further suspicion.

They returned to the lounge, Jane pulled the plug on the TV. The officers sat on the edge of the sofa, waiting to hear if the mysterious beeping noise would return.

Jane was disappointed. 'Hmm… It was certainly making that noise the other night.' Then, beep beep!

They looked at each other. 'See, I told you so!'

'Hey, I didn't disbelieve you.'

'Sorry Ash. What do you reckon?'

'Certainly sounds like a phone doesn't it?'

Jane nodded, 'That's exactly what I thought. It may be something, it may be nothing - I think we need to treat anything out of the ordinary here as suspicious. We need to bag this up and get it looked at by Forensics.'

'I don't think we've an evidence bag big enough for a TV though.'

Jane rose from her chair. 'Worry not, I picked one up on the way out of the station earlier. It's in the car, I'll get it.'

Jane held the bag open whilst her colleague placed the TV inside. The NIP was also collected.

The preliminary investigation was complete; they secured the property and returned to the station with their evidence.

Chapter 77

Tracy Hamilton was busy working in the lab, examining some plaster casts taken from outside a burgled property in New Bedford Road. An image appeared on her screen, she sat back and triumphantly punched the air. The image was an exact match. She clicked on it to reveal metadata behind the image. She wrote on a notepad, *Nike Air Max*. Size 8 she reckoned.

Her desk phone suddenly let out its loud ring, disturbing her concentration.

'Hello, Tracy speaking,' she almost sang into the handset.

The voice at the other end said, 'Hi Tracy, it's Jane Patterson here.'

'Hi Jane, what can I do for you?'

'I've a bit of an urgent request. We're working on a MISPER case at the moment and would like you to examine a TV that we consider a bit suspicious.'

'Hmm, sounds intriguing, why do you think it's suspicious?'

'Can we bring it in to you? We can show you.'

'Yeah sure, how long will you be?'

'Oh, about a minute, we're just in reception. Your rottweiler of a receptionist won't let us through without an appointment.'

Tracy knew Brenda on reception was only doing her job, but sometimes she came across as being unhelpful. 'I'll pop down and collect you, wait by the reception desk.'

Brenda glared at the visitors loitering in the reception area. Ashok placed the bulky TV across a pair of reception chairs whilst they waited.

A couple of minutes passed before an opaque glass door, behind reception, opened and Tracy appeared. Ashok picked the TV up again and the officers moved toward the turnstile gate. Brenda's guard was up.

'It's OK Brenda, will you sign the detectives in please, they've come to see me.'

Brenda pressed a button on the reception desk to allow them to pass through the turnstile gate. Jane thanked the frosty receptionist. Ashok manhandled the TV over the top of the gate to get it through to the other side.

Tracy walked down the corridor alongside Jane whilst her colleague followed, carrying the super-sized evidence bag. Tracy stopped and pressed a button on the wall to call the lift. Whilst waiting, she was keen to know what was going on and why a TV had become part of an investigation.

Jane was coming to the end of filling her in as they entered the lab. She concluded, '...and what's more, our MISPER is the wife of Steven Cooper.'

'Steven Cooper?' the scientific officer questioned, with a frown.

Ashok joined in the conversation, 'Yeah, do you remember that guy who disappeared a couple of years back?' 'Oh yes, I do, the white powder incident.' 'Yup, that's the one,' Jane confirmed.

'I seem to remember you had a dead cert suspect for that, didn't you?'

'We did have at the time but it wasn't him. We never solved that one, and it's now on the *cold case* pile.'

'Oh, I hadn't realised that. Do you think there's a link with Mrs Cooper's disappearance now?'

'We're keeping an open mind at the moment, but we're looking at anything out of the ordinary - this TV, for example... It's just... Odd!'

Tracy walked over to an empty bench, 'Ok, let's have a look. Can you put it up here please, Ash?'

The scientist pulled on some rubber gloves before opening the bag.

The TV had stopped beeping again on the way over in the car. Jane explained, 'We need to plug it in and wait a few minutes before unplugging. You'll see what we mean.'

The group chatted whilst Tracy made her visitors a coffee each. A good ten minutes had passed, so the scientist unplugged the TV. Sure enough the TV emitted its mysterious beeping noise.

'Ah, I see what you mean.' Tracy stood with folded arms, looking at the TV for a few moments. 'Listen guys, I'm going to deconstruct this and see what's going on inside. It's going to take some time, so why don't you leave it with me? I'll give you a shout when I have an answer.'

Jane was frustrated that there would be a further wait. 'You'll do it today though?'

'Oh yes, I'm as intrigued as you to know what's going on. I won't get a full report back to you before tomorrow, but I'll email you with a summary of what I find. Is that OK?'

'Thanks Tracy, that's perfect. Ash and I have only been given 24 hours to come up with something that would warrant further investigation - if there's something fishy with this, it would add weight to our case.'

Jane and Ashok left Tracy to begin her investigation. Back at the station, Jane instructed Ash to get photographic evidence of the speeding offence. 'We need to make sure it was Mrs Cooper at the wheel, hopefully the image will be clear enough.'

Ash started the evidential photograph request. They spent the rest of the day working on other cases.

* * *

It was almost 3.45pm when a notification ping sounded on Ashok's PC. He opened his email application to find an email from Hampshire Constabulary.

'Hey Jane, Mrs Cooper's evidential photo has arrived.'

Jane went over to her colleague's desk whilst he opened the image for a closer look. 'What do you think? Is it her?' He asked.

The image wasn't the sharpest and the light reflecting off the car windscreen obscured some of the face. 'I can't be entirely sure but, from what I can see, yes; I do think it's her. It would be a coincidence if a look-alike was driving Mrs Cooper's vehicle, wouldn't it?'

They'd barely finished their deliberations before the Chief Inspector, walked into the office.

'OK you two,' he said walking between their desks, 'Let's have an update on that MISPER case you're working on.' They all filed into his office and sat down.

'Right, what've we got? Anything?'

The detectives both started talking at the same time. Grant held his hand up. 'One at a time please, otherwise we'll be here all night. Ash, you start.'

The young DC carefully explained the house search and described the phenomena around the TV. He ended his report with '…it sounds like a mobile phone losing battery power to us.'

Grant turned to his DI, 'Anything to add, Jane?'

'Only that we've received the evidential photo of the speeding offence. I'm pretty sure that Mrs Cooper is the driver of the vehicle.'

The DCI thought for a moment. 'Hmmm, and when will we know what's causing this noise from the TV?'

Jane chipped in again, 'It's with Forensics right now sir, I'm expecting a summary report any time now. It may be nothing and unrelated to her disappearance, all the same though, it is odd.'

The inspector nodded in agreement. 'Why on earth would a TV have its own mobile phone?' he mused.

Jane sensed he was coming round to the idea of continuing the investigation. 'Our thoughts exactly, sir.'

'And who do you think our mystery informer was? Do you think he or she was referring to this TV thing in the message?' Ashok felt a little flushed, feeling guilty at the deceit.

Jane jumped in, 'We're not sure. We did a thorough search of all the rooms in the house, including the garage and the garden. There was nothing else out of the ordinary.'

'Right, as it stands, we've nothing. We wait for the report from Forensics. If that throws up something of interest, we'll investigate. Otherwise, tomorrow morning, we drop it and get back to solving some of the workload we already have. Understood?'

'Yes sir!' they both echoed.

'Well done though, keep me informed.'

The officers left Grant's office, keen to see if they had received an email from their friendly scientific officer. No email had arrived yet. Neither officer wanted to go home until they knew the results of the forensic examination. It was Jane's idea to take a break. 'Come on, I'll buy you a coffee at Orlando's. Perhaps we'll have heard from Tracy by the time we get back.'

Chapter 78

Margaret ran into the corridor outside Angus's room. Her voice boomed, 'Quick, quick! Somebody call an ambulance. Poor old Angus is not responding.' She ran back to the old man's room. He'd been through so much in recent weeks, it had apparently been too much. Margaret pulled back the bedcovers to reveal the old man's frail body, clad in pyjamas. She recalled her ABC of resuscitation and ran through the procedure, checking his airway first. There was no apparent blockage. She moved an ear close to his nose, sadly, there was no noticeable sign of breathing. His pallor was looking grey. 'Och noo Angus, dinnae leave us now.' She pushed a finger up under Angus' chin to check for a pulse in his carotid artery. Again, there was nothing noticeable.

'Och, noo!' she roughly pulled his pyjama jacket open. Following her first aid training, she started performing CPR on the frail body before her.

Niamh came running into the room. 'I've called an ambulance, can I do anything?' Already breathless at the effort of performing CPR, Margaret responded between pumps of the old man's chest, 'I may need... ye tae take... over from me... in a wee minute... lass.'

She kept going to the beat of the Bee Gees Staying Alive song playing in her mind. She remembered seeing this on a TV advert once.

Niamh stood anxiously looking on, Margaret paused briefly to check again for a pulse. Still nothing, but he did look less grey, she thought. She carried on doing her CPR, hoping the ambulance would turn up soon. 'Here my dear, can you take over for a while? Just do what I am doing will you?' Niamh moved in and took over from a breathless Margaret.

The ladies took turns to administer the potentially life-saving treatment. both hoping it wasn't too late. Paramedics arrived in just 12 minutes and immediately sprang into action. One continued CPR whilst the other prepared the defibrillator. The defibrillator made a small whining sound as it prepared its potentially life-saving charge. With an electrode in each hand, the taller paramedic shouted, 'Clear!' His colleague stood back whilst the electrodes were applied to the old man's chest. His body jerked off the surface of the bed as the electrodes discharged. Once more, the defibrillator whined, preparing another charge. The paramedic who was performing the CPR checked Angus's pulse again.

'He's back!'

Margaret could already see a bit of colour appearing on his nose. The paramedics continued to work their magic, applying patches to the old man's chest to link him up to a cardiograph. The machine beeped irregularly.

The tall paramedic administered an injection, the beep then seemed to settle down to a regular pace. His eyes remained closed. They worked quickly to prepare him for transportation to the Western General in Edinburgh.

With Angus hospitalised, the mood in the home was sombre for the rest of the day. Margaret maintained a vigil at the hospital. Waiting for news of their much-loved resident, everyone at the home was hoping he would soon pull through.

Chapter 79

David Davis was the newest member to join the Bedfordshire Police Scientific Services Laboratory, straight from university where he achieved a first in Forensic Science. He worked rotating shifts that repeated every three weeks. This week he was working the night shift. A shift he usually hated working. He was normally alone in the lab with the occasional visit from security patrols and individuals from other offices in the building. He never got used to the spooky noises some of the lab equipment made in the dead of night as evidence was processed. Another dislike was the mundane tasks he was left to do by the day shift. In particular, he seemed to be left more than his fair share of report writing with instructions that reports needed to be on whoever's desk by 8am the following morning. Tonight was different though. His colleague, Tracy, was still working on a job that came in during the day. She was just finishing an email when he arrived. 'You still here?'

'Yup, just finished for the night, I'm off home soon. Glad I've seen you though. I'd like you to examine this TV over here.' She waved her hand toward the enigmatic TV across the room.

'Come and see.'

The scientists approached the TV. Tracy showed and explained her findings so far. In particular, she drew his attention to a deconstructed mobile phone, crudely secured by tape inside the TV.

'I'd like you to investigate this further, see what happens if you dial into the phone, I want to know what it does. There are some SIM cards in the drawer over there but don't destroy evidence in doing so. There's a fair bet that the tape holding this in place has fingerprints on it. See if you can lift some prints. If you get something, run it through the fingerprint database, we might get a match.'

'Leave it with me boss, I'll have it all figured out by morning!' He was pleased that at last somebody had left an interesting case to investigate.

Tracy liked David and was glad to give him a chance to do some real scientific investigation.

He was already thinking what he would do, and he hardly heard Tracy say goodnight as she left for home. Fingerprints would be a good start. Instead of his normal routine of an early cup of tea he reached for the fingerprint kit stored on a shelf next to the stationery cupboard.

When he was alone in the lab, he often spoke to himself. 'Light, I need lots of light!' He moved some tripod mounted lighting, aiming it into the back of the TV to illuminate the contents. Still talking to himself, 'Hmm, fluorescent powder I think.'

He used a soft sable-hair brush, to gently dust some fluorescent powder onto the tape securing the phone. Results were negative, he swapped the bright working light with the ultra violet beam of a UV torch. He examined the surface of the tape carefully. Most of it appeared clean, but there was one point, where the tape was secured in a corner recess of the TV casing, that showed a good quality partial print. He remembered his training at uni, and carefully lifted the print onto clear tape. Keeping a steady hand, he transferred the print to a glass slide.

Once sealed, he placed the glass slide under a microscope. He took a digital photograph of the enlarged image. He then passed it through FIDA - Fingerprint ID Application. There was a chance a match could be found.

The bearded scientist turned his attention to the innards of the TV once more, looking for the location of the SIM card of the phone. An endoscopy camera was used to get a really close look without disturbing the suspicious installation. Taped in the base of the TV was the main body of the phone. Luckily, the SIM card holder was not covered by tape. He used some long tweezers with a bent end to carefully withdraw the SIM card. The fluorescent powder revealed no more secrets on the card, so he placed it in a sealed evidence bag.

He took the bagged SIM card over to the drawer which contained spare SIM cards and found an identical replacement. The replacement had the phone number related to the card written on a small sticky label on the back. David took a note of this before using the modified tweezers to insert the new card into the phone. A battery was present with the phone, but the keen scientist reckoned that this was probably flat. Thin wires linked the phone to the circuitry of the TV, he presumed that the TV would need to be connected to power for the phone to work. He applied power to the TV and reached for his own personal phone to make the call.

The temporary number was entered followed by the green phone icon. After a pause, he could hear the ring tone on his own phone. The deconstructed phone in the TV remained silent. After several rings, he received an automated message:

Your call cannot be answered at this time. A disappointing result.

The investigations were interrupted by a melodious fanfare from the PC that was running the FIDA enquiry. He logged back on to the PC and opened his email application to find a result from FIDA.

From: FIDAdonotreply
To: David Davis
Subject: FIDA Enquiry Number: BP35712 A match has been found for your enquiry:
Mr Michael David Lawson. with 95.8% probability.
* * * End of Report * * *

This was getting exciting now. He turned his attention back to the mystery phone. Tracy thought that its camera features might be being used for something - covert surveillance, perhaps. It would make sense then that a normal phone call would not be using the camera. He sat back in his lab chair and thought some more. He reviewed some of the Apps installed on his phone and came across the popular social media app face2face. 'I wonder?' He started the face2face app and entered the number of the new SIM card into the application. This time, he did have a response. The call was answered, and an image appeared on his phone showing a clear view across the laboratory. He walked in front of the TV, still looking at his phone and, after a short delay, he could then see himself on the screen.

He moved closer to the TV. 'Hello.' After a short delay, his phone echoed *Hello*, back. 'Well, I'll be damned,
whoever's behind this has been a naughty boy.'

Enough evidence had been gathered, it was time to get back to mundane tasks, there's a report to write.

Chapter 80

As usual, Jane was the first to arrive in the office the following morning. Eagerly, she booted up the PC on her desk whilst she made a hot brew. She heard the reassuring beeps from her machine just as she discarded her tea bag in the bin. She carried the steaming mug of tea back to her desk before clicking on her email application. Several more beeps emitted as emails arrived in her inbox. Most were run-of-the-mill information messages, notifying times of meetings, and a reminder to change her password. There was one that had arrived in the early hours of the morning though, that she was expecting.

From: David Davis
To: Tracy Hamilton;
Cc: DI Jane Patterson; DC Ashok Patel.
Subject: Forensic Examination of Samsung TV
Dear Tracy,

I've thoroughly investigated this TV. The deconstructed mobile phone has been installed to use the camera features. I can confirm that sound is also being picked up and transmitted using the face2face application.

I strongly suspect that this has been done to covertly observe and listen to activities and conversations local to this device.

I lifted a partial fingerprint from the tape holding the phone in position and have received a match with a 95.8% probability for a Michael David Lawson. I've added a full report to the case notes.
Regards,
David Davis
Scientific Officer
Bedfordshire Police

She slumped back in her office chair, which groaned a creaky complaint. 'I knew it!' She crossed her arms and sat thinking for a while. She thought, *a forensics team now needs to enter the house for a thorough examination.* She checked her watch. In her head, she rehearsed what she'd say to the Chief Inspector when he arrived. Her eager fingers danced over her keyboard as she checked his calendar. 'Blast!' It would be at least 11am before he was due to arrive in the office. Other thoughts came into her head, like, *Do I have the authority to authorise a forensic team to enter the house?* Probably not, she concluded. The outer office door flew open and in walked Ashok. Before he had time to greet her, 'Ash, come here, quick, you gotta read this.'

He stooped down to read the email, Jane tilted her screen to the side so he could see more clearly.

'Wow, I think you're on to something there.'

'I can't wait until the boss arrives. I want a forensic team in there. I daren't authorise it myself, what do you think we should do?'

Ashok was the more restrained of the two and would think things through carefully before acting. 'You're right, he would go potty if he didn't agree that action, especially with his boss on his tail to improve the clear up rate.' He looked up suddenly,

'Text him!'

'What?'

'Yes, send him a text. He might reply quicker and give the go ahead. I can't think why he would refuse. He might see it before he goes into his meeting, or whatever else he is doing this morning. If he does, he may reply and give the authorisation.'

Jane showed great dexterity in quickly creating a text message for her DCI. She read through it and corrected a couple of typos before sending it to Grant's mobile phone.

'There, it's done,' she slid her phone back onto her cluttered desk. 'What do you think's going on here, Ash?'

'I don't know. She was possibly a victim of some form of stalking or voyeurism. Who knows how long the device was there. Maybe it was a jealous or suspicious husband?'

'Hmm, possibly. What about industrial espionage?'

'How did you come to that idea?'

'Well, I read through the case notes for Mr Cooper, A couple of years ago he was involved in some nasty business at work. He nearly got the sack for passing on company secrets. They had an internal investigation which cleared his name. The blame was diverted to his manager who pleaded his innocence but he got the sack anyway.'

'Yeah, so how does that still tie back to Mr Cooper?'

'Supposing his line manager was innocent after all, and this other company gleaned these secrets through covert surveillance instead?'

Ashok looked doubtful. 'Now who's got the vivid imagination?'

'I suppose I have, I'm struggling to think of anything else though. If it was for sexual gratification, it wouldn't make sense for the TV in the lounge to be the main source of surveillance, would it?'

Her colleague adopted the pensive thought pose. 'Supposing the TV used to be in the bedroom?'

Jane pulled a bit of a face, 'Unlikely, normally you'd have your best TV in the lounge. It's more likely that when replaced, it would be relegated to the bedroom, not the other way round, don't you think?'

'Yeah, you're right.'

Jane's phone juddered around her desk showing a message notification. She grabbed the phone and traced her unlock pattern onto the screen. 'It's from the boss... Yay, he's given us the GO AHEAD!'

No time to waste, she picked up the phone and called Tracy Hamilton.

Ashok retired to his desk to look up this character *Michael David Lawson.*

* * *

Tracy had also read the email left by the night shift. *This is turning out to be an interesting investigation*, she thought. As if by some sort of extrasensory perception, her desk phone rang just as she was about to pick the handset up herself to make a call to her CID friends. It was quickly agreed that a team should be sent to investigate 34 Chatsworth Close today.

Chapter 81

Angus was the main topic of conversation at the home for the staff and some of the residents. Niamh was filling the dishwasher, 'It will be a pity if he never gets to see his poor wee niece again.'

Mary seemed agitated, 'Yes, just what's happening about her disappearance. I dinnae think the police have been in touch for some time now.'

This comment was met with some tutting and shaking of heads.

Niamh pressed the buttons on the dishwasher and enquired, 'Has Margaret been in touch? Is she still at the hospital? Does anybody know?'

Elizabeth was busy choosing vegetables for dinner, 'No news yet, I sent Margaret a text message earlier asking her to let us know of any changes in his condition.'

The carers were worried as the general morale within the home was noticeably down today. The only residents apparently unaffected by their peer's misfortune were those suffering from dementia.

Elizabeth had an idea. 'Tomorrow, I think we should take the minibus out. Let's give the residents a bit of an outing, it might cheer them up.'

Niamh loved an outing, 'Good idea!'

The carers discussed ideas and decided on a visit to Portobello beach for a gentle stroll along the promenade. The mood of the residents brightened somewhat when they were told.

* * *

Margaret had maintained a vigil at the hospital for several hours, and it was now approaching midnight. Medical staff noticed how tired she was looking and advised her to go home, citing the fact there was nothing she could do here. The night would be a difficult one for Angus.

'Is he going to be OK?'

A doctor in green scrubs gave his honest opinion. 'He's still in a critical condition... I can assure you he's receiving the best of care, we just have to hope and pray for him to pull through.

When he's stable, he may need an operation.'

'What sort of operation?'

'Well, we can't say yet, he may need a stent fitted or he may be fitted with a pacemaker.'

Reluctantly, Margaret called a taxi and went home.

Sarah would have been at the old man's bedside. But, the evil power of her captor's mind denied her of the plight of her poor Uncle Angus. The elderly man's potentially life-threatening condition was just one more tragedy waiting in the wings to blight this poor woman's life.

Chapter 82

Ashok was studying the information on his PC screen.

'Hey, come and look at this.'

Jane finished her call and rushed over to see what all the excitement was about. 'What've you found?'

'I searched the database for this Lawson character, and this came up.'

Jane viewed the message displayed on his screen.

WARNING: Information relating to this search is restricted. For more information regarding access, please contact: Detective Sergeant Crosby - West Bridgford Police Station, Nottinghamshire Police.

'How odd?' said Jane, 'I've seen nothing like this before, what do you think it means?'

'There's only one way to find out.' Ash closed the message down and searched the Police Personnel Contacts database for the details of DS Crosby.

* * *

It was midday as a large white van pulled up outside number 34 Chatsworth Close. Three forensic investigators alighted from the van and slid open the side door. One retrieved a roll of *Police Line - Do Not Cross* tape from a small hopper inside the van and taped off the property.

The other two investigators pulled on white paper coveralls with hoods. Shoe covers, latex gloves and dust masks completed the final accoutre. Each attached a digital voice recorder and body-cam to the front of their overalls.

'All set?' Tracy asked.

Her suited colleague nodded, 'Ready,' came the slightly muffled reply behind the dust mask. The third member of the team reached into the back of the van and handed an aluminium equipment case to each of his colleagues. 'There you go.'

Tracy accepted hers, 'Thanks Martin, we're going to make a start. Uniform should be here soon to keep the area secure. I want you to stop anybody entering until they arrive, then you can get yourself suited and booted to join us inside. Is that OK?'

Martin nodded in agreement and sat on the ledge of the van's side door to wait for a police officer to relieve him of this temporary duty.

Tracy led her fellow investigator down the path to the front door. It had been temporarily secured with a chunky padlock. She withdrew the key tucked inside one of her gloves and released the lock. The door was gently pushed open. They switched on their body cams before stepping over the threshold.

Twenty minutes passed before Martin joined the team meticulously working their way through each room of the deserted house. Each of them frequently making voice notes to describe which room they were in and what they were seeing as the search progressed.

The search continued into the following day. A young PCSO stood patiently outside the property. His boredom was occasionally punctuated by the odd inquisitive person walking past.

Chapter 83

Sergeant Crosby was busy writing a report when his desk phone rang. He picked it up before it got to the second ring and spoke into the handset. 'DS Crosby speaking.'

Ashok introduced himself on the other end of the line.

'How can I help you Detective Constable?' Crosby asked.

'We're working on a MISPER case here in Luton and a person of interest has come to light. We think you may be able to help.'

'Oh, really, who is it?'

'It's a character we identified by a partial fingerprint. His name is Michael Lawson.'

Crosby froze at the mention of this name, stunned into silence.

'Hello? You still there?'

'Um... Yeah, yeah sorry,' the detective replied.

'We tried to search for more information on the police database, but we got a message to say that information on this character is restricted and we should contact you.'

'Yeah, that's right, what's he done?'

'We don't know yet, but he's suspected of covertly observing an individual who's gone missing. We found his fingerprint in this person's house.'

'Really?'

'Yes, the print was found on some adhesive tape which held a camera in place inside the case of a TV. So, it wasn't left by a casual visitor to the house.'

DS Crosby's heart quickened as he wiped some perspiration from his jaw, deciding what to do next.

Finally, he said, 'Listen, this person is dangerous in ways you wouldn't believe. You and your team need to be very careful how you approach him. We knew him as Micky Lawson, but he has another name now.'

Ashok picked up on a change of the officer's demeanour since mentioning the suspect's name. 'Who is he now?' he asked.

'I know this person very well, a few years ago he was heavily involved in a case I was investigating. We tried to nail him but he is a slippery character and ended up with a suspended prison sentence, which was crazy, and a new identity under the Witness

Protection Scheme. Listen, I mean it when I say tread with caution, he's dangerous. His new name under the WPS is Mark Stewart.'

Somehow, that name rang a faint bell in Ashok's mind.

'Can we meet?' Crosby asked.

'Erm, yeah sure, where did you have in mind?'

'We need somewhere quiet, I would suggest somewhere in Leamington Spa, maybe the Justice Centre in Newbold Terrace.'

Ashok reached across his desk for a pen and scribbled the address down. 'When?' he asked.

'Just a minute,' Crosby consulted his Outlook calendar, 'Um, later today?' He finally decided, 'Say 4pm?'

'Yup, we can do that. We'll meet you at the front desk.'

'Good, I'll fill you in on all you need to know then.'

The call ended.

Crosby nervously considered what he might be getting back into as he sat staring blankly at his computer screen. Whilst never proved, he still thought Lawson, AKA Stewart, was responsible for the alleged suicide of his unfortunate colleague. He opened the bottom drawer of his desk and retrieved a large folder from within. The white label on the front read *Michael Lawson*.

* * *

'Does the name Mark Stewart mean anything to you, Jane?'

Jane looked over at her colleague. The name was vaguely familiar to her, but she couldn't immediately place it. 'No, who is he?'

'Well, it would appear that Mark Stewart and Michael Lawson are the same person. Apparently, he's in the Witness Protection Scheme and Mark Stewart is his new name. DS Crosby was very cagey about all this.'

'What do you mean?'

'He warned us we're dealing with a dangerous man. There was a definite change in his tone and attitude when I mentioned Lawson's name. We're to meet him later today in Leamington Spa, he said he would fill us in then. We need to leave here at about 2pm,' Ashok estimated. 'Our meeting is at 4pm. Meanwhile, I think we should try to find out who this Mark Stewart is.'

Jane was already entering the name into the search bar of the police database. A match was found. This Mark Stewart was serving a long prison sentence. He started his sentence before flat-screen TVs were all the rage so he was unlikely to be their man.

'I'll try the electoral roll,' said Ashok.

There were no matches for *Mark Stewart*. There was a Marcus Stewart, the closest match. At the bottom of the close match list were four entries for *M. Stewart*. All Misters, and a Reverend. He could be any of these. The very last entry stood out though; M. Stewart. 35 Chatsworth Close, Luton.

'Oh my God,' said Ashok slowly.

'What... What is it?' Jane asked.

'It's the neighbour!'

'The neighbour?'

'Yeah, you know, the helpful guy living next door. His name on the electoral roll is M. Stewart. I think his first name was Mark wasn't it?'

'Yes, I think it was,' said Jane. She looked at her watch, 'Come on, let's chat to our Mr Stewart before we leave for our meeting.'

Ashok grabbed his coat and followed his colleague out of the door.

It was a ten-minute drive to Chatsworth Close. Jane broke more than one speed limit en-route. 'This neighbour,' she began, 'There is more to him than meets the eye it would seem.'

'I agree,' said her colleague, whilst surreptitiously trying to hold on tight to his seat to steady himself.

The duty PCSO outside number 34 looked up as squealing wheels pulled into the close. The speeding car pulled up sharply behind the van. Neither officer noticed the scolding look from the PCSO as they alighted from the car. They ran down the side of the distinctive blue and white 'Police Line - Do Not Cross' tape to the door of number 35. Jane rang the bell. Mozart's Sonata played leaving no doubt that the bell was working. She peered through the frosted glass of the vestibule, looking for movement. Her ears were also tuned, listening for any signs of life within.

Ashok held his warrant card aloft so the PCSO could see that he was a policeman. 'Have you seen anybody arrive or leave this house today?' he shouted over to the PCSO.

'No sir, only the postman earlier.'

'No sign of life at all?'

'None at all, sir.'

Nobody came to open the door, so the officers resorted to looking through the downstairs windows at the front of the property. Jane looked down the side of the property, 'There's no car here.'

'I think he drove a van,' Ashok recalled.

'Yeah, that's right, probably for his business?' said Jane.

Ashok nodded, 'Yeah he was some sort of film producer or editor I seem to remember.'

Jane approached the side gate leading into the back garden. It was closed, she certainly wasn't going to do a repeat performance of her undignified ingress to the garden next door a few evenings ago. Grabbing the latch, she was pleased that the gate was not locked. The officers had a cursory look in the back windows and around the garden. Jane climbed the steps and tried the door to the wooden cabin in the garden, it was secure.

'Come on,' she said. 'There's nobody here. Let's check in on Tracy next door before we go.'

Jane showed her badge to the PCSO, and both officers ducked under the tape. The front door was ajar. Jane rang the bell. A white suited figure came down the stairs in response.

'Hi Jane,' came the voice from behind the suited figure's face mask.

'Hi Tracy, we were in the area so thought we'd pop in to see how things were going. Have you found anything yet?'

Tracy pulled the mask from her face, resting it on her forehead. 'Yes, I've just discovered that the TV in the bedroom has the same setup, a mobile phone with the camera pointing into the room.'

'Hell,' said Ashok. 'Do you think all this has a sexual motive?'

'It's looking that way,' Tracy agreed.

We also found something out,' said Jane. 'The partial print your team found, it belongs to the neighbour.' Jane nodded her head towards the house next door as she finished speaking.

'Interesting,' said Tracy.

'Have you seen anybody or any signs of life there today?' Ashok asked.

'Nothing,' said Tracy.'

'We'll ask around the neighbours to see if anybody else has seen, or knows anything. This afternoon we're meeting an officer in Leamington Spa. He has more information to share about our man next door. We won't disturb you any longer though, keep up the good work in there.' Jane smiled at the competent scientific officer as she finished speaking.

The officers departed to enquire at neighbouring properties. The enquiries were fruitless, nobody had seen any movement there for several days. 'Is it strange or just a coincidence that the whereabouts of both Mrs Cooper and our Mr Stewart, or whatever his name is, are both unknown?' Jane asked, as their journey to Leamington Spa began. They discussed various scenarios on the journey, including one that linked the neighbours in some sort of romantic relationship.

It was 3.35pm when Jane's car pulled up to the car park barrier at the Leamington Spa Justice Centre. 'We're a bit early, perhaps there's time to grab a coffee before our meeting,' she said as the driver's door window slid down. She leant across and pressed a button on the intercom post.

'Can I help?' A female voice echoed.

Jane introduced herself and Ashok. 'We have a meeting with an officer who is travelling down from Nottingham, erm... DS Crosby.'

The voice asked Jane to show her warrant card to the camera next to the speaker on the intercom pole. Finally, 'OK, that's fine, please drive to the far corner of the building to the visitors car park and enter via the door facing the car park.' 'Thank you,' Jane said as the barrier lifted.

Inside the building, they could put a face to the voice at the barrier as they were greeted at the reception desk.

'Come straight through,' the receptionist said whilst pressing a hidden button to release a door at the side of reception. 'DS Crosby has already arrived. Carry on down the corridor, he's in the refectory on the left. When you're ready, you can use Interview Room 3 for your meeting. The room is a little further down the corridor on the left.'

Jane completed the formality of signing both names in and she tore off a pass for each of them. A lanyard with a plastic sleeve was passed over the counter for each of them. 'Please hand them back in on the way out,' she said with a smile.

'Thank you,' said Jane,

The officers proceeded down the corridor, both in need of a cup of coffee.

'I hope the refectory isn't too big and crowded,' said Ashok. 'We don't even know what our friend looks like, do we?'

Neither need have worried, the Nottinghamshire officer was easily identified. He was sat at a table and the only person in there who wasn't wearing a police uniform.

'That must be him over there,' Jane pointed.

The detective was a thick set individual with dark wavy hair and a swarthy appearance. As they approached, it crossed Ashok's mind that all was needed was a scruffy raincoat and he would look just like the TV detective Columbo. Crosby was preoccupied with something on his mobile phone as they arrived at his table.

He looked up as Jane said, 'DS Crosby?'

'Oh hi,' he said, rising from his chair offering his hand.

'DI Jane Patterson,' she said and shook his hand. 'And this is my colleague, DC Ashok Patel.'

Crosby reached across to shake the DC's hand as well. He patted his hands on the side of his legs and said, 'Um… Let me get you two a coffee. Take a seat, I'll be right back.'

'Wow!' said Ashok as he craned his head skyward and looked around, impressed at the comparative opulence. 'They have a refectory here, it puts our tea room-come-refectory back home to shame, doesn't it?'

Jane agreed it was far grander than anything she'd seen in any other police station she'd been in.

Crosby returned with a tray of coffees in real cups, a jug of cream and a selection of sugar and sweetener sachets. He dug into his jacket pocket and produced some small packs of biscuits as well.

Goodness!' said Jane. 'We didn't expect to get fed as well.'

'I'm diabetic,' he said. 'It's always useful to have a sugary snack in your pocket, just in case.'

'So,' said Jane whilst munching a chocolate Hobnob.

Crosby held his hand up and looked around as if somebody might be listening.

'Can I call you Jane?'

'Yes, of course.'

'Do you mind if we wait until we get into the privacy of the interview room?'

She was a bit taken aback by the request but said, 'Oh, of course.'

'Fine,' said Crosby. 'I have the room booked for 4pm. We have time to finish our coffee, then we can talk.'

Coffees were finished over some small talk, which established how long each officer had served in the force.

Chapter 84

The three occultists had been joined by fellow brother Tarquin Masala. Masala was warmly welcomed into the vicarage. He chatted excitedly. 'I saw a news report, I'd no idea that the appeal for information was for our *Lady*... It wasn't until they displayed a photograph of her that I realised the likeness to our goddess Walpurga is uncanny.'

His colleagues concurred with him. Igor logged onto his laptop so that their victim downstairs could be observed. Tarquin marvelled at the sight of her, sitting relaxed, feet up, drinking wine, watching a soap opera on TV. Tarquin leant forward for a clearer view. 'She seems so calm about all this.'

'That's because, thanks to the Master here, she doesn't know what's going on, or, even who she is anymore,' Elias grinned wickedly.

Masala quickly caught on as to the reason for this, 'Ah, I presume, the Master has used his powerful mind to suppress any fears or thoughts she might have. She doesn't know she's being held captive, does she?' He looked at Igor, expecting a response.

Igor displayed a rare show of modesty by understating what he'd done. 'Well, I've made a few suggestions to her mind, just to keep her calm and happy whilst we wait for the big day, that's all.'

The group laughed at his comment.

'I do need her to be totally aware of the evening's proceedings and activities on the day. This is when we have to manage her reactions. I don't enjoy doing this, but we will need to strap her down to allow me to carry out my duties of consummating the marriage. When this has happened, she will be mine forever. I'll assert my will upon her once again, she'll live as my wife and take part in future acts to satisfy the demons of fire.'

'Aren't you afraid that she might be recognised somewhere? Surely there's a big police investigation going on, this could lead back to you,' Toby stated.

'I've got this covered. You remember the delivery of narcotics we had?'

Elias and Toby nodded.

'That aircraft will return to the same field after the event and, you, gentlemen will assist again to get it landed and safely away with a new cargo.' Igor was amused at the looks of confusion on his disciples' faces. 'The cargo being shipped out will be me and my new bride. We are to start a new life in France under different names. It won't be the first name-change I've gone through, so it'll be easy for me.'

Tarquin was impressed, he further massaged Igor's ego, 'Amazing! Your organisational skills are impeccable, you've thought of everything.' He genuflected towards his leader as he spoke.

They opened a third bottle of wine and finished it before Igor rose from his chair, 'Come, gentlemen.' He led them up to the bedroom where they each consumed a line of cocaine from a glass-topped dresser. Each man exchanged their clothing for a monk's habit. A ring of candles were lit. The four men sat inside the pentagram facing out. When settled, Igor began his Latin incantations to summon the *Demons of Fire* once again. The candles flickered and flared vigorously when the chanting began?

Chapter 85

Interview Room 3 was a tiny room. Crosby relieved his heavy burden of a large file, several inches thick and secured by a sturdy elastic band on to the table. He also dropped a pilot's case next to his chair. The three officers sat down ready to talk.

Crosby began with a grim warning, 'Listen guys, I don't mind telling you that your *person of interest*, is a dangerous man and, quite frankly, he scares me for reasons we'll discuss later. Just be careful, that's all, don't underestimate him.' Whilst opening the leather case on the floor, Crosby continued, 'OK, you go first, tell me what you've got and why he's of interest to you.' He retrieved a notepad from the case and sat poised with a pen, ready to take notes.

Jane recounted what they knew about the mysterious Mr Stewart.

'And that's basically where we are. We don't know that he's done anything other than indulge in some voyeurism or even stalking,' Jane concluded.

Crosby sat silently, finishing his notes. He finally put his pen down and leant back in his chair.

'I think you're right to suspect he may have something to do with the disappearance of…' - he consulted his notes - 'Mrs and possibly Mr Cooper. I tell you, this character is more slippery than a greasy weasel in a barrel. Let me tell you where I am with all this.'

For two hours, Crosby summarised the copious amounts of case notes he'd brought with him whilst Jane and Ashok made their own notes.

Mr Stewart, AKA Micky Lawson was not what they expected. It was explained that he had been arrested and charged as part of a major drugs bust. He was charged with intent to supply and detained in custody whilst the case was investigated. During this period, he turned *supergrass* to save his sorry arse from a lengthy prison sentence. The net effect of this was that he became public enemy number one in the seedy underworld of drug dealers. Several were brought in and prosecuted, but there were more out there. It became known that they'd been grassed up, so a price was put on his head.

Jane was curious, 'What sentence did he receive?'

You ain't gonna believe this, at the end of the case, the judge remanded him in custody whilst he reviewed the case to consider the help and cooperation he'd given to take some bad people off the streets. A month later, he was back in court for sentencing. His solicitor put in a final plea for leniency and stressed that he was a *marked man* now and should be afforded protection under the Witness Protection Scheme. Lawson was in the dock whilst the judge further deliberated. Finally, the judge said, '*Will the defendant please stand.*' Lawson stared at the judge for what seemed like half a minute. The court was in total silence. We all expected a custodial sentence of 20 years, or thereabout. This is the bit you won't believe, he got accepted on the Witness Protection Scheme and, a suspended prison sentence. The judge thought he'd served enough of a custodial sentence whilst being investigated, so basically, he let him disappear into the ether under a different name. The investigation team were gutted!'

A stunned silence followed before Jane commented.

'Unbelievable, you're right, he is slippery!'

'You mentioned on the phone about the death of your colleague?' asked Ashok.

Crosby paused, obviously moved and upset. 'We can't prove anything on that front, but my best mate, DS Cox was the original arresting officer. This all happened at an old warehouse. DS Cox, Phil, arrested him, read him his rights and told uniform to take him away. As the police van left, Phil...' Crosby paused as his voice wobbled. He composed himself and continued. 'Phil went back into the warehouse, climbed onto the roof and jumped off. He died instantly.'

Jane struggled to see the connection. 'Sorry to ask, but why do you think this was down to Lawson?'

'Just prior to Phil taking his life, one of the uniformed officers present at the arrest noticed a weird, intense eye contact between Phil and Lawson. He said Phil seemed to lose his way whilst reading Lawson his rights. He knew these off by heart so wouldn't get 'em wrong. After pausing, he started again. There was a similar intense eye contact between Lawson and the judge just prior to sentencing. Don't ask me how, but, we reckon Lawson can influence people and plant suggestions in their mind.'

The officers were silent whilst this information was digested.

Jane broke the silence, 'Wow... Really?'

'Yup. Of course, we can't prove any of this. But, I'm convinced, there's something weird, almost supernatural, about this piece of slime.'

Crosby eventually finished sharing his information. He secured the case notes back in the folder and produced another smaller folder from his case. 'I'm going to entrust you with these notes.' He slid the folders across the table to Jane.

'Thanks, you've been very helpful.'

'You're welcome - all I say is, be very careful of this man.'

The meeting ended and the officers walked back to the car park together. In the car, Ashok was first to speak. 'Well, what did you make of that?'

'This Mr Stewart or Lawson, whatever his name is, needs looking into. I wonder if he's returned home yet?'

Jane checked her text messages, the phone had buzzed a couple of times whilst in the meeting. She opened one from the Tracy and quickly read it.

She paraphrased to Ashok, 'It seems the Forensics team have finished their search of the house. Other than the TV, nothing else of interest was found. The TV will be deconstructed tonight, but she's certain the setup will be the same.'

Jane's fingers set to work texting back to enquire if the neighbour at number 35 had come back.

Less than a minute passed before a reply came back to say no. Both officers, minds racing, uttered together, 'We...' They both paused to let the other speak.

Jane resumed, 'I was going to say that we need to investigate number 35. First thing tomorrow, we should get a warrant and search the property.'

It had been a long day; they drove home to the sounds of Chill FM. Neither was really listening though as their minds were too occupied digesting the bizarre things they'd learned.

The journey back was a good one. It was 9.30pm and Jane was already back in her flat, showered and wearing her PJs. She snacked on a noodle pot whilst sitting on the floor of her lounge leaning against the sofa. She opened the case notes and began reading.

Crosby's name cropped up frequently, as did his best mate, Phil's. They were on the Drug Squad, and their team had carried out a lengthy surveillance and undercover operation as part of the investigation. The drug smuggling operation was a big one. Lawson, for one, was clearly implicated, but the team held out on any arrests to be made, hoping they could secure convictions on the main players. They needed to understand who was supplying them.

Jane's eyes were becoming unfocused. She looked at the clock, expecting it to be about midnight but was surprised to see that it was a little after 2.45am. She had just reached the bit in the case notes where the identity of one of the undercover officers had been compromised. His life was in danger, so the team had no choice but to raid the HQ of this enormous drug operation. An armed response unit was assembled. A warehouse and two properties were raided simultaneously. Several arrests were made, including Lawson.

The final document Jane read, detailed the last job that DS Cox would attend. It contained the tragic details of his death and an account from the uniformed officer who witnessed the extraordinary interaction between Lawson and Cox.

Jane decided it was time for bed. The strange thing was that once in bed, her mind did not shut down and it seemed an age before she actually drifted off to sleep.

Chapter 86

Jane's meandering thoughts during a fitful sleep raced in panic; an alarm was going off, there was a fire in her flat. She quickly woke, relieved to find no fire, just her alarm clock beside the bed dutifully waking her up with its monotonous tone. She'd managed very little sleep and was still tired. Whilst sitting on the edge of her bed, she stretched her arms up, reaching, to regain renewed energy. Over breakfast, she recalled the leads that must be followed today.

* * *

Ashok was already at his desk when she arrived in the office at 7.30am.

'Morning Jane.'

She dumped the case notes on her desk. 'Hi Ash. Right, how are we doing?'

He got up from his chair and retrieved a wad of printouts from the printer in the corner. He laid them on Jane's desk. 'What's this?'

'It's the paperwork to get a warrant for the neighbour's house. You need to sign it and then we can get the boss to sign it and get it processed.'

'Ah, good work.'

Ash patted the thick pile of case notes on Jane's desk. 'I guess we need to work through this lot.'

'We do, I've already started, I sat up till nearly 3am reading through them. It was an enormous drugs bust, it made the national news as the biggest haul ever seized, worth almost two million pounds on the street. Here's a question for you Ash, do you remember the neighbour having a partner?'

'In the back of my mind whilst we were investigating Mr Cooper's disappearance, I do remember reading something where Mrs Cooper referred to a best friend. I got the impression that she lived next door but she's since returned to Ukraine.' 'Yeah, that fits in with what I read in these case notes. She was in fact a failed asylum seeker and was due to be deported.' 'Due to? Why wasn't she?'

'Stewart, or whoever he is, intervened. They went to the Home Office to appeal and by the time the appeal was over, she'd been given indefinite leave to remain. There's a handwritten note in the margin of the case notes about this.'

'What does it say?'

'Well, it's basically highlighting another occurrence of leniency and suggests our friend can somehow influence people's minds.'

'You can't really believe all that can you? Surely it's just… well, a coincidence isn't it?'

'Whilst we wait for our warrant to enter the property, I think we should have a look round the grounds. Do me a favour, Ash.'

'Yup?'

'Go down and see the desk sergeant, ask him if he can spare a dog unit for an hour this morning. I'd also like to look in the wooded area at the end of the back garden.'

'Consider it done.' The young DC left the office to speak with the desk sergeant.

Jane continued reviewing some more of the case notes. Barely ten minutes had passed before she heard the familiar footfall of Chief Inspector Grant walking along the corridor. The door opened.

'Morning sir, can I get you a coffee?'

Grant paused en route to his office door beside Jane's desk. He peered over the top of his glasses. 'Morning Jane. Yes please, you know how I like it, you must want something.'

A few minutes later, Jane entered Grant's office carrying two steaming mugs of coffee.

He was busy reading through the request for the warrant and didn't look up. 'What's all this about?'

Jane spent the next half hour stating her case and summarising yesterday's meeting in Leamington Spa. Whilst the DCI read through a couple of documents from the case notes, Jane's smartphone buzzed in her pocket. She viewed the screen and noticed a new email from Forensics. The email confirmed a similar setup of a covert camera hidden in the second TV. Two more fingerprints were lifted from inside, and both were a match to Michael Lawson. Nothing else of significance was found in the house. Grant heard a jubilant but muted, 'Yes!'

'What's that?'

'Forensics have just confirmed that another TV in the house has been tampered with, they also found two fingerprints that match to our mysterious neighbour.'

'We need to find this Lawnton character.'

'Lawson,' corrected Jane.

'What? oh yes, I mean Lawson.' He'd heard enough, he scribbled a signature on the warrant request, 'OK, I'll speak to the super. Meanwhile, do what you have to do, it looks like you might be on to something. Good work!'

'Yes, sir. Thank you.'

Chapter 87

A Dog Section van was already parked outside number 35 when Jane arrived in her car with Ashok in the passenger seat.

'What are we looking for?' Ashok asked.

'You know what, I don't know, I just thought it would be a good place to start. There are some woods at the end of the garden that I'm interested in as well.'

'Really? What do you think might be there?'

'Who knows. A buried body, maybe two.'

'Two?'

'Yeah, remember, we never found out what happened to Mr Cooper. No body, nothing. Supposing our mysterious Mr Lawson is behind his disappearance. He's a common denominator in both cases, wouldn't you agree?'

The cautious reply to Jane showed that he didn't really believe in her conjecture. 'Yeah,' he said slowly, 'I suppose.' He paused to think of a reason Jane's theory could be wrong.

Ashok continued, 'It's unlikely though. The woods are full of dog walkers. Don't you think a dog walker or their beloved pooch might have stumbled across a buried body?'

'Maybe, but let's do it anyway, It'll pass the time till the warrant comes through.'

A uniformed officer alighted from the white van and approached Jane's car. 'Morning!' he said.

'Morning, officer?'

'Constable Turnbull, ma'am,' then he stated the obvious, 'Dog Unit!'

'Yes, so I see,' said Jane, slightly amused.

'What can me and Chunks do for you?'

'Chunks?'

'Yeah, my dog, a Cocker. It's Mr Chunks really, but he answers to Chunks as well.'

Jane smiled. *What a sweet, unusual name* she thought, before saying, 'I want him to inspect around this house and the wooded area at the end of the garden. We're waiting for a warrant to come through, giving us permission to enter the property. When that comes through, we need to give inside a good going over as well.'

'What exactly are we looking for?'

'Oh, I don't know, anything and everything... Drugs? A body?'

Turnbull baulked a bit at the mention of a body, 'Really?'

'Possibly,' said Jane. 'Shall we start?'

The dog handler retrieved a lively looking Cocker Spaniel from the back of his van. Ashok watched his enthusiastic tail wagging whilst a lengthy lead was attached to his harness. It was obvious from the start that Chunks was going to be very keen. In no time at all, he'd checked both Ashok and Jane out, as well as relieving himself over Jane's front nearside wheel.

'Thanks for that, Mr Chunks,' she said.

Apparently pleased that his little indiscretion had been acknowledged, his tail seemed to wag even faster.

The dog then began his search of the property, pausing at every bush, plant, and shrub in the front garden. All of them obviously passed examination with his highly efficient nose. Every so often, Turnbull would point to areas for inspection and offer encouragement to his four-legged partner.

The search moved to the back garden. No nook or cranny was left. The dog inspected everything, enjoying the task. It wasn't until the search moved down the garden when things took a different turn. The keen canine nose sniffed around the steps and entrance to the log cabin. He spent longer in this area than any other so far inspected. Suddenly, in front of the cabin doorway, he sat down, looked at his handler, then back at the door to the cabin.

'He's found something,' Turnbull said.

'What is it? Do we know?' Jane asked.

'We need to get inside, then he'll pinpoint what he's found.'

Jane pulled her phone out of her pocket and called DI Grant. Ashok listened to the half of the conversation he could hear.

'Hello sir... yes, we're at the house now with a dog handler. The dog's picked up something. There's a log cabin in the garden. Security is heavy on the door. The dog is indicating something around the door area, we need to get inside. Any news on the warrant?' A pause while Jane listened to the response. She ended the call with an 'OK sir, will do.'

Jane was frustrated. 'We've gotta do this by the book, he's going to see if he can expedite the warrant now. He'll call back shortly.' She then turned to the dog handler who was wrestling a dog tug toy with Mr Chunks. 'Can we look at the top of the garden, where it backs onto the woods?'

'Yeah, sure,' said Turnbull. Chunks obediently dropped the toy when commanded. The pair of them went up to investigate the perimeter fence. Nearing the end of the fenced area, Turnbull looked over, hearing Jane's mobile ring. After a short conversation, she hung up and beckoned them back.

'We've got a warrant,' she shouted over as they approached. 'I want to get inside that cabin. Off you go, Ash, break the door down.'

Ashok was slightly built, too slightly built to get through the secure door. The blacked-out windows were also secure with toughened glass. The dog excitedly patrolled the bottom of the doorway with his sensitive nose. He frequently paused and looked up at his handler to indicate a continued strong interest. In fact, he seemed almost more keen to gain access than Jane.

Ashok abandoned his attempt to gain entry. 'It's no good, we need to get uniform down here with the Big Red Key.'

Half an hour later, a patrol car arrived. Two burly officers looked forward to the challenge of gaining access to the cabin. A dozen attempts were made before the door even showed signs of giving way. Some splitting and cracking noises came from the sturdy frame encasing the door. The other officer took over, three more bashes and the door swung open.

'Thank you, gentlemen,' Jane said. She looked at the dog handler, 'OK let Chunks do his work.'

The interior of the cabin was dark and there was a musty, damp smell inside. Officer Turnbull stood in the doorway's threshold and allowed the dog free access off the lead. His little tail wagged, confirming the pleasure he had in doing so. The dog handler looked around at the array of technology. Computers and monitors were on the desk and attached to the wall. A shelf to the left festooned with what must be hundreds of CDs or DVDs, he couldn't tell which from the doorway. A large poster was to the right, he'd no idea who the lady was on the poster, some Greek goddess maybe. He read the caption at the bottom *Saint Walpurga*, whoever that was. Chunks suddenly stopped and sat. He looked at the desk drawer then up to his handler.

'Good boy,' said Turnbull. He stepped inside the cabin, found a light switch, and gently opened the drawer to look inside.

'Anything?' came Jane's call from outside.

'Erm, yeah, we've hit the jackpot!'

'What is it?' she entered the cabin, tripping over the edge of a rug in the middle of the floor.

'I'm no expert, but I reckon Chunks here has found some cocaine, a lot of cocaine. Good boy!'

Jane peered into the drawer, Ashok quickly joined them. 'Wow,' said Ashok as he counted four plump plastic bags full of white powder.

'Hmm,' said Jane. 'It would seem that our Mr Lawson hasn't been behaving himself, has he?'

Their attention was then diverted towards the behaviour of the dog. He was clawing frantically at the edge of the rug that Jane had just tripped over. Turnbull pulled the rug aside to reveal the bare boards of the floor. They stared curiously at the crudely painted pentagram that was partially revealed.

'Just a minute,' said Jane, stooping low to examine the floor. 'What's this?'

They studied the centre of the pentagram to see a straight join running across several of the floorboards. The dog handler removed the rug completely to reveal a flush brass handle inset into the floor. Mr Chunks was very excited and was sniffing profusely at the narrow gap bordering a trapdoor.

Ashok pulled at the ring embedded in the brass handle and pulled. Nothing moved, the trapdoor was too heavy or stuck. On a shelf, next to some black candles, Jane found a small toolbox. She looked inside and found a pair of pliers. 'Here, try these,' she said as she passed them to Ashok.

Once again, Ashok tried pulling at the brass ring. Finally, the door creaked opened.

Chunks wanted to get in there, but for his own safety was held back by his handler.

The officers peered into the void that had opened up in the floor. The dank, damp smell intensified. Despite the centre light in the cabin being on, the shadows below would reveal none of the secrets within.

'I've got a torch in the van,' Turnbull said. 'I'll get it.' He secured the excited Mr Chunks to a post on the veranda outside the cabin.

In his absence, Jane took a better look around the cabin. 'You know what I think?' 'What's that?' Ashok replied.

'I reckon our mystery Mr Lawson worships the devil.'

Ashok nodded in agreement, 'It sure looks that way.'

Turnbull returned and shone the torch down the gaping hole. Things still weren't clear, just a sea of cobwebs reflecting the light straight back out.

'Somebody's going to have to go down there,' Jane said hinting at her colleague.

Ashok rose to the challenge, 'I guess that somebody's gonna be me.'

'I've got some paper overalls in the van, if you like,' the well-equipped dog handler offered.

Ashok was grateful for the offer and was extra pleased that the overalls also had a hood. Jane produced a pair of latex gloves, 'Here, wear these as well.'

The young detective gingerly lowered himself into the hole until the floor of the office was waist high to him. Jane was mildly amused to see her partner's antics, he looked as if he was trying to swat a bothersome wasp away, when in fact he was just clearing away the mass of cobwebs in preparation to fully submerge himself into the dark depths of the floor void. Ashok slithered around, eventually disappearing from sight.

'Can you see anything?' Jane shouted down the hole.

The reply was muffled, 'Not yet!'

A few minutes passed when Jane heard her colleague mutter something inaudible.

'Pardon? What did you say?'

'Oh my God, No…'

'What is it? What've you found?'

'I'm coming out!'

A hot and flushed Ashok reappeared, laying flat on his back.

'What is it? What's down there?' Jane asked.

'I think we might be investigating a murder now.'

'You've found a body?'

'No, I think I've found two.' Ashok stood and climbed out of the hole.

'Two?' Jane questioned.

'Yeah, I'm pretty sure that's what they are. They're hidden over there, below the entrance steps, both in body bags.' Jane was straight on her mobile phone to call the DCI.

'Hello sir, our investigation has just got more serious. This is to be confirmed, but we think we've just found two bodies at the Lawson property.' She paused as she listened to the response. 'Yes sir, we need a forensics team and a pathologist down here straight away.'

Whilst making the call, she studied the large poster on the wall. Placing the mobile phone back in her bag she said, 'Ash...'

Her colleague was struggling out of the dirty paper overalls, 'Yeah, what is it?'

'Look.'

Ash turned his head to follow where her eyes were looking. 'Remind you of anyone?' she asked.

Ashok studied the poster, 'Good God! It's a dead ringer for Mrs Cooper, I'd not noticed it before.'

Jane had a very uneasy feeling about yet another coincidence.

Chapter 88

The police investigation moved on rapidly, following the gruesome discoveries beneath the foundations of the log cabin.

A pathologist attended, but his physical size rendered it impossible for him to examine the suspected bodies beneath the floor. A decision was taken to remove the small terrace and steps at the front of the cabin to gain access. After a preliminary peek inside each body bag, the pathologist confirmed their suspicions.

A forensics team was now crawling all over the property, including inside the main house. Other items were retrieved from the exposed floor void. Evidence bags containing computers, laptops and DVDs were removed from the site. These items were handed over to a specialist team for examination. As evening closed in, lighting was erected in the garden, allowing the team to work on through the night. The area that once contained the steps up to the cabin was tented off to preserve any evidence in case inclement weather closed in.

* * *

Chief Inspector Grant addressed his team at the station. 'It looks like we have two unexplained deaths, probably murders. We know that we've two MISPERS. The pathologist needs time to examine the bodies. Jane, how's that going? Can we expect post-mortems to happen tonight?'

'Yes sir, PMs will be conducted by Mr Jackson Olewiler tonight. I'm going over to the morgue straight after this meeting, just to see if I can get an early sign on identities of the deceased.'

'OK, do that. Ashok, you've helped to put what we have together, I want you to carry on working closely with Jane, supporting the SIO and her team. Now then Jane, can you tell us what we've got?'

There were 20 detectives assembled in the incident room. Grant took a seat as Jane walked to the front of the room.

'OK, Earlier today, DC Patel discovered two body bags concealed below an outbuilding of number 35 Chatsworth Close. We were there as part of a MISPER investigation. Sarah Cooper has not been seen since she left her house, number 34 Chatsworth Close, nearly two weeks ago. Mysteriously, Mrs Cooper's husband also disappeared about two years ago. No trace of him was ever found. The pathologist has briefly looked inside the bags and confirmed we have two bodies.'

Jane continued to fill the team in on their investigation so far. She gestured towards the back of the room and continued, 'Please make yourself familiar with the bagged items of evidence at the back of the room. I'd like to know if there is any significance to the crossbow recovered next to the body bags. Our main person of interest is Michael Lawson, AKA Mark Stewart. We know he's a dangerous man and should not be underestimated. A recent picture is on the info-wall. Any questions?'

One detective put his hand up.

'Yes?'

'Are you thinking that the discovery of two bodies will solve both MISPER cases?'

'No, both bodies according to the pathologist have been dead a long time, way before Mrs Cooper disappeared. Hopefully, I'll know more after the PM results come out.'

Chief Inspector Grant watched the DI's confident performance, thinking she would go far.

'Meanwhile, I want to know where Mrs Cooper's car is. I also want to know where Lawson's vehicle is. Jonesy,' she pointed at the ginger-haired detective, 'I want you to follow that up, details of both vehicles are on the info-wall.'

'Yes ma'am.'

'Stamford!' she called as she pointed to a nerdy-looking detective sitting at the far end of the conference table.

DC Nick Stamford nervously said, 'Yes ma'am?'

'As our resident technical expert on mobile phones, I want you following up on Lawson's phone - I need to know where it might be and when it was last used, OK?'

'Yes ma'am.'

'I would also like you to liaise with the Computer Forensics team. Let's see if they come up with something.' She looked around at those assembled, 'Jacky!' she called. The petite frame of DC Jacky Potts looked up from her note taking, 'You're pretty good on the technical stuff, I want you to team up with Nick on this.'

'Yes ma'am, will do.'

'Thank you ladies and gentlemen,' she concluded.

The room broke into a hubbub of conversation. Sub-teams were already forming, tasks being shared and accepted throughout.

Jane grabbed her coat and bag before looking around once more at the crowded room. She was pleased to see people getting organised. Sub-teams were already talking and discussing items of evidence gathered so far. 'Come on Ash, let's go.'

Chapter 89

Jane drove round the back of the Luton & Dunstable Hospital and parked in a space reserved for police cars.

Neither had attended a post mortem before so both were nervous. Ashok pressed the button on the door access system. The door lock buzzed and they filed through the heavy security door.

A portly figure appeared at the far end of the short corridor. Dressed in scrubs, white wellingtons and rubber gloves, a muffled voice spoke from behind a surgical mask.

'Detectives, welcome, come on through.'

As they approached the pathologist, Jane introduced themselves.

The pathologist reciprocated the introduction, 'Jackson Olewiler. I'm just about to look at your two bodies, are you ready?'

They both nodded nervously.

He swung a door open. 'Here, you can watch from the viewing gallery.'

The pathologist followed them into the glass-fronted room overlooking the cutting room. He pulled the surgical mask away from his face, 'The room's miked up so we can talk to each other whilst I'm conducting the PM. Ask any questions as we go. I'll record my findings as we proceed and let you know if I find anything that might help your investigation. Is that OK?' The officers nodded.

'Have either of you ever attended a PM before?' Both shook their heads.

'Ah... OK' he pointed to a small grey metal cupboard. 'Sick bags in there. The bathroom is through that door over there.'

He turned on his heel, 'Let's get started then.'

The confident pathologist left the room. The detectives sat down in what looked like theatre seats, it was as if they were about to watch a performance.

The cutting room was brightly lit. A counter top skirted two sides of the room, one side looked like a giant filing cabinet. Ashok counted five columns of three oversized drawers. The centre of the room was dominated by four operating tables, two of them occupied with a cadaver bag.

Jackson appeared the other side of the glass wall. He looked up to the viewing room, 'Can you hear me?' They both nodded.

'Erm ... I can't hear you.'

'Sorry, yes, we can hear you.'

'Splendid! Let's do this then, I'll start with this one first,' he lightly patted the smaller looking dark green body bag. He repositioned his mask and adjusted a Madonna-style microphone to the side of his face.

An assistant stepped forward and slowly undid the fastenings along the top of the bag. He gently pulled the folds of the bag down to reveal the contents, a blackened, shrivelled, corpse.

Jackson spoke as he worked. 'This is a female, remarkably well preserved. The body was deposited in the bag very soon after death, I would say. This has helped preserve the contents in an almost mummified state.'

'How long ago did she die?' Jane asked.

'Hmm, difficult to say exactly, but I would say years rather than months,'

'Any indications of her age at death?'

He examined various parts of the body and looked inside the mouth. 'I would estimate that we have a 35 to 45-yearold here. I'll need to run some biomechanics on bones. The bone structure should give a more accurate result plus or minus three years.'

Jane was quickly taking notes. 'Thank you.'

'Right, let's see if we can establish a cause of death.'

His assistant carefully cut the grey tracksuit and other clothing from the corpse, then helped to remove the body bag so the corpse was lying unclothed on the table. Clothing was deposited in a clear plastic evidence bag.

The pathologist started a visual inspection of the body first. 'Skull appears intact, no obvious signs of impact. Eyes have decomposed to a state that's unlikely to reveal any clues.' He looked closely at the front of the neck, 'Hmm, there does seem to be some deformation around the front of the neck.' The assistant passed a camera. Jackson took several pictures of the throat area from different angles.

'What are you thinking? Strangulation?'

'Too soon to say for certain, I need to examine the Hyoid bone and larynx for damage.'

The assistant swung a tray of surgical instruments over the table. Ashok looked away as a scalpel was used to expertly open up the trachea and surrounding area.

'Ah yes, here we are.'

'What is it?'

'I can see Hyoid bone and laryngeal fractures. Typical injuries that can occur with manual strangulation. I would normally look for other indications like petechial haemorrhages on the face and eyes for example, but the condition of the body is too far gone. So that's the best you're going to get as to the cause of death at the moment. I'll request a toxicology report as a matter of thoroughness.'

'Is there anything that might help us identify the body?'

'I'll carry out a DNA test, but that's only useful if her DNA is recorded somewhere. Hold on a minute,' he went back to the body bag and started searching amongst the detritus inside. 'Ah, this might help.'

Jane was eager to know what he had found. 'What is it?' Ashok sat quietly, obviously not enjoying the process.

Jackson held some tweezers aloft, gripping some black matter from the bag.

'What is it?' Jane repeated.

'After death, certain changes in the body occur. There's an amount of shrinkage that takes place as it dries out. Skin sloughs off. If I'm right, this blackened item here was once skin on the victim's hand. It's all brittle and crispy at the moment.'

Jane was impatient, 'How does that help us identify the victim?'

'Simple, we'll try rehydrating it. With luck we may get some fingerprints.'

The assistant left the laboratory and quickly returned with paraphernalia to hydrate the crispy skin sample.

The pathologist began wielding the scalpel again, opening up the thorax. Jane watched with interest while Ashok excused himself, muttering something about needing the bathroom. Several organs were removed from the chest cavity. The state of each made them mostly unrecognisable. Each organ was placed in a tray and weighed. The assistant recorded weights of each as they progressed.

'It's as I thought, decomposition of these organs will make it virtually impossible to carry out more tests.'

Ashok resumed his seat in the viewing room just in time to see and hear the pathologist start up a powered bone saw. It looked and sounded like a dentist's drill, but with a small circular saw attached. The assistant placed a full face mask over both of their heads. Jackson started sawing through the top of the skull.

'I need to get back to check some stuff if you don't mind.'

Jane made a dismissive wave and Ashok left the viewing room again. She smiled to herself, realising her colleague just didn't have the stomach for gore.

Jane reached into her bag when she heard her mobile frantically buzzing, demanding attention. She swiped the screen to answer the call.

'DI Patterson.'

She recognised the voice on the other end as belonging to DC Stamford. 'Hi Nick, what've you got?'

'It's Lawson's mobile phone, I contacted the mobile phone company and they were very helpful. Lawson's mobile was last detected yesterday by a mast in, wait for it… Hampshire!' 'That's where Mrs Cooper picked up a speeding ticket, isn't it?'

'Yeah. There's something else ma'am.'

'What's that?'

'The mobile phone company faxed me a map, circling the area where the mobile phone could be'

'Yes, and?'

'I checked and that speeding ticket was picked up just outside the area indicated on the map. Coincidence or what?'

Jane thought for a moment. 'No, Nick, not a coincidence. Good work. Who's coordinating the ANPR search?'

'That was Jones, ma'am.'

'Yes, put him on will you?'

Jonesy's Welsh accent was next to speak on the phone.

'Yes ma'am?'

'Jonesy, I want you to liaise with Nick please, he's some interesting information that might lead to the whereabouts of Lawson. I want you to get Hampshire traffic police to focus on this area looking for Lawson's and Mrs Cooper's vehicles.'

'Will do ma'am, anything else?'

'No Jonesy, that's all for now. Keep up the good work, thanks.'

Jane diverted her attention back to the PM again.

About ten minutes later the pathologist had completed his task and was ready to move on to the second body.

Once removed from its protective bag, Jane could see that it was in a similar state to the first. Still alone in the viewing room, she watched and listened.

'We've a male here, looks like a jogger by what he's wearing. I would say this person's death was more recent than our mystery lady over there, by several months, maybe a year, I'd say.'

Jane looked at the clothing, a black or navy running vest, trimmed with a white border around the neck and armholes, some black running pants, grey socks and white trainers with fluorescent orange soles.

'Is there a make on those trainers?'

The pathologist looked, 'Yes, Asics.'

'Thanks.' Jane grabbed her mobile phone again. This time, her thumbs danced over the screen, typing out a text message to Ashok.

'Ash, do you still have the old case notes for Mr Cooper on your desk? If you do, check what clothing Mr Cooper was thought to be wearing when he was last seen. Call or text me when you know J.'

Jackson bagged the clothing up and added it to the growing collection of evidence bags on a bench at the side of the room. The body was laid on its back whilst he carried out his visual examination.

'No obvious signs of trauma, as far as I can see.'

He looked at his assistant, 'Can you help me turn the body over please?'

The two carefully rearranged the corpse so it was face down. Immediately he spotted something. He leaned over for a closer examination of the back of the neck.

'Hmm.'

'What? What is it?'

'There seems to be some injury to the foramen magnum. Pass the forceps, please.'

The assistant passed over some forceps. He struggled to extract what looked like splintered wood from the corpse.

'It's no use. Whatever it is, it's in too deep. We have to open up the skull and go in from that way.'

'What is the foramen magnum?'

'Ah sorry, the foramen magnum is the hole at the base of the skull where the spinal cord passes through into the brain.' Jane added to her notes.

Out came the bone saw once more. A neat line was cut around the top of the skull before removing the lid to reveal the shrivelled brain inside.

The brain was carefully removed and placed in a stainless steel dish.

Jackson examined it closely in silence, occasionally pulling and poking at the contents of the dish. 'Well, there's your cause of death.'

'What've you found?'

'This brain has received some severe trauma. There appears to be splinters of wood and small shards of metal throughout. There's a hole at the base of the skull, which was the entry point for what looks like an arrow or crossbow bolt. If the victim was standing at the time of impact, I would say that the trajectory of the missile was from below.'

'Crossbow bolt, did you say?'

'Yes, that's what it looks like.'

The significance of the crossbow in the floor void of the log cabin now became clear.

Jane's phone buzzed as a message arrived.

'Black long legged shorts, navy running vest trimmed with white edging, trainers with bright orange soles, no make specified and grey socks with a red 'W' logo on the side, Wilson I think.'

'Jackson,' she called. The pathologist looked up, 'Can you check the socks you bagged up and tell me if there is a make or logo on them, please?'

The assistant didn't need to look, he remembered, and spoke for the first time. His voice was soft and barely audible, but Jane could just hear him. 'They're Wilson socks. I recognise the 'W' logo.'

'Thank you.'

Her phone buzzed again, another message from Ashok. 'Any update?'

Jane quickly typed a reply,

'I think the second corpse is the body of Mr Cooper.'

The pathologist had moved onto the chest cavity and was weighing the organs from the body - 'I'll ask for a toxicology report and get a DNA profile for this one as well.' He examined the hands closely. 'Hmm, I might get a half decent fingerprint off this one. It's quite well preserved. I'll add anything I get to my report. You should have it by tomorrow afternoon.'

'OK Jackson, that's perfect. I think I've seen and heard enough, thanks. How long will it take to see if you're able to get fingerprints off of our lady there?'

'The skin sample is soaking in a saline solution. I reckon we might have something in 24 hrs.'

'Great, thank you. Can I take the clothing bags with me?'

'Sure, I'll get Colin here to bring them round to you.'

'Thanks Jackson, I'll look out for your report.'

With the help of the assistant, Jane packed the evidence bags into the boot of her car.

Chapter 90

Time was running out in the race to find Sarah. The investigating team were meeting to update themselves on progress. Jane chaired the meeting with the Chief Inspector by her side.

'We've had some test results back. I can confirm that after a DNA match, one of the bodies recovered is that of Mr Steven Cooper, the husband of Mrs Cooper. He disappeared a couple of years ago. Cause of death was massive brain trauma from a crossbow bolt to the base of the skull. The pathologist said he would have been dead before he hit the ground. This might explain the crossbow found close to the bodies. Lawson's prints are all over it. Mr Olewiler has done some great work and managed to rehydrate the skin from the hands of the female body, enabling him to get some fingerprints from the body. We got a match on the fingerprint database. We can now confirm the female body is that of Ms Karyn Kedjerski. She was originally a failed asylum seeker from Ukraine. The report states that cause of death was probably through manual strangulation. She died several months before Mr Cooper. We believe she was the partner of Lawson. I think if we find Lawson we'll find Mrs Cooper, hopefully still alive. How are we getting on trying to trace the whereabouts of Lawson?'

Stamford began, 'We've an area in Hampshire that has been highlighted by the mobile phone company. It's about 12 square miles in total. Lawson has used his phone frequently over the last couple of weeks, all in this general area.'

'Thanks Nick, keep on it, see if we can narrow this area down.'

'Will do, ma'am.'

'What about vehicles? Anything back from ANPR?' Jonesy looked up. 'Nothing yet ma'am.'

'OK, keep on it Jonesy.'

'There is one thing you may not have heard, ma'am.'

Jane looked over at DC Geraldine Golding. The normally quietly spoken detective raised her voice to be heard. 'I got this information just before we started this meeting.'

'What is it Geraldine?'

'Because of the TV appeal for information Crimestoppers have had a response. A shopkeeper, Mrs Gladys Robinson, has left a message claiming that Lawson has recently been shopping at her corner shop.'

'Where's the shop located?' Jane was excited at this potential breakthrough.

'It's in a small village called King's Somborne. I Googled it. It's in Hampshire, not too far away from the A30.'

'That's interesting. Ash, where was that speeding ticket issued again?'

Ashok went to the back of the room to check the evidence table. He picked up the plastic sleeve containing the speeding ticket. 'Let's see, it was on the A30, er…just outside Stockbridge.'

Stamford looked up after examining the OS map provided by the phone company. 'And,' he began, 'King's Somborne is just on the edge of where the phone company say Lawson's phone was last used.'

Jane was about to speak again when Stamford broke in excitedly, 'King's Somborne is just three miles south of Stockbridge on this map!'

'Well, that narrows it down, doesn't it?' Jane felt the investigation had just taken a great leap forward. 'It look's like our focus has moved to Hampshire. Any news from Computer Forensics?'

'Yes ma'am, I have the report here. There's nothing much on hard disk drives, but it does say that the Dark Web has been frequently used. Details of a Dark Web session are encrypted and deleted at the end of the session. It's virtually impossible to get anything from that. There's some incriminating evidence on the DVDs we seized though.'

'What's that?'

'Well, he's been covertly observing his neighbour for what looks like several years. That was the purpose of the mobile phones installed in the TVs. There are recordings of Mrs Cooper and her husband having sex. There are more recordings of Mrs Cooper alone, presumably after she lost her husband. In most of these, she's in various states of undress.'

Jane looked disgusted. 'Oh, the poor woman. Do you think any of these recordings have been shared on porn sites?'

'It doesn't give any sign here, but not impossible.'

A general discussion followed. A young DC seemed to have analysed the facts and concluded the discussion. 'I think this Lawson guy has some sort of master plan. I reckon he wanted his neighbour for a specific purpose, something he was working on for several years, remember the satanic connotations? If you think about it, we are fairly certain he's responsible for Mr Cooper's death. He needed him out of the way for whatever reason. Once isolated, Mrs Cooper became vulnerable so, in rides Lawson on his white charger, Mr Nice Guy, offering help and support, gaining her confidence each day. She fell for it and he could finally implement his master plan. I reckon that he wouldn't want to put this plan in jeopardy by publishing these recordings on a porn site, in the unlikely event that things get back to her and his plan is ruined. Whatever, we conclude that she's in grave danger.'

'I agree, we need to find her as soon as we can. Great work everybody, keep at it, we will meet again tomorrow evening.'

The meeting broke up and Jane turned to Ashok, 'Fancy a trip to Hampshire?'

'You bet!'

She grabbed her bag and coat. 'I'll pick you up at 6.30am tomorrow morning. Oh, and bring an overnight bag, we may need to book into an hotel.'

Grant stood nearby listening in to plans. 'I'll give someone at Hampshire Constabulary a courtesy call, just to let them know you are following leads on their patch. They should give you any support you might need down there.'

'Thank you. We may not get back for tomorrow evening's meeting though.'

Grant held his hand up, 'No matter. Just check in regularly so we can keep each other informed. I'll chair tomorrow's meeting if you can't. Well done so far, it looks like we might solve several crimes here, The Super will be pleased. Off you go, and remember that this Lawnton character is dangerous.'

'Lawson, sir.'

'Oh yes, Lawson. You will call for backup if you need it, won't you?'

'Of course, sir.'

Chapter 91

King's Somborne was a sleepy Hampshire village unspoilt by time. Jane drove through slowly, thinking the village shop would be easy to spot on the main through road. At the point where they were about to drive out of the village again, Ashok noticed a weathered sign by the road. He suddenly pointed, 'Look there! That sign, *The Olde Shoppe*, it's to the left.'

Jane turned the corner in the direction indicated. The road almost doubled back on itself until it finally opened out onto a village green area, complete with a pond. The shop stood opposite the green, there was a parking space at the front of the quaint looking building.

The officers got out of the car and walked up to the shop door. Jane pushed it open and a loud *ding* announced their arrival.

The far end of the shop was taken up with a small post office counter. The front area of the shop was laid out mini-supermarket style, selling mostly groceries, but it also included a small hardware section. Nobody manned the checkout area. The only customer was at the post office counter, an elderly lady, wrapped up well in the unlikely event that the weather might take a turn for the worst. She was having a good old natter with the elderly-looking post office clerk.

Gladys Robinson diverted her attention to see who had entered the shop. She ended the conversation, 'Well it's lovely to see you Maud. Do give my regards to your husband, I hope he feels better soon. I'd better go now, I have customers.'

Maud put her purse into her shopping bag, 'Yes, of course. Bye Gladys, I'll see you next week.'

The elderly shopper walked with a stoop and was supported by a walking stick. 'Morning,' she politely nodded, as she passed the detectives.

'Good Morning;' they said in unison.

Ashok did the gentlemanly thing and opened the door for her.

'Thank you young man, bye bye.'

'Mrs Robinson?' Jane enquired as she approached the post office counter.

How can I help you?' she asked, surprised that this stranger knew her name.

Jane showed her identity badge as Ashok arrived by her side, also reaching for his. 'I'm Detective Inspector Jane Patterson. This is my colleague Detective Constable Ashok Patel. We're from Bedfordshire Police and we are responding to your message left on Crimestoppers.'

'Oh my,' the lady said. 'That was quick and you've come so far.'

'Can we talk?' Jane asked.

'Yes, of course, what would you like to know?'

'Would you mind if we closed the shop for a short while so we can have a proper chat?' Jane enquired.

'Doh, where are my manners?' Mrs Robinson said. 'I expect you would like a cup of tea as well.'

'That would be very nice, do you mind?'

'No, of course not my dear, give me a minute, will you?'

The shopkeeper slid a bolt across to release a doorway on the end of the counter. She passed through into the shop and the substantial door closed after her with a reassuring clunk.

Looking at Ashok she said, 'Would you be kind enough to release the front door catch and turn the *closed* sign to face outwards, young man?'

Ashok secured the front door. Mrs Robinson beckoned Jane through a door marked *Private*. 'Come straight through when you're ready,' she called back, as they passed through the door.

Jane entered a cosy-looking sitting room.

'Sit right down, dear, I'll be back with the tea.'

The kind shopkeeper reappeared a few minutes later carrying a tea tray. The cups made a gentle chinking sound in response to her slightly shaky hand. She placed the tray on a large coffee table, 'There we go my dears, milk and sugar's there. I'll let you pour it how you like it.'

Jane started pouring the welcome beverage out from the large teapot.

Once settled with their tea, Jane began, 'We'd like to ask you a few questions about this man who you say has visited your shop recently.'

Ashok searched through a folder of papers and produced a picture of Lawson to show the shopkeeper.

'Yes, that's him.'

'When did you first see him?' Ashok asked.

'Oooh, I can't say for sure, but he's been in a few times over the last couple of months, I would say.'

'When was he last in?' Jane asked.

'Just a couple of days ago.'

'What sort of things does he buy?'

'He spends quite a lot here when he comes, wine, tea, coffee, you know, stuff like that.'

'Anything else?' Jane prompted.

'He has a lot of those ready meals from the freezer, you know, meals for one. I rather got the impression he lives alone and doesn't like to cook. Oh, and some toiletries too on the last visit.'

'Toiletries?'

'Yes, he had some soap and deodorant. He might have a lady somewhere,' she chuckled.

'What makes you say that?' asked Ashok.

'Well, his choice of deodorant wasn't exactly for a man, more for a lady, I would say.'

Jane and Ashok looked at each other. This could be encouraging news that their MISPER might still be alive.

'How does he pay for his goods?' Ashok enquired.

'Always cash, something he doesn't appear to be short of either.'

'What makes you say that?' asked Jane.

'I remember one day when he came in, I put his goods through checkout. It came to 80 something pounds I think. He took out a big roll of banknotes from his back pocket to peel off a couple of £50 notes to pay the bill. Now, I work in the post office and I'm used to seeing large amounts of cash. I would say that he had upwards of several hundreds of pounds in that wad of notes!'

'Interesting,' said Ashok.

'Does he arrive on foot?' Jane asked.

'No, he always comes in a big white van, like a transit sort of size.'

Jane continued, 'I don't suppose you recall or remember the registration do you?'

'Oh no, usually cars park side on so, I wouldn't have seen this. I doubt I'd have remembered anyway.'

'Any ideas where he might be living or staying?' Jane asked.

'Sorry dear, none. I wouldn't think it's too far from here though… We're not exactly in the town centre, it's mostly locals that shop here. Those with cars would prefer to drive to the big supermarkets. I can't compete with their prices I'm afraid.'

'Mrs Robinson, can I ask you to take one more look at his picture and can you tell me how sure you are that this is the same man?'

'Oh, a 100% sure, I can show you if you like.'

'Show us?' Ashok questioned.

'Yes, I still have him on CCTV footage. I checked it before I made the Crimestoppers report.'

The detectives looked at each other, not believing their luck.

'Can we see?' Jane asked.

'Yes, of course, follow me.'

Mrs Robinson rose from her chair and led them into a small office at the back of the post office.

Ashok looked on, impressed at the shopkeeper's technical knowledge. She quickly navigated through menu options on the computer used to record CCTV footage.

'The post office insisted I have this installed, otherwise they wouldn't let me have the post office counter. We have a lot of elderly people living nearby and they need a post office you know, as we have no bank.'

She clicked on various files until she found the one she was interested in. 'Ah yes, here it is.' She fast forwarded through the video until she reached the point where a white van was visible through the shop window. A man got out of the van and entered the shop. The image was not clear initially, as he was too far away. The officers were frustrated with a view of the back of his head. The footage continued, he got closer, and then Mrs Robinson hit the pause button just as his full face came into view.

The detectives leaned in closer for a better look.

'Mrs Robinson, I could hug you,' Jane said.

'It's him, isn't it?'

'I do believe it is,' Jane said.

'Mrs Robinson,' Jane began, whilst retrieving a business card from her bag. 'We're looking for this man. Until we find him, there's a possibility he might come in again. Just serve him as you would normally do, don't let on that you've spoken to us.
Do you understand?'

'Ooh yes dear, this is very exciting isn't it?'

Jane was slightly amused at this budding Miss Marple character. 'If he comes back, I want you to call me as soon as you can on this number. Can you do that?'

'Yes, yes dear, of course I can, no problem.'

Ashok produced a data stick from his pocket, 'Can we have a copy of that footage please, Mrs Robinson?'

Ashok was especially impressed when she asked, 'Has it been checked for viruses before I plug it in?'

'Yes,' was the reply. 'It gets scanned every time I plug it into my PC back at the station.'

Reassured, she plugged the data stick into the USB port on the front of her PC. Once again, she showed her technical skills to produce a copy of the video footage that they'd just viewed.

Back in the car, Jane called the new information in to the team back in Luton. There had been no new developments to report back to Jane. 'Keep plugging away,' she said, before ending the call.

'What a remarkable lady Mrs Robinson is,' Ashok said.

'Yeah, often older people are left behind with new technology, but not this lady.'

'Where to now?' Ashok asked.

'Let's just think for a minute,' Jane started. 'We've had an ANPR alert out for both Mrs Cooper's vehicle and Lawson's, haven't we?'

'Yeah, but nothing's come back.'

'Why's that, do you think?' Jane queried.

'I dunno. Maybe we've just been unlucky?'

'I don't buy that. OK, maybe Mrs Cooper is being held somewhere against her will so her vehicle may not have been on the road. We know that Lawson has been using his though, as our shopkeeper sleuth has seen it pull up outside her shop.'

'Maybe he has a different vehicle we don't know about,' Ashok offered.

'Hmm, possible I suppose. Or, maybe, he has false plates to avoid detection.'

'That's a good likelihood,' said her partner.

'In which case, he's going to be harder to find. OK, let's think about Mrs Cooper's vehicle, an old Nissan?'

'Primera,' Ashok reminded her.

'Yes, an old model, wasn't it?'

Ashok consulted the folder of paperwork he had, 'Ah, here it is, yes, this one has an 03 plate. You don't see many around these days. We could ask the local boys to look out for Primeras.'

'You know what though, I have a hunch that this car's not been on the road since her disappearance.'

'Where do you think it is now?' Ashok asked.

'Certainly off road, maybe a garage. It's quite rural around here, it could be on farmland somewhere, in a barn maybe. I dunno, I guess, I just feel it in me water,' she joked.

Ashok held his hands up, 'Woah, information overload.'

'That reminds me,' Jane said.

'What does?'

'I need the toilet after all that tea. It's time to speak to the boys down at the local nick.'

Ashok smiled as he punched the postcode for the local police station into the satnav.

Chapter 92

There was an air of excitement between Igor and Toby at the vicarage. Elias pretended to be excited, but his deepening animosity towards Igor prevented it. Instead, he put up a good pretence of eagerness. It was the day before the event, attendees were arriving regularly and setting up camp in the grounds of the venue. Tarquin was administering these. Sales of tickets and narcotics were going well; Igor stood to be a rich man at the end of this.

Sarah was still heavily drugged and completely unaware of the fate that would befall her tomorrow. The three plotting occultists were meeting in the lounge.

Igor was updating Toby and Elias with details for tomorrow. 'I'll need some help tomorrow morning first thing. She will be sedated; a mild dose of ketamine should do it. The effects will have worn off before the evening. Then, when she's subdued, you two must leave me with her. I'll need to dress her in her ceremonial gown,' he nodded towards the back of the door. Hanging on the door was a pure white muslin gown. 'It will show up crimson blood perfectly, don't you think?' Both men nodded. 'Once she's been prepared, we'll wrap her in warm blankets ready to transport her to the chapel in my van. Elias, you can drive us there. Toby, you can help me with her in the back of the van, you know, keep her still and make sure she comes to no harm. We can lay her on the mattress from her bed for the short journey. At the chapel, we must carry her in and secure her to our makeshift altar.' Igor was positively relishing the thoughts of tomorrow.

'You, Toby, will be by my side. It's important everything goes off without a hitch. Should she put up too much resistance, I'll need you to restrain her. As a last resort, I'll leave a prepared syringe with you. If you need to, plunge the needle into her thigh and squeeze the plunger in. It'll contain enough ketamine to quieten her down. At the stroke of midnight, I will emerge from the vestry door. My appearance will be enough to evoke fear and panic in her eyes, she'll probably scream as well. You, Toby, will read out our marriage vows' - Igor reached into his briefcase and passed a manuscript - 'here, practise this before tomorrow, it's in Latin.'

Toby took the single page manuscript and started reading to himself.

'Which brings me to you and your duties, Elias.' His less than willing disciple looked up. 'There comes a point during the ceremony where she needs to say '*I do*'. You must tell her what she should say, she may resist and need some persuasion. I want you to hold the sacrificial knife to her throat if need be, until she complies. When Toby has finished, I want you to take charge of the sacrifice. You know what to do, don't you?'

'Yes Master.'

Igor flashed an evil look. 'Make sure she can see you, I want to see some terror in those eyes as you approach with the sacrificial knife.'

Elias assured him that this would happen.

'Well, gentlemen, any questions?' There were none. 'Come then, we've earned a generous line of cocaine each.'

Soon after the three were robed and once again sitting back-to-back within the pentagram.

Chapter 93

Detective Inspector Jim Savage of Hampshire Constabulary welcomed the visitors from Bedfordshire into his office. 'First things first, can I get you a tea or coffee?' The officers placed their order and Jane asked for directions to the toilet. Her return coincided with the arrival of three paper cups of steaming coffee. Savage began, 'Norm (referring to DCI Grant) called to say you were down this way investigating a case. A MISPER that blossomed into a murder I understand. What's it all about? How can we help?'

Jane spent the next 45 minutes going through the case before concluding, 'We have just visited the shopkeeper, Mrs Robinson, who has positively identified Lawson. She even provided us with a video, bless her.'

'It looks like he's holed up somewhere local, doesn't it?' said Savage.

'We think so,' Ashok replied.

Jane added, 'We have had ANPR alerts out for his and Mrs Cooper's vehicles, but no sightings have been made of either.'

'We can only assume that they are being stored off road somewhere or maybe one or both are using false plates,' said Jane.

Ashok added, 'We thought that as a lot of the local area was quite rural, the vehicles might be located on a farm or in a barn somewhere.'

'What about the TV appeals?' Savage asked.

'The only response of any use was from Mrs Robinson. Whilst we still don't know where he is, it has narrowed the search area down somewhat,' said Jane.

Savage said. 'Yes but it's still a huge area.' He thought for a moment, 'I think the farm or field idea is a good call so I'm going to ask uniform to increase patrols around these areas. We can talk to some of the locals to see if they've seen anything suspicious or noticed any strangers about.' He reached for his phone, 'I'll ask our eye in the sky to assist.'

Jane waited while he explained his needs to *Hawkeye 1*, she assumed this to be the call sign for helicopter support. His call finished and Jane said 'Thank you Jim, that'll be a great help.'

He removed a business card from his top drawer and passed it over to Jane, 'Call me if there are any developments we need to know of, or if you need backup at any time.' Savage then rose from his chair indicating that it was time for the visiting officers to leave. Opening the office door he asked, 'What will you do now? Are you going back to Bedfordshire or will you stay local?'

'We are staying,' Jane said, 'I saw one of those budget hotels on the way here. We'll book in there.'

'Keep me posted,' the DI said as they walked down the corridor towards the station exit.

Fortunately, the hotel had rooms available. They dumped their bags in their rooms before going to a local country pub for a light lunch.

Conversation between them over lunch was minimal, Jane was busy making notes on her iPad and Ashok was engrossed catching up with emails on his smartphone. The time was frequently punctuated with incoming text messages and phone calls between members of the team back at base. Jane had an idea and called to speak with one of the team, affectionately known by colleagues as Tuffers.

DC Colin Tufnell had been with the force for 35 years. It was no secret that he intended to retire this year. Most of his time was now spent in the office, he didn't take part in the physical side of some of the investigations and was happy to see his time out sitting at a desk as a researcher. His mind was as sharp as ever though and he loved digging about in case notes and on the PND (Police National Database) looking for links and leads.

Jane listened on her phone until the quietly spoken Tuffers answered. 'Hi Colin, it's Jane,' she began. 'I want you to do something for me. I want you to grab the case notes, you know, the ones on my desk from Nottingham. I want you to trawl through them with a fine tooth comb, I'm looking for any link to a property, address or associate in the Hampshire area. Call me straight away if you find something, won't you? Thanks Colin,' Jane ended the call confident that if there was anything to find, Tuffers will find it.

After lunch Jane and Ashok decided to return to the local nick where they spent the rest of the day on a hot desk, trawling through the PND and some of the paperwork they had brought with them. Ashok updated the online case files with the CCTV footage from Mrs Robinson. They then skyped in to join the evening meeting. Halfway through the call Jane suddenly tutted.

'What's up?' Ashok asked.

'Both my phone and iPad have run out of battery power. Come on it's been a long day, my chargers are back at the hotel, I suggest we make our way back, we can grab something to eat on the way. I'll charge my devices up overnight ready for the morning.'

Later that evening, back in the CID office at Luton Police Station, only one member of the day shift team was still in attendance. Totally engrossed in the mountains of paperwork by his side and all around his desk, Tuffers was still searching for a connection to Hampshire. He liked a challenge and was one of those people who had the tenacity to continue where others have long given up. This strategy had worked well, and he often stumbled over vital clues and links that others have missed or failed to connect.

The breakthrough he was looking for came at about 9.30pm. Reading through some background information on Michael Lawson, Tuffers discovered that Lawson had an aunt. She was married to a vicar and lived in a vicarage just outside the village of King's Somborne. *That's the village mentioned in the meeting yesterday,* he thought.

Logging back onto his desktop computer he accessed various databases to see if he could find more information about this aunt. The uncle had retired as a vicar, he was in his 70s. He discovered that he had passed away shortly after. The aunt passed away a couple of years later. He thought for a moment. Normally a vicarage would be owned by the church, surely the couple would have had to vacate it after retirement. Some more research and he discovered that the church was no longer in use. A local historical society stated that the church was in a state of disrepair since lead was stolen from the roof in 2005. He checked up on the Land Registry to see what happened to the vicarage. In 1996 ownership changed from the Anglican Diocese of Winchester to the Reverend Clarke. Scrolling down, another change of ownership occurred in 2004. Tuffers spoke to himself as the new and current owner's name appeared. 'Well I never, Mr Michael Lawson.' Excited by this discovery, Tuffers reached for his phone to call his superior in Hampshire.

It was a little before 10pm, Jane and Ashok were at an out of town retail park enjoying a dinner at Nando's. Jane had no idea that Tuffers was trying to reach her on the phone at the moment they decided to head back to the hotel.

Tuffers was frustrated to hear the call going straight to voicemail. He left a message,

Back in her room, Jane put her phone and iPad on charge. She was tired and forgot to power the phone up - this meant she'd be unaware of any contact from her team until the morning.

Chapter 94

Jane rarely woke up late, always relying on her alarm clock. This morning was different, she forgot to set an alarm on her charging phone. Her deep sleep was instead interrupted by a knock at the door of her room. She got straight out of her bed, checking her watch on her way towards the door. Her reflection in the mirror showed she was in no decent state to receive visitors at the moment. She put her eye to the security viewer in the door and could see her colleague, dressed and ready to take on the day.

'Hi Ash, I'm running a bit late,' she called through the closed door. 'Go get some breakfast downstairs, give me 20 minutes, I'll be down to join you.'

'OK,' came the reply. Ashok was coming to the end of his buffet style full English breakfast when 25 minutes later Jane appeared at his table. 'Good morning, grab some breakfast, it tastes even nicer when the company's paying for it.'

'Yes, sorry Ash, I overslept a bit.'

She looked over at the choice of breakfast. Still feeling full from last night's dinner, she decided on just a yoghurt and a piece of fruit. Ashok had poured a coffee for her.

'Sleep well?' he asked.

'Like a log apparently. I'd better check my phone.' She took the phone from her bag and powered it up. The phone emitted a *ding* sound, notifying a voicemail message. She also noticed a missed call.

'It looks like Tuffers tried to call me.' She called Voicemail and listened to his message. 'He thinks he's found something, he's asked me to call him back.' She checked her watch; it was just coming up to a quarter to eight. Colin was usually a nine till five guy. He must have worked late last night though by the timing of the message. Hoping that he was still keen to share what he had found, he might be in early this morning, she called his number at the station. She was disappointed to hear Tuffers' voicemail greeting.

'Hi Tuffers, it's Jane. Sorry I missed your call last night, my phone died. Please call me when you get in and tell me what you've found. Thank you.'

It was a waiting game now, time for more coffee. Whilst on her third cup, Jane decided to fire up her iPad, maybe Tuffers had updated the case notes before he left for the evening. The hotel wi-fi was slow, but eventually she could check online. She was disappointed that after all that effort to get logged on, her enquiry was fruitless.

'Come on Ash, let's check out and grab a hot desk down at the local nick.' They collected their belongings and left the hotel.

It was a little past 9am when a young administrator, with false eyelashes that Ashok had never seen the likes of before, showed them to an unoccupied desk in the main office. 'You can use this one for as long as you like.' She wheeled another chair across so they could share the space. Ashok was sure he felt a draught every time she blinked.

Jane thanked the young lady. She was prompted by the time shown on the wall clock to reach for her phone. Tuffers would be in the office now. She was just about to press the button to call him when her phone started ringing. It was Tuffers, he'd beat her to it.

'Hi Colin, sorry I missed you last night. What've you got for me?'

She remained silent whilst listening to his report. Ashok strained to hear too, but the background noise in the office made it difficult.

'Colin, that's brilliant, thanks mate. What's the address?' She grabbed her pen from a pocket in the side of her handbag, Ashok reached in his pocket and pulled out his notebook. Jane wrote the address in it, speaking out loud as she wrote, 'The Vicarage, St Hugh's Lane, King's Somborne. Thanks again Colin, we'll be in touch.'

Jane ended the call and sat back in her chair.

Ashok looked on expectantly. 'Well?'

Jane filled him in. 'We need to speak to DI Savage on this one. We're gonna need backup.'

Chapter 95

Sarah looked up as she heard the key turn in the lock of the heavy wooden door. Igor appeared first, carrying a white garment draped over his arm. His two followers entered afterwards.

Igor gave an enthusiastic greeting, 'Good morning, my dear. Today, is our special day.' He stood on the wooden landing studying her reaction.

Bewildered at this sudden intrusion, Sarah looked up, enquiringly, 'What? What's happening?'

'Today, we will start a whole new life together,' he announced, as if she should be receiving this as good news. She showed no emotion when returning his gaze. Disappointed that she didn't seem to share his enthusiasm, he tried to put a positive spin on the situation. 'Just think, no more being cooped up down here. After today, we'll be together, abroad... somewhere sunny.' There was still no visible reaction from his prisoner, he was now getting annoyed at her lack of appreciation, after all he'd done for her!!!

Igor unhitched the rope holding up the wooden steps and gently let them down to the floor. The men descended the steps. Sarah backed away fearful of their intentions.

She was worried, 'What do you want? What's happening?'

'Don't fret my dear, today's our special day... the beginning of a whole new life for us.'

Frightened, she cowered back until she was sitting on the bed, she pulled the duvet up to her neck so only her head could be seen.

Igor laid the ceremonial garment over the back of the armchair and held his hand out to take the case from Elias. He carried the case to the kitchen area and out of Sarah's sight. He prepared a hypodermic syringe of ketamine. *Not too much*, he thought, he needed her to be alert and aware of this evening's proceedings.

'OK gentlemen, now is the time.'

Elias and Toby advanced towards Sarah, one each side of the bed. She looked terrified. 'What's going on? What are you doing?'

They pulled back the duvet and grabbed an arm each. She started screaming and struggling to get free. She tried kicking out but was restricted in doing so to any great effect because of the duvet. Igor arrived at her left-hand side. She saw the needle in his hand and she screamed a desperate plea... 'Get off me!! Nooo! Don't!'

She turned her head to see the point of the needle come closer. Her final scream came as the needle entered the pale flesh in her upper arm. Igor, eyes wide and nostrils still flaring at the delight of this treatment of his intended, pushed the plunger of the syringe to discharge the clear liquid into her arm. She let out a couple more final throes until her whole body went limp and her eyelids closed.

'There, she'll rest for an hour or two, time enough for me to prepare her.' He turned to his two followers. 'You must leave me now, close the door on the way out.'

Elias and Toby obediently left their Master with his comatose prize.

Ecstatic at what he was about to do, he prepared his bride. Whilst Sarah was petite, he still found it a struggle when removing her clothing. His eyes feasted on the naked spectacle before him, whilst he bathed her and dried her body ready for her robe.

Finally dressed in the white shroud, he studied his beautiful bride in awe.

Chapter 96

Savage was quick to respond to Jane's request. He stood at the front of the briefing room addressing the team of eight burly uniformed officers. 'Thank you for assembling so quickly. 'I'd like to introduce you to DI Jane Patterson from Bedfordshire. This is her shout, she'll be the officer in charge of today's mission.' Savage looked over at Jane and said, 'Jane, perhaps you would like to brief the team.'

Jane stood up, she'd done this before back in Luton station but she knew most of the officers there. This was a little different, and she was nervous. She took a sip from the plastic cup of water she was carrying as she approached the centre front of the room. 'Thank you, sir,' she acknowledged, before turning to those assembled in the room. 'Thank you all for sparing the time this morning.' She gave a potted history of the case to those assembled. Holding up an A4 picture she said, 'This is our target. Michael Lawson was his birth name but following a court case he turned *supergrass* and, as a result was granted a new identity under Witness Protection. More recently, he's been living in Luton under the name of Mark Stewart.'

One of the officers present raised his hand to ask a question.

'Yes,' said Jane.

'I thought Witness Protection was a closely guarded secret, where the identity of a person would never be disclosed for that person's protection.'

'Normally, that's the case. What I haven't told you yet is that we believe this Lawson character to be responsible for two murders; the disappearance of Mrs Sarah Cooper and we strongly believe that he is tied up with the occult. We found items relating to witchcraft when searching his home. He was originally arrested in Nottinghamshire for drug offences. The arresting officer read him his rights before he was carted off to the station. This officer, previously of sound mind, promptly re- entered the building, climbed up onto the roof and jumped. He died at the scene.'

A gasp and a few puzzled looks came from the team. 'That's not all. Lawson stood trial for serious offences, offences that would normally guarantee a lengthy custodial sentence. He got a custodial sentence alright, but the judge suspended it, and granted him entry to the Witness Protection Scheme.' There were more puzzled looks of disbelief. 'Look, I know what you must be thinking. I can't explain it either. It's strongly thought by those who know him better than I do, that he has some way of controlling others with his mind. He possibly did this to the judge hearing the case.' Jane was worried that she might cause the team to doubt her credibility by these bizarre claims, so she carried on presenting the facts. 'On to today's mission then, we have received information that he might be hiding in a property close by. Today, with your help, I'm hoping to pick him up. I've been warned that he's extremely dangerous. You are to avoid eye contact with him as it is thought this is how he can influence the minds of others. We also hope that his arrest will help find the whereabouts of our MISPER, Mrs Sarah Cooper. I should add that one of the bodies found on Lawson's property, back in Luton, was Mr Cooper, her husband, who also disappeared under mysterious circumstances a couple of years ago. Any questions so far?'

The room was silent. 'OK, this is our target address.' Ashok rose from his seat and placed an acetate image on an illuminated wall board. 'This is the vicarage that was associated with St Hugh's Church. There are only two properties in St Hugh's Lane, the church, which is apparently in a state of disrepair and no longer a place of worship, and the vicarage opposite. Lawson owns the vicarage, it was passed down to him when his aunt passed away.'

A member of the team butted in, 'What leads you to believe he's hiding out there?'

'I can't guarantee that he is, but we do know he has been in the area. We have CCTV footage from a local shop and know that he's shopped there recently. On a positive note, he's purchased feminine items which leads us to believe a female, possibly Mrs Cooper, might be with him.'

DI Savage stood up again. 'OK, thanks Jane.' He turned to the team. 'You've heard he might be dangerous, so be careful out there. I suggest you have a covert look at the place before deciding on an entry strategy. Two of you should cover the back.' The DI motioned a hand towards the most formidable looking member of the team because of his 6 foot plus height and stature. 'Constable Bonetti here will, if required, use the enforcer on the front door to gain rapid entry.'

Bonetti nodded, flashing a perfect set of white teeth through his big black bushy beard. He liked that job.

Savage looked over at the only female member of the team. 'Bridgette, if our MISPER is in there as well, I'd like you to look after her.'

Bridgette nodded in agreement. 'Yes sir.'

The DI looked at Jane. 'If she's there, do we know if she might be being held against her will or do you think she is with him by choice?'

'We're pretty sure that it was not her original intention to be with him. She was due to go to Edinburgh on the day she disappeared, but we've evidence, in the form of a locally issued speeding ticket, that she ended up in Hampshire on that day. Is she with him by choice? Well, that's a good question, she may well have also fallen victim to his unusual powers and be under his control.'

Still finding this hard to take in Savage just said, 'Um, right, OK.' He turned to his team, 'OK, unless there are any more questions, I suggest we do this. Get your PPE gear on and the vehicles loaded. Be ready to leave at 11.45am.' The meeting disbanded.

Chapter 97

It was a cool, damp April morning when the short convoy of police vehicles pulled off the main road into St Hugh's Lane. Not knowing the area, Jane agreed to follow the van transporting the team to the property. She arranged beforehand that the convoy would stop out of sight of the vicarage, whilst Jane and one of the officers would approach on foot to recce the house first. The front vehicle stopped just a few yards in. Jane pulled up behind it.

Police Sergeant Talbot, the minibus driver, got out of his vehicle and beckoned Jane to follow. The two officers, thankful for the cover supplied by the spring growth in the hedgerow, cautiously walked along the lane towards the entrance of the vicarage.

Jane peered through a gap in the hedge and noticed a grey Nissan Primera. She reckoned it had been parked there for some considerable time, as the birds had covered it in excrement whilst nesting in the branches above. Jane pulled some foliage aside to reveal the registration plate. A sharp intake of breath. 'That's Mrs Cooper's car,' she quietly informed the police sergeant next to her.

They moved a little closer. A white van was also parked behind the trees on the other side of the entrance to the property. This had obviously not been parked up for long, as the birds had left only a tiny amount of evidence on this vehicle. Jane wondered if this could belong to Lawson, but from the road she couldn't see the registration plate.

The two officers paused just before the entrance to the property and stood observing for few minutes, looking for signs of life within. There were no lights on, just a small upstairs window open. Jane studied the open window for a minute or two before saying, 'It might be the wind, but I'm sure I saw the net curtain in that upstairs window move.'

Talbot focused on it, 'Yes, I saw it too, as you say, it might just be the wind.'

Talbot's radio burst into life. 'Is everything OK, skipper?' a voice asked.

Jane looked at him, 'You happy to proceed?'

Talbot nodded. He pressed a button on his radio to answer the call. 'Yeah, everything's fine, come on up, we're going in.'

The rest of the raiding party, led by PC Bonetti, arrived on foot a couple of minutes later.

Ashok stood next to Jane, unable to contain his excitement. 'Did you see the car? It's hers, isn't it?'

Jane nodded, 'Yeah, I think it is, let's hope she's safe inside.'

Talbot looked at Jane, 'Are you ready ma'am?'

'Yes, let's do this.'

Bonetti, despite his size, ran sprightly up to the front door closely followed by the rest of the raiding party. Jane and Ashok brought up the rear, ready to dash in when it was safe to do so. Talbot grasped the swinging arm on the big brass door knocker. He gave half a dozen loud knocks, 'Police! Open up now!' he shouted.

They listened for any sounds of movement, there were none. Talbot checked to see if the door was unlocked, it was secure so he signalled to the eagerly awaiting Bonetti to force an entry. Three hefty strikes at the door with the *big red key* was all that was needed. The door bounced open, vibrating violently in protest at the trauma it had just suffered. Shock and awe tactics were employed with the noisy entrance, 'Police! Stay where you are!'

In a well-rehearsed procedure, the team entered the house. Jane heard several shouts of 'Clear!' as the officers checked each room for occupants.

Satisfied that the house was empty, Talbot called the visiting officers inside for a look round. 'Nobody home,' he said as Jane and Ashok walked into the hallway, pulling on rubber gloves to avoid contaminating evidence.

Jane and Ashok started downstairs, moving from room to room, looking for recent signs of occupancy. The kitchen was the most telling, as water in the kettle was still warm.

One of the uniformed officers called from the hallway. 'Ma'am, you might want to see this.'

Jane rushed towards the hallway where a young PC nodded towards the door under the stairs. 'In there,' he said.

The door was slightly ajar, she noticed a key in the lock as she approached it. Her initial thoughts were that it was a cupboard for storage. Using just a finger, she gently pushed the door open to reveal the wooden landing and stairway beyond. The interior was in darkness. She located a light switch just inside the door. Jane flicked the switch and surveyed at the scene that was suddenly bathed in light below.

'Look at this, somebody's been living down here. There's a bed, a kitchenette, I'll bet that door in the corner is a bathroom.' said Jane, as Ashok arrived by her side. They carried on taking in the scene before them from their lofty vantage point. Jane pointed to an armchair, 'Look! That's a pile of ladies clothes there, isn't it?'

Ashok noticed the rope trailing down the wall behind them. 'What's this?' He started tugging on it. A creaking noise below attracted their attention. Ashok kept pulling on the rope, and said 'Look, the steps are lifting.'

Jane now understood, the car, the lock on the cellar door, the elevated steps and ladies clothes. 'Somebody's been kept prisoner here. I'll bet it was our MISPER.'

Ashok lowered the steps again, they both descended to have a better look round. The place was fully equipped to live in, it had food, water and a bathroom. The only odd thing was that there was no mattress on the bed. A pile of discarded bedclothes suggested that there was once a mattress there. The keen-eyed DC called, 'Over here, look at this.'

Jane looked over, Ashok was studying the small occasional table next to the armchair.

On the table was a hypodermic syringe. Jane carefully picked it up, looking at it in better light. 'It has a residual clear liquid in it,' she said before placing it back on the table. Without wanting to disturb any potential forensic evidence, the officers had a cursory look round to see if there was anything that might lead to providing the identity or location of whoever was held captive down here. There was nothing.

Back in the hallway Jane spoke with Sergeant Talbot. 'Can you call this in to your guys please? I think what we have here is a crime scene. We need Forensics to go through that cellar with a fine-tooth comb for a start.'

Talbot's team continued their search of the house. A young constable called from the upstairs landing, 'Ma'am, there are some items of interest up here.'

Jane and Ashok went upstairs. They noticed the thin net curtain over the landing window flutter in the breeze.

The constable led them into one of the bedrooms, 'First, there's this,' he pointed to an open drawer at the top of a bedside table.

Jane moved over to look inside, 'What is it?' she asked as she observed what looked like a black or navy leather bound case.

'Can you see the embossed logo in the corner there?' the constable shone his maglite in to make it clearer.

Jane screwed her eyes up to make out the logo, 'Smith… and… Wesson… It's a gun?'

Not wanting to touch the case for fear of destroying fingerprint evidence, the constable grasped each side of the drawer and removed it from the bedside table. He bounced it gently as if gauging its weight, 'Correction, ma'am, it's just a case, not heavy enough to contain a gun.' The constable gently pushed the drawer back into the top of the table. 'That's not all, look at this.' He led them into another room, stepping aside to let them view the scene.

Jane looked around with a deja vu feeling as she observed a scene reminiscent of Lawson's cabin back in Luton. A large pentagram was painted onto the bare floorboards, surrounded by candles.

There was also a small glass-topped table with a white powder residue on top, 'I'll bet this is cocaine,' said the constable.

Jane remembered that cocaine was also discovered in Lawson's den back home, so had to agree.

'Right!' she said, 'I've seen enough, I want everybody out of here and a forensic team in here right away. Ashok, check out that van outside will you, whose is it? I want a name and address of the owner. Oh, and check out the church building opposite, though I doubt anybody is there as the brambles seem to have taken over, making access impossible.'

The officers left the property, gathering back at their vehicle. The entrance to St Hugh's Lane was cordoned off with *Police Line - Do Not Cross* tape. They waited for the forensic team to arrive.

'What are your thoughts?', Ashok asked.

'I'm worried, I think he may have Mrs Cooper held captive somewhere.'

'It's been a long time he's had her, if he has.'

'Yeah, that's what worries me. I wonder why he has her. Remember the sexual content of some of the DVDs that the slimy pervert has recorded over the years. I think he's executed a very devious plan to get her all to himself. He got rid of his current partner, then Mr Cooper. He then bided his time until he could somehow lure her away to end up here.' 'But where is he now?' Ashok asked.

Jane sounded despondent. 'Who knows? The search moves back to square one I'm afraid.'

Chapter 98

Sarah was slowly coming round from her drug-induced coma. She opened her eyes to see her old neighbour standing over her, smiling.

'Ah, welcome back my dear.'

She tried to move but couldn't, something was restraining her arms and legs. She pulled at the restraints, twisting her body and struggling as she did so. No longer under the influence of previous restrictions imposed on her mind, she slurred, 'What's happening? Why are you doing this?'

Her desperation amused Igor, 'Don't struggle my dear, you'll only hurt yourself.'

Toby entered the chapel and walked down the aisle between the rows of pews.

Igor looked up. 'Ahh, Toby, how are things going down at the main house?'

'Tarquin has everything under control. New guests are arriving in a steady stream.'

Igor was pleased, 'Good, good and sales?'

'Oh yes, visitors are picking up their orders. It's a good job you purchased some extra as that supply is also selling well.'

'Excellent. What do you think of our bride here?'

Sarah lay there whimpering, tears flowing down her cheeks, 'Please...please, release me. Let me go and I won't say anything or go to the police.'

Igor turned to her, 'We can't let you go yet my dear. Tonight, we are to be married.'

'What? Are you crazy? Let me go now!' She again pulled violently at her restraints.

Her constant struggling to free herself from the uncomfortable position, securely strapped within the confines of the pentagram, led her to realise that she was naked beneath the thin cotton gown she was wearing. The horror struck her! She herself had not dressed like this, so somebody must have done this for her. Her confused mind was still fuzzy, needing more time to recover from the shot of ketamine she'd been given earlier in the day. Peering through her puffy tear-filled eyes she could make out she was in some sort of church. Struggling caused chafing on her wrists and ankles. She finally decided efforts to free herself were futile.

Toby stood with folded arms observing their special Walpurgisnacht guest. Her arms and legs were secured at the lower four points of the pentagram, her head occupied the fifth point at the top.

'Where's the dagger, Toby?'

Toby walked towards a heavy oak door at the side of the chancel, *probably a vestry*, Sarah thought. He entered and quickly re-emerged, holding a black leather case before him in both hands. 'Here it is.' He walked over to a shelf with a carved sculpture of the Virgin Mary, he moved the sculpture aside and rested the case in its place.

Sarah was suddenly filled with more dread hearing the word *dagger* mentioned. 'What's happening? Why've you got a dagger? What are you going to do?'

Igor was delighted to see the fear on the face of his prize. He gently patted her shoulder, 'You'll find out later this evening, my dear.'

Again, she pleaded with the two men. 'I'm not your *dear*! Let me go. I'll just walk away, I won't go to the police, I promise... I promise.' *A ridiculous statement to make* she thought, but she was desperate and would try anything to escape. *Surely somebody, the police or her uncle will be looking for me?* She was confused and didn't know how long she'd been held captive by this monster... these monsters as there were more than one. *What did he mean, they were to be married? What was the dagger for?* Her empty stomach fluttered nervously at the new thought that she might later die at the hands of these evil people.

Igor approached her, bringing his face to within an inch of hers. She smelt his fetid breath as he spoke, 'Sleep my dear, sleep.' She obediently moved on to another place at the command.

'Come, let's leave her to rest. I'd like to go down to the main house and see what's happening there.' Igor and Toby left the little chapel.

Sarah lay motionless on the uncomfortable makeshift altar that had become her resting place. Somewhere in oblivion, she was unaware of their departure.

Chapter 99

Jane and Ashok sat in a Hampshire Police incident room. News from the forensic search of the vicarage was coming in all the time. Traces of ketamine and cocaine were reported. It was confirmed that there were signs that the cellar had been occupied, probably by a female, for some time and that at least three others, thought to be male, were also living there.

Jane researched ketamine and its uses. She was worried that it had long been used in veterinary practices to anaesthetise animals. More recently, its use on the social scene had grown with individuals seeking the *detached high* its use provides. Presumably, she mused, it would be an ideal drug to disable a person as well.

The current whereabouts of the group were unknown, it was possible they were no longer in the local area but it was decided to focus locally, until evidence suggested the search should widen. Mobile police units were updated with vehicle details, a general warning was put out advising an armed response presence before any suspect vehicle stop.

A debate took place to decide whether to put out an appeal for information on local radio. The debate concluded that as a firearm was possibly involved; it was best not to involve members of the public lest they put themselves in danger.

Local patrols were increased by drafting in extra mobile units from Berkshire and Dorset. Traffic police increased ANPR observations on main artery routes through the area. It was a waiting game until something significant was reported either from forensic tests or the *eyes on the street*.

Jane heard DI Savage's voice in the corridor outside. 'Well, Chief Inspector, good to see you, how are you?'

This was followed by the familiar voice of DCI Grant, 'Hello Jim, I hope you're taking good care of my officers.'

'Come and see for yourself, they're in the incident room right here.'

They entered the room and DI Savage announced, 'This is DCI Grant from Bedfordshire Police everybody.'

'Good evening, sir,' said Jane and Ashok in unison. Several of Savage's team acknowledged his arrival as well. 'How's the investigation going?' Grant asked.

Savage looked over at Jane, 'I'll let you fill the DCI in.'

Jane took centre stage a little after 9pm. She spent the next hour with a comprehensive summary of how the investigation was going. She concluded that the priority was to find out where Lawson was holed up, 'Hopefully when we've found him, we'll find Mrs Cooper as well.'

The room was silent for a few moments, Grant ended the silence. 'Well done all of you, it's a worrying development that a firearm is potentially involved, so we must call on the special skills of SO19.'

'Already arranged,' said Savage.

'Good, good,' said Grant, 'This Larson character sounds dangerous!'

'Lawson,' said Jane.

'What? Oh yes,' said Grant, 'I mean Lawson. It looks like you have all bases covered, I guess we must play a waiting game to see if our field based team come up with anything. Good work everybody, carry on, thank you for updating me.'

Grant and Savage retired to Savage's office, *probably for a good chinwag behind closed doors* Jane thought. She reached for her mobile and speed dialled to speak to the Luton team.

Two team members were still working hard. Speaking to Jacky first, there was nothing to report. Before ending the call, Jane asked, 'Is there an update from Tuffers?'

Jane listened as she heard Jacky shout across the office, 'Tuffers, I've got the boss on the phone, have you got anything to say?'

Ignoring reference to being called the *boss*, Jane faintly heard Tuffers respond.

Jacky said, 'Just putting you through ma'am.'

'Thanks Jacky.'

The familiar voice of Colin Tufnell came on. 'It might be nothing ma'am, but you remember that poster in Lawson's den?'

'Yeah,' said Jane, 'Walpurg… something wasn't it?' 'It's pronounced *Valpurgis,*' said Tuffers.

Jane repeated, 'Val Purgis,' with emphasis on the Val. As she did so, a uniformed constable had just entered the incident room.

He looked over as Jane practised the name, his comment drew her attention. 'Flippin' 'eck, talk about a coincidence.'

She spoke into the phone, 'Hang on Colin, there's somebody here who might know something.' She cupped the mobile phone in her hand, looking at the constable, 'What do you mean coincidence?'

'Well,' he began, 'Traffic have brought in this German tourist downstairs, he was involved in an RTA, a head on collision, no doubt driving on the wrong side of the road.'

'Yes,' said Jane, 'but what's the coincidence?'

'He's more than twice the legal alcohol limit, he can't speak or understand English very well but he keeps tapping his watch saying Val Burgess, Val Burgess.'

Other ears in the room pricked up.

'We assumed he is trying to tell us he is late for a meeting with somebody called Val Burgess.'

Jane resumed speaking to Tuffers, 'Gotta go Colin, something interesting has just come up, once again you're a star.'

Before she could end the call, Colin said, 'There's another thing you need to be aware of ma'am.'

'What's that?'

'Members of the Black Magic community celebrate this event and, Walpurgisnacht is tonight, midnight to be precise!'

This was getting more interesting by the minute. Jane asked Tuffers to hang on and turned her attention to the uniformed constable.

'Where's our drunk driver now?'

'He's in a cell, making a lot of noise shouting but nobody down there knows what he's saying. There was a passenger in the car, a female, I believe she could speak English.'

'Where is she now?'

'She gave her nose a bit of a bash in the accident and was taken to A & E for treatment, I think it was broken.'

'We need to speak to these people urgently. Can we interview our German friend downstairs along with a conference call with an interpreter?' said Jane.

'Sure thing,' the constable said. 'Give me 20 minutes to arrange it and I'll call you down.'

She praised her Luton team. 'That's a great effort and thanks for staying late Colin, there's not much else you can do tonight, so I suggest you and Jacky get off home now, we'll no doubt speak tomorrow.'

The call ended and she turned to Ashok, standing by her side. 'What do you think, Ash?'

'I think it looks promising, it's all we've got at the moment.'

'Yeah, I want you to grab one of Savage's team and go down to the hospital to see if you can find his travelling companion, she might be able to help us before our drunk friend downstairs.' Ashok was turning on his heel as she quickly added, 'Listen Ash, let me know as soon as you get something, won't you?'

'Yes of course.'

Jane looked over at the DI's office. Grant and Savage were chatting when she tapped lightly on the door.

She heard Savage call, 'Come in.'

Jane entered and the two senior officers looked up. She announced, 'I think we've got a bit of a lead.'

* * *

Twenty minutes later, Jane sat opposite Herr Schmidt. She was interviewing via a German interpreter who was speaking on a conference phone on the desk between them. Schmidt was agitated and Jane also heard reference to Walpurgis which could easily have been mistaken for Val Burgess. The German was protesting and gesticulating, constantly referring to his watch as if he had to be somewhere.

Jane introduced herself and Herr Schmidt to the interpreter. She asked the interpreter to explain that they needed to ask some questions. Schmidt fell silent whilst the interpreter spoke. When he had finished, the German started his protestations once again. Jane held her hand up shouting for quiet. He understood that alright and temporarily stopped his gesturing.

The interpreter translated what the prisoner was saying. 'He's wondering why he's being held in this way. It's his belief that apart from a minor collision, he's done nothing wrong. He also wonders where his wife is, she was travelling with him in the car.'

Jane thought for a moment, as impatient as she was to find out about his final destination this evening he needed to be reassured that his wife was in good hands. Through the interpreter, she explained that his wife was being cared for at the local hospital. It was further explained that she had an injury to her nose.

The German nodded and quietened a little. Again, he asked why he was being detained.

Jane explained that he'd broken English law by driving under the influence of too much alcohol. It was standard procedure that he be held in custody until he was sober enough to be interviewed and charged for the offence. He shouldn't expect to be released until tomorrow at the earliest.

This last bit of information set him off again, he was red-faced and banging the table. The uniformed officer standing by the door stepped forward ready to restrain the man should he need to.

Jane raised her voice to be heard over the angry outburst,

'Tell him the longer he drags this out the longer he'll be here.'

Once again, hearing dialect in his own language, he quietened for a moment.

'OK,' Jane began, and using the correct pronunciation she said, 'ask Mr Schmidt what he knows about Walpurgis.'

Schmidt looked across sharply at her when he heard Walpurgis mentioned.

The interpreter posed the question and waited for the reply.

'He is surprised you know about Walpurgis, but it is a special night for Saint Walpurga and he is to attend a special event to celebrate Walpurgisnacht. He says he's paid a lot to attend and travel for this and that he and his wife need to be at the venue before midnight.'

Jane knew that his attendance would not be possible, but didn't yet say so for fear of another outburst. Instead she asked, 'Where is this event due to take place?'

The German shrugged his shoulders and spoke some more.

'He's saying he does not have the address but was using the satellite guidance system in his Mercedes to get him there.'

Damn, thought Jane, another delay. She was unlikely to get more information from Herr Schmidt, so he was led, protesting once again, back to his cell for the night. She thanked the interpreter and closed the call.

A call to Ashok also drew a blank, Mrs Schmidt was having some minor surgery to have her nose re-set.

Back upstairs in the incident room she asked, 'Can we find out where Mr Schmidt's car is? Has it been recovered yet?'

One of Savage's team got straight on it. Meanwhile, Jane asked to see on a local map where Mr Schmidt's accident took place. Another of Savage's team assisted, pinpointing the spot on an OS map on the wall. They studied the surrounding area looking for potential sites that this event might take place, there was nothing obvious. DCI Grant approached, 'Any joy with our drunk driver yet?'

Jane shook her head, 'I'm afraid not sir, I think there's a connection but he didn't know where he was going exactly and was relying on his satnav to get him there. I'm afraid we're running out of time.' She looked at her watch, it was after 10pm now, 'I think that whatever's happening tonight might come to its climax at midnight. If Mrs Cooper is still alive and part of this, I fear she may be in mortal danger.'

Jane heard gentle scratching noises as Grant gently stroked his chin. 'OK, keep doing what you're doing. Let's hope we get a break soon.'

'Yes sir, I'm waiting to hear from the vehicle recovery team, with a bit of luck the address is still programmed into Mr Schmidt's satnav.'

The DCI returned to Savage's office.

Chapter 100

The small chapel was dimly lit by several candles, Sarah lay on her makeshift altar listening to faint scratching noises of rodents scurrying around somewhere nearby. She hated mice, which added to her fears. The only respite from these feelings occurred when she occasionally drifted off to sleep, succumbing, for short periods, to the after-effects of the cocktail of drugs she'd been given since being held captive.

Sarah was awakened by the sound of the creaking chapel door followed by voices. The chapel was suddenly bathed in brilliant light. She screwed her eyes up against the glare and momentarily struggled to see where the source of the light was. She hadn't noticed before but, suspended from a large oak beam supporting the roof of the chapel were two spotlights. They were akin to those you might see in a theatre. Both were focused on the altar.

Igor stood over his quarry. 'Hello my dear.' He clasped his hands in front of his body looking as if he was standing in front of a goal protecting himself from a pending free kick. 'Not long now, my dear, then it will all be over.'

Sarah squirmed fruitlessly against her restraints. Her voice reflected increasing levels of desperation. 'I told you, I'm not your dear! Let me free now... You're evil... EVIL!!!'

Igor was delighted with the fighting spirit of his intended bride. He turned to Toby, 'I think we were wise to do this away from the main party,' then, looking back, he gently shook his head. 'Scream all you want my dear, nobody will hear you here.'

She was now inconsolable, between sobs she uttered, 'I... just ... want... to die... just let me... die now... please... I beg... you! Let me die!'

This outburst did nothing but to excite her captor, whose smile broke into a full grin.

'Come,' he beckoned to his acolytes, 'We must check the cameras are working.'

They covered Sarah's body in a black satin sheet for the screen test. She shook uncontrollably beneath the cover and listened to the conversation, which included a phone call. Gatherers in the main house looked up as the giant screen above suddenly came to life, bathing the room in a pleasant atmospheric light. They saw the image of their shrouded star guest for the night and several points of the pentagram were visible around the cover.

After a successful equipment test, the large screen returned to its standby mode. There was some excited chatter as the room darkened once more. Noise soon subsided and scenes of debauchery in the room resumed.

Final preparations resumed in the chapel prior to the midnight ceremony.

Sarah felt a tug at the satin cover as it was removed. Once again, she screwed her eyes up against the bright glare of the studio lights. She whimpered and repeatedly asked what was going to happen to her. Her eyes were dry and rimmed red from the trauma she'd endured. There were no more tears, they'd long ago dried up.

Igor stood over her, his eyes wide with anticipation, his nostrils flaring. 'Not long to wait now my dear, soon, you'll be indoctrinated into a new life with me by your side.'

Again she struggled against her restraints, 'You're insane! I'll not be by your side... I'd rather die!!!'

A look of displeasure momentarily appeared on the evil occultist's face, 'The latter option can be arranged,' he mocked before emitting a loud haughty laugh which echoed around the chapel. His cacophony of laughter died down. His persona quickly changed from sinister to gentle. He patted her left arm, 'Rest my dear, it's going to be a late night.'

A door opened, Toby and Elias emerged from the vestry, both dressed in their hooded cowls. 'Master,' Toby called out. 'It's time for you to prepare yourself, come to the vestry, I'll assist you,' the two men retired to the privacy of the vestry. Elias remained in the chapel.

Sarah's observations of her captors led her to think that Elias was the underdog in all this. She was willing to try anything to escape and decided to appeal to his apparent better, weaker, nature.

'What's your name?'

The shadowy figure lurking in the apse remained silent.

Her shaky voice called out again, 'Hello? Please talk to me, I'm afraid.'

Elias looked over, remembering what happened when he last went against Igor's instructions. Reluctantly he warned. 'I shouldn't be talking to you, the Master wouldn't like it.'

Sarah didn't give up, 'He's not here right now so he won't know we're talking, will he? I suppose you know that you're culpable in all this, keeping me captive, drugging me.' Her minder remained still, with no comment.

'If you help me escape, now, we can go together to the police. I can explain how you saved me... I'll tell them that your role in all this was minor... or, if you'd prefer, you can set me free and then disappear yourself, I can be very vague about your identity to the police.'

Still no response.

'Please... please... help me!'

The shadowy figure emerged from the apse and approached her.

'Let me advise you. There is no escape from this for any of us. You do not know the powers our leader possesses. If we were to escape from all this, trust me, he would find us. Should this happen, our fate at his hands would be worse than death. He has forced those disloyal to him to inflict painful and barbaric tortures on themselves. This treatment can last for hours, even days, before they eventually succumb to the torment and die. Trust me, just do as he says.'

The noise of the vestry doorknob turning silenced Elias, he quickly turned and walked back into the apse. Toby emerged from the room and he joined him. 'The Master looks magnificent; we now just wait until it's time to begin.'

Sarah was shaking at the chilling advice she'd just received.

Elias looked at Toby, 'Have you got the sacrifice ready?'

A sharp intake of breath came from the altar, the men looked over at their ashen-faced prisoner. 'Sacrifice? What do you mean sacrifice?'

Elias grinned, this was just what the Master wanted to see. In his perverse way, he thrived on another's terror.

'Yes, I'm prepared, the ceremonial dagger is over there on the shelf.'

Elias nodded, 'Very well.'

Sarah tried to reach out to these two sinister characters. 'Please let me go... I've done nothing, let me go and we can all walk away from this.'

'But my dear, this is your special night, you are the chosen one and will marry the Master,' said Elias in a mocking tone.

'No! I will not!' she remonstrated.

'We'll see.' Elias then turned away, signalling the end of this little spat. He checked his watch and announced, 'Just a little under 45 minutes and the show will begin.'

Chapter 101

The atmosphere in the incident room was tense. Jane was hoping and praying that traffic officers could locate Herr Schmidt's damaged vehicle. They hoped that the satnav would reveal its last programmed destination. It was 11.20pm when a phone in the incident room started ringing.

A scruffy-looking detective nearby picked up the phone, 'Yeah, ok, wait…' he reached for some paper and pulled a pen from his top jacket pocket. Jane listened along with everybody else in the office. 'Ok, ready,' he fell silent as he wrote on the scrap of paper, 'brilliant, thanks guys.' He replaced the phone on its cradle then holding up the piece of paper he read out a postcode.

A flurry of activity began when several officers started tapping on their computer keyboards, using the internet to match the postcode to an address.

'Got it!' echoed across the room. 'It's Batstone House, it's on the edge of Humber's Wood in Stockbridge.'

Jane was curious, 'What sort of place is it?'

One of Savage's team volunteered some detailed information, 'It's an old manor house ma'am. It was constructed in 1776 but was destroyed by fire in 1826. The place lay in ruins for many years until the land was purchased by Lord Lancaster, he demolished the original house and built a much grander house to replace it.'

Jane was eager to get to the point. 'Thank you, detective?'
'DC Stokes, ma'am.'

'Can we skip to present day please?'

'Sorry ma'am, yes of course. Today, the house is owned by a heritage trust. During the summer, June to September, it's open to paying visitors at weekends. At other times, it's available for weddings, parties and corporate events. I drive past this site every morning. It looks like the caravan club is having an event there at the moment.'

'Thank you, Detective Stokes, I bet this is our event.' Jane looked to DI Savage, 'Can we get a team together? We need to pay Batstone House a visit, hopefully SO19 will get here very soon.'

A uniformed officer said, 'Already here ma'am, they're standing by in the canteen.'

'Perfect, let's do this.'

Savage rallied the team together. 'Get your PPE gear on everybody, we need to leave in ten minutes.'

The team prepared themselves for the raid. Stab vests were worn, SO19 were notified, all available units in the station were mobilised. DI Savage produced protective clothing for Jane and Ashok.

Ten minutes later a convoy of vehicles left the secure parking compound at the police station. Led by a transit van full of burly uniformed officers, another similar vehicle carrying SO19 officers followed close behind. Bringing up the rear was Jane, Ashok and DCI Grant travelling with Savage's team.

Jane checked her watch, 'How far's this place?'

Savage estimated, 'Not far, we should be there in about ten minutes.'

She calculated that their ETA was ten minutes to midnight, *cutting it a bit fine*, she thought.

Chapter 102

Sarah was suddenly aroused from her stupor by the bright studio lights coming on once more. She sensed something bad was about to happen to her; she shuddered whilst screwing her eyes up against the harsh glare. Slowly, her eyes became accustomed to the brightness and could see more clearly. Her constant pleas to be released fell on deaf ears.

Elias pulled on the vestry door handle; the door creaked open revealing the dim flickering light of candles within.

Back in the hall the giant TV screen once again bathed the room in light. Those assembled fell silent to view the image of their special guest tethered within the pentagram on the makeshift altar. Some excited chattering, cheering and clapping began as the show was about to begin.

Sarah screamed loudly as a grotesque creature on all fours suddenly emerged from the vestry. 'What is it? What is it? Get it away from me!'

Toby and Elias were amused as they saw this new personification of the Master scamper around the chapel.

Sarah watched the horrific creature, she could recognise what appeared to be a goat's head, the shoulders and front legs were covered in goat's skin. She was repulsed by what she saw, trying to work out what this inhuman form was, it was nothing like she'd seen before. Only when glimpsing the creature's chest did she think it could be human. The back legs of the creature were cloven hoofs. The strange creature came to a standstill by her side and suddenly spoke. 'Hello my dear, the time has come for us to be joined in matrimony.'

Sarah recognised the voice, this wasn't some sort of animal as she first thought it was Mark, her neighbour. She screamed, 'Noooo! Let me go now!'

The viewers in the hall were enjoying the show, applauding and cheering at the sight of their Master appearing from the vestry. Similar cheering occurred when they saw and heard the terror in their special guest's voice.

Sarah attempted to back away from her evil captor and was further repulsed when he suddenly raised his grotesque figure to full height; he was naked from the waist down. She quickly turned her head away.

'Get away from me!' she screamed.

The evil occultist's nostrils flared whilst he smiled at the terror his appearance had invoked in her.

Toby approached, holding a long, thin leather case before him. He opened the case and held it towards Elias. Elias reached in and pulled out the sacrificial dagger, holding it point up to resemble an inverted religious cross.

Sarah's eyes widened at the sight of it, convinced that this was going to be her demise. Death would be a welcome release from the trauma of all this. Her tear ducts finally found the final dregs that now filled her eyes and trickled down her face.

Those assembled in the hall were not disappointed at the spectacle before them. Aroused, some resumed their perverse activities with each other. A few just lay there, their dilated pupils evidencing the over indulgences of narcotics. Most watched in awe as their Master held his arms aloft and began his Latin chanting, summoning the fire demons once more.

Sarah listened to her evil neighbour perform his ritual. Her peripheral vision noticed the lit candles around the small chapel flicker and flare as if in response to his incantations. Her breathing was becoming difficult, as if she were suffering a panic attack, not helped by the mucus congestion she was feeling in her nose. Some of the chanting was directed towards the sacrificial dagger. Elias gently laid the dagger on the altar between her legs, she flinched, wondering if he was about to inflict pain and injury upon her as he did so.

Bowing, as a clear mark of respect towards his Master, Elias withdrew backwards into the shadows. Sarah heard the chapel door open, closely followed by an animal bleating. Elias reappeared at the end of the altar, under his arm was the small goat with terror in its eyes.

The Master ended his chanting and nodded towards his two followers. Toby stepped forward towards Elias, holding a silver chalice in his hand. Elias reached for the dagger. Toby pulled the goat's head back. Elias drew the knife across the poor creature's throat. The goat let out a final gurgling sound as it suffered its fate. Toby held the chalice under the goat's throat to collect the blood draining from the wretched animal.

Sarah watched in horror, repulsed at the event she'd just witnessed. She screamed as her white garment was splattered crimson red by the initial spurts of blood from the sacrificial goat. The animal fell limp as life drained from its body.

Viewers in the hall were again galvanised to the big screen. The cruel sacrifice was received well. They watched as Toby passed the chalice to the Master. Igor held it aloft, chanting in Latin once more before putting it to his lips to drink some of the warm goat's blood. He passed the chalice to Toby who also drank, leaving a visible residue on his top lip. Elias did the same before passing the chalice back to the Master.

The grotesque occultist turned to Sarah. 'Now, my dear, it's your turn.'

Doing her best to resist, she turned her head away and struggled furiously against her restraints to avoid taking the unpleasant draft being forced upon her.

Igor tried a couple of times to administer the blood to his bride without success. Toby stepped forward to hold her head still, ready to inject the ketamine into her arm if he needed to. She clamped her lips shut, still resisting. Toby pinched her nose until she finally opened her mouth, gasping for breath. At this opportunity, Igor quickly administered the goat's blood into her mouth. Sarah violently choked, retched and vomited causing a red sticky pool to collect under her neck and head.

The white garment she was wearing was further stained.

Chapter 103

The convoy of police vehicles drew to a stop about 50 metres in front of the large house. The surrounding area was scattered with a range of camper vans, caravans and tents. There were no people to be seen, lights shining through windows at the front of the house were the only signs of life.

An SO19 officer alighted from one of the minibuses in front, he carried his Heckler & Koch MP5 in front of him, and approached the vehicle occupied by Jane.

'OK ma'am, I suggest we recce the house first, just to get an idea of what we're dealing with. If the outside is secure, I plan to go straight in the front door, my officers will go in first, followed by DI Savage's team. When we've secured inside, you can join us.'

Jane nodded, 'Very well, secure the place as quick as you can, we believe somebody may be in danger as we speak.'

'No problem, ma'am.' The officer turned back to address his team now gathered outside the van in front.

Jane watched the team split up to perform the outside recce. Frequent radio bursts reported an *All-Clear* status. The armed response team regrouped. Savage's uniformed officers joined them for a briefing. The SO19 skipper informed both teams of the plan to gain entry, silently and swiftly. The groups split up. Two armed officers fronted up the team at the front door, closely followed by the uniformed officers. Other armed members ran around the sides of the house to cover potential exits around the back.

The senior officers and Ashok alighted from their vehicle and started walking towards the front entrance, Grant suggested they approach walking on the grass verge rather than the gravel which crunched underfoot. They stopped at the foot of the steps leading up to the front door.

An SO19 officer had his ear to the door. He listened carefully for a few moments, looked over to his teammate and nodded his head briefly. The same officer gently twisted the door handle. The handle creaked as he did so. He pushed the door, they wouldn't need the big red key tonight, the door was unlocked.

Light from an indirect source appeared along the opening crack of the door. Officers took cover as the door was pushed to swing open on its own. The vestibule area was deserted. Armed officers slipped inside quietly. Uniformed officers waited to be beckoned in. Senior officers climbed the stairs and also entered the outer hallway. The most apparent thing that suggested something illegal was happening here, was the strong smell of cannabis that was obviously being smoked somewhere. Light filtering out of the hall doorway had a hazy appearance.

The officers advanced to discreetly look through the gap in the hall doorway. The team waiting behind them watched with bated breath. Jane's radio burst into life. 'You'd better come and see this ma'am, before we break the party up.'

Jane looked at her fellow officers, 'Come on, let's see what's going on.'

The detectives stayed in the shadows as they moved forward to see inside without being seen. The scene before them could only be described as one of depravity. Many of the party goers were in various states of undress, indulging in various acts of sexual gratification. There were singletons, couples and groups interacting with each other. Some wore masks and others wore bizarre fetish style outfits. It was now obvious where the sickly-sweet smell of cannabis was coming from, as several occupants could be seen smoking it. An individual, about 3 metres away from Jane's vantage point, unaware that he was being watched, was consuming a line of white powder from a stone windowsill. This was an orgy on a grand scale. The attentions of many seemed to be directed to the part of the room that was not visible from the outer hallway. There was a flickering of light indicative of a TV screen. *Perhaps they're watching pornography,* Jane thought. Then it came, a scream like none she'd ever heard before. Jane stepped back and ordered the armed officers and their backup team in.

The officers ran through into the hall. The SO19 officers shouted above the raucous screams for everybody to be still and to put their hands behind their heads. Jane could still hear a female in distress. Armed officers were poised, ready to shoot anybody who might be a threat to the team. Other armed officers entered the hall from outside, backup was needed as there were too many people to control.

Jane was disturbed to still hear shouting and desperate pleading. She moved forward to investigate. The pleas were coming from the TV sound system. On the large TV screen in the hall, she could see a distressed female, tethered within a crude pentagram. The unfortunate female was surrounded by three men, two wearing cowls and one looking more creature-like. The female's face momentarily appeared on the screen. Jane immediately recognised their MISPER. It was a worry for Jane that

Mrs Cooper was splattered with crimson stains that could only be blood!

A melee ensued. Despite armed police shouting and screaming at them for order, desperate individuals were scrabbling around trying to locate discarded clothing or anything to cover themselves up. Why covering up should be important now, following their exhibitionist ways just two minutes ago, Jane didn't know. Others were overcome by the excesses of narcotics.

Jane stepped back into the relative quiet of the vestibule area. She requested two officers to go through the rest of the house room by room. 'We've got to find her. I think this is being streamed from another room.'

Savage paced up and down talking into his mobile phone, requesting more backup from neighbouring forces.

Officers inside the hall continued trying to gain control of the situation. Power was removed from the TV screen.

Jane entered the hall once more. The occupants, many still in a state of undress, were being asked to lay face down with hands behind their heads until backup arrived. Armed officers were still poised ready to react with lethal force to any threat.

Frequent bursts of radio traffic blasted out from the search team reporting the status of each room they entered. Most were reported as *Clear,* in others, they were greeted with more scenes of debauchery. The surprised occupants of these rooms were gathered and led downstairs to the hall.

Still no sign of Mrs Cooper or Lawson though. Some backup officers arrived whilst Jane turned her attention to the large TV screen and its associated equipment. She traced the attached cables and discovered that they led outside, through a window next to the ostentatious fireplace, dominating the wall behind the TV screen

Jane stood aside to allow more uniformed officers to surge through the entrance door to the hall. When a gap appeared in the influx, she darted through into the vestibule area and headed for the front door. An officer guarding the door challenged her as she exited, thinking she was one of the partygoers.

She produced her warrant card. With no time to waste, she ran around the side of the building looking for the cables she'd seen inside. In the darkness, she tripped on a low hedgerow, falling to the ground, 'Damn! There goes another pair of tights!' she cursed. Undeterred she pulled herself up to continue looking for the tell-tale cables. She passed by the chimney stack and found the cables exiting from the hall. Using her phone as a temporary torch, the cables were routed along the side of the building towards the back of the house. She picked up one of the cables to use as a guide and followed its path. The overcast night sky gave no clues as a terrace at the back of the house opened up into a blackness beyond. Still using the cable to guide her route she continued to trace its path. The moon briefly reflected in some water as it appeared in a break in the clouds. Her peripheral vision could pick out an approaching tree line. The guiding cable curved around behind the thick trees and then she saw it. A dim light in the front tower of the small chapel was clearly visible about 25 metres further on.

This is it, I need backup, she reached for her radio. It was a shock to discover the radio wasn't there. 'Oh flaming hell!' She muttered, 'I must have dropped it when I fell!' Her mobile phone was her only option. Her hands shook whilst she prepared the phone to make a call. Signal strength was dangerously low, she prayed that it was enough to make a call.

Ashok was still in the hall, pleased to see reinforcements arriving to help restore order. He felt his phone buzzing in his pocket. Recognising Jane's number, he answered the call. He stuck a finger in one ear to block out the noise and placed the phone to his other ear. 'Hi Jane, where are you?'

The reply he heard was punctuated by strange atmospheric noises and Jane's voice drifted in and out. Ashok detected panic and urgency. He heard mention of the TV, something about cables and a chapel before the call abruptly ended.

Jane looked at her phone, dismayed that the call had ended prematurely, she had no signal at all now and hoped that Ash had understood her message The tree line provided good cover
as she carefully approached the chapel. She paused just of a short ten metres dash to the chapel door. She listened intently, hoping to hear some backup approaching from behind.

The noise she heard was not from behind though, it came from the chapel in the form of a bloodcurdling scream. This was followed by a raised female voice. It wasn't entirely clear what was being said, but it was obvious shouting, pleading and more screaming.

Jane couldn't ignore this, despite the dangers, she felt she must go in. Hoping that backup was imminent, she sprinted to the chapel doorway. The distressed female's voice was clearer now,

'Get away from me! HELP! Somebody please HELP ME!!! Why are you doing this to me?' This was followed by the guttural cry, 'I'd rather die!' punctuated with uncontrollable sobbing.

Jane, almost thankful for the cacophony from within, could turn the large metal latch securing the door without being heard. She gently opened the door to get a restricted view inside.

Chapter 104

Ashok found the Chief Inspector talking to DI Savage.

'Have we found the woman yet?' asked Grant.

'No, not yet, and more worryingly, sir, DI Patterson has disappeared.'

Grant looked over to the doorway. 'Is she not in the hall there?'

'No sir, I had a garbled phone call from her a minute ago. The call was intermittent but she said, with a sense of urgency I might add, something about the TV, some cables and a chapel. I can't reach her on the radio.'

Savage looked over the young DC's shoulder, on the wall behind him was a diagram of the house and its grounds. 'A chapel, you say? Let's have a look.'

The three detectives examined the hand drawn picture of the grounds on the wall. Ashok pointed to a three-dimensional representation of the house, 'Here's the house and the front door.' The main gate and drive up to the house were clearly visible. 'Apart from a gatehouse, there are no buildings out the front of the house.' He traced his finger up the pictorial representation following the shore of the lake, which extended northwards. 'Look! There are some buildings around the other side of the lake.' The first he located was labelled *The Crypt/Folly*, then DI Savage stabbed a finger to the left of this to indicate another building called *The Chapel*.

'Right,' said Grant, 'I want a team, including SO19 officers up there NOW!' He thought for a moment before stabbing a chunky finger on the diagram, 'Send a team to this other building, the Crypt/Folly, as well.'

Savage and Ashok left Grant examining the picture as they left to organise the teams. Within minutes later four SO19 Officers, and four uniforms from Savage's team, split into two raiding parties. Ashok joined the team heading for the chapel. One of Ashok's team produced a powerful torch from a clip on his belt. Guided by the light the men ran around the side of the house, looking for the chapel.

They hadn't gone far when they heard the familiar sound of static coming from one of the police radios. The noise came from the other side of a low hedgerow. Ashok's heart was in his mouth, as his immediate thought was that Jane had been injured.

The officer carrying the torch heard the noise as well. As if to help find the black-coloured radio on a dark night, the radio burst into life. It was Savage, asking for a status report!

The powerful beam was aimed in the noise's direction, the radio was on the ground beyond the row of hedges.

One of the uniformed officers reported back, 'I think we've located the officer's radio, we are now searching the locality for any signs of DI Patterson.'

'OK, keep me informed of developments, won't you?'

'Will do, sir.'

A quick recce of the local area was made, in case the DI was laying injured. Ashok called out. There was no response.

The torch beam picked up a disturbed area of soil near the base of one of the hedgerow saplings, a couple of footprints were leading away from the area.

'Look here, she probably tripped in the dark and dropped her radio.' Agreement was unanimous, 'Quick, we've got to get to that chapel.' Ashok and the team forged ahead into the inky blackness behind the house.

Following the beam of light, Ashok felt something underfoot. 'Wait!'

The advancing team halted and looked round. Ashok felt around in the damp grass and located a trailing cable. 'I've found a cable, Inspector Patterson mentioned cables in her call to me. I'll bet this is the cable used to relay TV signals back to the house. If we follow it, it'll most likely lead to this chapel.'

The team moved forward once more, using the route of the cable as a guide.

Chapter 105

Jane observed a grotesque looking creature, half animal and half human standing with his back to the door, arms held aloft. He was speaking loudly, Jane thought in Latin. It wasn't until he stepped slightly aside that she could see and then hear his whimpering victim.

She retrieved the police baton from her utility belt. She sensed others were also present inside, she extended the baton and used it to push the door open a little more. Two robed individuals kneeling each side of the makeshift altar came into view.

Toby noticed movement by the chapel door. The Master was oblivious to this, too busy feasting his lustful eyes on the prize he had worked years to win. Toby got up and quickly moved towards the door. *It must be someone from the main house trying to get a front-row seat no doubt.* He thought.

With her cover blown, Jane had no choice but to enter the chapel and try to save Mrs Cooper from an unpleasant fate. She swung the door back and burst through into the chapel, halting Toby's advance. Her shouts echoed around the small chapel, 'Police! Stay where you are!'

It was only then that Igor's attention was drawn to the commotion at the doorway.

Sarah looked over. Jane noticed how red and puffy her eyes were, 'Oh thank God, thank God! Please help me, he's going to rape me!'

The strange creature pointed at Jane and shouted angrily. 'Stop her! Get her, now! Kill her!!!'

Toby advanced towards Jane. He grabbed the arm that was wielding the baton. Even though her attacker was a good foot taller, Jane gained a quick advantage using her martial arts training. She extended her other arm, catching the robed figure sharply, with her palm, under his chin. She felt his jaw crack and give way sideways. At the very least, it was dislocated. The robed figure yelled out in pain as his head snapped back.

Igor started yelling like a demented idiot. He directed his wrath and orders at Elias. 'Quick, cut her loose! Quick, you incompetent fool!'

Elias grabbed the sacrificial dagger and started cutting through the bonds that had restrained Sarah. Igor continued berating his disciple. 'Do it quickly, I say quickly, you idiot!'

Toby recovered his balance. He still had a hold on Jane's right arm, he turned into her and attempted to get her in a headlock. He released his grip on her arm. It was his biggest mistake. Jane rammed her baton hard from behind between his legs, he screamed out in pain and buckled at the knees falling to a kneeling position before her. She followed up with a blow to his nose, another crack was heard, followed by copious amounts of blood flowing from his nostrils. Toby fell to the floor, blocking the way forward. She attempted to move over her assailant's battered body but he was not done yet. He grabbed her leg as she stepped over. The baton fell from her grasp, landing on one of the pews, she fell heavily onto her opponent, both were now wedged between two rows of pews. Momentarily, neither could move. Jane frantically felt around, trying to locate her baton without success. Toby was writhing around, trying to get the upper hand, until Jane was face down with this brute of a man on top of her. She felt a sharp pain in her ribs and rolled over a bit feeling to find its source, dreading that she might have been stabbed. To her relief, she discovered the reason for the pain was a small can of pepper spray, in her utility belt.

Currently, she was in no position to administer the spray, she needed to roll over on her back to do so. Toby didn't notice as she removed the spray from the belt, but as he sharply pulled her arms back, she had no option but to drop the small can of spray; it rolled slowly beneath one of the pews.

More screaming came from above, 'No! Help me... Please help me!' Jane then heard a door slam closed; the screams became muffled.

Jane continued her struggle and attempted to turn over on her back. It was useless; he had her securely pinned down. She tried a different tactic, the oldest trick in the book, playing dead. She allowed her body to fall limp and remained still. It worked. Thinking that she'd perhaps lost consciousness, Toby shifted his weight and relaxed his hold on her. He pulled on her stab vest to roll her over onto her back.

Jane felt spatters of blood on her face, his voice full of vitriol, 'Now you must die bitch!'

Jane's eyes opened just as he attempted to apply her baton across her windpipe. She scrabbled around with her left hand under the pew and located the can of pepper spray. She wriggled and turned her head before he could apply any real pressure on the baton. Pulling her hand out from beneath the pew, she pressed the button on top of the pepper spray can and directed a generous dose into his face.

Toby screamed out in pain. Apart from stinging his eyes, he inhaled some of the spray, further adding to the nasal discomfort he was feeling. Jane was still pinned down. She felt around blindly on the floor and picked up the baton he'd dropped. She directed a sharp blow to his temple before poking it hard into his sternum. That was enough; he fell back, rubbing his eyes, moaning and groaning, humiliated that he'd been beaten.

Jane kicked him away so that she could pull herself up. Just in case he decided to rise again for another assault on her, she completed the job by handcuffing one of his hands to some sturdy pipework at the base of a large cast iron radiator.

She looked around the chapel and was dismayed to see that the altar was now empty. Sarah's bonds were still gently swinging beside the crudely built structure. There was no sign of her captors, either. It wasn't possible that they'd left through the front door as they wouldn't have got past unnoticed during the scuffle. Jane remembered hearing a door slam, there was only one more door in the chapel, the door to the vestry.

She ran and stood to the side of the carved oak door. Holding her baton at the ready, she twisted the chunky cast iron latch ring before pushing the door open. The heavy door opened. There was no noise from within. She took a quick look into the small room. The cursory glance revealed an empty room apart from a flickering light from a candle on a wooden desk.

'Mrs Cooper! Can you hear me?' There was no response.

Jane entered the room. She held the candle aloft, she could see that the walls were covered with oak panelling. *There's nowhere to hide in here*, she thought. She diverted her attention to outside the room and noticed that the distance between the doorpost to the outside wall was greater on the outside than it was inside the room. Back inside the room she started knocking on the oak panelling running down the side of the room. It sounded hollow, but there was no apparent way to get behind it.

She examined the desk, which was butted up to that side of the room. *There's nothing odd here,* she thought. The left-hand side of the desk contained three drawers, the top drawer was empty, the middle drawer was slightly open but also empty. The bottom drawer wouldn't open at all. Jane pulled the middle drawer completely out, hoping it would give her some access to the bottom drawer. It did! What she saw inside was ingenious, probably hundreds of years old and still working, she found a latch. A spring, loaded wooden peg protruded through the side of the desk into the oak panel at its side. Pulling the peg back, Jane put some pressure onto the back panel, which slid along effortlessly to reveal a passageway. Eight stone steps led down to the subterranean passage. Jane felt a sudden chilly breeze blowing up from the dark, dank void. In the distance, she could hear the faint remonstrations of a distressed Mrs Cooper.

Gingerly, she started down the stone steps. The only light in the passage was coming from the room she'd just left. There was a new fear to face now; reaching out in front of her she had to clear a path through the entanglement of cobwebs that remained in the passageway. She hated spiders and at one point frantically brushed away at her neck as she felt one of the arachnids crawl along it. Speed was of the essence, she didn't want to spend a moment longer down here than was absolutely necessary. She gritted her teeth and ploughed on, using her baton to clear the entanglement of webs whilst feeling her way with the back of her hand brushing on the side of the passage wall. The passage seemed to be curving away to the left. Ahead was still an inky blackness. She frequently paused to brush off spiders creeping over her. She hurried as fast as she could. Voices shouting and screaming at the end of the passage became louder. Her eyes were now fully accustomed to the dark; a faint glimmer of light ahead was becoming evident. As Jane approached the end of the passage, she could see another set of stone steps ascending back up to ground level. She looked up and could see a burning torch supported by a bracket at the top of the steps. With her baton at the ready, Jane slowly advanced up the first couple of steps. She did her best to survey the room. As she did so, Mrs Cooper's distraught voice was clear to hear, but she was out of view from Jane's vantage point.

She studied the gloomy room carefully trying to work out what this place was. As far as she could see, in the dim light, the back wall opposite was constructed from bricks. She could slowly make out regular arched patterns in the brickwork. Satisfied there was no immediate danger, she ascended the rest of the steps. At the top, she paused to determine the layout of this strange room. There was a very high ceiling, supported centrally by brick built pillars. She reached out to feel the form of the wall opposite; the arches seemed to sink deep into the wall. Realisation dawned, she was in a crypt. She quickly withdrew her hand and turned towards the voices she could hear. The interior was L-shaped. With her back to the wall, she edged along preparing to peer around the corner. There he was, Lawson, wrestling with Mrs Cooper to restrain her once more. With her baton held high, ready to strike, 'STOP! POLICE!'

The evil-looking creature had hold of Sarah's hair to prevent her escaping. With his other hand, he reached out for a glass container resting on the base of one of the brick arches. He threw it, smashing the container to spill its contents on the stone floor between him and Jane. He then reached for another burning torch on the wall nearby. Initially he held the torch before him, making lunging actions towards his pursuer. Jane watched the light show that was created as several cobwebs combusted and fizzled around the crypt. She drew her baton hand back in preparation to knock the flaming torch from his hand, but before she could strike, the evil occultist threw the torch to the floor. This immediately ignited the liquid that had pooled on it.

Jane felt a waft of heat from the wall of fire as it erupted. It was now impossible to get close enough to strike him with the drawn baton. She watched, helpless, as he produced a dagger and held it to Sarah's throat. Terrified, Sarah pleaded for help, but Jane felt powerless to do anything. It was then that Jane noticed a spot of red light dancing on the forehead of this evil man.

'Armed Police! Drop your weapon!' came an intimidating command from behind. This was followed by the thundering noise of a gunshot which echoed around the crypt. Jane watched as a crimson stain spread down Sarah's white gown. Her initial thoughts were that a member of SO19 had shot the victim by mistake.

'Take cover!' came a shout from behind. 'Get down ma'am, there's an unidentified assailant in the room!'

Jane ducked down, watching the scene play out before her, feeling powerless that there seemed nothing she could do to save Mrs Cooper. She then saw the evil occultist drop to his knees, Sarah sidestepped away from the flames. The crimson stain on her gown was Lawson's blood.

A voice came from behind, 'Get down, lady! Armed Police!' Sarah went to the far end of the room and crouched down behind one of the supporting pillars.

Lawson fell forward into the flames; his body was quickly consumed by the inferno. Perhaps it was apt that his life was ended by the fire demons!

It was still somewhat of a mystery as to how he got shot. Another shout from an SO19 officer, 'Drop your weapon, come out with your hands up, NOW!'

A hooded figure appeared to Jane's right, out of sight of SO19 officers. Jane looked over as the robed stranger brought his hand up to the side of his head. Jane warned SO19, 'There he is! He's got a gun!' Before the officers could react, another shot rang out. Sarah screamed again, Elias immediately dropped to the floor, the gun fell from his hand, clattering across the ancient flagstones.

It was then that more SO19 officers entered the crypt. The rescue was complete.

Chapter 106

There was a certain irony attached to the fact that Sarah was just waking up from yet another sedative. This one, however, was administered legitimately two days ago in the early hours of the morning by a medical team at the Royal Hampshire County Hospital.

It was now late afternoon on the third of May and bright sunshine was streaming through the window of the hospital room. Sarah looked down at her wrists, they were still bound, but this time with dressings to cover the minor cuts and bruises she'd received during her ordeal. She shuddered as a flashback to those events that caused the injuries. A tube was attached to her left arm, which dropped from a drip hanging on a hook by her bed.

She closed her eyes once more and relived some moments she felt in most danger. Confused, it suddenly dawned upon her she still might be in danger. Her eyes suddenly snapped open as she heard a noise. The door to the room opened, and a person peered around the door. Seeing that Sarah was awake, she entered the room.

Nurse Florence Owusu let out a high pitched 'Hello honey. It's good to see you back with us again.'

Any fears that Sarah had that she might still be in the clutches of evil quickly melted at the welcome sight of this jovial person.

'Where am I?'

'This is the Royal Hampshire County hospital.' The nurse moved to adjust the window blinds so that the sun was not too bright in her patient's eyes. She pushed the window open a little. 'Let's have a bit of fresh air, shall we? I need to take your temperature and blood pressure. Then, if you're up to it there's a whole lotta visitors waiting outside to see you. Just relax for a minute.' She wrapped the blood pressure cuff on her arm and placed the digital thermometer in her ear.

'I must call my uncle, he's elderly and lives in Scotland - he'll be wondering where I am. Visitors? Who?'

'Well, I don't rightly know all of them, but I think the police is amongst them. You've even got an officer guarding your door. A fine young man he is too.' She spoke softly, 'I wish I was ten years younger, I can tell you.'

This time Sarah caught some of the infectious laugh and joined in - she hadn't had cause to laugh for a long time.

Her checks finished, 'There we go darling, all normal, I expect the doctor will be in to check you over later. Now then, they tell me there's one special visitor waiting to see you, are you up to it?'

Sarah was filled with some trepidation, it would be some time before she could trust others, 'Special visitor? Who is it?'

The infectious laugh again, 'Yes, I think you're gonna like seeing this one. You just have to wait and see who it is, shall I send them in?'

Sarah was unsure, 'I... I must look a mess! I don't know if I'm ready for visitors, is it the police?'

Florence folded her arms and looked at her patient,

'No, this one ain't the police. Let's see what we can do.'

Florence put her hand in her uniform pocket and produced a purple scrunchie. She skilfully bunched Sarah's hair back and applied the scrunchie, 'There you go.' she stood back to view the impromptu coiffure. 'Pretty as a picture, now then, are you ready for this visitor?'

Sarah, still looking pale from her ordeal managed a smile for Florence, 'Thank you, you're very kind.'

'Just doing my job darlin. Are you ready?'

Sarah nodded, 'Yes, OK.'

A few minutes passed after Florence left. Sarah watched as the door opened. The young PC guarding the door stepped inside the room, 'Excuse me ma'am, you have some visitors,' he stood holding the door open.

Puzzled as to who it could be, Sarah listened as wheels of a wheelchair squeaked on the shiny floor whilst negotiating the doorway. Sarah burst into tears, this time, tears of happiness, as dear old uncle Angus was wheeled into the room.

'Oh uncle, I thought I'd never see you again.'

'Aye lass 'twas the same for me, it's been so long I thought you must surely be gone forever. It's thanks to Margaret that I got here.'

Tears rolled down the old man's face and then Margaret joined in. The two ladies greeted each other with an embrace.

'I could nae believe it when the police called me yesterday to say that you'd been found safe and well.'

Margaret blew her nose on a tissue before speaking, 'We were so worried about your dear old uncle, he took a turn for the worse you know. I think it was the stress of not knowing what had happened to you. He ended up on the coronary ward. We all thought he wouldn't come out.'

'Aye,' uncle chipped in, 'I suppose you could say I'm bionic now.'

Margaret patted the old man's shoulder, 'Yes, He's been fitted with a pacemaker, it saved his life.'

Sarah looked at her uncle with sad eyes. 'Oh uncle, I'm sorry I wasn't there for you when you needed me.'

'Och, dinnae worry aboot that my dear, I'm just glad you're here now.'

Sarah swung her legs over the side of the bed and despite still feeling a bit wobbly on her feet she stood and give her uncle a hug and kiss.

With Sarah back in bed, Angus put on a serious face. 'I have nae been told details,' he began, 'but a young detective outside from Luton,' he looked up at Margaret for a prompt.

'Inspector Patterson?'

'Yes… that's her, a wee young lass. She helped to track you down. She just wouldn't give up one of her colleagues said.'

Margaret then picked up the story, 'She's a wee slip of a girl and apparently she gave one of your captors a bit of a beating, put him in hospital.'

Angus described the young DI. 'Yes, she's 5 foot nothing in her stockinged feet and her opponent towered above her! A plucky wee lass she is, I'm sure she must have some Scottish blood in her somewhere,' he quipped.

The happy moments and discussion continued when a sudden chill descended upon the room. Margaret turned to pull the window shut. Nobody noticed the shimmering apparition that had appeared in the corner of the room. Sun shining through the tree branches gently swaying in the breeze gave the impression of flames flickering at the base of the apparition.

Chapter 107

It was a bittersweet conclusion for Sarah. Yes, she'd escaped the clutches of evil but was devastated to find out the fate of Steven, her husband. Steven's body was eventually released by the coroner. As sad as it was, Sarah was at least able to have a proper funeral and closure for losing her husband.

She felt a little guilty for thinking the worst about her best friend Karyn and the way she just left with no explanation.

A lot of the trauma was brought up again during the several months of the police investigation. In particular, she was sickened to learn of the vile voyeurism of her perverted neighbour. Eventually, the police investigation was concluded.

Sarah remembered DI Jane Patterson when she was involved in the investigation of Steven's disappearance. So grateful was she of the young detective's dogged determination, it was only that, that saved her from a fate worse than death.

The Chief Constable was also grateful for the young inspector's efforts, awarding her a commendation. Jane accepted the award on behalf of the team. The Chief Superintendent and Chief Inspector Grant were both very happy. The multiple crimes that had been solved, immensely improved the division's clear-up rates.

Two of the event organisers were dead. One murdered the other, before committing suicide himself. The battered Toby received a lengthy custodial sentence for his part in the kidnapping of Sarah. Multiple arrests and prosecutions took place for possession of narcotics; some of these received cautions, others received suspended prison sentences. Some custodial sentences were also handed down for the supply of narcotics.

Lawson's assets were seized as the proceeds of crime. With his estate, this amount exceeded £1.2 million.

Police helicopters intercepted a small Piper Cub aircraft that covertly slipped into UK airspace the day following the Main Event. It was forced down at Biggin Hill. A drugs dog indicated there may be drugs in the aircraft. The pilot was taken into police custody. The drugs were long gone, but the pilot admitted that he was here to pick up human cargo: a newly married couple due to start a new life in Europe.

Sarah could no longer live at the property in Luton. It held too many bad memories. She instructed an agent to sell it. With the proceeds, she purchased a little cottage in Burntisland, just a short bus ride from her dear old Uncle Angus. The cottage was mostly warm and cosy but did suffer from frequent icy chills, even on warm days. The problem was investigated by various tradesmen but no apparent cause was ever found.

Acknowledgements

I am grateful for the help advice and encouragement of Diana Diggins at Eventispress; your guidance has been invaluable. A special thanks to my friend Ying Li; you did a fantastic job. I couldn't have done it without you. Thanks to Gary Arnold for some stunning graphics. Thanks also, Ian Pulham, Brian Kerr and Rod Hart.

If you have enjoyed reading The Main Event then author Peter Arnold would be really grateful if you would leave a review on Amazon.

BV - #0033 - 290424 - C0 - 203/127/20 - PB - 9781739328627 - Matt Lamination